THE MUSIC

OF

THE MOST ANCIENT NATIONS,

Procession of Assyrian Musicians to meet the Conquerors returning from Battle.

(From a bas-relief in the British Museum.)

THE MUSIC

OF

THE MOST ANCIENT NATIONS,

PARTICULARLY OF THE

ASSYRIANS, EGYPTIANS, AND HEBREWS;

WITH SPECIAL REFERENCE TO RECENT DISCOVERIES IN
WESTERN ASIA AND IN EGYPT.

By CARL ENGEL.

BAAL.

WITH ABOUT 100 ILLUSTRATIONS.

BOOKS FOR LIBRARIES PRESS
A Division of Arno Press, Inc.
New York, New York

First Published 1909
Reprinted 1970

STANDARD BOOK NUMBER:
8369-5279-0

LIBRARY OF CONGRESS CATALOG CARD NUMBER:
73-114875

PRINTED IN THE UNITED STATES OF AMERICA

PREFACE.

IT is not without hesitation that I offer to the public the present contribution to the history of music. I am fully aware that, in having to express myself in a language which is not my mother tongue, I labour under considerable disadvantage. Nevertheless, I venture to hope for the reader's indulgence on this point, for the following reasons.

For years I have taken every opportunity of ascertaining the distinctive characteristics of the music not only of civilized but also of uncivilized nations. I soon saw that the latter is capable of yielding important suggestions for the science and history of music, just as the languages of savage nations are useful in philological and ethnological inquiries.

As I proceeded, I became more and more convinced that, in order to understand clearly the music of the various modern nations, it was necessary to extend my researches to the music of ancient nations. Thus my attention was directed to the Assyrian monuments in the British Museum. All the facts which I have been able to gather from them must be considered as a new addition to our history of music, and one by no means unimportant to the musician.

If from the music of ancient nations important

hints may be obtained respecting the music of the
various modern nations, on the other hand, an exact
acquaintance with the latter greatly facilitates the
proper appreciation of the music of any ancient
nation, such as the Assyrian.

For these reasons I venture to hope that my book,
notwithstanding its shortcomings, may be received
with indulgence by those interested in the subject of
which it treats.

Should this hope be realized, I purpose soon to
publish a work on National Music, on which I have
for a considerable time been occupied.

Respecting the illustrations in the present book, I
have to add that those relating to Assyrian music, as
well as several illustrative of Egyptian music, have
been copied from the antiquities in the British
Museum. Some, which have been derived from
other sources, are specified n the list. Moreover,
for drawings of most of the Egyptian musical instruments, I am indebted to Sir Gardner Wilkinson's
'Manners and Customs of the Ancient Egyptians,'—
a work which deserves the special consideration of
all interested in the history of ancient music.

1864.   C. E.

PUBLISHER'S NOTE TO THIS ISSUE.
(Which is an exact facsimile of the 1864 edition).

Fig. 6, page 38. Assyrian Lyre. The strings, as stated in the
letterpress, should be shown tied round the front bar. This is
shown in the British Museum slab.

Fig. 9, page 44. Assyrian dulcimer. The end of the dulcimer
away from the performer has been somewhat unskilfully mended
in the example at the British Museum and in joining the slabs
a portion showing the bridge is wanting. This should have been
shown in the illustration given.

1909.

CONTENTS.

CHAPTER I.

THE OLDEST RECORDS ON MUSIC.

CHAPTER II.

MUSICAL INSTRUMENTS OF THE ASSYRIANS.

CHAPTER III.

ASSYRIAN MUSICAL PERFORMANCES.

CHAPTER IV.

MUSICAL SYSTEM OF THE ASSYRIANS.

CHAPTER V.

MUSIC OF THE ANCIENT EGYPTIANS.

CHAPTER VI.

MUSIC OF THE HEBREWS.

LIST OF ILLUSTRATIONS.

MUSIC

OF

THE MOST ANCIENT NATIONS.

CHAPTER I.

THE OLDEST RECORDS ON MUSIC.

Representations of musical instruments on ancient sculptures and paintings—National music applied to ethnology—Monumental records referring to Assyrian music—The ruins of Nimroud, Khorsabad, and Kouyunjik—The extent to which the characteristics of Assyrian music can be ascertained from the representations of the instruments—The gradual development of music from its most primitive state, demonstrated by a comparison of the music of modern nations in different stages of civilization—The earliest musical instruments—Examples of musical scales in use among nations in different stages of civilization—The earliest development of vocal music—The degree of progress in music attained by the Assyrians—Their accomplishments in other arts.

IT is unnecessary for the purpose of this work to notice the mythological accounts and legends found among different nations respecting the origin and early development of music. Neither need I trouble the reader with a reiteration of the oldest records on this art given in Holy Writ. With these I may presume every one to be acquainted; at all events a reference to Burney's ' History of Music,' or any similar work, will at once supply the inquirer with such information. My object is to submit a few observations which are not to be found in those books, but which seem to me useful as introductory to the following pages, because they indicate the

B

point of view from which the music of the Assyrians, as an art, ought to be considered, in order to be properly understood.

Before proceeding further, it must be observed how much new light has been thrown on the state of music of different ancient nations by the various interesting researches and discoveries made in the course of the present century. Not only have we become better acquainted, by means of sculptures and paintings, with the musical instruments of several ancient nations, but in some instances the actual instruments have been discovered in tombs or other places, where, protected from the destroying influences of air and damp, they had remained almost unchanged during a marvellously long period. It seems indeed almost incredible, but it is nevertheless a fact, that in one of the famous sepulchres at Thebes an Egyptian harp was found, with catgut strings which, when touched, still emitted sounds, though the instrument had been immured and mute probably about three thousand years.

With the musical instruments of the ancient Egyptians especially we have become more intimately acquainted during the present century, by means of sculptures and frescoes, which not only furnish representations of instruments, but also show us their use in musical performances, and display the peculiar customs of the people among whom music was common.

Besides the music of the ancients, we have become gradually more familiar with that of contemporary nations in every part of the globe;—at all events, more attention is paid now to national music than formerly, though this subject does not in my opinion yet receive that consideration which it deserves.

Hitherto it has been almost entirely disregarded by musical *savants*. Sir John Hawkins, in the preface to his 'History of Music,' says: "The best music of barbarians is said to be hideous and astonishing sounds. Of what importance then can it be to inquire into a practice that has not its foundation in science or system, or to know what are the sounds that most delight a Hottentot, a wild American, or even a more refined Chinese?" I have transcribed Hawkins's own words, because he precisely expresses the prevailing opinion, not only of his own day, but also of the present time. I think, however, a few moments' reflection will convince the reader of its fallacy. The study of national music is especially useful to the musician, because it enlarges his musical conception, and secures him from one-sidedness and an unwarranted predilection for any peculiar style or any particular composer.

Many national tunes are delightfully beautiful, and are therefore eminently fitted for improving the taste and preparing it for a higher appreciation and a judicious cultivation of what is refined and beautiful in art. Our best composers, as might be expected, have been fully aware of this; indeed, they have been the most ardent admirers of national music, and have not unfrequently evinced this by imitations of national tunes, or by adopting them into their works. Handel's beautiful Pastorale in the 'Messiah' owes it origin to a song of the Italian *Pifferari*,—Calabrian peasants, who, according to an ancient custom, make their appearance in Rome about Christmas, to perform their pastoral melodies before the shrines of the Holy Virgin; — Mendelssohn also is indebted for the theme of the admirable Scherzo in his

Symphony in A minor to a well-known Scottish melody.

And though the music of some nations may appear to us harsh and rude, it not infrequently gains upon us when we have, so to say, become reconciled to its unpolished exterior, and are no longer unable to catch its true spirit. This may be said to be the case, for instance, with the music of the Hungarians and Wallachians, which, however strange and unsatisfactory it may appear to the ear of those not accustomed to it, has great charms for the initiated.

Moreover, national music which may seem to us entirely devoid of beauty, possesses generally some characteristic peculiarities in rhythm or modulation, which afford valuable hints to the reflecting musician; so much so, that, when judiciously employed and ennobled in musical composition, they may be made to produce new and charming effects.

Likewise a knowledge of the nature and construction of the numerous musical instruments used by different nations may be, and indeed has often been, suggestive in inventing and improving our own instruments.

Even if it were true that the music of those nations only which have cultivated this art scientifically, could be considered worthy of being inquired into, it is evident that the contempt with which Hawkins speaks of the music of the Chinese is inconsistent with his own dogma, since they, as well as the Hindoos, Persians, Arabs, and several other nations, all of which are entirely ignored by him, actually possessed musical systems long before our own was developed.

Again, in an ethnological point of view, an acquaintance with national music must be, I should think, interesting. There are sometimes striking resemblances in the musical scales, in peculiarly characteristic modulations, or in the construction and employment of the musical instruments, between two different nations, so that the ethnologist may perhaps find therein hints, either affording him additional evidence in substantiating a preconceived theory, or perhaps even suggesting some entirely new investigation. Thus, though the remarkable resemblance of the music and musical instruments of the Japanese with those of the Chinese cannot be considered as a sufficient proof that these two nations derived their civilization from the same source, yet in combination with other evidence it may point to a conclusion almost irrefragable.

And as in their songs the people express generally their innermost feelings and aspirations, national music would even on this account alone be highly interesting to the intelligent mind, because it exhibits the true character of a nation.

Moreover, a knowledge of it is an especial assistance in investigating the music of ancient nations such as the Assyrians or the Egyptians, and it is for this reason that I have thought it necessary to say thus much on a subject which most otherwise appear irrelevant.

Concerning the music of the Assyrians little or nothing is to be found in our musical literature; nor could it be otherwise, since the discoveries which give us some insight into its character are of very recent date. These are almost the only sources from which information can be obtained; and as they are yet very limited, the result of an investigation of them must necessarily be in many points unsatisfactory. However, as regards a nation such as the Assyrians, who played for a long time an important part in the

history of the world, and whose power, wealth, enter-
prise, and military greatness, as recorded in the
Bible, have been, so to say, brought before our eyes
through recent discoveries,—any investigation which
is likely to assist in throwing additional light upon
its state of civilization cannot but be interesting.
Besides, through the music of the Assyrians we may
also possibly become better acquainted with that of the
Hebrews, so often mentioned in the Bible, on which
many treatises have been written, but which nevertheless is so imperfectly understood that even the meaning
of frequently-occurring musical terms and expressions,
and the nature of some of the most usual Hebrew instruments, have not been exactly ascertained.

The discovered monuments of the Assyrians, on
which the musical instruments are represented, consist of bas-reliefs. Most of them are at present deposited in the British Museum. They have been
obtained from three extensive mounds near the river
Tigris in Asiatic Turkey. These mounds owe their
origin to the natural accumulation of rubbish and
earth over the ruins of destroyed edifices. They are
known as the mounds of Nimroud, Khorsabad, and
Kouyunjik.

Nimroud, situated about twenty miles to the south
of the town of Mosul, was explored in 1847 and 1850
by Mr. Layard, and the discovered bas-reliefs have
been transmitted to the British Museum.

Khorsabad, about ten miles to the north-east of
Mosul, has been excavated by M. Botta, French
Consul at Mosul. Most of the sculptures obtained
by him are at present in the Louvre.

The mound of Kouyunjik, which is believed to
contain the ruins of the ancient city of Nineveh, is

situated in the immediate vicinity of Mosul, on the opposite bank of the Tigris. Mr. Layard, in his 'Monuments of Nineveh,' observes that many of the sculptures from this mound were, when discovered, in too advanced a stage of decay to bear removal, and have already perished. A valuable collection was, nevertheless, secured by him, and is now exhibited in a separate gallery in the British Museum. Another very interesting series of slabs from Kouyunjik has recently been obtained, also for the British Museum, by Mr. Hormuzd Rassam, and by Mr. Loftus, who excavated the mound in 1853 and the two following years, under the direction of Sir H. C. Rawlinson, who resided at that time as British Consul-General in Bagdad.

According to the opinion of the most competent judges on Assyrian history, the period in which these monuments were executed commences about 1000 years B.C. The musical instruments represented thereon must of course be older, and may have existed many centuries before that time. This appears the more probable when we consider that they were used at religious and popular ceremonies, and in representations of historical events of earlier times.

It may perhaps be objected· that from the mere representations of the instruments, which moreover are, in not a few instances, imperfectly preserved and partly obliterated, but little reliable information respecting the characteristics of Assyrian music can be gathered. However, it must be borne in mind that musical instruments are often so constructed as to permit only the use of certain intervals or combinations of sounds. This is the case with several of the Assyrian instruments, as I shall endeavour

hereafter to explain. Besides, almost all these instruments are yet in existence in different parts of
the East, and are played upon by the people almost
precisely in the same manner as we see that they
were handled nearly 3000 years ago by the Assyrians. And it is remarkable also that several of the
peculiar customs or ceremonies with which music
was connected, according to the representations on
the Assyrian sculptures are yet to be found in the
East. I trust a consideration of these facts will make
it appear less presumptuous in me if, from an examination of the slabs, in connexion with other suggestive hints which will be noticed afterwards, I
venture to come to a definite and certain conclusion
respecting the nature of the musical system of the
Assyrians.

There is another point with reference to our oldest
records on music, on which it seems to me necessary
to say here a few words. Nothing is more usual
than the notion that, in order to trace the art of
music from its most primitive state and to observe
its gradual development, we must commence our
inquiries by penetrating the most remote periods.
This, however, is erroneous, as I shall have soon
an opportunity of proving. Indeed it will be seen
that among the most ancient nations known to us—
the Assyrians as well as the ancient Egyptians and
Hebrews—music had already attained a degree of
perfection considerably higher than we meet with in
many nations of our own time.

A clear idea of the gradual development of the
art of music, from its most primitive condition to
that degree of perfection in which it at present exists
among ourselves, may be best obtained by examining

the music of contemporary nations in different stages
of civilisation. At the same time it is necessary to
compare the music of several nations standing in the
same scale of civilisation, because climate, the usual
occupations of a people, and other circumstances, are
here not without a modifying influence. Thus, in
order to ascertain how music reveals itself in its
earliest infancy, we ought to observe it not only
among the natives of the Fuegian Archipelago, or
the Esquimaux, but also among the natives of Aus-
tralia, of New Guinea, and others in a similarly low
state of civilisation, who are placed in a part of the
globe which impels them to pursuits and habits different from those which we find among the former.

Some knowledge of this kind seems to me absolutely requisite for an unbiassed examination of the
music of an ancient nation like the Assyrian. If we
were to consider it only from the level of our own
highly cultivated music, starting with the assumption
that the musical system of the Assyrians must have
been similar to our own, though less perfect—that
they possessed scales and rhythmical constructions
similar to ours, though probably much more incomplete—that their musical compositions must have
been the less good the less they resembled the compositions of Mozart and Beethoven—if we were to
commence our enquiries from this one-sided point of
view, we should be led to partial and unsatisfactory
conclusions.

The reader will therefore do well to bear in mind
the following brief observations, which result from a
comparison of the music of the different nations of
the present time, as I have just indicated.

Vocal music, regarded historically, takes precedence

by its antiquity of instrumental music. There exist even at the present time a few savage tribes who, though possessing a number of songs, are almost entirely unacquainted with musical instruments. If they accompany their vocal effusions at all, it is only with the rhythmical sounds produced by clapping of hands, or by beating pieces of wood together. Generally, however, the most uncivilised nations at present existing employ for this purpose some rhythmical instruments, especially the drum and the rattle. The invention of these instruments is very naturally accounted for. Indeed it is not improbable that man was led by the animating effect of the regular accompanying sounds of his steps, in walking while singing, to invent such instruments to heighten the effect of his songs, especially in processions and dances. At all events it is not surprising that we meet with them at an earlier period than with any others. The variety in construction, shape, and size of the different kinds of drums, found in almost every part of the world, is indeed remarkable. It would almost require a separate work to describe them.

A step further, and some rude wind-instruments make their appearance. The pipe, generally made of reed or wood, appears at first without finger-holes, and only capable of emitting one or two notes. Similarly incomplete is the horn or trumpet, usually constructed of the horn of an animal in which a mouth-hole has been cut; or consisting of pieces of wood fixed tightly together, like the Swiss *Alp-horn* and the *Lure* of the Scandinavians; or made of the tusk of an animal, as the large ivory trumpets of the negroes of Western Africa, which are simply the hollowed tusks of elephants.

Another step further and we find, in addition to those already mentioned, some rude wind-instruments formed by a combination of a number of pipes, such as the double-pipe and the Pandean-pipe (the *syrinx* of the ancients). The latter especially is to be found among many savage tribes in different parts of the globe. This instrument is particularly remarkable as being the first producing a series of notes of different pitch, and therefore the first on which a melody, or what may be called a tune, could be played. But it must not be supposed that in the rudest instruments of this kind any regular order of succession of notes is observed. On the contrary, the notes succeed each other without any systematical arrangement whatever.

Next we meet with instruments consisting of a series of pieces of sonorous wood, which are made to vibrate by being beaten with a stick or hammer, like our harmonicon. The invention of instruments of this description seems to have suggested itself to many nations at a very early stage of musical progress; nor is this to be wondered at, considering that sometimes a merely rhythmical instrument like the drum, when made of hard wood or any other particularly sonorous substance, will emit a distinct tone instead of a confused sound. The effect accidentally produced by a few such drums beaten at the same time must have soon directed man's attention to the invention of a united series of wooden slabs of different pitch. It is therefore not surprising that instruments of the harmonicon species should exist in many different parts of the world. Some savage tribes possess them at present in a very imperfect state; but generally we find them improved by the addition of some contrivance for increasing the sound, like our sounding-board. The negroes use gourds for this purpose. What I have said of the notes of the syrinx applies also here. Where these instruments exist in a most primitive condition, no regular succession of intervals is traceable, but the relation of the notes to each other is seemingly quite unpremeditated and accidental. However at present there are but few nations so little advanced in music as not to possess some kind of order in the notes produced on their instruments, or what might be considered as some approach to a musical scale. The following examples, selected from a number which I obtained by an examination and careful comparison of the instruments to which they appertain, may further elucidate my observations :—

1. Syrinx.—Tonga Islands.

2. Another.

3. Another.

4. Zanze.—Senegambia.

5. Vissandschi.—Congo.

6. Zanze.—Guinea.

7. Syrinx.—Ancient Peru

8. Pipe.—Ancient Mexico.

9. Gambang gangsa.—Java.

10. A kind of Harmonicon.—China.

11. Balafo.—Senegambia.

12. Balafo.—Mandingoes.

Nos. 1, 2, and 3, are the notes of three syrinxes from the Friendly or Tonga Islands in the Pacific Ocean. The syrinx No. 1 was brought by Captain Fourneaux from Tongataboo (formerly called the Isle of Amsterdam), and is the same which has been described in the 'Philosophical Transactions of the Royal Society,' vol. lxv. Nos. 2 and 3 are from instruments in the British Museum : the former consists of nine pipes, and the latter of ten, which, when blown with an unusually strong breath, produce other notes besides those above indicated. No. 2 may be considered as belonging to the diatonic scale of A major, and No. 8 to that of D major. The arrangement in the succession of the notes may perhaps have been suggested by the notes of some birds: at least such is the impression produced upon the hearer when the pipes are sounded in a moderately fast time. Nos. 4, 5, and 6 show the notes of three *zanzes*. The zanze (in different parts of Africa known also by the names of *ambira, marimba, ibeka, vissandschi*, &c.) is a favourite instrument of the negroes, especially of those in Senegambia and in Upper and Lower Guinea. It consists of a wooden box on which a number of sonorous slips of wood, or tongues of iron, are fixed in such a position as to admit of their being made to vibrate by pressing them down with the thumb or with a stick. Of the above instruments No. 4 consists of slips of wood or cane ; the others have tongues of iron. They are in the possession of Victor Schœlcher, Esq., who kindly permitted me to examine his interesting collection of musical instruments. The succession of the notes in these three instruments appears, as will be observed in the above examples, to be quite arbitrary.

No. 7 shows the intervals of a syrinx, called
huayra-puhura, of the ancient Peruvians. Several
instruments of this kind, made either of reed or of
stone, have been discovered in ancient tombs. The
present one, which may be seen in the British
Museum, contains a double row of reed-pipes, of
which one is open below, and the other closed.

No. 8 shows the intervals of an instrument of the
ancient Mexicans, a kind of flageolet with four finger-
holes.

No. 9 shows the intervals of the *gambang gangsa*, a
kind of harmonicon with metal plates, from Java;
and No. 10 the intervals of a Chinese instrument of
a similar description, but made entirely of wood. It
will be seen that these instruments have the notes of
our diatonic scale, with the exception of the intervals
of the *fourth* and *seventh*. The two semitones of our
diatonic scale are consequently wanting, and there
are only five different notes in the compass of an
octave. On the other hand there are two *minor thirds*
which in our diatonic scale do not occur, viz., from
the third to the fifth, and from the sixth to the
octave. As I shall have afterwards to refer to this
peculiar scale, which is to be found in several Asiatic
nations, and which existed evidently in former ages
with others where at present only a few traces of its
former existence are perceptible, I may add that I
have given it, by way of distinction from the diatonic scale, the name of *pentatonic* scale.

It is remarkable that the music of the ancient Inca
Peruvians, and of the Aztecs in Mexico, was also
founded upon this scale, as will be seen indicated in
the notations Nos. 7 and 8, and as I could further
prove by corroborative evidence. This fact may be

suggestive to the ethnologist, as pointing to an early connexion between the American Indians and Asiatic nations.

Nos. 11 and 12 exhibit the intervals appertaining to two *balafoes* of the negroes of Senegambia. The Mandingoes, from whom the second of these has been obtained, are, it will be remembered, a people widely spread through Western Africa, and somewhat more advanced in civilization than most other negro tribes. The fact that on the balafo, which is a species of harmonicon, we meet with our diatonic scale (and I could point out other nations even less advanced than the Mandingoes who are acquainted with this scale), may tend to the conclusion that this scale naturally suggests itself wherever sufficient progress in music has been made for the adoption of any distinct and regular succession of intervals. Even if we assume that, where we find this scale among uncivilized nations, it must have been derived from Europeans, as is in many instances undoubtedly the case, it proves at all events that there exists very universally a natural susceptibility for it, and that it is therefore a less artificial scale than theorists have frequently declared it to be. However, I hope to show that it is not the *only* scale with which a nation must necessarily become acquainted in its musical progress.

After the invention of the syrinx and the harmonicon, the next important step in the development of instrumental music was the discovery that upon a single pipe different notes are producible by means of finger-holes. A great variety exists of such instruments, blown with the mouth, or with the nose, as the nose-flutes of the Society and Feejee Islanders, and the *poogyee* of the Hindoos. I could point out several nations or tribes who, when first visited by Europeans, possessed such instruments, though they were entirely unacquainted with stringed instruments. There is, however, one stringed instrument which, among some savage nations, is found at a very early stage of musical progress, and before the invention of wind-instruments with finger-holes. This is merely an elastic stick bent with one or two strings, like a bow. Indeed it is very probable that the bow used in the chase and in war suggested this instrument, which in its turn seems to have led to the invention of several others, in which the shape of the bow is more or less discernible. We may then consider this primitive bow-shaped stringed instrument as the great ancestor of the harp, lyre, and other similarly constructed stringed instruments.

In most instances, however, those nations who are only acquainted with one stringed instrument construct this by stretching some strings over a hollow piece of wood or a calabash. The strings, usually consisting of the fibre of some plant or the hair of some animal, are played upon either with the hand or with a *plectrum* made of wood, bone, or any other suitable substance. In a more perfect condition an instrument of this description greatly resembles our *dulcimer*. It may therefore be considered the parent of the latter, from which again ultimately have sprung the harpsichord, spinet, pianoforte, and all similar instruments.

Important progress in the development of instrumental music was made by the invention of the finger-board, or neck, by means of which a series of different notes is obtainable on one string, merely by

c

shortening it more or less, as is the case with the guitar, lute, tamboura, and others.

Stringed instruments played with a bow are the least universal. They are however met with not only throughout Europe, but also among the Chinese, Hindoos, Japanese, and other Asiatic nations.

The invention of keyed instruments, like our pianoforte and organ, is entirely European, and of comparatively recent date. The rudiments of these instruments, however, have existed in Asia from a very remote period. The Chinese, as well as the Japanese, possess two distinct instruments which in construction bear a remarkable resemblance to our organ. One of these, the *cheng* of the Chinese, consists of a box or bowl, into which a number of tubes of different length and pitch are inserted. Each of these tubes contains a small metallic tongue, like the so-called *free-reed* stops of our organ, or like our accordion. The instrument is made to sound by being blown with the mouth through a kind of spout at the side of the bowl, and the tubes have holes to be played upon with the fingers. In Laos and Siam there is also a species of organ constructed on a principle similar to the *cheng*, though entirely dissimilar in outward appearance.

In indicating the order in which the different kinds of instruments make their appearance in the development of music, I do not of course intend to imply that this order necessarily occurs in every nation, but only that it is the most usual. Extraordinary influences not unfrequently produce exceptions: thus an uncivilized nation coming in contact with a civilized one is most likely to adopt the inventions of the latter, without experiencing the gradual degrees of progression which in the course of time led to these inventions. The Hottentots in South Africa—a people particularly ingenious as well as fond of music—having become acquainted with the violin through the Dutch boors who settled among them, soon contrived to construct similar instruments, and learned to play them ; so that at present a rude kind of violin is not uncommon among the Hottentots, and may be considered as one of their national instruments, although they are unacquainted with several others which have usually preceded the invention of stringed instruments played with a bow.

The earliest development of vocal music is closely connected with that of instrumental music. The melodies of songs are not unfrequently performed by the people on their instruments, and melodies originally invented on instruments are often adopted as tunes of songs by being wedded to words. Certain characteristics in national songs—as, for instance, a peculiar succession of intervals, a frequent occurrence of certain groups of notes, passages, or modulations—can therefore be frequently traced to some favourite instrument which, from the nature of its construction, suggests or perhaps demands these characteristics. For this reason it is often possible, solely from an exact acquaintance with the musical instruments of a nation, to determine with much certainty the chief characteristics of its vocal music.

The songs of savages in the lowest scale of civilization are generally confined to the compass of few notes, seldom extending beyond the interval of the *fifth*. Sometimes, however, a sudden transition into the octave occurs, especially in sudden exclamations, or where a word naturally dictates an emphatic raising of the voice. The *fifth* especially plays a prominent part in primitive vocal music. As far as I have been able to ascertain from an examination of many songs of this description, derived from different nations, it appears that, with respect to their more or less frequent occurrence, the intervals range in the following order:—*Prime, fifth, third, second, sixth, octave, fourth, seventh.* But it must not be supposed that each interval is distinctly intoned: on the contrary, in the transition from one interval to another, all the intermediate intervals are slightly touched in a way somewhat similar to a violinist drawing his finger rapidly over the string from one note to another to connect them; and as the intervals themselves are seldom clearly defined, it will easily be understood how nearly impossible it is to write down such songs in our notation so as to convey a correct idea of their natural effect. In instances where the *major third* is not distinctly intoned, it sometimes gives the impression of *minor;* and I have reason to believe that many songs have been written down in *minor* by collectors which would have been more properly written in *major.*

Savages are generally very imitative. Their dances are often representations of the peculiar motions and gambols of certain animals; and the *motivos* of their songs have not unfrequently been derived from a similar source, especially from the songs of birds. Sometimes this can be distinctly traced. As as an example I shall only mention the *Aangitsch songs* of the natives of Kamtschatka, which derive their name as well as their origin from a wild duck (*Anas glacialis*) which appears in Kamtschatka at a certain season in large flocks. The notes of this bird are—

but the same pitch is not constant in all birds of this description, some emitting the notes higher, some lower. It may easily be imagined what a variety of melodious sounds must be produced from a whole flock of these birds. This explains also how it happens that the *Aangitsch songs*, which form a particular class of national songs of the Kamtschadales, are very different from each other, although all have been derived from the same source.

We should however err were we to infer, as some speculators have done, from such facts, that in a primitive stage of the art all vocal compositions consisted only of imitations or adoptions of sounds derived from the animated world. The power of creating an expressive melody is an inate gift which the most primitive savage may possess as fully as the most highly civilized man. Susceptibility for music is, in a greater or less degree, natural to all men, and is not dependent on the state of civilization which has been attained. The savage thus gifted, however little in some respects he may be elevated above the animal, is likely, when influenced by strong emotions, to be led by a natural impulse to give vent to his feelings in musical phrases improvised at the moment, without any external aid. If these phrases, or rather melodies, are particularly impressive and pleasing to others, they are soon caught and retained in the memory, and further circulated among the people. Such is usually the origin of national songs, which, however, as they mostly are only traditionally preserved, frequently undergo, in the course of time, considerable alterations by additions, extensions, or otherwise.

With respect to the form of vocal music in its infancy, I must not omit to notice the usual combination of voices in which two or more sing alternately, or in which a chorus responds to a leader, who is more generally the chief or superior of the party than the superior musician. This mode of singing has been observed in many uncivilized nations. We find it, for instance, among the New Zealanders, in dragging their canoes overland; among the palanquin-bearers in Hindoostan ; among the negro slaves in Brazil, when employed in carrying heavy burdens ; among the Egyptian boatmen on the Nile. And such is also the oldest form of vocal performance recorded in the Bible. After the miraculous escape of the Jews through the Red Sea, and the destruction of the pursuing enemy (about 1500 b.c.), "Miriam the prophetess, the sister of Aaron, took a timbrel in her hand ; and all the women went out after her with timbrels and with dances. And Miriam *answered them*, Sing ye to the Lord, for he has triumphed gloriously ; the horse and his rider hath he thrown into the sea" (Exodus xv. 20). Again, about four centuries later, when David returned from the slaughter of the Philistine Goliath, "the women came out of all the cities of Israel, singing and dancing, to meet King Saul, with tabrets, with joy, and with instruments of music. And the women *answered one another as they played*, and said, Saul has slain his thousands, and David his ten thousands" (1 Sam. xviii. 6). From the construction of some of the Psalms it appears also that the Jews practised alternate singing of this nature during their religious observances in the Temple. I may cite as an example the cxxxvi. Psalm, with its regular repetition of the sentence, "for his mercy endureth for ever." Later we find in the Christian Church a similar form, which has been preserved until the present time in our antiphonal responses.

There are so many noteworthy facts relating to the earliest development of the art of music, as observed among different nations that I should gladly have extended my observations on this branch of my subject, were this the proper place for so doing. However, the above sketch, imperfect though it be, will, I believe, be sufficient to prepare the reader for an unbiassed examination of the music of the Assyrians, Egyptians, and Hebrews, which is the chief object of this book. I may add that those who desire to learn more about national music will find information and drawings of foreign instruments in a work shortly to be published in which I have endeavoured to show that an acquaintance with the characteristics of the music of different nations may be an assistance in ethnological researches, as well as in the study of musical composition.

The Assyrians, as we learn from their monuments, not only possessed a variety of pulsatile, wind, and stringed instruments, but they also understood how to employ different kinds of stringed instruments in concert, either in mere instrumental performances or in connexion with vocal music. Moreover they were acquainted with the use of the finger-board, by means of which a great number of distinct notes are attainable on a few strings, like those on the guitar or mandoline. We may therefore conclude that their musical acquirements were considerably in advance of those of some nations of the present day.

Progress in music is generally slower than in other arts, because much depends on the auxiliary aid of musical instruments, which require to be invented or improved previous to the music which is performed upon them being advanced. We may therefore conclude, from the progress which the Assyrians had made in music, that they must also have progressed considerably in other arts, and must have attained a degree of cultivation in taste and social refinement altogether remarkable. This conclusion is corroborated by the accounts of the Assyrians which we find in the Bible, and confirmed by the sculptured bas-reliefs to which I have alluded. The same opinion is held by scholars who have made the history of the Assyrians their special study. Mr. Bonomi, in his interesting work on Nineveh, has given a graphic account of the high state of perfection to which several of their arts had attained. Of sculpture he says, "The most striking facts that present themselves to our imagination, in contemplating the remains of the Assyrian palaces, are the perfection to which the art of sculpture had arrived at so remote a period, and the important evidence they afford of conversance with the most refined arts of life, both indicating a pitch of civilization that we should find it difficult to reconcile with the most extended scheme of chronology, if at the same time we were bound to suppose that the first settlers in the land were in a parallel state of ignorance and degradation with the inhabitants of New South Wales, or with those of the back-woods of America. The Scriptures, however, afford ample evidence of a primitive civilization, especially in the knowledge of the working in metals, and of other refined arts (Gen. iv. 17, 21, 22), even before the Deluge ; and this testimony, we apprehend, sufficiently accounts for any degree of proficiency we find in the works of art of these remote ages, and for that early civilization of the human family which the contemplation of these sculptures suggests."

Again, with respect to other accomplishments, we are told, " The Assyrians were able to work the hardest as well as the softest substances, with a view to their employment in building or other purposes. This is proved by the jasper or crystal cylinders, and by the bas-reliefs sculptured on gypsum or siliceous basalt. They were acquainted with glass and various kinds of enamels. They could bake clay for bricks or vases, the quality of the clay varying in fineness according to the purpose for which the vases were intended. . . . The Assyrians were also acquainted with the art of founding, of working, and even hammering out various metals ; the latter branch of manufactures having acquired great perfection among them, as can be seen by the little statue of the bronze lion, the nails, calf's head, &c. The metal most frequently used appears to have been copper, as was the case with all people of antiquity. . . . Among those who traded in ' blue cloths and embroidered work ' with Tyre, Ezekiel (xxvii. 24) enumerates the merchants of Asshur, or Assyria. In these stuffs, gold threads (Pliny, viii. 48) were introduced into the woof of many colours, and were no doubt the ' dyed attire and embroidered work ' so frequently mentioned in Scripture as the most costly and splendid garments of kings and princes. The cotton manufactures were equally celebrated and remarkable, and are mentioned by Pliny as the invention of Semiramis, who is stated by many writers of antiquity to have founded large weaving establishments along the banks of the Tigris and Euphrates. The silken robes of Assyria, the produce chiefly of the looms of Babylon, were renowned long after the fall of the Assyrian empire, and retained their hold of the market even to the time of the Roman supremacy. Frequent allusions are found in classic authors to the brilliancy and magnificence of the Babylonian carpets, which were embroidered with symbolic figures, together with animals and conventional forms. . . . Copper constantly occurs in their weapons, and most probably a mixture of it was used in the materials of their tools. They had acquired the art of making glass, an invention usually attributed to the Phœnicians. Several small bottles or vases of this substance, of an elegant shape, were found at Nimroud and Kouyunjik. The well-known cylinders are a sufficient proof of their skill in engraving gems. Many beautiful specimens of carving in ivory were also discovered—an interesting illustration of a passage in Ezekiel (xxvii. 6), where the company of Assyrians are described as the makers of the ivory benches of the Tyrian galleys: 'The company of the Ashurites have made thy benches of ivory, brought out of the isles of Chittim.' Some tablets of ivory from Nimroud are richly inlaid with blue opaque glass, lapis lazuli, &c.''[1]

In concluding these introductory observations, I

---

[1] Nineveh and its Palaces, by Joseph Bonomi, London, 1853, p. 323 &c.

shall only point out that the music of the Assyrians,
though evidently greatly inferior to our own, yet
appears to have attained to a degree of perfection
which it could have reached only after a long period
of cultivation. It is not at all probable that music
should have attained such a degree of perfection by
cultivation during the existence of one nation, however extended the period of this existence may have
been. We are therefore reasonably led to infer that
the Assyrians derived their music in an already
somewhat advanced state from some other nation or
nations unknown to us, and that they only further
developed what had been transmitted to them. This
view may appear merely conjectural. I trust, however, that a perusal of the following pages will convince the reader that it is not advanced without some
plausible reason. Moreover the oldest records on
music in Holy Writ also tend in some measure to
confirm my hypothesis.

CHAPTER II.

MUSICAL INSTRUMENTS OF THE ASSYRIANS.

The harp—Traces of the ancient Oriental harp in Europe—the Assyrian lyre and the Nubian kissar—The Assyrian dulcimer and the Persian santir—The asor—The tamboura or guitar—The double pipe—The trumpet—The drum—Assyrian bronze bells found in the ruins of Nimroud—Tambourine and cymbals— Remarks on the dancing of the Assyrian musicians—Traces of some other Assyrian instruments—Conjectures on the antiquity of stringed instruments played with a bow—Some peculiar similarities between ancient Asiatic and European instruments—The names of musical instruments.

THE Assyrian bas-reliefs chiefly represent historical events, religious ceremonies, and royal entertainments. It is therefore very probable that the Assyrians possessed several popular musical instruments which are not represented on these bas-reliefs, because they were not employed on occasions such as those alluded to. And it may be thus explained how it happens that we do not meet with certain instruments which we naturally might expect to find, and of which I shall say a few words presently. Further discoveries may also bring to light some others hitherto unknown. However, those known to us are sufficiently numerous and various to afford an insight into the characters of Assyrian music. With these I shall now endeavour to make the reader acquainted.

THE HARP.

The frame of the Assyrian harp was about four feet high. The performer held the instrument before his breast, and played while standing or walking. It must have been light, because women as well as men carried it in processions, while singing, and even while dancing. This is shown in our frontispiece, which represents a procession meeting a conqueror. In this illustration may also be observed some difference in the several harps, which is chiefly occasioned by the more or less ornamented tassels which are appended to the lower part of the frame. These appendages make the instrument appear nearly half as large again as it really is. The upper portion of the frame contained the sounding board; two sounding-holes, somewhat in the shape of an hour-glass, are seen on one side. Below them are the screws, or tuning pegs, arranged in regular order. The strings run from these pegs down to the horizontal bar of the frame, round which they are fastened; and the tassels alluded to appear to be united to the strings so as to form a prolongation of them. On some of the harps also the horizontal bar is represented with dots similar to those which show the tuning pegs in the upper portion of the frame.

Fig. 3.   Assyrian harp.

The strings were perhaps made of silk, like those which the Burmese use at the present time on their harps, or they may have been catgut, which was used by the ancient Egyptians, one of whose harps thus strung as I have already mentioned, has been exhumed.

The greatest difference in the construction of the Assyrian harp as compared with our own is that the front pillar, which in our harp serves to resist the tension of the strings is entirely wanting in the Assyrian harp. It may perhaps be inferred that on this account the frame was not calculated to resist any great tension of the strings, and that consequently the sound of the instrument must have been weak and poor. However, some of the Burmese harps, as well as several other instruments similarly constructed, emit, as I can attest, notes far more clear and sonorous than one might be lead to expect from their appearance. Moreover, if the Assyrian harp was not made entirely of wood, but partly of metal or ivory, which is very probable, it may have had strength enough to resist a considerable tension of the strings, and to permit of their being screwed up very tightly.

The drawing (fig 4) represents an eunuch playing the harp. The slab from which it has been sketched is remarkably well preserved, and every part of the instrument appears very distinct. In several points it is, as will be observed, different from the harp represented in fig. 3. The appendages seem to consist only of cords, the ends of which are untwisted, or of one row of tassels; while on the former there are four rows. Also the shape of the frame differs, as well as the number of strings and pegs. The

manner in which the performer places the little
finger of his right hand under the lowest bar of the
frame is peculiar, This was probably done to keep
the instrument more steadily in its right position.
It must however, have pre-
vented his using the right
hand with the same facility
as the left.

It is difficult to determine
from the bas-reliefs what was
the usual number of strings
of the Assyrian harp, since
almost all the representations of it are in too imperfect
a state of preservation for the
strings to be exactly counted.
Besides, the Assyrian sculptors may very probably have
thought it unimportant to
represent scrupulously the
right number. This is also
proved by the fact that on
most harps the number of
the tuning pegs is not in
accordance with the number
of the strings. Of four harps,
on which both are sufficiently
distinct to be ascertained, I
found one with 21 strings

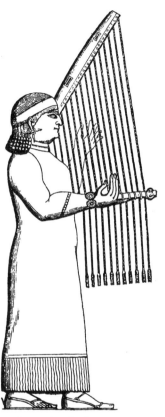

Fig. 4.   Assyrian harp.

and 15 pegs ; another with 21 strings and 12 pegs ;
a third with 23 strings and 17 pegs ; and a fourth
with 14 strings and 26 pegs.

Generally the Assyrian sculptors were very exact,
even in minute details ; of this the monuments afford

ample evidence. We have therefore good reason to apprehend that in all the musical instruments which have only a small number of strings, which are easily discerned, we may accept their representations as reliable in every respect. Thus, an instrument with three strings would certainly not have been represented as having four or five, although they considered it immaterial whether they gave an instrument with 10 or 20 strings a few more or less.

Some harps may probably have been strung differently from others. For reasons which I shall explain when I speak of the musical system of the Assyrians, I am inclined to believe that they had usually 25 or 26, 20 or 21, 15 or 16, 10 or 11 strings.

The non-existence of the front pillar in the Assyrian harp is a peculiarity found in all the harps of Asiatic nations. The ancient Egyptians constructed all their harps, of which they possessed a great variety, on the same principle. As the harp of this construction appertains pre-eminently to Eastern nations, I shall designate it the *Oriental harp*, for the sake of distinguishing it from the differently constructed European harp.

At the present time the harp is much less common among Asiatic nations than it was in former ages. It is, however, a favourite instrument in Burmah, and in the countries situated between Hindoostan and China. The Burmese harp, called *saun*, has thirteen strings of silk. To the ends of the strings are attached tasselled cords, which are bound round the curved upper part of the frame in a way which admits of their being pushed up or down. By this means the instrument is tuned, as the tension of the strings can be thus increased or diminished at pleasure. The cords are made to serve also as ornamental appendages, as in the Assyrian harp. And this mode of tuning was practised by the Assyrians in some of their stringed instruments. In Persia, where the harp is now but rarely met with, it was formerly a well-known instrument. Sir Robert Ker Porter has given us some careful illustrations of it in his sketches from the celebrated old sculptures which exist on a stupendous rock, called Tackt-i-Bostan, situated in the vicinity of the town of Kermanshah. These sculptures are said to have been executed during the lifetime of the Persian monarch Khosroo Purviz, towards the end of the sixth century of the Christian era. They form the ornaments of two lofty arches, and consist of representations of field sports and aquatic amusements. Some boats are filled with women playing upon harps, resembling in construction those of the Assyrians. As an instance how unreliable communications by travellers respecting music sometimes are, I may mention that in Bunting's 'General Collection of the Ancient Music of Ireland,' vol. i., which is prefaced by an elaborate 'Historical and Critical Dissertation on the Harp,' a drawing of this harp-concert transmitted to the author by a military officer, "who took a sketch of it on the spot on his return from India," exhibits the harps with the addition of large front pillars. Through such want of exactness, incorrect notions are not unfrequently promulgated.

Interesting engravings of some Persian harps of a more recent date than those just alluded to may be seen in Mr. Lane's edition of 'The Arabian Nights' Entertainments.' The Persian harp, called *chang* in

Persian, and *junk* in Arabic, is now almost entirely fallen into desuetude. Mr. Lane received the two drawings from which his engravings are derived from Sir Gore Ouseley. The harps are about 400 years old, and resemble in the principle of their construction all other Oriental harps. The Oriental harp is now but seldom found out of Asia. The negroes in Western Africa and in Soudan possess, however, an instrument which bears a strong resemblance to it, or rather to some of the harps which we see represented on Egyptian monuments. The negroes in Senegambia and Guinea call it *boulou*, or *ombi*, and use strings made from a kind of creeping plant, or from the fibrous root of a tree. The Oriental harp does not exist among European nations at the present time; but there are indications of its having been formerly in use, at least among some of them. The Finns preserved it the longest. They called it *kantele*, or *harpu*, and it was the instrument on which, according to a beautiful old mythological tradition, the Finnish god Wäinämöinen played, like Orpheus, with such irresistible effect, that men and animals became alike enchanted; the wildest beasts of the forest lost their ferocity; the trees did not venture to move their branches; the brook retarded its course, and the wind its haste; even the "mocking echo" approached stealthily and listened with the utmost attention to the heavenly sounds.

According to Herr Neus,[2] there existed in Esthonia up to the beginning of the present century wandering minstrels who accompanied their old songs and improvisations on the *kantele*. The last popular

---

2 Ehstnische Volkslieder herausgegeben von Neus. Reval, 1850.

minstrel, much respected and everywhere heartily welcomed as "the old singer," died in the year 1812, at an advanced age, and with him the Oriental harp of the Finns seems to have become extinct.

To avoid any misunderstanding, I must mention that the Finns have another old national instrument called *kantele*, consisting of a wooden box, over which five strings are stretched. This *kantele* is still often met with in Finland, and Dr. Clarke saw it also in the hands of the Laps in Lapland, who belong to the Finnish or Ugrian races.[3] It bears, however, no resemblance to the *kantele* before-mentioned, and is a species of dulcimer rather than a harp.

Considering that the music of some of the Celtic nations possess peculiarities which remind us of that of Asiatic nations, and that the earliest harps of the Scotch and Irish, with which we are acquainted from old monuments, bear a greater resemblance to the Oriental harp than those of a later date, it appears very probable that the Oriental harp pre-ceded the European, and that the latter has been derived from it. Some facts mentioned in Mr. Con-ran's book on Irish National Music tend to strengthen this impression. For instance, in describing some ancient representations of Irish musical instruments, he mentions one which forms an ornamental com-partment of a sculptured cross near the antique church of Ullard, in the county of Kilkenny, "which," he says, "from the style of its architecture, and the workmanship, is evidently more ancient than the like monument at Monasterboyce, known to have been

---

3 Travels in various Countries, by E. D. Clarke. London, 1810. Part III., Sec. i., p. 439.

erected prior for 830. In this ornament the figure is represented as playing upon a harp which rests on his knee; and it cannot fail to be regarded with interest, as being the first specimen of a harp without a fore pillar that has been hitherto discovered out of Egypt."[4] It must be remembered that the Assyrian harp was discovered subsequently to the publication of 'The National Music of Ireland.' Its author might, however, have known the Persian *chang*, the Burmese *saun*, and the Finnish *kantele*, all of which are specimens of the Oriental harp discovered in other countries besides Egypt.

Such resemblances may be accidental. It is quite possible that two nations may, independently of each other, invent harps which are alike in their principal features. If, however, in addition, the peculiarities of the other instruments, as well as the chief characteristics of the music itself, are also somewhat similar in different nations,—as is actually the case in some Celtic and Ugrian nations in relation to some Asiatic nations,—it is almost impossible to regard such resemblance as merely accidental.

If the reader has carefully examined the harps represented in our frontispiece, he will have observed on the under side of the upper portion of the frame a small semicircular incision, which on the bas-relief has the appearance as if a piece had been accidentally broken out. It occurs, however, on each harp in this representation, always in the same part of the frame, and must therefore have been made purposely. In some harps on other slabs it does not appear. Possibly it may have been intended to

---

[4] The National Music of Ireland, by Michael Conran. Dublin, 1846, p. 96.

indicate a sounding-hole existent in that part of the upper bar.

THE LYRE.

The lyre appears to have been a favourite instrument with most ancient nations whose musical instruments are known to us. By the Greeks and Romans its invention, as I need perhaps scarcely remind the reader, was ascribed to Mercury, who, according to their mythological traditions, constructed it from the shell of a tortoise which he chanced to pick up on the bank of the Nile.

Of the Assyrian lyre, representations of three kinds occur in the sculptured monuments, differing in shape as well as in the number of strings. The first of these (fig. 5), from a slab forming part of M. Botta's excavations at Khorsabad, is so far corroded as to render the number of its strings uncertain. Eight can be counted, and there is space for about two more, so that we may conjecture the number to have been ten. The performer carries the instrument before him by means of a band slung over his right shoulder, and he seems to employ both hands in twanging the strings, marching firmly on at the same time, as if his music were in time with his steps.

A lyre of a very different appearance, though of the same construction as the preceding one, occurs on one of the bas-reliefs from Kouyunjik (fig. 6). It is in the hands of a female; or perhaps the performer is one of those beardless effeminate personages, called eunuchs, who are so frequently represented as attendants on Assyrian monarchs in their various pursuits and entertainments. It has been remarkably well preserved, and its five strings, as well as the

mode in which they were fastened round the front
bar of the instrument, are distinctly seen. The front
bar is curved, probably for the sake of facilitating

Fig. 5.   Assyrian lyre.   Fig. 6.   ssyrian lyre.

the tuning of the strings. For the same reason the
position of the front bar in the lyre fig. 7 is slightly
oblique. The strings were, undoubtedly, tied round
the bar so as to allow of their being pushed upwards
or downwards; in the former case the tension of the
strings increases, in consequence of the slanting position of the front pillar on which they are moved;
the notes become therefore higher. On the other
hand, if the strings are pushed lower down, the pitch

of the notes must become deeper. This is similar to
the contrivance for tuning some of the lyres which
are at present in common use in Nubia, Abyssinia,
and one or two other parts
of Eastern Africa, and
which bear also in other
respects a remarkable re-
semblance to the Assyrian
lyre, as well as to that of
the ancient Egyptians.

In most of the Assyrian
representations the body
of the instrument is not
seen, because it rests on
the side of the performer
furthest from the spec-
tator. Its construction was
most likely similar to that
of the Nubian lyre.

The strings on the lyre
fig. 7 are partly oblite-
rated and indistinct; four
seems to have been the
number. All these lyres
were probably played with

Fig. 7.   Assyrian lyre.

a small plectrum as well as with the fingers. The
performer fig. 6 appears to hold something in his
right hand, which undoubtedly is intended to represent a plectrum. Here also part of the body of the
instrument is visible, showing it to have been nearly
square in form.

The Nubian lyre, called *kissar*, is made of wood
and leather. Its body consists of wood, hollowed in
the form of a bowl, and covered with sheepskin. The

cover is generally pierced by three sounding-holes equidistant from each other; sometimes there are more.

The kissar has five strings of catgut, usually made of the intestines of the camel. To prevent their

Fig. 8   Nubian lyre, called Kissar.

coming in contact with the body of the instrument, a kind of bridge made of wood is placed near the end of the body upon which the strings rest. It is played with a small plectrum, made of a piece of leather or horn, and fastened with a cord to the instrument. The plectrum is held in the right hand, and the strings are struck with it, while the performer twangs some strings with his left hand, using the plectrum and his fingers either alternately or together. Sometimes the body of the kissar is made square instead of circular. Six or even more strings are also sometimes used; but five is the usual number. A kissar from Abyssinia, deposited in the East India Company's Museum, is so far different from the common Nubian Kissar, that its body is square, without sounding-holes, and it has ten strings, which rest upon a large wooden bridge 5 inches long and $2\frac{1}{2}$ inches high. On the bridge are small pieces of leather between the strings, to keep them separate from each other, and to prevent their coming out of their position when twanged. Each string is wound round the front bar, and also at the same time round a small piece of hard wood, about an inch and a half in length, by means of which the tension of the strings can be regulated and maintained, as the pressure of the little pieces of wood on the front bar prevents the unwinding of the strings. A plectrum, made of horn, about 3 inches long, is affixed to the instrument by a leathern thong.[5]

I shall reserve some additional observations respecting the kissar, which is especially interesting on account of its apparently high antiquity and its close resemblance to the Assyrian lyre; for in our subsequent inquiries they will afford assistance in elucidating the nature of the musical system of the Assyrians.

---

[5] The Abyssinians have a tradition, according to which the *kissar* was introduced into Ethiopia from Egypt, by Thoth, or Hermes, at a very early period.

THE DULCIMER.

This is another of those instruments of which we have positive evidence of their having existed in Asia at very remote times. In Europe it is at present less common than it used to be about a century or two ago. On the continent we sometimes meet with it among the country people at their rural rejoicings and dances. In Hungary and Transylvania it is employed by the gipsy musicians in their little bands, when they wander from village to village to entertain the people with their favourite national melodies. In Germany it is called *Hackbret*, or *Cimbal*.[6] It consists of a trapeziform or square box, about 4 feet long and 18 inches broad, which contains the sounding-board, at the right and left of which are the iron screws for tuning. The compass embraces about three octaves. The strings are of wire, and there are two or three in unison for each tone. It is played with two little sticks having small oval knobs at each end. One side of the knob is covered with soft leather or felt, and is used in *piano* passages, which produce an agreeable effect, somewhat resembling the sounds of the Æolian harp. When played *forte*, the sound is too confused to be pleasant, as there are no means to stop the vibration of the strings, such as for instance the dampers on our pianoforte.

The English dulcimer seems to be somewhat dif-

---

[6] The name must not be mistaken for *cymbal*, which applies to a certain instrument of percussion. The German *claricimbel*, now out of use, was a kind of spinet. The French called it *clarecin*, and the Italians *cembalo*. Some of J. S. Bach's admirable concertos are written "a due cembali."

ferent, if we may rely on a description of it in Gras-
sineau's 'Musical Dictionary' (London, 1740), which
is as follows:—"An instrument with wire strings, of
a triangular form, strung with about fifty strings,
cast over a bridge at each end, and the acuter gradually the shorter, the shortest about eighteen inches,
and the longest about thirty-six ; struck with little iron
rods. The bass strings are doubled, and its sound
is not disagreeable. To be played on it is laid on a
table before the performer, who with the little iron
rod in each hand strikes the strings."

I may add, that I have seen in England dulcimers
in form almost exactly like the German Hackbret. The
Italians call the dulcimer *salterio tedesco*, which seems
to indicate that they consider it of German origin.
The Persians possess, however, a dulcimer called *santir*,
which in construction and in the mode of its treat-
ment is almost identical with the German Hackbret.
Its high antiquity in Persia is testified to some extent
by the representation of a Persian lady playing on the
santir, of which Hommaire de Hell, in his 'Voyage
en Perse,' has given a sketch taken from an illustration which is known to be very old. And it is remarkable that this oldest santir known to us bears a
string resemblance, even in some minor points, to
some of our oldest known dulcimers, such as that, for
instance, of which a drawing is given by Luscinius
in his 'Musurgia,' published in the year 1536, which
Sir John Hawkins has copied in vol. ii., of his
'History of Music.'

The Assyrian dulcimer (fig. 9) is in too imperfect
a state on the bas-relief to familiarize us intimately
with its construction. The slab representing a procession, in which this instrument occurs, appears to

have been injured and slightly repaired afterwards; the defect extended over a portion of the dulcimer, and it cannot be said that in repairing it much musical knowledge has been evinced, for it never can have existed as represented. What appears most strange is, that the sculptor seems to have neglected to represent the bridge over which the strings, to

conclude from the delineation, must have run before they took a vertical direction. The representation of the strings is also curious; the further ones being made to appear in front of those nearest the spectator; perhaps, however, only because, if the sculptor had faithfully adhered to nature, he could, as he gives us a side aspect of the instrument, have

Fig. 9.   Assyrian dulcimer.

shown only one string, since they lay all strictly parallel, similar to those on our dulcimer or on the Persian santir. It may have been then the desire to show as much as possible of the instrument which occasioned this odd disregard of perspective.

In the frontispiece this dulcimer is shown, with the imperfection alluded to, exactly as it appears in the bas-relief; while in the woodcut, fig. 9, all the strings are shown as the sculptor evidently would have exhibited them, had not the figure of the preceding performer in the procession been in his way. It seems strange that the strings do not run across the instrument as on our own dulcimer, but apparently in a straight line from the player,—in fact, as on a grand piano. The performer, therefore, must have struck them sideways with his plectrum.

This, however, we learn with certainty, that the Assyrian dulcimer contained a number of strings— in the present instance *ten*—which were played with a plectrum; that the instrument was ornamented with tassels ; and that the performer carried it before him, most likely fastened by a band round his body, holding the plectrum in his right hand. And he seems to use also his left hand in performing, either by twanging the strings, or, perhaps, only for checking any undesirable continued vibration of the strings.

Among the different species of dulcimers at present in use in the East the *kanoon* must be noticed, which differs from the santir not only in form, but also in the circumstance that the strings are of lamb's gut, and are twanged with two small plectra, one attached to the forefinger of each hand ; while the strings of the santir are of wire, and are struck with two little sticks. These instruments appertain especially to the Arabs and Persians. The Chinese and Japanese have also several instruments which may be considered species of dulcimers. The *kin* or "scholar's lute" of the Chinese, which, according to tradition, was the instrument upon which the great philosopher Confucius and the sages of antiquity used to play, and which is consequently held in high esteem, has strings of silk. The *yang kin* is, however, furnished with brass strings, which are struck with two small hammers, like our dulcimer. Similar to the *kin* are some kinds of the Japanese instrument called *koto*. The strings of the *koto* are generally twanged with small plectra fastened on the fingers of the performer.

We meet also in Europe with several old instruments which greatly resemble the dulcimer, though they are not played like it, but rather like the guitar or mandoline. The most remarkable of these are the *kantele* and the *gussli*. The kantele, an instrument of the Finns, to which I have already alluded, page 35, has five metal strings, which are played with the fingers, but which cannot be shortened in playing, as those of our guitar or violin, the instrument having, like the dulcimer, no finger-board.

The *gussli*, an old national instrument of the Russians, is played like the *kantele*, which it also resembles in form. At present its wire strings embrace from two to three octaves; but in former times it possessed only five strings, like the kantele.

In chap. iii. v. 5 of the Book of Daniel the *dulcimer* is mentioned among the six instruments which the Babylonians used in their idol-worship. It must, however, be remembered that not much reliance can be placed on the translation of the text, as far as the names of musical instruments are concerned; the translators, unacquainted with the original instruments, would naturally adopt the names of those of our own instruments which they thought most likely to have resembled them, and would prefer adopting names universally known to obscure ones.

THE ASOR.

This instrument differs too much from every instrument of our own at present in use for me to compare
it to any one of them. I have therefore preferred to
apply to it the name of a Hebrew instrument called
asor, to which it seems to be more nearly related than
to any other.

The *asor* of the Hebrews was, it is generally supposed, a species of *nebel*, of an oblong square or triangular shape, mounted with ten strings, which were
struck or twanged by means of a plectrum. The information which has been transmitted to us regarding
this instrument is, like that regarding most others
of the Hebrews, too meagre to convey an exact idea,
of its construction; but, as far as it goes, it indicates a similarity with the Assyrian instrument in
question. If, on such slight grounds, I venture to
apply the name of the Hebrew instrument to the
Assyrian, the reader should bear in mind that it is
rather for want of a more appropriate name, than
from a conviction that the two instruments were
identical.

The engraving fig. 10 exhibits so faithfully the
characteristic features of the Assyrian asor, as to
render a minute description superfluous. I shall,
therefore, only briefly direct the reader's attention
to the following facts :—

The strings are placed horizontally one above the
other at regular distances. The lowest string is the
shortest, producing the highest note, and the upper-
most string is the longest, producing the deepest note.
From the gradual increase in length of the strings,

in counting from the lowest upwards, we may conclude that they were tuned in a regular order of intervals, or in a certain scale. The performer holds with his right hand a long plectrum, not at one end as is usual, but in the middle. The plectrum was probably of wood or ivory. From the position of the strings, the performer could not have struck them as those of the dulcimer are struck, but he must have twanged them with the plectrum. The left hand seems to have been chiefly occupied in checking the vibration when its discontinuance was considered necessary.

On the front bar of the instrument are seen a number of little dots, which probably represent the screws or pegs round which the strings were fastened, and by means of which they were tuned. To the bars are affixed tasselled cords, which hang down considerably below the instrument, and which evidently served for no other purpose than as ornaments.

The front bar is surmounted by a small hand, which may have been of carved ivory, or, perhaps, of metal. In an interesting communication in the *Athenæum* on the Assyrian sculptures in the British museum, it is suggested that the hand served as a stand to hold the written music. There is, however, no evidence in support of this supposition.

The asor was supported by a belt passed over the shoulder of the performer, so that he had both hands at his disposal when required for the execution of his music.

The asor seems to have been pre-eminently a favourite instrument with the Assyrians, or, at least, with the higher classes of this nation, because it is

introduced more frequently in their sculptures than
any other, and when it occurs it is generally at the
entertainments and sacred rites of the monarchs.   It
never appears in combination with other stringed or
wind instruments, and never singly, there being
always, at least, two together.   On a few of them
the strings are suffi-
ciently distinct to be
counted ;   of these
some have ten, others
nine, one has eight,
and one six strings.
As the number of the
tuning pegs is seldom
in accordance with
that of the strings,
no great reliance can
be placed on the re-
presentations so far
as this point is con-
cerned, and my pre-
vious   observations
respecting the indif-
ference of the sculp-
tors in representing
the number of strings
of the harp may also
apply here.   Still,

Fig. 10.   Assyrian asor.

there is reason to conclude that the six strings of
one of them exhibit the exact number which the
instrument contained at an early period ; since, from
the evident care with which they are indicated,
from the smallness of their number, and from the
corresponding number of the tassels depending from

E

the frame where the strings are fastened, it is not likely that this representation would be inaccurate. The instrument is delineated on a brick obtained from the ruins of Nimroud, and now in the British Museum. As the relics from Nimroud are ascertained to be some centuries older than the others, it may be conjectured—and is, indeed, suggested by the instruments themselves—that the asor had at an early period only six strings, and that, in the course of time, the number was gradually increased to ten, which is the highest hitherto found.

I believe ten to have been the highest number of strings with which the asor was provided ; partly because this is strictly in conformity with those numbers —be they smaller or greater—which most frequently occur on other Assyrian and ancient Asiatic instruments, and partly because the Hebrew asor was, as its name implies, a ten-stringed instrument; and as such it is mentioned in Psalms xxxiii. 2, and cxliv. 9.

The frame of the Assyrian asor certainly appears to have been weak, and but little fitted for resisting any strong tension of the strings. Mr. Layard observes :—" Like the Egyptian harp, it had no cross-piece between the upright bar and the flat board or base ; it is difficult, therefore, to understand how the strings could have been sufficiently tightened to produce notes.[7] Mr. Bonomi expresses a similar opinion, and suggests, " either the sculptor has altogether omitted the column to resist this tension of the strings, or the angle formed by the body of the instrument and the arm is not faithfully repre-

---

[7] Nineveh and its Remains, by Austen Henry Layard, 2 vols., London, 1849, vol. ii. p. 412.

sented."[8] These impressions seem to have originated
in the assumption that the frame of the asor was constructed of wood. But the portion which constitutes
the angle may have been partially, if not entirely, of
metal, which would afford great power of resistance.

If the strings were made of silk, like those of the
Burmese harp *saun*, and the Chinese *kin*, or scholar's
lute, they were, on account of their elasticity, well
fitted for being twanged with a plectrum. The employment of silk for strings was probably an invention of a very remote age in Asia, because in nations
cultivating the manufacture of silk, like the Assyrians, its adoption for this purpose must have suggested itself very soon, and perhaps earlier than
that of catgut or wire. At all events, we find silken
strings used in some Asiatic instruments at present
in use, which we know to be of high antiquity.

THE TAMBOURA.

This instrument is at present in use, especially in
Persia, Hindoostan, and Asiatic Turkey; it is also
found in Egypt. M. Villoteau, the intelligent musician, who was a member of the Scientific Expedition
which accompanied Napoleon Bonaparte to Egypt,
has given us the most circumstantial information of
it which we possess. He saw and examined in
Egypt not less than five kinds of tambouras, which
differed from each other principally in size, in a
slight variation in the shape of the body, in the
number of their strings, and in a few other similar
points.[9] But they all have the following characteris-

---

8 Nineveh and its Palaces, by Joseph Bonomi, London, 1853, p. 254.

9 The *tamboura* bears no resem-

blance, except in name, to the *tambourine*, which is, it will be remembered, a small hand-drum.

tics in common:—The strings are of wire, and are sounded with a plectrum usually made of tortoise-shell, or of the hard portion of an eagle's or vulture's

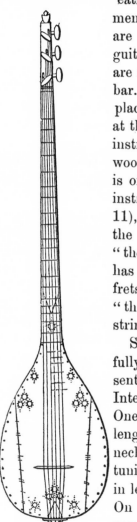

Fig 11.
Tamboura bouzourk.

eather. The neck of the instrument is remarkably long, and there are frets or stops on it, as on our guitar. The neck and finger-board are formed of only a single straight bar. Half the tuning pegs are placed in front, and the other half at the right side of the head of the instrument. The oval body is of wood, without sounding-holes, and is often highly ornamented. The instrument here represented (fig. 11), M. Villoteau describes under the name of *tanbour bouzourk*, or "the great Persian tamboura." It has six strings and twenty-five frets, while the *tanbour charqy*, or "the Oriental tamboura," has five strings and twenty-one frets.

Some elegantly shaped and taste-fully ornamented tambouras were sent from Turkey to the London International Exhibition in 1862. One of these, I found, was $4\frac{1}{2}$ ft. in length, the body one foot, and the neck $3\frac{1}{2}$ ft. It had 35 frets and 8 tuning pegs. Another, about 4 ft. in length had 44 frets and 9 pegs. On this instrument three strings were always tuned together in unison; on the other, always two.

The frets are made of catgut cords wound tightly round the neck, generally four times for each fret, and neatly fastened. These frets are arranged at short distances from each other, corresponding to the Arab system of *one-third tones*.

In Egypt the tamboura is at present not much in use; it is, in fact, scarcely ever seen in the hands of the Egyptians themselves, but only in those of the Turks, Jews, Greeks, and sometimes of the Armenians residing in that country. The ancient Egyptians, however, possessed an instrument which greatly resembled it.

We may perhaps acquire a more exact acquaintance with the tamboura if I add here Mr. Bonomi's description of a Syrian one which he examined. "The instrument is 3 ft. 9 in. long, and its elegantly shaped sounding-board is $6\frac{3}{4}$ in. wide; it has ten strings of small wire, forty-seven stops, and is invariably highly enriched and inlaid with mother-of-pearl. The tamboura is in common use upon the shores of the Euphrates and Tigris."[10]

The tamboura of Hindoostan differs chiefly from those described in having no frets, and is generally of an extraordinarily large size; indeed, the neck is in some instances so long, that it seems impossible for the performer to reach with his hand the highest part without shifting the instrument on his lap. The body is usually formed of a large gourd, lacquered and richly ornamented. In the interesting collection of Oriental musical instruments in the East India Company's Museum, London, are several tambouras of this description, remarkable not only on account

---

10 Nineveh and its Palaces, by J. Bonomi, London, 1853, p. 231.

of their enormous size—one of them being about 4½ ft. long, with a body nearly 20 in. in diameter— but also on account of the very tasteful designs in gold and harmonious colours with which they are embellished. So beautiful are some of these designs that they have been copied by artists as patterns for various purposes. The tamboura is used by the Hindoos either as a *solo* instrument for instrumental performance, or for accompanying the voice. It is chiefly found among the wealthier classes, who are in the habit of displaying it in their rooms like a piece of elegant furniture.

The Assyrian instrument, for which I have adopted the name *tamboura* on account of its resemblance to this instrument, occurs only once on the monuments hitherto discovered, and is so indistinct as to show

neither the tuning pegs nor the strings. Perhaps it had only two strings, to which were affixed the two tassels which are seen (fig. 12) hanging down from the higher part of the neck; and it was probably played with a plectrum.

This instrument is also represented in the hands of two little images, about 3½ in. high, formed of baked clay, of which the engraving (fig. 13)

Fig. 12.   Assyrian tamboura.

represents one. Several small figures of a similar
substance have been found, almost all of them in
the ruins of Susa, but without musical instruments.

They are supposed to be
images of the Assyrian
Venus, Mylitta, or Astarte.
That the little idol with
the tamboura was intended
for Mylitta, as patroness of
the art of music, is doubtful
but possible.

If we turn to Asiatic
countries at a greater distance from that part of
Asia where Assyria was
situated than those men-
tioned, we find there also
instruments which differ
in some respects from the

Fig. 13.   Assyrian image.

tamboura, yet not very materially. The most remarkable of these are the *san heen* of China, and the
samsien of Japan. These two instruments are almost
identical, each having a body without sounding-
holes, three strings which are played with a plectrum, a long neck, and three long tuning pegs.
The body of the *san heen* is round and the belly
consists of the skin of the tan snake. The body
of the *samsien* is square, and this constitutes in
fact almost the only difference between the two instruments. M. Hommaire de Hell saw among the
Kalmucks in the vicinity of the Caspian Sea a somewhat similar instrument with three strings. This
latter instrument may be considered almost identical
with the Russian *balalaika*, an instrument said to be

of high antiquity, and to have been originally derived from the East.[1]

Among the few European instruments resembling the Assyrian tamboura must especially be noticed the *calascione*, found among the peasantry in Southern Italy; the two catgut strings of which, extending over a long neck with frets, are also played with a plectrum. This is the same instrument as that mentioned by Dr. Burney in his 'History of Music' (vol. i. page 196) on account of its resemblance to a certain instrument of the ancient Egyptians, represented on an obelisk.

The high antiquity of the tamboura among the Egyptians is proved by the fact that a figure of it is found among the hieroglyphs, meaning *nofre*, "good;"[2] which also seems to indicate that it was at an early time held in much favour. It occurs in representations of concerts of the eighteenth dynasty, which dates, according to Sir Gardner Wilkinson, from B.C. 1575 to 1289. Some of the hieroglyphs in which it occurs are, however, at least 600 years earlier.

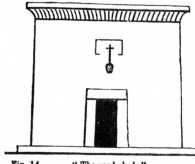

Fig. 14.   " The good abode."

The engraving fig. 14 represents the front of an Egyptian house with an hieroglyphic inscription over the door, consisting of a tamboura and a bracket, which signifies "the good abode." It appears

1 Stimmen des russischen Volks in Liedern und übersetzt von P. v. Goetze. Stuttgart, 1828, p. 37.

2 An Introduction to the Study of the Egyptian Hieroglyphs, by Samuel Birch, London, 1857, p. 225.

to have been the custom with the Egyptians, as it is
at the present time in some European countries,
to write over the entrance of the house the owner's
name, or some significant sentence.

The tamboura affords the best proof that the
Assyrians as well as the Egyptians had made considerable progress in music at a very early age;
since it shows that they understood how to produce
on a few strings, by means of the finger-board, a
greater number of notes than were obtainable even on
their harps.

THE DOUBLE PIPE.

This instrument was well-known to the Greeks
and Romans, and they employed different kinds,
some having only one mouth-hole, and others having
two, but placed so near together as to enable the
performer to blow upon both pipes at the same time.
The pipes are either of equal length, or one is shorter
than the other. Probably the purpose of one of the
pipes was in many cases only to produce an accompanying tone similar to the drone of the bag-pipe,
while the other served for the performance of the
melody and of passages. At least I have found
many double-pipes thus constructed, which are at the
present time in use in different parts of the world.
As an instance may be noticed the double-reed-pipe,
called *arghool*, of the modern Egyptians, in which
one of the tubes is considerably longer than the
other and serves as a drone. The Egyptian boatmen are in the habit of using the *zummárah*, another
species of double-pipe, in which the tubes are of equal
length.

The ancient Egyptians also possessed a double-pipe, of which I shall, however, reserve any observations until I proceed to point out the affinity which apparently subsisted between the music of the Egyptians and that of the Assyrians.

The accompanying engraving (fig. 15) represents an Assyrian female playing on a double-pipe, which, from the direction in which the two tubes are placed, seems to have but one single mouth-hole. No finger-holes are seen, but although they are not discernible on the slab from which the engraving has been derived, they probably existed on the instrument itself This we may almost accept as certain, partly on account of the progress which the Assyrians had made in instrumental music, so evident in the construction of some of the stringed instruments just described,—and partly also because it is ascertained that the Babylonians possessed a single pipe with two finger-holes. In the pipes of the ancient Egyptians also finger-holes were used. Judging from certain indications in the representation, the Assyrian pipes and flutes consisted of several pieces fitted together, which could be separated, as is the case with our flute.

Fig 15.   Assyrian double-pipe.

One of the most curious double-pipes at present
extant in Asia is the *poogyee* of the Hindoos already
alluded to, the tubes of which are inserted into a
gourd, and are blown with the nose instead of with
the mouth. As the use of the nose-flute originated
in the religious doctrine of the Brahmins that a
person of superior caste is defiled by touching with
his mouth anything which has been touched by the
mouth of an inferior, this instrument is probably of
high antiquity in some parts of Asia. On the Assyrian sculptures, however. it does not occur.

THE TRUMPET.

This is another instrument which was known, as
might be expected, to every ancient nation with
whose musical instruments we are acquainted. The
tube is, however, not wound in an oval form like
that of our trumpet, but is either quite straight or
slightly bent, and in shape somewhat resembles the
horn of an animal, from which, in fact, such instruments in old times were made, as they are at present
by some semi-civilised nations.

The Hebrews employed trumpets made of rams'
horns. Metal trumpets, however, were also used by
them, and we are informed in the Bible (Numbers,
chap. x.) that Moses made trumpets of solid silver,
on which various signals were blown to call the
several ranks and divisions of his people together on
certain occasions.

The winding of the tube is said to have been first
adopted about four centuries ago. When people
began to construct trumpets of greater length, they
found it more convenient to double the tube once

together: thus originated the long trumpets which were formerly used in Germany. They had a kind of wooden bridge inserted between the two parts of the tube, to prevent their pressing together and injuring each other. Sometimes the tube was wound in various directions, in order to make the instrument more handy and manageable. At present the tube is twice doubled, in an oblong shape, and the instrument is consequently only half as long as it used to be, and easier to manage. It is pre-eminently a military instrument. In the cavalry service, where it is especially employed for promulgating orders, the branches of the tube which are in contact are generally protected by a strong cord wound round them, which, with its gay colours and hanging tassel, serves at the same time as an ornament.

With the Assyrians there was no necessity to adopt any such form as that just described, since their trumpet was too small to be inconvenient in a straight shape. In some parts of Asia this shape is retained at the present day, although the tubes are sometimes of an immense length. This applies especially to the enormous trumpets used by the Buddhist priests in Thibet, as well as by the Kalmucks, in their religious performances. With the latter the trumpet usually employed is far too long and too heavy to be held up by the performer; in processions there are usually attendants in front, who carry it before him, while in the temple it rests upon a frame, so that he needs only to raise it slightly when blowing. I have seen also large straight trumpets from Hindoostan; they are, however, chiefly used in Nepaul, and a few other mountainous districts in the north, where the people possess robust lungs capable of producing the full tone. These trumpets are often wound in different shapes, as, for instance, coiled like a serpent, or with the projecting head of a tiger, &c.

It is unnecessary for our present purpose to submit a detailed description of our own trumpet. I shall confine myself, therefore, to pointing out that its length, if the tube were straight, would be about eight feet. On such a trumpet, without the recently introduced auxiliary means of pistons and cylinders, only a limited numbers of intervals are obtainable.

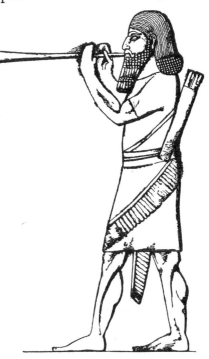

The Assyrian trumpet (fig. 16), judging from its short length, was only suited for pro-

Fig. 16.   Assyrian trumpet.

ducing three or four notes, appertaining to the Triad, or Common Chord.

The accompanying representation is remarkable for the faint indication of the *bell* of the trumpet, which must probably be attributed to the imperfect state of preservation of the slab on which the instrument appears. On a portion of a trumpet occurring on another partly corroded slab, the bell is distinctly apparent (fig. 17). This trumpet greatly resembles the trumpet of the ancient Egyptians, as well as that of the Hebrews which is represented on the famous arch of Titus in Rome. Small though the compass of the Assyrian trumpet must have been, it was well suited for military purposes, or for conveying orders where works were executed by a large number of men. On such occasions we find it was actually used ; its few notes were quite sufficient, because by means of various rhythmical arrangements a great number of signals, easily distinguishable, could be produced, each of which would convey a distinct meaning.

Fig. 17.   Part of an Assyrian trumpet.

THE DRUM.

We meet with various kinds of drums on the Assyrian sculptures, which, however, have this feature in common, that they are covered with skin only on their upper part, and that they are beaten with the hands instead of with drum-sticks.

The woodcut (fig. 18) represents a female with a small drum fastened to her person, whether suspended by a band over her shoulders or round her waist is not ascertainable from the sculpture, of which the woodcut is a faithful sketch. She beats the drum with both her hands, much in the same way as such little hand-drums are at the present time played upon by females in the East.

Small drums, more or less similar, are indeed to be found in most Asiatic countries. They may be

divided into two classes, viz., those which, like the
Assyrian drum, are covered with skin at the top
only, and those which are of a barrel-form, covered
with skin at both ends. The former kinds are
usually designated by the name of *tubla*. They are
also frequently beaten with
sticks instead of with the hands,
and sometimes two together are
used, one producing a deeper
sound than the other. The *tabl
shamee*, or *Syrian drum*, is used
by the modern Egyptians in
their wedding processions, and
in the processions of Dervishes.
It is, according to Mr. Lane,
"a kind of kettle-drum, of tinned
copper, with a parchment face,"
and is carried, by a band suspended round the neck of the
performer. The Assyrian tubla
may very possibly have been at
least partly of metal, and the
dots round it near its upper rim
may have been the bright and
ornamental heads of the nails
with which the skin was fastened.

Fig. 18.   Assyrian drum.

The other class of Oriental small drums consists
of those which are of a barrel-form, covered at each
end with skin, carried obliquely, and beaten with one
hand at each end. Such drums are best known by
the name *tom-tom*. Some of them are almost identical with a drum common among the ancient
Egyptians. This is especially the case with the
mridang, kholé, and *dholkee* of the Hindoos, the

berri of the Singhalese, and several others. The *pukwauz*, often used by the Hindoo dancing girls at their performances, or nautches, is also of the same description; but with this difference, that it is sur-rounded with cords, under which are little moveable pieces of wood, by which the sound is regulated. This appears to me worth noticing, because there is evidence that some of the drums of the ancient Egyptians also possessed such a contrivance. It may perhaps have exist-ed also in the Assyrian drum (fig. 19), which from its shape was particularly adapted for it. This drum was about three feet in length, and was beaten with the hands, like the other.

Fig 19.
Assyrian drum.

A third kind of Assyrian drum ap-pears on the monuments, too indistinct for me to venture to submit a sketch of it. Though similar to that carried by the female, fig. 18, it appears to be of a larger size and somewhat spherical below.

BELLS.

Small Assyrian bells have been found by Mr. Layard, and are exhibited in the British Museum. Mr. Layard gives the following short account of them when describing the various relics which he brought to light from a newly-discovered chamber at Nim-roud:—"The first objects found in this chamber were two plain copper vessels or caldrons, about $2\frac{1}{2}$ feet in diameter, and 3 feet deep, . . . filled with curious relics. I first took out a number of small bronze bells with iron tongues, and various small copper ornaments, some suspended to wires. With them were a quantity of tapering bronze rods, bent into a hook, and ending in a kind of lip. The caldrons contained about eighty bells. The largest are $3\frac{1}{4}$ inches high, and $2\frac{1}{2}$ inches in diameter; the smallest $1\frac{3}{4}$ inches high, and $1\frac{1}{4}$ inch in diameter."[3]

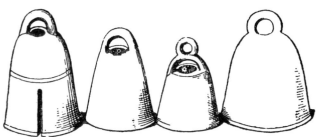

Fig. 20.   Assyrian Bells, found in the ruins of Mound Nimroud.

Most of them have a hole at the top, in which probably the clapper was fastened. This is especially the case with the smaller ones; and it is remarkable that some of the large bells used at the present day in China are also open at the top. One of the Assyrian bells in the above engraving has a slit upon the rim upwards, which was most likely filed after its discovery for the purpose of ascertaining the exact composition of the metal.

Small bells were known also to the Egyptians and Hebrews. The Egyptian bells, which have been discovered in tombs, are of bronze, and some of them resemble those of the Assyrians. In the ancient Egyptian necklaces of gold and silver, imitations of bells may be also seen. Among the Hebrews we know

---

3 Discoveries in the Ruins of Nineveh and Babylon, by A. H. Layard, London, 1853, p. 177.

from Exod. xxviii. 33, 34, and Ecclus. xlv. 9, that small golden bells were attached to the lower part of the robes of the high-priest in his sacred ministrations. In Zech. xiv. 20, "bells of the horses" are mentioned, which probably were fastened on the bridle or upon the forehead of the horses, as we find them at the present time in many countries. In the mountainous and wooded districts of Germany and Switzerland the cattle are provided with bells to prevent their straggling.

In several of the bas-reliefs the Assyrian horses are represented wearing on the neck a little bell with a clapper, very similar in shape to those in the above engraving. It appears to have been a usual custom with the Assyrians to decorate their horses in this manner. On one of the Assyrian sculptures in the British Museum, two spirited horses drawing a chariot have each of them about half-a-dozen of these bells, varying in size, affixed to the lower part of their collars.

Richly caparisoned horses are seen on the Assyrian monuments having head-stalls ornamented with appendages which, if not intended for short tufted plumes, probably represent those small hollow metal balls enclosing loose pieces of iron, which are called in French *grelots*, and in German *schellen;* and are used in Germany especially on the harness of sledge-horses to prevent accidents by announcing the proximity of the rapid and noiseless sledge, and to contribute at the same time with their cheering harmony (being tuned in the triad or common chord) to the hilarity of the drive. *Grelots*, to conclude, from their similarity with rattles, must be of very high antiquity, probably older than bells. They are at present in use in different parts of the East. The Japanese instrument *soezoew* consists of a cluster of them attached to a handle. The Copts, in Egypt, who are Christians, use the *maraoueh* in their religious ceremonies. This consists of a disc of silver, round which are attached a number of *grelots* made of copper, and to which is affixed a long handle. *Grelots* have also been found in tombs of the ancient Mexicans.

Small bells were used in America before its discovery by Europeans, as is proved by a copper bell discovered in one of the tombs of the ancient Peruvians, and now preserved in the Museum of Antiquities in Lima. The resemblance between this Peruvian bell and the little hand bell called *drilbu*, which is used by the Buddhist priests of Ladak in their sacerdotal functions, seems to me worth notice. The *drilbu* is about 6 inches in height, including the handle. Mr. Cunningham, who has given a drawing of it in his work on Ladak, remarks, " It is represented in the left hand of the great Lama Skyobba Jigten, of the red sect, and it is placed on the throne at the feet of the great Dai Lama Navang Lozang. The bell is formed of a very white brittle-looking metal."[4] Again, the Brahmins of Hindoostan use a little bell in their religious ceremonies, similarly shaped and as elegantly ornamented, called *ghunta*.

The invention of our large church bells is generally attributed to Paulinus, Bishop of Nola in Campania, A.D. 400; whence the term " campana " is supposed to be derived. It may be that church bells were first used by Paulinus, and that from Italy

---

[4] Ladak, Physical, Statistical, and Historical, by Alexander Cunningham, London, 1854, p. 373.

F 2

they were introduced into other European countries, but in Asia they appear certainly to have been known, and used for religious purposes, long before the Christian era.

In Barrow's ' Travels in China ' is given a drawing of " the great bell of Canton, 20 feet in diameter, and 16 inches thick ;" and Mr. Halloran saw near Ningpo, in a large pagoda, " an enormous bell of a very sweet tone, suspended from the rafters of the roof, having its lower edge curiously scalloped, and its outer surface entirely covered with inscriptions, and ornamented in high relief."[5] Similar large bells are found in other Asiatic countries, especially where the Buddhist religion has been diffused. In Siebold's celebrated work on Japan, drawings of several large elegantly-shaped bells are given ; and Mr. Tronson saw, near one of the Japanese temples, "a belfry with a large bell suspended, deep and heavy, and richly carved." " This," he states, " is struck at different hours of the day with a heavy wooden mallet, and the sound, mellow and sonorous, is heard far away over the water."[6] And Mr. Oliphant, when speaking of " the celebrated temple of Dai Cheenara," about ten miles from Yedo, says, " In the court was a ponderous bell, swinging in a handsome belfry of carved wood, on a massive pedestal. In Japan the bells never have tongues or clappers, but are always struck from without by a piece of wood conveniently suspended."[7] Mr. Winter, in his

---

[5] Eight Months' Journal, by A. L. Halloran, London, 1856, p. 117.

[6] Personal Narrative of a Voyage to Japan, by J. M. Tronson, London, 1859, p. 348.

[7] Narrative of the Earl of Elgin's Mission to China and Japan, by L. Oliphant, London, 1859, vol. ii. p. 198.

description of "the Golden Pagoda" at Rangoon, mentions a large Burmese bell, under which, he says, he was able to stand upright with ease. He informs us, "There is, in a pagoda in Maulmain, a great bell suspended in the usual way between two posts; it has an inscription in the Burmese character. . . . . The bell is suspended in front of the temple; and when an offering has been made, or some religious duty performed, it is generally struck by the devotee once or twice with a deer's horn, several of which are usually placed near the bell."[8]

Large bell-foundries exist in Chinese Tartary. The French missionary, M. Huc, who visited them, observes, "The magnificent statues in bronze and brass, which issue from the great foundries of Tolon-Noor, are celebrated not only throughout Tartary, but in the remotest districts of Thibet. Its immense workshops supply all the countries subject to the worship of Buddha with idols, bells, and vases employed in that idolatry."[9]

A further description of these bells is unnecessary, especially as a Chinese bell from a Buddhist temple near Ningpo may be seen in the ethnological department of the British Museum. In the official 'Synopsis of the Contents of the British Museum' (London, 1856), we are told, "On the top is the imperial dragon, the national emblem of China, crouching, and forming the handle. Beneath this is the orifice where the clapper has been placed." If this really was the case, it must be considered as quite exceptional, since the large bells in the Buddhist temples

---

[8] Six Months in British Burmah, by Christopher Winter, London, 1858, p. 30.

[9] Travels in Tartary, Thibet, and China, by M. Huc, vol. i., p. 35.

are usually without a clapper, being struck with a wooden hammer or a kind of mallet.

Moreover, bells with clappers are frequently fixed on the outside of the sacred edifices. On the famous "Porcelain Tower" in Nanking (built of white bricks having the appearance of porcelain), a number of such bells were affixed to the projecting corners of its different stories. Mr. Halloran describes a Chinese pagoda in the vicinity of Shanghae, octagonal in shape, and consisting of eight stories, each of which "is provided with a covered verandah, having a projecting roof, at the corners of which are hung small bells of different tones; and as there are sixty-four of them, which are kept in almost constant motion by the wind, the sound they produce is exceedingly pleasing, greatly resembling the wild melody of the Æolian harp."[1]

The Chinese declare their bells to be of very high antiquity, and assert that they used them in numbers, arranged according to a certain scale, so far back as more than 2000 years B.C. The oldest Chinese bells known had not, however, the round form of the present ones, but were nearly square. Sonorous stones were also used, suspended, like the bells, in a large frame. A glance at the drawings of these bells and stones, by Amiot, Laborde, and others, might convince us, if there were any doubt on the subject, that a regular succession of intervals, or some kind of scale, was observed in their arrangement, since we see them gradually increasing in size from the highest to the lowest.

Moreover, also, at the present time similar sets of

---

[1] Eight Months' Journal, by A. L. Halloran, London, 1856, p. 124.

bells (as well as sets of gongs) are by no means uncommon in Asiatic countries. When Lord Macartney, with his suite, witnessed in Peking the anniversary of the Emperor of China's birthday, a concert was performed which consisted principally of "sets of cylindrical bells, suspended in a line from ornamented frames of wood, and gradually diminishing in size from one extremity to the other, and also triangular pieces of metal arranged in the same order as the bells. To the sound of these instruments a slow and solemn hymn was sung by eunuchs, who had such a command over their voices as to resemble the effect of the musical glasses at a distance."[2] Captain Yule mentions that he saw, near a pagoda in Burmah, a number of attuned bells which were struck by the visitors of the pagoda on the conclusion of their prayers, and which reminded him of the village chimes of England.[3]

I suppose the few facts which I have stated will be considered sufficient to prove that our large church bells, as well as our sets of bells, or *carillons*, are not originally European and Christian inventions, as has been often asserted; but that to Asia must be conceded the origin of the bell, and its uses for sacred purposes.

It is true, some travellers and missionaries, struck with the similarity of the ceremonies in the Buddhist temple with those of the Roman Catholic Church, have thence drawn the conclusion that the former must have been adopted from the latter. The

---

[2] An Authentic Account of an Embassy from the King of Great Britain to the Emperor of China, by Sir George Staunton, London, 1797, vol. ii. p. 255.

[3] A Narrative of the Mission sent by the Governor-General of India to the Court of Ava, by Captain Henry Yule, London, 1858, p. 178.

Buddhist religion is however older than the Christian. At all events it is evident that bells were used in Asia in religious worship long before the Christian era. It is impossible to determine with certainty the purpose for which the Assyrian bells that have been found were used. Considering that in ancient times bells were specially used in religious ceremonies, it appears probable that this was also the chief use made of them by the Assyrians. The difference in size, varying in a great number, though all were found in the same place, seems to indicate that they were also originally arranged in regular order, in conformity with a certain scale or peculiar succession of intervals. When I examined them in the British Museum I observed that in almost all the clapper was missing. I found, however, one in which it had been preserved, which gave me hope that I should hear at least one Assyrian sound—a sound which once perhaps had vibrated in honour of the famous Baal himself. My hope, however, was not realized; the clapper, adhering fast to the inner side of the bell, strenuously resisted any attempt of mine to restore it to its former function; besides, the bell itself was in so corroded a condition as would probably have precluded any response to its clapper.

TAMBOURINE.—CYMBALS.

These two instruments occur in a group of four musicians, given by Mr. Bonomi in his third edition of 'Nineveh and its Palaces,' of which the engraving (fig. 21) is an enlarged copy. As the sculpture from which it has been derived is not shown in the British

Museum, it was probably in too dilapidated a condition to be exhibited.   Nevertheless, from Mr. Bonomi's carefulness, we may rely on the strictest fidelity having been observed in sketching the details of the instruments.   It is therefore worth noticing that the two lyres of this group are the same in form as two

Fig. 21.   Assyrian musicians, with tambourine, cymbals, &c.

of those previously described.   Each has five strings, exactly the number which we had reason to expect.

The tambourine appears to be almost precisely like that now used by us, which was already known to the ancient Egyptians.   The cymbals were either flat circular plates of metal, or (although this is not indicated in the representation) they may have been concave in the middle like our cymbals, and like those which have been found in Egyptian mummy-cases.

The performers appear to mark the time with their feet. Probably they are dancing to their music, as is the case with several other performers represented on the Assyrian sculptures. In some instances these dancing musicians take part in religious ceremonies, which shows that sacred dances were in use with the Assyrians, as we know them to have been with the ancient Chinese, Egyptians, and Hebrews. Soon after their departure from Egypt the Hebrews performed sacred dances before the golden calf, doubtless after the manner of the Egyptians (Exod. xxxii. 19). In Psalms cxlix. and cl. the people are admonished to "praise the name of the Lord in the dance." David himself "danced before the Lord with all his might" (2 Sam. vi., 20), although it would appear from Michal's sarcastic reproach that this manifestation of

religious zeal was considered derogatory to the dignity of a king. Sacred dancing was also admitted in the primitive Christian Church, and is still continued in some Roman Catholic countries.

The Assyrians had also a kind of cymbal which was funnel-shaped, resembling the Egyptian *darabukkeh* drum. It appears probable that there was some contrivance in this peculiarly-shaped instrument for increasing the loudness and the rhythmical effect of its sound.

Fig. 22.   Assyrian cymbals.

Pipe from Babylon.—The instrument next deserving
of notice is a little pipe of baked clay which was found
by Captain Willock in the ruins of Babylon, *Birs-i-
Nimroud*, and which has been presented by him to
the Museum of the Royal Asiatic Society. It is about
three inches in length, and has only two finger-holes,
situated side by side, and consequently equidistant
from the end at which it is blown. The opposite
end has no opening : the instrument in this respect
resembles a whistle. If both finger-holes are closed,
it produces the note c ; if only one of them is closed,
it produces e ; and if both are open, it produces g.

Besides these notes, one or two others are obtainable by some little contrivance : thus, by blowing
with unusual force, the interval of a fifth, g, may be
raised to that of a sixth, a. But the fixed and natural
notes of the instrument are only the tonic, third, and
fifth. Moreover it is remarkable that the third which
is obtained by closing the left finger-hole is about a
quarter-tone lower than the third which is obtained
by closing the right finger-hole. Perhaps it was intended for the *minor third*. It may have been originally more flat, and might perhaps be restored to
its former pitch, if it were advisable to submit the
pipe to a thorough cleaning.

The accompanying engraving exhibits the instrument full size. That it is a genuine Babylonian relic
admits, in my opinion, of no doubt. It resembles, in
material and workmanship, several other articles
known to be of Assyrian manufacture ; and several
little idols have been found embedded with it, which

are similar to those obtained from the Assyrian
mounds.

This is, as far as I am aware, the oldest musical
instrument hitherto discovered which has preserved
its original condition;
yet it is constructed of
so fragile a material
that were it to fall
from the hand to the
ground it would most
likely be destroyed for
ever. But its notes can-
not have been clearer
two thousand years ago
than they are at the
present day. They
constitute the intervals
of the common chord,
either major or minor.
No doubt the feeling
for musical concord is
innate in man, like the
feeling for melody. It
probably caused the Babylonians to adopt for their
little wind instrument those intervals which together
constitute the harmonious Triad, and which, even
when heard in succession (arpeggio), produce an effect
similar to that most consonant chord.

Fig. 23.   Pipe from Babylon.

The shape of this instrument appears to be intended to represent the head of an animal. It is singular that the little flageolets and whistles of the
ancient American Indians, of which many have been
found in tombs, especially in Mexico and in Central
America, are also of pottery formed to represent

animals, and bear besides, in other respects, much resemblance to the Babylonian pipe.

Traces of other Instruments.—I have already suggested that further discoveries will probably bring to
light several other Assyrian instruments. At least
there are some which we might have expected to see
on the bas-reliefs, but which have not yet been found.
The *single pipe*, for in-
stance, seems to have
been known to all an-
cient nations. There has
been discovered in the
ruins of Susa a figure in
baked clay, representing
a female playing upon a
pipe (fig. 24). It may
possibly be of a more
recent date than those
before described; there
seems to be even some
doubt whether it is really
of Assyrian origin, as it
bears but little resem-
blance to the Assyrian
figures. However this
may be, there can at

Fig. 24.   Pipe from Susa

least be no doubt that the pipe was well known to
the Assyrians at an early period, especially as they
possessed the double pipe, which it must have preceded. Besides, it is a well-known fact that pipes
and flutes were in common use in Asia Minor and in
Syria. The Gingras flutes used in Caria and in
Cyprus, in songs of lamentation, in honour of Adonis,
are especially famous.

The *syrinx*, or *Pandean pipe*, was also known to most ancient nations, and was probably the instrument whose invention is ascribed in Genesis to Jubal, and which in the English translation is rendered *organ*. Travellers tell us that it is at present in use in Syria and other Asiatic countries, especially by the lower classes. It may have been also with the Assyrians a popular though perhaps but little esteemed instrument, and this would account for it not appearing on their monuments. We might also expect to meet with an Assyrian trumpet, consisting of the horn of some animal, such as we are informed in the Bible the Hebrews used on certain solemn occasions; and perhaps also the conch-trumpet, called in Hindoostan *sankh*—an instrument undoubtedly of high antiquity, and used in the temples of the Brahmins as well as in those of the Buddhists.

The *bagpipe* is also very universal throughout Asia, though at present not so much in use as it seems to have been in former ages. The earliest evidence which we have of its existence in Asia is a representation dating before the Christian era. This curious relic, to which I shall afterwards recur, was discovered in the ruins of Tarsus, Cilicia. A Hindoo bagpipe, called *titty*, brought from Coimbatoor, may be seen in the East India Museum, London; and a drawing of a similar instrument is given in Sonnerat's 'Voyage aux Indes Orientales,' where it is called *tourti*. Mr. Hill found the bagpipe in the hands of Chinese musicians in Maimatchin, the famous trading-place on the border of Mongolia.[4] Sir William Ouseley met with it in Persia, where it is called *neï*

---

[4] Travels in Siberia, by S. S. Hill, Esq., London, 1854, vol. ii. p. 64.

ambánah (from *neï,* a reed or pipe, and *ambánah,* a bag), and where also "it appears to have been more general in former ages than at present."[5] The same may be said of the Egyptian bagpipe, *zouqqarah,* which is now of but rare occurrence.

In the Persian concert, sketched from a bas-relief of the sixth century of the Christian era (mentioned page 33), one of the musicians plays upon a bagpipe. Moreover we know that the Romans were acquainted with this instrument, and most likely the Greeks also. There may be some reason for supposing that it was likewise known to the Assyrians, if we remember that most commentators on Hebrew music are of opinion that it was one of the Hebrew wind-instruments mentioned in Holy Writ. Among the instruments of the ancient Egyptians it has, however, not hitherto appeared.

Again, the *sistrum,* which we find so frequently in the Egyptian representations, and of the use of which among the Hebrews there are many indications, might likewise be expected to have existed among the Assyrians. Of the Egyptian sistrum, which was especially used in religious services, and which is seen usually in the hands of females, I shall hereafter say a few words when noticing the Egyptian instruments. The sistrum has not hitherto been found on Assyrian monuments, unless we may surmise that the little instrument shaped like a sickle, in the right hand of a small statue of hard stone, is intended for one. This statue, which will be remembered by visitors to the Assyrian antiquities in the British Museum, was found

---

[5] Travels in various Countries of the East, more particularly | Persia, by Sir W. Ouseley, London, 1819, vol. i. p. 241.

by Mr. Layard in the mound of Nimroud, and is supposed, according to the official guide-book of the Museum, to represent Sardanapalus the Great. If this be so, the instrument may perhaps be an emblem of dominion, like the crook of Osiris, mentioned by Sir Gardner Wilkinson,[6] which it also resembles in shape. Mr. Bonomi, however, describes the statue as that of a high-priest in his sacerdotal dress;[7] and it appears therefore not improbable that the instrument is a kind of sistrum which may have been used by the Assyrian priests in their religious processions and dances, as it is at the present time employed by the priests of a Christian sect in Abyssinia. There may be seen, on close examination, about twenty divisions in the crook, which were perhaps so many separate and jingling pieces of metal; and though the instrument differs essentially in shape from the usual Egyptian sistrum, it must be remembered that the sistrum generally attributed to the Hebrews is also different in appearance. However, far from wishing to

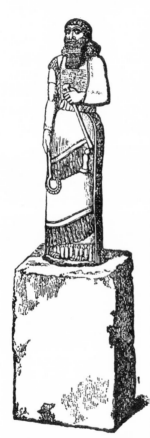

Fig. 25. Assyrian high-priest.

---

[6] The Manners and Customs of the Ancient Egyptians, by Sir G. Wilkinson, vol. v. p. 267.

[7] Nineveh and its Palaces, by J. Bonomi, London, 1853, p. 291.

express a decided opinion, my object is only to suggest
the great probability that the sistrum also was one of
those hitherto unascertained but nevertheless commonly used instruments of the Assyrians.

THE ANTIQUITY OF THE INSTRUMENTS OF THE VIOLIN KIND.

Stringed instruments played with a bow seem to
have been unknown to the Assyrians as well as to the
Hebrews and Egyptians. It is true some historians
mention Hebrew instruments played with a bow, but
they have in translating apparently mistaken the
plectrum for a bow. On the other hand, there are
indications of the existence of a kind of violin in Asia
at a very remote period. M. Sonnerat tells us that
the Hindoos maintain that the *ravanastron*, one of
their old instruments played with the bow, was invented about five thousand years ago by Ravanen,
a mighty king in Ceylon.[8] The most characteristic
instruments of this description at present extant
in Asiatic countries are the *urh-heen* of the Chinese,
the *kokiu* of the Japanese, the *sarangi* and the *sarinda*
of the Hindoos, the *kemangeh* and *rebab* of the Arabs
and Persians. It is not at all improbable that some
instrument of this species may have been known to
the Assyrians also.

In describing the Assyrian instruments I have repeatedly pointed out some remarkable similarities in
form or construction between ancient Asiatic and
European instruments at present in use—similarities
which, in my opinion, are too peculiar and striking to
be accidental, and which therefore indicate a common

---

8 Voyage aux Indes Orientales, par M. Sonnerat, Paris, 1806,
vol. i. p. 182.

origin. The object which I had in view will become evident when I proceed to explain the musical system of the Assyrians. I mention this here because the following observations might otherwise be considered irrelevant.

Among the Hindoo instruments played with a bow, and also among those which are played with a plectrum, are certain kinds in which the body exhibits on its sides a curved outline, similar to that of our violin and its relations the tenor, violoncello, double-bass, &c. Besides, I have frequently seen instruments from Hindoostan which had a double set of strings, one set above the other, the upper consisting of catgut and the lower of thin wire strings. Now this peculiar contrivance was also formerly applied to several of our own instruments. The *viole d'amour*, for instance, a favourite instrument some centuries ago, was provided with fourteen strings, seven of catgut and seven of wire, the latter placed under the former, and tuned in unison with them, or in octaves. The catgut strings only were played upon, and the object in placing the wire strings under them was to increase their sonorousness—it being a well-known fact that if of two sonorous bodies tuned in unison, or in octaves, one is made to sound, the other will also sound without being touched. Thus the pitch of the note of a church bell may be ascertained by playing upon a flute under the bell. As soon as the note which is that of the bell is blown, the bell will begin to vibrate, emitting softly the same note. The Hardanger peasants in Norway have at the present day a fiddle with a number of thin wire strings placed under the catgut strings. It is not surprising that the Hindoos should be aware of this sympathising nature of notes of equal vibrations; but that they should have applied it in their stringed instruments precisely in the same way as we have done, seems to me suggestive. In the *thro* of the Burmese, and the *kemangeh roumy* of the present Egyptians, the resemblance to our violin is even greater than in the Hindoo instruments above mentioned. I should think no one who is acquainted with the history of our music, and with the music and habits of Asiatic nations, could entertain the opinion that these Oriental instruments have been originally derived from Europe, or must be imitations of European instruments. Although the name of the Egyptian instrument (*kemangeh roumy*, " a Greek violin ") seems to indicate either that it was introduced into Egypt from Greece, or that in Egypt it is considered as a violin specially belonging to Greece, it must also be remembered that the Greeks possessed at an early period several instruments in common with Asiatic nations; and although it may be impossible to ascertain with any degree of accuracy the time when the Hindoo, Burmese, and Egyptian instruments which I have alluded to were invented, there are sufficient reasons to apprehend that they existed prior to ours.

I must not omit to state that most modern musicians who have written on this subject express an opinion the very opposite to mine. This is, I think, owing to their having followed the well-known 'Résumé philosophique' of M. Fétis, prefixed to his 'Biographie Universelle des Musiciens.' I have frequently observed instances in our musical literature where the opinion of a theorist of reputation has been adopted and repeated by others without their having ascertained that it was well founded.

Fétis, in his 'Résumé,' asserts that stringed instruments of the violin kind are a European invention; and he believes them to have had their origin in the Russian *gudok*. The following extracts, translated from three different works of this author, will show better than any explanation that he was but superficially acquainted with the music of Eastern nations when he made that assertion.

In the 'Résumé philosophique' ('Biographie des Musiciens,' Bruxelles, 1837, tome i. p. 83) he writes as follows:—"If we have borrowed much from the East, as regards the taste for ornamentation in melody, and with respect to musical instruments; on the other hand, we have made known to the East the class of instruments played with the bow. For the bow originated in the West. Having passed through Italy into Greece, the viol was carried into Asia Minor, and afterwards into Persia and Arabia, where it became the *kemangeh roumy*, of which several varieties were afterwards formed, by being invested with an Oriental character. The *rebab*, a rude imitation of the same class of instruments, was long afterwards brought back by the Crusaders to Europe, where it received the name of *rebebbe;* and, after having undergone various modifications in form, in the material of its construction, and in the number of strings with which it was mounted, it became the rustic fiddle called *rebec*."

In a later treatise on the same subject, contained in 'La Musique mise à la Portée de tout le Monde,' Bruxelles, 1839, page 121, M. Fétis points to the Welsh *crwth*, instead of the Russian *gudok*, as the instrument from which all others of the violin kind are derived. He says:—"All the researches made with a view to discover whether the nations of antiquity were acquainted with instruments played with the bow have been fruitless; or rather, it has been proved, almost to a certainty, that they were entirely unknown. It is true, a certain statue of Orpheus, holding a violin in one hand and a bow in the other has been cited; but, on closer examination, the violin and bow were found to have been added by the sculptor who repaired the statue. Passages from Aristophanes, Plutarch, Athenæus, and Lucian have also been quoted, in which some writers find proofs of the existence of the bow among the Greeks; but the most superficial investigation will suffice to show how little ground there is for this assumption. There is no doubt that the instruments with a sounding board, a finger-board, and with strings raised by a bridge, and made to vibrate by a bow, originated in the West; but in what century, and in what part of Europe they were invented, are questions not easily answered. We find in Wales an instrument which has existed there from the earliest times under the name of crwth. It is nearly square in form, has a finger-board, and is played with a bow. In England it is regarded as the parent of the different kinds of viol, and of the violin."

Again, in a subsequent work entitled 'Antoine Stradivari, précédé de Recherches historiques et critiques sur l'Origine et les Transformations des Instruments à Archet,' Paris, 1856, M. Fétis says:—" Hindoostan, the country whence we derive the most ancient monuments of a well-developed language, of an advanced civilization, of a philosophy in which all varieties of human thought have their expression, of a poetry eminently rich in all its branches, and of a music in which the extreme sensibility of the natives finds expression—Hindoostan has, it appears, been the birthplace of the instruments played with the bow, and has made them known to other parts of Asia. This does not admit of a moment's doubt, as the instruments are actually in existence, bearing unmistakable marks of their Indian origin. If we wish to find the instrument played with a bow in its original state, we must take it in its simplest form, where no art has been employed to render it more perfect. Thus we find it in the *ravanastron*, formed of a cylinder of sycamore wood, partly hollowed." After mentioning two other Hindoo instruments, the *ruana* and the *omerti*, both belonging to the violin class, M. Fétis says:—If we compare the *omerti* with the Arab instrument called *kemangeh à gouz*, we at once perceive that the latter took its origin from the former." And further on he observes:—" Truth to say, the *rebab* is only a modification of the *ruana* of the Hindoos, the only difference being in the form of the body of the instrument."

I may now leave it to the reader to form his own opinion as to the value of the statements of M. Fétis. We have already seen that instruments of the violin kind are also known to the Chinese and other Asiatic nations, and I shall presently submit to the reader's judgment some evidence from which it appears highly probable that the musical instruments of the Arabs were originally derived from the Chaldees and Assyrians.

THE NAMES OF MUSICAL INSTRUMENTS.

The circumstance of many of our European instruments having nearly the same name in different languages would appear to be to some extent an indication of their having been derived from the same source. I shall notice a few instances which occur to my mind, and I must leave it to the philologist to explain or to enlarge upon them. To the musician such investigations would most likely prove useful, and certainly interesting. Thus, it might perhaps be easily ascertained in how many languages the word *pipe*,—German *pfeife*, French *pipeau*, Gaelic *piob*, Welsh *pib*, Swedish *pipa*, Dutch *pijp*, &c.,—can be recognised. Or the word *harp*,—German *harfe*, Finnish *harpu*, Icelandic *haurpa*, Hungarian *hárfa*, French *harpe*, Spanish *arpa*, Anglo-Saxon *hearpe* or *earpe*, &c. Of the lute,—German *laute*, Italian *liuto*, French *luth*, Dutch *luit*, Swedish *luta*, Spanish *laud*, Arabic *el oud*,—we know with some certainty that it is the Arabic instrument from which the others have been derived. The *guitar* is said to have been brought from the East to Spain by the Moors. In Germany it has hardly been known for a century. The inhabitants of some mountainous districts in Germany had, however, from time immemorial, a somewhat similar instrument called *zither*; in Persia, Hindoostan and other Asiatic countries, we find the *sitar*; in Nubia the *kissar*; in ancient Greece the *kithara*; and might not also the name of the Hebrew instrument with which David subdued the "evil spirit" of Saul, the *kinnor*, be related to these? This appears less improbable if we remember the similarity of the name of the Hebrew trumpet *keren* with the Greek *keras*, the Latin, *cornu*, the French *cor*, the German *horn*, the Welsh *corn*, the Persian *karnaï*, the Hungarian *krüt*, the English *horn*, &c.

This instrument undoubtedly was originally made of the horn of an animal, and hence the name. Indeed, many recurrences of the same names are easily accounted for. Nevertheless, by a closer investigation of them, some new light might probably be thrown on obscure questions relative to the history of music. For instance, in the Hebrew *bárdáhi* some clue is afforded to the original home of the Celtic *bard*. We are informed in the 'Asiatic Researches,' that " the usual name in India for a bard is *bhát*. It is not a. Sanskrit appellation, though asserted to be derived from it. But the original name, as it was pronounced several hundred years ago, was *bárdai*, or *bárdáhi*, though some think it a different name applied to the same class of people. . . . The title of *bárdáhi* is translated 'musician' by Abul Fazil. His functions, both in the field and at home, were exactly those of the ancient bards of the West,"[9] &c. And it is a remarkable fact that the further we extend such enquiries, the more forcibly we are directed to the East as the cradle of our music. It would, however, be out of place to enlarge here upon this subject.

---

[9] An Essay on the Sacred Isles, by Captain F. Wilford, Asiatic Researches, vol. ix. p. 76.

CHAPTER III.

ASSYRIAN MUSICAL PERFORMANCES.

Various combinations of musical instruments—Description of the Assyrian bas-reliefs in the British Museum on which musical performers are represented—Other representations of Assyrian musicians briefly described—The characteristics of the performances—Fondness of the Assyrians for music—Their songs—Music employed in their religious worship—Court bands of the kings—Rhythmical character of the music—Oriental music of the present time—Choruses of the dervishes—Call to prayer of the Muëzzin—Character of the Assyrian instrumental accompaniments—Harmony not entirely unknown to the Assyrians.

In order to show the combinations of musical instruments used by the Assyrians in their concerts, and also on what occasions music was specially introduced, I propose now to give a short description of those bas-reliefs in the British Museum which represent musical performances. Most, if not all, of these stony records were originally coloured. On some of them, when discovered, the colours were partially preserved; and there are even now a few in the British Museum on which a red tint is still distinctly visible, bearing witness to the correctness of the prophet's description of the Assyrian palaces, and the "men portrayed upon the wall, the images of the Chaldeans portrayed with vermilion." (Ezek. xxiii. 14). The colours actually found upon the bas-reliefs are, according to Professor Rawlinson, only four, viz., red, blue, black, and white. "The red is a good bright tint, far exceeding in brilliancy that of Egypt. On the sculptures of Khorsabad it approaches to vermilion, while on those of Nimroud it inclines to crimson or lake tint. It is found alternating with the natural stone on the royal parasol and mitre; with blue on the crests of helmets, the trappings of horses, on flowers, sandals, and on fillets; and besides, it occurs, unaccompanied by any other colour, on the stems and branches of trees, on the claws of birds, the shafts of spears and arrows, on bows, belts, fillets, quivers, maces, reins, sandals, flowers, and the fringe of dresses."[1]

It is to be regretted that the colours have not been preserved on the musical instruments; otherwise we might perhaps be enabled to ascertain therefrom whether the frames of the harps and lyres were entirely of wood or partly of metal,—whether the little dots observable on the lower bar of the frame in some of the harps were tuning-pegs or merely ornamental brass buttons,—whether the indentations on the inner side of the upper part of the frame in some of these instruments, noticed page 36, are meant for sounding-holes, or whether they are dilapidations in the sculptures; whether the *plectra* used by the performers were of wood or ivory, and several other such points. Unimportant as any information of this kind may appear, it is sometimes of great assistance in inquiries relating to the music of a nation of antiquity.

Most of the instruments have ornamental appendages; and from the recorded wealth and luxury of the Assyrian monarchs, we may suppose the tassels

---

[1] The Five Great Monarchies of the Ancient Eastern World, by George Rawlinson, London, 1862, vol. i. p. 451.

on the harps and other stringed instruments of the
musicians playing before the king to have been of
rich silk in various splendid colours, interwoven with
gold; and the frames themselves to have been embellished with elegant devices, and lacquered, as is the
case with the instruments employed at the present
day by the higher classes in Persia and Hindoostan.

The following is a description of the most remarkable scenes in which musical performances occur:—

No. 1. *Harp and drum.*—The king with his queen,
at a banquet under a bower of vines, are waited upon
by attendants, four of whom are fanning them with
fly-flappers, while others hand refreshments. At the
further end are two musicians, facing the king; the
first, an eunuch, is playing upon a harp; the other
beating with both hands a sugarloaf-shaped drum,
like the one which is represented at page 64 (fig. 19).
The dimensions of the slab only allow the hands to
be seen. It is therefore possible that other musicians
took part in this concert who were represented on
another slab which obviously joined this one, and
contained additional figures. [*From Kouyunjik.*]

No. 2. *Lyre, harp, and double-pipe.*—The subject of
this representation appears to be a religious ceremony.
Two personages, perhaps royal chamberlains, each
with a long stick in his left hand, which he holds in
the middle, are standing before some vessels, probably
used in sacrifice. At a first glance, one might suppose these men to be indicating the time to the musicians; but this is very unlikely, because it could not
be nearly so well done by two as by one alone. There
is a greater probability that the sticks were used as
rhythmical instruments. They appear each to consist
of two pieces united, which may have been loosely

fastened together so as to produce a rattling noise
when shaken. However, the manner in which the
men have the right arm placed over the left, tells
against this conjecture; since it was scarcely possible
for them in this position to move their sticks, far less
to use them for a rhythmical purpose in combination
with the musical instruments. Facing these men, on
the opposite side of the vessels, stand the musicians.
The first plays upon a lyre with five strings, as represented in fig. 6, page 38; the second upon a harp;
and of the third only the instrument, a double-pipe,
is seen, as the slab does not embrace more of the
representation, which undoubtedly extended to another
slab united to the present one, and which may have
represented one or two more musicians. [*From Kou-*
yunjik.]

No. 3. *Two asors.*—Return from the bull-hunt.—
The king, with a cup in his hand, is standing near a
prostrate wild bull, and seems to perform some religious ceremony, by pouring out a libation above the
slain animal, or by drinking out of a sacred cup in
honour of the gods. He is surrounded by attendants,
one of whom shades him with a parasol, while another
fans him with a fly-flapper, and a third is approaching
him in an attitude of respect. Two performers upon
asors celebrate his victories over the wild beasts, or,
perhaps, execute a solemn composition appropriate to
the sacred ceremony in which he is engaged. They
are standing side by side, and each holds the plectrum
in his right hand in precisely the same oblique direction over his instrument as if they were going to
twang the strings both at the same moment. It is
singular that the sculptor has represented the left
hand of the second performer as in front of the strings

of the instrument of the first performer, undoubtedly with the object of showing it more distinctly than it could possibly have been seen in its proper position behind the strings. Such a disregard to natural truth by the sculptor, in order that no part of any object which he considered as of greater importance than others should be hidden, may be not unfrequently observed in the Assyrian bas-reliefs. The wild bull of Assyria must have been a formidable and noble animal. We see it depicted in deadly strife with the lion;[2] and the king performed over each the same religious and musical ceremony, when he had been successful in the chase. Neither of these animals is any longer found in the country where, in former times, their figures were adopted as symbols of power and nobleness. [*From Nimroud*].

No. 4. *Two asors.*—Here the king is represented standing before an altar and pouring a libation over some dead lions, which he probably has just slain in the chase. Two musicians with asors, beardless and juvenile in appearance are standing on the opposite side of the altar, and are probably singing a hymn with instrumental accompaniment, in praise of the courageous achievements of the king in his battle with the lions, or in honour of the gods for having protected him in his daring pastime. [*From Kou-yunjik.*]

No. 5. *Two asors.*—Return from the lion-hunt. The king, accompanied by four archers, besides other attendants, with the slain lion at his feet, holds a cup in his right hand, in a similar way, and probably for the same purpose, as indicated in our previous

---

2 See Layard's Monuments of Nineveh, First Series, Pls. 46 and 48.

description of the return from the bull-chase. The
two royal minstrels in the present scene stand side
by side, as all the asor-players on the different slabs
are represented. However, in the bas-relief before
us the instrument of the nearest performer does not
exhibit on its fore-pillar the usual imitation of a
hand, which has been noticed, p. 48; but terminates
instead in a human head, which is, as Mr. Bonomi
suggests, " probably to indicate that the bearer is the
chief musician, or the leader of the chorus; for we
apprehend that the *two* in this sculpture, as in all the
representations of battles, sieges, hunts, &c., are put
for the many." [*From Nimroud*].

No. 6. *Two asors and a drum.* Triumphal return
of the victors from the battle-field. The king is
approaching in his chariot, preceded and followed by
soldiers on foot and on horseback. Warriors are
carrying the heads of slain enemies ; others are
counting them. Three musicians are celebrating the
victory with song and instrumental accompaniment.
The first two are bearded men playing upon asors ;
while the third, a beardless and juvenile-looking person, is beating a drum with his hands. The latter
instrument is nearly obliterated, but seems to have
been similar in shape to the small drum represented in the wood-engraving, fig. 18, p. 63. [*From
Nimroud*].

No. 7. *Four asors.*—This slab contains nothing but
the half-length figures of four performers on the asor
two and two together. Of the first two the instruments are incomplete ; they extended apparently to
an adjoining slab. The head-dress of one these

---

3 Nineveh and its Palaces, by J. Bonomi, London, 1853, p. 252.

musicians, shown in the accompanying engraving
(fig. 26), is remarkable.   In a short description of the
slab in the 'Athenæum' (London, August 17, 1861),
these musicians are sur-
mised to be priests : "one
has a monstrously ele-
vated head-dress, not un-
like that remarked by
Egyptian antiquaries as
characteristic   of   the
people of Upper Egypt,
which, when combined
with the mitre usual in
Lower Egypt, constituted
the peculiar crown seen
in so many of the Egyp-
tian   portraits   of   monarchs after the union
of the kingdoms."

If I may hazard an
opinion, I should con-
jecture, from his distinctive head-dress and dig-
nified attitude, that the
above musician was the

Fig. 26.   Head-dress of Assyrian musician.

king's chief bandmaster, or director of music.   [*From
Kouyunjik.*]

No. 8. *Three lyres.*—On this slab four bearded
men are seen traversing a mountainous country.
On the tops and sides of the hills a few trees are
represented to indicate a woody district.   Three of
the men are playing upon lyres, while the fourth,
a warrior, is carrying in his right hand a short stick
surmounted by a knob, or a mace; he is following

the musicians, and appears to be their superior. The dress of the men and the shape of the lyres are exactly as shown in the engraving (fig. 7, p. 39). [*From Kouyunjik*].

No. 9. *Two trumpets.*—Removal of a colossal bull. —Whoever has paid a visit to the Assyrian monuments in the British Museum will remember the colossal bulls and lions, with human heads and eagles' wings,—expressive symbols of wisdom, power, and swiftness,—which originally were placed on the two sides of the chief entrances of the magnificent palaces of the Assyrian monarchs, and also of the entrances to some of the inner halls.

The slab now under consideration commemorates the conveyance of a human-headed winged bull to the royal palace, under the superintendence, or at least in the presence, of the king, who is seen standing in his chariot, which has been drawn by the attendants to the summit of a mound. Numerous workmen, directed by overseers, are occupied in removing the bull, which has been laid sideways on a kind of sledge. Some officers are standing on it, engaged in giving orders to the workman by means of clapping their hands and other signs. They are assisted in this operation by two men with trumpets, one of whom is just in the act of transmitting commands to the most distant workman in front of them. [*From Kouyunjik*].

No. 10. *Two trumpets.*—Removal of a human-headed winged bull.—The chief features of this representation are similar to the preceding one. The king is, however, not present, and the scene is near a river or lake, which obviously is intended to indicate the district of the country from which the bull was brought to the palace. Workmen with spades, picks, saws, and ropes, are busily engaged in the removal of the heavy mass, under the direction of officers, whose commands are transmitted by signs and trumpet-signals.

I must not omit to mention that in the official 'Synopsis of the Contents of the British Museum,' the above trumpets are noticed as "speaking-trumpets." Such an instrument is however different in appearance from the trumpets here exhibited. It especially requires a large aperture which entirely covers the mouth, and in which the lips can be moved freely, so as to insure a distinct enunciation of every word. An examination of the monuments must convince any one that the Assyrian sculptors took great care to exhibit any characteristic peculiarities appertaining to a figure or object which they were representing. I need only notice the great fidelity evinced in representing the muscles in the limbs of bulls and lions. This is also curiously exemplified in the representation of a claw in the tuft at the end of the lion's tail. The existence of such a claw in the tail of the living animal had been repeatedly asserted and doubted, but it has recently been ascertained to be a positive fact. For some interesting information on this and similar subjects, in further corroboration of the conscientious exactness observed by the sculptors, I must refer the reader to Mr. Bonomi's book on 'Nineveh and its Palaces.' From such facts the conclusion may be drawn, that if the instruments in question were speaking-trumpets, the sculptors would not have omitted to indicate the large aperture constituting the mouthpiece; there is, however, not the slightest

H

trace of it in the representations of any of the trumpets, although some of the sculptures are in good preservation.

Besides, trumpet signals are better fitted for transmitting orders to a great distance, than verbal messages through a speaking-trumpet, because they are more distinctly heard. And it must also be remembered that the ancient Egyptians and Hebrews had trumpets like those of the Assyrians; and that the Hebrews used them for signalling, in the same manner as the Assyrians, is a fact known from Holy Writ. [*From Kouyunjik.*]

No. 11. *A tamboura.*—We have here a scene which may perhaps refer to some peculiar national custom or popular festival. Two mummers, most likely mimes, clothed in lions' skins, and wearing masks resembling the head of the lion, are dancing to the music of a man who plays upon a tamboura. One of the dancers is carrying a whip in his right hand, which he used, perhaps, to produce a rhythmical accompaniment to the music of the tamboura. Similar customs exist at the present time in European countries. In some of the villages in Germany, for instance, grotesque mummers perform a peculiar dance at Whitsuntide before the houses, to the rhythm produced by the cracking of a number of whips. Three or four men with whips, who may be said to represent the band of musicians, accompany the dancers; they are generally so well practised together as to perform with much precision, producing a variety of animating rhythmical effects. [*From Nimroud.*]

No. 12. *Seven harps, one dulcimer, two double-pipes, and a drum.*—Procession of instrumental and vocal performers to meet the conquerors on their return

from the battle-field.—This is the largest and most
interesting assemblage of musicians which has been
discovered. I have therefore selected it for the
frontispiece to this book. It consists of eleven performers upon instruments, besides a chorus of singers.
The first musician—probably the leader of the band,
as he marches alone at the head of the procession—is
playing upon a harp. Behind him are two men, one
with a dulcimer and the other with a double-pipe;
then follow two more men with harps. Next come
six female musicians, four of whom are playing upon
harps, while one is blowing a double-pipe, and another
is beating a small hand-drum covered only at the top,
of the kind described at p. 63. Close behind the
instrumental are the vocal performers, consisting of a
chorus of females and children. They are clapping
their hands in time with the music, and some of
the musicians are dancing to the measure. One of the
female singers is holding her hand to her throat, in
the same manner as the women in Syria, Arabia, and
Persia are in the habit of doing at the present day,
when producing, on festive occasions, those peculiarly
shrill sounds of rejoicing which have been repeatedly
noticed by Oriental travellers. Dr. Clarke says,
"They are caused by trilling the tongue against the
roof of the mouth, without the utterance of any distinct words. Yet this singular mode of expressing
joy is all that constitutes the *Alleluia* of the ancients.
When Lord Hutchinson first entered Cairo, after the
capture of the city, he was met by a number of
women who greeted him with *Alleluia;* they accompanied him through the streets, clapping their hands,
and making this extraordinary noise in a loud and
shrill tone. It seems to be a constant repetition

of the same syllable *al*, uttered with the utmost rapidity."[4]   Besides being singularly illustrative of modern Oriental customs, the Assyrian procession under our consideration is also especially interesting on account of the resemblance which it bears to some musical processions of the Hebrews on similar occasions mentioned in the Bible.   I shall remind the reader only of David's reception by the women after his victory over the Philistines; and of that of Jephthah by his daughter and her companions, after his return from the battle against the children of Ammon (Judges xi. 34).   Also, on the solemn occasion of the conveyance of the ark into the City of David, the procession seems to have been very similar to that of the Assyrians here represented.   "David and all Israel played before God with all their might, and with singing, and with harps, and with psalteries, and with timbrels, and with cymbals, and with trumpets" (1 Chron. xiii. 8); and it was on this occasion that "David danced before the Lord with all his might" (2 Samuel vi. 14).   [*From Kouyunjik.*]

In addition to those enumerated I have seen a few other representations of Assyrian musicians, of which a brief notice will suffice.   The first is a performer on the harp, engraven on one of those little cylindrical seals which may be seen in the British Museum.

The second is a procession with instruments of music, in connection with a ceremony apparently sacrificial, before two altars.   It occurs on an obelisk in white calcareous stone, which was found near the

---

[4] Travels in various Countries, by E. D. Clarke, London, 1810, Part ii. Sect. ii. p. 121.

centre of the mound of Kouyunjik, and which also is now exhibited in the British Museum. But it is so much dilapidated that I could not distinguish with certainty more of the musical instruments than one or two asors.

The third is an engraving of two performers on lyres, given in M. Botta's work, 'Monuments de Ninive,' from a much corroded slab found in Khorsabad. The men, who seem to be singing while marching and twanging their lyres, are dressed like soldiers, with an appendage to their tunics, as represented in fig. 5, p. 38, which, according to Mr. Layard, was a kind of ornament somewhat resembling the Highland *philibeg*, and which was only worn by a certain class of soldiers.[5]

The fourth is a scene in which some singers and drummers are introduced, and of which also I have seen only a drawing, viz. in Mr. Layard's work entitled 'Discoveries in the Ruins of Nineveh and Babylon.' It is there described as representing "Assyrians cutting down the palm-trees belonging to a captured city." The drums are like those to which I have alluded (p. 64) as a third kind of Assyrian drum. It is worthy of notice that we find rhythmical sounds of the drum here employed apparently for the purpose of facilitating the execution of some menial labour.

CHARACTERISTICS OF THE PERFORMANCES.

I shall now state in a few words what may be adduced from a comparison of the different repre-

---

[5] Nineveh and its Remains, by A. H. Layard, London, 1849, vol. ii. p. 336.

sentations which I have described, respecting the
characteristics of the Assyrian musical performances.
It must be remembered that the monuments are not
all of the same age. Thus the king on slab No. 9 is,
according to our authorities on Assyrian history,
Sennacherib, during whose reign, about 720 B.C.,
the bas-relief probably was made; while the king on
slab No. 4 is Ashur-bani-pal, the grandson of Sennacherib. Again, the sculptures derived from the
mound of Nimroud are supposed to be several centuries older than those which are from Kouyunjik.
If we possessed more ample information on Assyrian
music than we do, it might have been of use for the
history of music to arrange these stony records
according to their age, as far as this is ascertainable. With our present limited knowledge, however,
nothing satisfactory could be gained by such an
attempt. I shall therefore consider here the instruments only, without further reference to the time to
which their existence can be traced in each individual instance.

We have seen that the Assyrians employed in their
musical performances stringed, wind, and pulsatile
instruments in combination. Moreover, we find the
stringed instruments greatly predominating, and any
loud rhythmical instruments but sparingly employed.
In this respect their music evidently differed from
that of the ancient Egyptians, in whose bands various
kinds of instruments of percussion are of frequent
occurrence. The Hebrews also used, besides loud
trumpets, several noisy rhythmical instruments, even
in religious ceremonies, which are seldom met with
in the Assyrian bands. Their music must consequently have been pre-eminently soft and senti-

mental in character, like that of several Asiatic nations at the present time. Captain Yule relates that when the military band of the English Embassy to the Court of Ava was playing European music to the Burmese, " they listened with more curiosity than enjoyment; the music was too loud for their taste."[6] On the other hand, their own music, as well as that of the Siamese, is described by most travellers as usually soft; and that it must be so, may be also concluded from the nature of their musical instruments, with the same certainty that the character of Assyrian music may be determined from the Assyrian instruments.

The stringed instrument most frequently used by the Assyrians was, it appears, the asor; after this the harp and the lyre seem to have been the most common. It was the custom to use two or more instruments of the same kind, probably more for the purpose of insuring greater fulness and brilliancy of tone than for the sake of increased loudness. For the same reason we employ a number of violins together in unison in our orchestras, although the music executed may be quite *piano*.

The Assyrians were obviously very fond of music and it was probably never wanting at their festivals and public entertainments. The power of music to increase the solemnity and grandeur of any public festivity is, indeed, so great and so universally felt, that it would have been extraordinary if the Assyrians had not, like other nations, made use of it on such occasions. Of the luxury and magnifi-

---

6 A Narrative of the Mission sent | to the Court of Ava, by Captain H.
by the Governor-General of India | Yule, London, 1858, p. 128.

cence displayed by them at festivals, we have some casual records in the Bible and Apocrypha. In the Book of Judith, for instance, it is related that, when the King Nabuchodonosor had conquered the King Arphaxad, he celebrated his victory in Nineveh, "and banqueted, both he and his army, an hundred and twenty days" (Judith i. 16). The employment of music at banquets and feastings was also customary among the Hebrews, as, indeed, it was with all ancient nations. Jesus, the son of Sirach, says: "A concert of musick in a banquet of wine is a signet of carbuncle set in gold. As a signet of an emerald set in a work of gold, so is the melody of musick with pleasant wine" (Ecclus. xxxii. 5, 6). And in praise of Josias he says that the remembrance of him is "sweet as honey in all mouths, and as musick at a banquet of wine." (Ecclus. xlix. 1).

Isaiah alludes to the fondness of the Babylonians for music, when exclaiming, "Thy pomp is brought down to the grave, and the noise of thy viols: the worm is spread under thee, and the worms cover thee" (Isaiah xvi. 11). And from a passage in Daniel it would appear that in Babylon hymns in praise of the gods were sung at the royal banquets. (Dan. v. 4, 23.)

Moreover, there can scarcely be a doubt that the Assyrians had also their funeral songs and lamentations, either entirely vocal, or perhaps with the accompaniment of flutes. The introduction of music by the Hebrews at funerals and on occasions of mourning is often mentioned in the Bible. King David himself composed a dirge upon the death of Saul and Jonathan (2 Sam. i. 17). From a sentence in St. Matthew ix. 23,—"And when Jesus came into

the ruler's house, and saw the minstrels and the
people making a noise, he said unto them, Give
place : for the maid is not dead but sleepeth,"—it
would appear that it was a Jewish custom to introduce music on such occasions. Forkel mentions that,
according to Maimonides, even the poorest Hebrew
husband was expected to engage at the funeral of his
wife at least two flute-players, and a hired female
mourner.[7]

It would seem from the beautiful Psalm cxxxvii.,
that the Babylonians must have found pleasure in
listening to the music of the Jews :—

"By the rivers of Babylon, there we sat down ;
yea, we wept when we remembered Zion.

"We hanged our harps upon the willows in the
midst thereof.

"For there they that. carried us away captive
required of us a song ; and they that wasted us required of us mirth, saying, Sing us one of the songs
of Zion.

"How shall we sing the Lord's song in a strange
land?"

Bedford, in his 'Temple Musick,' suggests that
"the service in the Temple at Jerusalem was regular
and orderly, without confusion and disturbance, and
where every one knew his part without interrupting
another; and this made the Babylonians so very
desirous to hear the same, that, when they had led
the Children of Israel captive, they required of them
a song, and melody in their heaviness, saying, Sing
us one of the songs of Zion."   It is, however, more

---

7 Forkel's Geschichte der Musik,
vol. i. p. 127.

8 The Temple Musick, by Arthur
Bedford, London, 1706, p. 37.

probable that they considered their own music quite
as good, if not superior to that of the Hebrews; and
their principal motive for inducing their captives to
sing, and for encouraging the continual practice of
music, was undoubtedly, as indicated in the psalm,
to preserve them in a cheerful and healthy condition
through the mighty influence of music, of which
influence the Babylonians themselves were fully convinced.

Music was especially used by the Assyrians and
Babylonians in their idol-worship, and in supersti-
tious ceremonies of a religious character. This is
obvious from the sculptures, but is also to some
extent confirmed by the mode of worship paid by
command of king Nebuchadnezzar to the golden
image, which is supposed to have been Baal:—

"Then an herald cried aloud, To you it is com-
manded, O people, nations, and languages, that at
what time ye hear the sound of the cornet, flute,
harp, sackbut, psaltery, dulcimer, and all kinds of
musick, ye fall down and worship the golden image
that Nebuchadnezzar the king hath set up." (Dan.
iii. 4, 5.)

The kings appear to have maintained at their
courts musical bands, whose office it was to perform
secular music at certain times of the day, or on fixed
occasions. Of king Darius the Mede we are told
that, when he had cast Daniel into the den of lions,
he "went to his palace, and passed the night
fasting; neither were instruments of musick brought
before him" (Dan. vi. 18); from which we may
conclude that his band was in the habit of playing
before him in the evening.

A similar custom prevailed also at the Court of

Jerusalem, at least in the time of David and Solomon; both of whom appear to have had their royal private bands, besides a large number of singers and instrumental performers of sacred music, who were engaged in the Temple. When David, in gratitude for services received from Barzillai the Gileadite, invited the old man to go with him to Jerusalem, and to abide there in comfort at the King's expense, Barzillai replied, " I am this day fourscore years old, and can I discern between good and evil? can thy servant taste what I eat or what I drink? can I hear any more the voice of singing men and singing women? wherefore then should thy servant be yet a burden unto my lord, the king?" (2 Sam. xix. 35.) Taking into consideration the circumstances under which this was said, there can scarcely be a doubt that Barzillai here alludes to the royal band; nor is it surprising that David, with his fondness for music, should have enjoyed musical performances in his palace of a different character from those introduced into divine service.

Solomon himself mentions his private orchestra in his reflections on the vanity of worldly pleasures and luxuries :—" I gat me men singers and women singers, and the delights of the sons of men, as musical instruments, and that of all sorts." (Eccles. ii. 8.)

Great as the fondness of the Assyrians for music appears to have been, the practice of this art as a profession can scarcely have been held by them in high estimation, but was more likely considered as unmanly and effeminate, to judge from the representations of musical performances, in which many of the musicians are eunuchs. These personages un-

doubtedly were singers as well as instrumentalists;
this may be concluded from their attitude, and from
the nature of their instruments, which in some instances could scarcely have been used otherwise than
for accompanying the singing. Their *sovrano* voices
must have imparted a peculiar brilliancy to their
performances. And it may be supposed that some
of them greatly excelled and attained renown and
riches.

RHYTHM, HARMONY, AND UNISON.

The questions which, in contemplating the Assyrian
vocal performances with instrumental accompaniment, would, most likely, first suggest themselves to
the musician, are—" How were the songs constituted,
and was the accompaniment in harmony or in unison?" On these I shall now submit a few observations.

In nations which have not brought the cultivation
of music to so high a degree of development as it has
attained with us, it may be observed that in vocal
compositions the words are often treated as of
greater importance than the music, and the latter
appears to be subservient to the former. The songs,
therefore, partake more of the nature of *recitative:*
they cannot be properly divided into bars, because
the rhythm is entirely dictated by the accentuation
and emphasis demanded by the words. This is usually
the case with the vocal music of uncivilized nations,
although some of them, naturally gifted with an
extraordinary susceptibility for rhythmical order,
have been almost instinctively led to the invention
of symmetrically-formed melodies of the nature of
our airs or tunes.

On the other hand, among nations with whom
music has been highly developed as an art, we not
unfrequently find the words entirely subordinate, in
order that the form of the vocal composition may be
worked out freely and unimpeded. In proof I need
only mention our fugues and similar compositions,
written in a strictly prescribed form, in which the
words are generally distorted in a most merciless
way. In our operas, especially in those of Italian
composers, the words often stand only for so many
unmeaning syllables upon which the notes are sung ;
and even the prevailing emotion conveyed by the
words is not always expressed in the music.

Gluck, the great musical reformer, fully appreciated the advantage of regarding poetry in combination with music, as of nearly equal importance ; and
thus he treated the words in his immortal operas.
Other distinguished musicians have adopted his views,
and created master-works. Some recent composers,
however, under the notion of extending and improving Gluck's principle, have, for the sake of the
words, injudiciously neglected the distinctness and
beauty of form of the music. Their compositions
are indeed, so far as rhythmical construction is concerned, not very different from the music of uncivilized nations—consisting merely of various phrases,
each perhaps beautiful in itself, but not forming
together an entire whole, or, in other words, not constituting a work of art producing a distinct total
impression.

In Asiatic nations, especially, the songs are generally of a nature which renders it almost impossible
to write them down divided into bars of equal duration. It is true that in some of the collections of

national airs this is by no means evident. A little closer investigation, however, would show that the tunes have been not unfrequently altered by the European collectors, in order to bring them into conformity with our usual divisions into bars. Hamilton Bird, who had lived for about twenty years in Calcutta when he published his collection of the 'Airs of Hindostan,' candidly states in his preface, "It has cost the compiler great pains to bring them into any form as to time." Similar accounts could be given relating to other oriental countries; but it will, perhaps, better answer our purpose if I insert instead a few specimens of vocal compositions of the nature alluded to :—

CHORUS OF THE MEWLEWI DERVISHES.

più mosso.

. . . . Hëi Jar!   Hëi Dost! Dscha-ni men Dscha-

Maestoso.

na - ni men! Ger   A - lim jan dschümle Ta - bi   ban ba-sched

Hal - li   no - - kü-ned   müschki - li ma   il - la

Hv, Hu, Hu, Hu . . . .

più mosso.

Hëi Jar!   Hëi Dost! Dscha-ni men Dscha-na - ni men!

CHORUS OF THE MEWLEWI DERVISHES.

Lento.

Bischnew   es . . . nëi   tschün . . . hi - kia -

- - jet mi - küned. . . . . . Be-li Ja -

ri . . men! es dschü - dai - - ha hi - - kia - -

- - jet mi - küned . . . . . Be - li Ja -

The above two choruses of the Mewlewi Dervishes
are taken from the Abbé Stadler's reliable collection.
They form part of those choruses which are usually
performed at the religious dances of the above sect
of dervishes in Constantinople. It will be observed
that, in order to convey a correct impression of their
rhythmical character, several peculiar means have
been resorted to in committing the music to paper,—
such as the frequent employment of pauses, of different kinds of bars, and of indications of change in
the time.

In the second chorus, in which a certain phrase is
several times repeated, and which greatly resembles
a kind of chant used in the Jewish synagogues in
Germany, it has been found necessary in several
instances to extend the duration of the last note of
the bar into the following bar, to avoid in the notation a continual change in the time of the several
bars.

The following piece is the Mahomedan 'Call to
Prayer' of the Muëzzin, from the minaret of the
mosque, as given in Mr. Lane's 'Manners and Customs of the Modern Egyptians:'—

CALL TO PRAYER OF THE MUËZZIN.

Al - - lá - - hu ak - bar. Al -

- lá - hu ak - bar. Al - lá - hu ak - bar.

Al - lá - - - - - - - - - - - - - - - hu ak -

- bar. Ash-ha-du an lá i - lá - ha il - lal - láh.

Ash - hadu an lá i - lá - ha il - lal - láh. . . . .

. . . . Ash-ha-du

an - na Mohamma - dar rasoo - lu - láh. Ash-ha-du

an - na Mohamma - dar rasoo - lu - láh. . . . . . .

I

Hei - ya 'alas - sa - láh.   Hei - ya 'a-las - sa - láh.

Hei-ya 'a - las - sa - láh.   Hei-ya 'a - lal - fe - láh.

Al - lá - hu ak - bar.   Al - lá - - hu ak -

- bar.   Lá - i - lá - ha il - la - láh.

The 'Blessing of the Priests,' as at present sung
in the synagogues of the Spanish and Portuguese
Jews, is believed to be identical with that used some
thousand years ago in the Temple of Jerusalem. If
this be really the case, undoubtedly it must have
undergone considerable change in the course of time.
Nevertheless, it bears unmistakeable resemblance to
Oriental vocal compositions, as is also the case with
several other ancient melodies in the collection of
Jewish sacred tunes published by De Sola and Aguilar,
—from which it has been derived :—

HEBREW 'BLESSING OF THE PRIESTS.'

Adagio maestoso.

Ye - - - ba - - - - - - - -

- - - re - - - - - - - che - cha -

- - - - - - - - - - - - -

The specimens of ancient melodies in Sulzer's 'Schir Zion,' which are used in the synagogues of the German Jews, are of a similar character. Moreover, the resemblance of the mode of singing, or rather chanting, in the synagogues, to the vocal performances of the Persians and other Eastern nations is unmistakeable, and shows, to some extent, how tenaciously the Jews have preserved ancient usages connected with their religious observances. That the singing of the ancient Hebrews, as well as that of the Greeks and other nations of antiquity, was of a similar nature, is the impression conveyed by the accounts of their music which have been transmitted to us.

Such, especially, must have been the songs of the Assyrian minstrels, whom we see entertaining the monarch probably with recitals of historical events and the glorious deeds of his forefathers, or of his own achievements ; particularly as these recitals were, most likely, often extempore performances, like those which are sung at the present time on similar occasions in chivalrous nations of the East.

For certain solemnities they may probably have had more measured melodies, consisting mostly of notes of an equal duration, like those which the Chinese and some other Asiatic nations use in their Buddhist worship. The vocal performances of the ancient Hebrews appear also to have been sometimes less chant-like, and more resembling a tune; we may suppose that they were modified according to the occasion on which the music was employed, as well as to the particular metre of the poetry to which it was wedded.

Respecting the instrumental accompaniment employed by the Assyrians, it may be concluded that it was certainly not always in unison with the voice, but frequently in harmony. To judge from the construction of the instruments, the harmony must, however, have been very primitive in comparison with our own.

Harmony is not so artificial an invention as has often been asserted. The susceptibility for it is innate in man, and soon becomes manifest wherever music has been developed to any extent. Children of the tenderest age have been known to evince delight in hearing *thirds* and other consonant intervals struck on the pianoforte; and it is a well-ascertained fact that with several savage nations the occasional employment of similar intervals combined did not originate from an acquaintance with European music, but was entirely their own invention. Nor is this surprising, if we consider that each single tone of a melody may be said to contain a harmony in itself, a harmony produced by the soft derivative tones or *harmonics* which are generated with the predominant tone.

If travellers not unfrequently assert that they have not observed any traces of harmony in the music of a nation, it must be remembered how few favourable opportunities they generally have for exact investigations. Moreover, they must naturally oftener meet with opportunities of witnessing vocal performances without instrumental accompaniments, such as simple national songs, or dance-tunes played upon a single instrument only, and accompanied perhaps by instruments of percussion for the purpose of rhythmical effects. And from what they thus casually witnessed, many have come to too hasty a conclusion on the characteristics of the music of a whole nation.

Besides, some may, in their inquiries, have been influenced by the preconceived notion that the music of nations in a low state of cultivation must be entirely without harmony. This opinion, originally promulgated by most of our writers on the history of music, who evidently were but little acquainted with the music of any other nations at present existing, but those of some European countries, has been, naturally enough, widely accepted, and repeated without any further investigation into its truth.

The music of Asiatic nations especially is usually described as being exclusively in unison. It is, however, noteworthy that, in some of the accounts in which this opinion is expressed, facts are related which rather tend to prove the contrary. Amiot, for instance, in the 'Mémoires concernant les Chinois,' states that the performances of the Chinese are always in unison, while in the course of his dissertation it becomes evident that his statement must be received with caution. And this impression is strongly confirmed by the information obtained from some other sources. Tradescant Lay says of the Chinese *pepa*, a species of guitar with four strings, "It is often used at festal rites of a religious character, and accompanied by the three-stringed guitar (*san heen*) ; so that we see something like music in parts, though of a very humble kind." Of the latter instrument he observes, " The sounds of the *san heen* are low and dull, which adapt it for the purpose of subduing the shrill sounds of the *pepa* by something like a bass. Performers do not appear to have anything like a score,—one plays from memory or in learning from notes, while the other accompanies him according to the best ideas of harmony he is master of." Of another instrument, the *yue kin*, or full-moon guitar," he says, " I once saw a musician at one of the strolling theatres who displayed a great deal of execution upon it, with very pleasing effect. On another occasion it was used as an accompaniment to the *urh heen* (a species of fiddle), and as the musician understood his business, the result had something peculiarly merry and exhilarating about it." The Chinese dulcimer, *yang kin*, is furnished with brass strings, which are struck with two small hammers. " When touched by a skilful hand, it yields a very gay and lively combination of harmonious and melodious sounds."[9]

A Hindoo morning concert, in which the *surinda* a stringed instrument played with a bow ; the *choutara,* a kind of guitar with four wire strings ; the *surod,* also a kind of guitar, but very different from

---

[9] The Chinese as They Are, by Tradescant Lay, Esq., London, 1841, pp. 76-83.

the preceding one in appearance ; and the *dara,* a kind of tambourine, were used, is described by Mr. Prinsep as follows :—" The *surod* is the leading instrument, and is sounded with a plectrum, like other native guitars. The *surinda* plays in unison with it, while the *choutara* forms a kind of bass accompaniment, or rather performs the same office as the drone among wind instruments. The men's voices occasionally chime in with the air, and again leave room for some *ad libitum* movements of the chief performer, who exerts all his energy in rapid impassioned execution."[1]

Even the bagpipe with its drones, an instrument almost universal, not only in European but also in Asiatic countries, produces a kind of rude harmony, and is unfit for performances in unison. The same may be said of several other wind instruments found in Asia. Of the Chinese *cheng,* already noticed (page 18) Mr. Lay observes, " By covering the first set of tubes with the forefinger, and breathing softly into the mouth-piece, a most charming *concentus* of sweet sounds is heard, with the harmonic divisions of the octave and twelfth, as the impulse is augmented. By stopping the second and third groups respectively, we get harmonies of three and two sounds which are loud and effective."[2]

The Assyrians were evidently much more civilized, and had made greater progress in music, than many nations of the present time which are no entirely unacquainted with harmony. The construction of their stringed instruments, especially the

---

[1] Benares, illustrated in a series of Drawings, by James Prinsep, Esq. Calcutta, 1830.

[2] The Chinese as They Are, by Tradescant Lay, London, 1841, p. 89.

harps, the strings of which they touch with both
hands at the same moment at different parts, as well
as the use of the double-pipe, indicate that they produced together different notes which appeared to
them agreeable in concord. Herein consisted, however, probably, their entire harmony. For a sys-
tematic combination of a fixed number of different
parts, each having its own individual course and
forming a melody by itself, their instruments were
too incomplete.

Neither could we expect to find among them a
harmony subjected to the same rules as our own, even
if they had been considerably further advanced in
music than was the case. For our own theory of
harmony is by no means so strictly founded upon
natural and universal laws, that any other nation
must by a progressive cultivation of music, be ultimately led to its adoption as a matter of course. It
is, in fact, continually undergoing changes. Scarcely
three centuries have elapsed since Monteverde ven-
tured to introduce, for the first time, the chord of the
seventh on the dominant without preparation into our
harmony, which previously consisted only of consonant chords, interspersed occasionally with a *discord
of suspension.* The harmony in some of our old
madrigals and similar compositions appears to us
antiquated and quaint. Modern composers have,
not unfrequently with admirable effect, made use of
combinations of chords which until recently were
considered as incorrect and quite inadmissible. Instances of this kind occur in Beethoven's instrumental
compositions.

I have already noticed the remarkable resemblance
of the Nubian *kissar* to the Assyrian lyre. I shall

presently give a few examples of the usual accompaniments on the kissar, from which it will be seen that they consist of certain rhythmical groups of notes, which are repeated during the song. The Assyrian accompaniments on the lyre must have been similar; not only on account of the likeness in the construction and capability of the two instruments, but also because such accompaniments are the easiest to execute, and would most naturally suggest themselves to the performer; and also because they are similar to some accompaniments which are employed by Asiatic nations on stringed instruments at the present day.

Vocal music in harmony requires more musical experience and efficiency than simple instrumental harmony used as an accompaniment. The execution of the Assyrian choruses was therefore most likely usually in unison, and in octaves, when men, women, and children were singing together; though it is not improbable that some harmony, consisting of short sequences of *thirds*, or perhaps even of some *consecutive fifths*, may have been now and then introduced.

Such combinations of intervals have actually been found in use in several uncivilized nations when Europeans first came in contact with them,—nations whose degree of musical cultivation was far below that to which the Assyrians had evidently attained.

CHAPTER IV.

MUSICAL SYSTEM OF THE ASSYRIANS.

Resemblance of the Assyrian music to that of other ancient Oriental nations—The pentatonic scale—The present existence of the pentatonic scale in various Asiatic nations evidenced by tunes from China, Siam, Java, Hindoostan, Burmah, and Japan—High antiquity of the pentatonic scale in Asia—The order of intervals in which the Assyrian stringed instruments appear to have been usually tuned—Traces of the pentatonic scale among the ancient Greeks—The intervals of the Nubian kissar—Subdivisions of the whole tone—Diffusion of the pentatonic scale—The pentatonic scale of the ancient American Indians—Traces of the same scale in the music of the Scotch and other Celtic races—The peculiar character of the Assyrian music—The probable musical notation of the Assyrians.

A CAREFUL examination of the evidences relating to Assyrian music, which I have been able to collect, has convinced me that their musical scale must have been similar to that of other ancient Asiatic nations, and, furthermore, that traces of this scale, which differs from our own, are even at the present time apparent.

I purpose now to explain first the characteristics which distinguish this scale from the diatonic scale employed in European music; and afterwards to give the reasons from which I deduce that it was used by the Assyrians and other ancient Asiatic nations.

The reader may be assured that I have exercised the utmost caution in admitting in confirmation of any opinion only those musical examples whose genuineness is indisputable.   The musician has therefore an opportunity of drawing his own conclusions from them, should he not concur in those advanced by me. I think this especially desirable, since an independent and unbiassed examination is the surest means of attaining the exact truth, which is my only aim.

It would be a mistake to suppose that the music of the various ancient Asiatic nations was in every respect alike. This is as little the case at the present time as it was formerly, although from the accounts of many travellers we might be led to surmise the contrary. The actual fact may best be explained by a reference to our own music as practised in different European countries. The musician seldom finds any difficulty in distinguishing compositions of Italian masters from those of the French, Germans, and others. In the popular folks-music, generally originating with and traditionally preserved by the rural population, the peculiar character of the national music of a civilized country is usually more strongly marked than in the compositions of educated professional musicians; because the musicians do not confine their studies to the music of their own country, but learn also from celebrated masters of other countries. The character of their music is consequently often influenced and modified by what they admire in, and perhaps involuntarily adopt from foreign music. Thus it may be explained why, for instance, the Swedish, German, and Hungarian national tunes are more widely different from each other than the works of modern celebrated composers appertaining to Sweden, Germany, and Hungary.

Notwithstanding these differences, the music of most European nations possess certain distinct cha-

racteristics in common, which stamp it with a kind
of family likeness. The principal features consist in
the circumstance that it is almost always founded
upon the diatonic scale, and exhibits a symmetrical
arrangement of rhythmical notes.

THE PENTATONIC SCALE.

If an intelligent Chinese or Hindoo musician, on a
cursory visit to Europe, were to hear the music of
different European countries, he would in all probability only observe those peculiarities which appertain to all European music, and which distinguish
it from that of his own nation; and it might take
some time before he would be enabled to perceive
the differences which exist in the music of various
countries.

It is therefore not surprising that many European
travellers should have described the music of several
Asiatic countries as the same; since in Asiatic music
are to be found certain characteristic traits which
convey to it what I have called a family likeness.
The most remarkable of these is that the melodies
are frequently founded upon a scale differing essentially from our own, and consisting of only five
tones, wherefore I have given it the name of *Pentatonic Scale.*

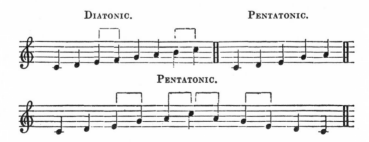

DIATONIC.   PENTATONIC.

PENTATONIC.

In order to show exactly the nature of the pentatonic scale, I have also written down our diatonic scale, which, it will be remembered, consists of five *whole tones* and two *semitones*. The two semitones are from the *third* to the *fourth*, and from the *seventh* to the *octave*, as indicated in the example by brackets. This scale, which appears here in c *major*, consists therefore of only seven different intervals,—the *octave*, which is considered as identical with the *prime*, has been added merely to show the second *semitone* before mentioned. The above example exhibits the five intervals of the pentatonic scale, assuming c to be the *tonic*. It differs from the diatonic scale inasmuch as the intervals of the *fourth* and *seventh* are wanting. Consequently the two diatonic semitones do not occur : we have instead two *minor thirds*, as will be seen in the example, in which the pentatonic scale is represented ascending to the octave and descending to the prime.

In the communications of travellers, relating to musical performances, inadvertent indications are now and then met with that the pentatonic scale is in use at the present time in various parts of Asia. Some travellers describe it so distinctly as not to be mistaken, while others allude merely to some peculiarity in the music which appeared to them a defective scale. The following extracts from some well-known books of travel may serve as instances in proof.

Mr. Tradescant Lay, in describing the Chinese stringed instrument called *pepa*, observes, " The player generally avoids the half-note. I asked my instructor why he did this, but the question confounded him greatly."[1] Again, Sir George Staunton says that " to

---

1 The Chinese as They Are, by Tradescant Lay, London, 1841, p. 77.

Mr. Huttner, a good judge of music, it appeared that
the Chinese gamut was such as Europeans would
call imperfect, their keys being inconsistent." A
little further on the same author distinctly tells us,
" The Chinese, in playing on instruments, discovered
no knowledge of semitones."[2]
The pentatonic scale of the Siamese is described,
rather obscurely, in Finlayson's ' Journal' as follows:
—" My friend Captain Dangerfield, himself an adept
in musical science, remarks that the music of the
Siamese differs from that of all barbarous tribes in
being played upon a different key to that, if I understand him right, which characterizes the pathetic
music of certain European nations."[3]   Doctor Ruschenberger relates that he heard a Siamese minstrel
performing an air, " which might have been mistaken
for Scotch, had we not been assured that it was
Siamese."[4]   Barrow, while in Cochin China, heard
on a certain occasion some national airs of that
country, of which he remarks, " One in particular
attracted our attention, whose slow melancholy movement breathed that kind of plaintive softness so peculiar to the native airs of the Scotch, to which, indeed,
it bore a very close resemblance."[5]   Again, the
Honourable Mountstuart Elphinstone mentions that
in Afghanistan he witnessed performances of the
national songs and dances of that country, when " a

[2] An Authentic Account of an
Embassy from the King of Great
Britain to the Emperor of China,
by Sir G. Staunton, Bart.,
London, 1797, vol. ii. p. 262.
[3] The Mission to Siam and
Cochin-China, from the Journal
of the late George Finlayson,
Esq., by Sir Th. Stamford
Raffles, London, 1826, p. 290.
[4] Narrative of a Voyage
Round the World, by W. S. W.
Ruschenberger, M.D., vol. ii. 37.
[5] A Voyage to Cochin-China,
by John Barrow, London, 1806,
p. 295.

love-song was sung to an extremely pretty melody, very simple, and not unlike a Scottish air."[6]

One other testimony will suffice. It is from a recent traveller in the north of China, whose statements are perhaps all the more suggestive because he shows himself incompetent duly to appreciate the works of great musical composers. He says, "None of those grand conceptions bestowed on the world by Mozart, Mendelssohn, Donizetti, Hummel, Handel, or Beethoven, to nearly all of whose masterpieces I have lent my enraptured attention, ever produced in me such unspeakable emotions of tenderness and plaintive melancholy as those which arose as I sat one midnight long ago on the banks of a Highland loch during the fishing season, when all nature seemed to be lulled to rest under the burnished silvery light of a summer moon." In this lovely place his musings were suddenly interrupted by a Scotch tune, 'Mackrimmon's Lament,' played on a bagpipe by one of the fishermen in a distant boat. "Though before and since those happy days I have been dinned, delighted, and distracted by pibrochs, strathspeys, and all the variations which can be appended to the entire catalogue of Celtic music, the air which threw me into an almost cataleptic state on that night remains preserved in my memory in all its original simplicity and unalloyed genuineness of half-civilized natural impression, as told in pure pathos by a few notes on a simple instrument. Mackrimmon's Lament, 'We return no more,' continually interposes between my judgment and the favourable verdict I might

6 An Account of the Kingdom of Caubul, by the Hon. Mount-   stuart Elphinstone, London, 1839, vol. i. p. 311.

give in regard to any modern symphony or elaborate production of a civilized and cultivated mind." Could we have stronger evidence of a close resemblance between Chinese and Scotch popular melodies than the assertion of this enthusiastic admirer of 'Mackrimmon's Lament' that he has met with it again, to his great surprise, at a Chinese funeral procession? He relates: "For many years I had not heard again my melancholy favourite, and little expected to do so until I revisited 'the land of brown heath and shaggy wood;' when, one spring afternoon, riding along the banks of the Peiho above Tien-tsin, the old sound suddenly overwhelmed me; and, though the notes I anxiously sought to catch were not exactly the same, and did not succeed each other in quite the identical rhythmical order, yet the resemblance was sufficiently startling and complete to accomplish the return of the spell."[7]

This resemblance to the songs of Scotland, which we find so often alluded to, is quite inexplicable, as there are also in these unmistakeable traces of the pentatonic scale. I shall afterwards have to say a few words on this subject, which I touch upon here only for the sake of explaining the remarks of the traveller I have quoted.

Similar accounts are not unfrequently met with in descriptions of Asiatic countries and their inhabitants. In order to ascertain how far they are well founded, I collected and compared as many authentic melodies of those countries as I could obtain. I shall now transcribe a few examples from

---

[7] Travels on Horseback in Mantchu Tartary, by G. F. Fleming. London, 1863.

my collection to show that the impressions of the travellers cited are confirmed by the music itself, which
has been transmitted to Europe through different
channels.

CHINESE AIR

CHINESE AIR—' Moo-lee-wha.'

The first Chinese air is taken from Du Halde's
well-known work on China.[8] It was afterwards reprinted in Rousseau's 'Dictionnaire de Musique,'
through which it has become more known to the

---

8 Description de l'Empire de la Chine, par le P. J. B. Du Halde.
A la Haye, 1736.

K

musical world. However, by some oversight, a wrong note has crept into the copy printed by Rousseau, viz., in the third bar the interval of the seventh, f, occurs. This circumstance has given rise to some curious conjectures among learned musicians. Dr. Burney observes "f natural comes in so awkwardly as to raise a suspicion that it has been inserted by a mistake of the engraver."[9] Dr. Fink, the late editor of the Leipzig musical journal called 'Allgemeine musikalische Zeitung,' instead of referring to Du Halde's work, where he might have convinced himself that Burney has conjectured rightly, takes some pains to prove that the introduction of the *seventh* in the bar where it occurs must be quite in accordance with the rules of modulation in Chinese music; and he is rather bitter against Burney for having suggested the probability of a misprint, where he himself finds just exactly what he would have expected to find.[1] I mention this as an instance how learned musicians, when defending a certain theory of their own, are sometimes apt to endorse statements in confirmation thereof, which, with less prejudice, they would see were quite erroneous.

The Chinese air in praise of the flower Moo-lee I have transcribed from Barrow's 'Travels in China,' a work in which several other Chinese melodies are given, all of which are characterized by the pentatonic scale.

The following song, called *Sian Chok*, has recently been published in an interesting article on the musical notation of the Chinese, by the Rev. E. W. Syle, in

---

[9] Burney's History of Music, vol. i. p. 31.
[1] Erste Wanderung der æl-   testen Tonkunst, von G. W. Fink, 1831, p. 72.

the Journal of the China Branch of the Royal
Asiatic Society, Shanghai, 1859. I insert it here to
show that the specimens of Chinese music collected
by different persons, and in different parts of the
empire, all bear the same characteristics, as far as the
scale is concerned.

CHINESE AIR—'SIAN CHOK.'

A number of Siamese tunes, transmitted to Europe
by Captain James Low, of the Madras Army, have
been published in the 'Journal of' the Royal Asiatic
Society,' vol. iv., London, 1837. From these I have
selected the following two specimens, to give the
reader an idea of the character of Siamese music :—

SIAMESE AIR.

THE KING OF SIAM'S MARCH, 'Phriyadun.'

The King of Siam's March, it will be seen, consists of only four different intervals; but it is evidently founded upon the pentatonic scale, like all the other Siamese melodies in the collection of Captain Low.

In Java, which derived its earliest civilization from India,[2] we meet with the same scale, as may be seen

---

[2] The Natural History of the Varieties of Man, by R. G. Latham, London, 1850, p. 152.

in Sir Stamford Raffles' 'History of Java,' where
some Javanese tunes are given, of which the following
is a specimen :—

JAVANESE AIR—'SURUNG DAYUNG.'

A number of Javanese melodies, all, like the above,
strictly founded upon the pentatonic scale, have been
published in Crawfurd's 'History of the Indian

Archipelago.' In this book we find also a letter
from Dr. Crotch, referring to a collection of Javanese
musical instruments brought to England by Sir
Stamford Raffles, in which the writer says, "The
instruments are all in the same kind of scale as that
produced by the black keys of the pianoforte." These
instruments are now deposited in the British Museum,
where I have had an opportunity of convincing
myself that they are, as Dr. Crotch intimates, tuned
in the pentatonic scale, which is, in fact, the order of
intervals represented by the black keys on our pianoforte.

With respect to the music of Hindoostan, I must
observe that the largest collections of native melodies
which we at present possess have been derived from
Calcutta and its immediate neighbourhood. They
were written down by European musicians who lived
in that city as organists and professors of music. I
must say that I have found scarcely any traces of
the pentatonic scale in these collections. In some
instances the cause may perhaps be ascribed to the
circumstance that the collectors considered anything
which appeared defective to the unaccustomed European ear as accidental mistakes of the performers,
and they may, therefore, have taken the liberty of
making alterations which they deemed improvements
when committing the music to paper. Some of them,
indeed, indicate this clearly enough in their observations prefacing the collections.

It is also very probable that now and then alterations may have been introduced unintentionally.
Tradescant Lay remarks, " In my travels I sometimes
wrote down the airs that I heard among the natives ;
but though I took much pains to learn them accu-

rately, I always found they had lost something of their peculiarity when played upon the violin."[3]

M. Villoteau, the French musician before-mentioned, relates that during his sojourn in Cairo he took some lessons from an Arab music-master, in order to become thoroughly acquainted with the musical system of the Arabs. While writing down certain melodies which his teacher sang, they appeared to him now and then out of tune, and he therefore took care to rectify in the notation the apparent defects. However, afterwards, when he sang to his teacher what he had written down, he was told that he was singing wrong notes. This led to a dispute between the two musicians, each maintaining that the ear of the other must be at fault. Thus they went on until at last it struck M. Villoteau that the intervals of the Arabic scale must be different from those of our own, and that therefore they appeared wrong to him; and he found this to be the case. A less intelligent musician, perhaps, would not have discovered this, and would consequently in his notation have entirely obliterated the characteristics of the music. It is therefore always hazardous to draw conclusions from examples obtained through one or two channels only.

There can, however, be no doubt, as will be seen presently, that our diatonic scale is at the present time found in some parts of Asia, especially where the people have come more in contact with Europeans.

NATIONAL AIR FROM CHUMBA.

Moderato.

3 The Chinese as They Are, by G. Tradescant Lay, London, 1841, p. 81.

The above air, from Chumba in the northern part
of Hindoostan, is taken from Vigne's Travels.[4] It is
strictly pentatonic. But I ought to mention that in
some other tunes communicated by the same traveller,
also from the north of Hindoostan, the pentatonic
scale is only partially apparent. Nevertheless, there
can be no doubt that this scale is used in Hindoostan at the present time, although perhaps not
so universally as formerly. Sir William Ouseley hints
at this fact by observing, "Many of the Hindoo
melodies (to use the words of an excellent musician)
possess the plaintive simplicity of the Scotch and
Irish."[5]

An interesting collection of Burmese melodies was
some years ago presented to the Royal Asiatic Society
in London by Mr. Fowle, who resided for many years
in Rangoon. It contains thirty different pieces,
which, according to Mr. Fowle, include all the
principal popular tunes of the Burmese : most of
them are of considerable length. I shall therefore
transcribe only the commencement of the first of
them :—

---

[4] Travels in Kashmir, Ladak,
Iskardo, the Countries adjoin-
ing the Mountain-Course of the
Indus, and the Himalaya North
of the Panjab, by G. T. Vigne,
London, 1842.
[5] Sir W. Ouseley's Oriental
Collections. London, 1797.

AIR FROM BURMAH.

It will be seen that the interval of the *seventh* occurs several times. In the phrase of bar 12 and 13, which repeatedly occurs in the course of the piece, this interval must, however, be considered as the *third*, and appertains therefore also to the pentatonic scale, because the phrase is not in C major, but in G major.

From a letter of Mr. Fowle to the Secretary of the Asiatic Society we learn that these melodies have been arranged for the Burmese *thro*, a kind of violin which I have already noticed. This may account for the fact that but few traces of the pentatonic scale are perceptible in them. Besides, the manuscript has been written hastily, or by an inexperienced hand, as is proved by the many mistakes and oversights by which the musician is every moment puzzled. It can therefore be used only with great caution.

The employment of diatonic passages in these Burmese melodies seems to me, however, authentic, as it is not likely that the collector would have allowed himself so great an alteration of the music as their unwarrantable introduction would involve. The same may be said of the choruses of the Dervishes and the ' Call to Prayer ' of the Muëzzin, which I have given. There are, however, various indications which I shall notice presently, suggesting that the pentatonic scale was at an early period in use in Western as well as in Central Asia.

In Japan also we might expect to meet with this scale, considering the great resemblance of the Japanese musical instruments to those of the Chinese, as well as the circumstance of these two nations possessing much in common in religion and usages.

Although we have several accounts relating to Japanese music, scarcely any tunes of reliable authenticity have been published. The following one, which appeared a short time ago in 'All the Year Round' (London, May 11th, 1861), has been obtained from the Japanese envoys, who, with a suite of seventy officers and attendants, recently visited the United States of America. A gentleman who had frequent opportunities of hearing the singing of these foreigners, took, as he informs us in the above-mentioned journal, much care to commit several of them faithfully to paper. Of these the following is the only specimen hitherto published:—

JAPANESE SONG.

It will be observed that this melody is also constructed upon the pentatonic scale. It is, however, not in *major*, like most melodies of this kind, but in *minor*—*f-sharp* being the tonic.

Nothing, in my opinion, could more clearly prove the universal diffusion throughout Asia of the penta-

tonic scale than the unanimity in the observations
of so many different travellers and other persons
acquainted with Eastern nations, particularly as most
of these gentlemen possessed but little musical knowledge, and were evidently unable to account for the
cause of the peculiarity in the music which they
noticed. It seems to me, therefore, unnecessary to
add here any more examples of modern Asiatic music,
especially as I have mentioned several books in which
a number of tunes are given, to which the reader can
easily refer, should he desire further proof in confirmation of my opinion.

Some musicians may possibly object to my designating this series of intervals a *scale*. According
to our usual definition of this word, no wider steps
than from one *whole tone* to another are admissible ;
and such a progression is considered the most natural.
It must, however, be remembered that in our scales
the steps are not all equidistant from each other.
Our diatonic series consists of *whole tones* and *large
semitones ;* and even in our chromatic scale all the
intervals are not exactly equal in succession, some
being *large semitones* and others *small semitones*.
Again, our minor scale is constructed in various
ways : some composers employ, as a rule, the *major
sixth* and *major seventh* in ascending, and the *minor
seventh* and *minor sixth* in descending ; others prefer
the *minor sixth* and *major seventh* both in ascending
and descending. In this instance a step is actually
introduced which exceeds a *whole tone*. The Wallachians in their national music employ two such steps
(embracing a *whole tone* and a *small semitone*) in the
minor scale, viz., one from the *minor third* to
the *superfluous fourth*, and another from the *minor*

sixth to the *major seventh.* There is no reason why this succession of intervals also should not be considered as a real scale; natural it certainly is, as it has been, so to say, adopted instinctively.

Moreover, the difference between the *large semitone* and the *whole tone* in our diatonic scale is about equal to the difference between the *whole tone* and the *minor third* of the pentatonic scale. The latter scale, therefore, cannot be considered less irregular than the former. In short, instead of defining the word *scale*, so as to be applicable to our diatonic and chromatic orders of intervals only, as is often done, it is in my opinion more correct to consider it in a sense which allows of its being applied as well as any other fixed series of intervals upon which the music of a nation is founded.

ANTIQUITY OF THE PENTATONIC SCALE.

I shall now endeavour to show that the pentatonic scale was in common use in Asia at a very early period. In truth, we might reasonably expect this to have been the case, considering that it is so widely spread, and that it is more simple than any other scale.

There is no doubt that children, in their first attempts to sing our diatonic scale, will not unfrequently find a difficulty in producing the semitone from the interval of the *third* to the *fourth*, and they are apt to skip from the *third* at once to the *fifth*, omitting the *fourth* altogether. Now, this is exactly a pentatonic succession of intervals, which impresses itself upon the musically uncultivated mind all the more easily, because it is especially melodious as well as characteristic.

The tenacity with which Oriental nations adhere
to old customs is well known. Indeed, almost
everything with them is of high antiquity. On
sculptured monuments we see representations of
manners and ceremonies which are still in existence,
and much light has been thrown upon the Assyrian
bas-reliefs by a reference to modern Eastern customs.
Music in Asia has been from time immemorial associated with religious observances and solemn ceremonies; and any alterations were, of course, considered highly objectionable. It is true the Chinese
and Hindoos maintain that their music was in old
times in a higher state of perfection than it is at present. Such a belief, however, exists in many nations,
and may be classed with the usual traditional belief
in a former period of universal happiness and perfection.

But granting the music of the Chinese and Hindoos
to have been once superior to what it now is, still it
was most likely not different in its principal characteristics, because it has not been subject to European
or other foreign influence. If, therefore, it is at
present less perfect, we may conjecture it to be all
the better qualified for affording us an idea of what
it was originally. These conclusions may appear
hazardous, but they are corroborated by several facts
which I shall briefly notice.

It must not be supposed that semitones were
unknown to the ancient Asiatic nations; on the
contrary, we find in their music even smaller divisions than our chromatic scale, at least in theory
if not in practice.

Of the early history of Chinese music we possess
an account by the French missionary Amiot, who,

during his abode in Peking, made it part of his mission to collect as much information on this subject as he could possibly obtain. He consulted a large number of old Chinese treatises on the science and history of music, of which a list is given in the book containing the result of his investigations.[6] We learn from them that the ancient Chinese divided the octave into twelve equal parts, like the semitones of our chromatic scale, which were called *lu*.[7] Their scale, as commonly used, consisted, however, of only five notes, which were called *koung, chang, kio, tché,* and *yu,* and which corresponded to our *f, g, a, c, d.* *Koung,* or *f,* was considered to be the normal key, as we consider our *c;* and it was from *koung* that the above order of intervals was transposed to any of the other keys, in a similar way as we change the scale of C major into that of G major, F major, &c. The intervals of the *fourth* and *seventh* were called *pien-koung* and *pien-tché.* The former was identical with our *e,* and the latter with our *b.* These two intervals they employed only in exceptional cases, or rather, nearly in the same way as we introduce chromatic intervals into our diatonic scale. Several of the ancient Chinese musical instruments contain only the pentatonic scale, and are purposely thus constructed. The *hiuen,* an ancient wind instrument of an oval shape, had five holes through which the notes *koung, chang, kio, tché* and *yu,* were emitted. A similar instrument is still used. The highly esteemed *kin,* the favourite instrument of the venerated Confu-

---

6 Mémoires concernant l'Histoire, les Sciences, les Arts, les Mœurs, les Usages, etc., des Chinois, par les Missionaires de Pekin, tome sixième. Paris, 1780.

7 There is, however, this difference, that the twelve Chinese divisions were strictly alike, while our chromatic scale consists of large and small semitones.

cius, was also similarly tuned. Another very ancient one, the *ou*, in the shape of a crouching tiger, possessed six notes, corresponding to our *f, g, a, c, d, f.*

Several of these instruments are no longer in use, or have become gradually changed. The Chinese, even at the present time, construct instruments in which they purposely introduce the pentatonic scale only. Of this kind is the one mentioned at p. 15, which is deposited in the Museum of the United Service Institution. The Chinese harmonicon which Dr. Burney saw in Paris, in the possession of the Abbé Arnaud of the French Academy, was of a similar construction, as is evident from the description of it given in Burney's ' History of Music.'[8]

The following ancient Chinese hymn " in honour of the ancestors," was, according to Amiot, annually performed on a solemn occasion, in presence of the emperor. The ceremony took place in a large hall of the imperial palace, in which the portraits of the former emperors were ranged on the walls. Near the entrance, on the right and left, stood the instrumental performers; opposite the entrance stood the singers; in the middle of the hall the dancers, whose office it was to perform at a given signal some sacred evolutions. Upon a table were placed various articles used as offerings and libations. When everything was thus duly prepared, the emperor, amidst the deepest silence, entered the hall. Then at a signal on the large drum, *taokou*, the hymn, slow and solemnly sung, commenced. During the performance, the emperor knelt at assigned places, brought his offerings, and burnt incense in honour of his

---

[8] Burney's ' History of Music,' vol. 1. p. 32.

ancestral relations, whose spirits were supposed to be present during the solemn ceremony. All was conducted according to strictly prescribed rules, and the three parts of the hymn did not immediately follow each other, but there were intervals of silence between, until a signal directed the recommencement of the music.

ANCIENT CHINESE HYMN IN HONOUR OF THE ANCESTORS.

Grave.   **First Part.**

See hoang sien Tsou,   Yo ling yu Tien,

Yuen yen tsing lieou,   Yeou kao tay hiuen,

Hiuen sun cheou ming,   Tchoui yuen ki sien,

Ming yn ché tsoung,   Y ouan see nien.

Second Part.

Toui yué tché tsing,   Yen jan jou cheng,

Ki ki tchao ming,   Kan ko tsai ting;

Jou kien ki hing,   Jou ouen ki cheng,

L

Ngai   eulh   king   tché,   Fa   hou   tchoung   tsing.

Third Part.

Ouei   tsien   jin   koung,   Tê   tchao   vng   Tien,

Ly   yuen   ki   yu,   Yuen   cheou   fang   koue,

Yu   pao   ki   tê,   Hao   Tien   ouang   ki.

Yn   tsin   fan   hien,   Ouo   sin   yué   y.

The Hindoos at a very early time divided their scale into intervals smaller than our semitones, of which there were twenty-two in the compass of an octave. These intervals were called *sruti*. The notes of the common scale were *sa, ri, ga, ma, pa, dha, ni,* which, according to Sir William Jones,[8] correspond to our, *a, b, c, d, e, f, g,*—and according to Captain Willard,[9] to our *c, d, e, f, g, a, b.* From these intervals a great number of modes are formed, by substituting a different interval for the key-note, or *tonic,* in much the same way as our old church modes were formed ; and also—which is more re-markable—by treating certain intervals either as unessential parts of a scale, or by actually omitting them. The following specimens of scales, from Sir

---

[8] On the Musical Modes of the Hindus by Sir William Jones ; Asiatic Researches, vol. iii.

[9] A Treatise on the Music of Hindoostan, by Captain A. Willard. Calcutta, 1834.

William Jones's essay on the musical modes of the Hindoos, will explain this more clearly :—

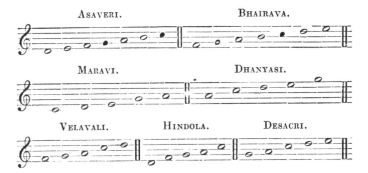

In the above two scales called *Asaveri* and *Bhairava*, the intervals written in black notes are considered merely as additions or ornaments. The other scales,—*Maravi, Dhanyasi, Velavali, Hindola,* and *Desacri,*—are all strictly pentatonic, and do not require further explanation. I might have selected several more of the same stamp, but I consider this unnecessary, as Sir W. Jones's essay is easily accessible to everyone.

The *rags* and *raginees* are ancient Hindoo melodies, composed upon certain fixed scales. Captain Willard says, " *Rags* and *raginees* are divided into three classes : first, *sumpoornu,* or those which comprise all the seven notes, in their course, in any determinate succession whatever ; second, *khadoo,* or such as are composed of six notes ; and third, *oodoo,* whose extent ranges to but five notes ; and hence it is said that no *rag* or *raginee* is confined within limits whose extent is less than five notes."[1] This account requires but little comment, after what we have already seen. Suffice

---

[1] A Treatise on the Music of Hindoosta by Captain A. Willard, p. 56.

it to notice that the extension of the pentatonic scale into the octave, which requires a sixth note, is not unusual, as might be expected.

The following old Hindoo melody, called *hooly*, is a spring song upon the god Krishna. It was communicated to Herr von Dalberg (the German translator of Sir W. Jones's essay on the Modes of the Hindoos) by Richard Johnson of Calcutta, the friend and fellow-labourer of Sir W. Jones :—

'Hooly.'

Tu - me - ra   aus - ser   laa   ger - hat.

I do not hold myself responsible for the correctness of the words of any of the songs. I give them as I find them, judging that, although of no importance for our present inquiry, they may nevertheless perhaps be of some interest to the reader.

The characteristics of the music of the Singhalese were formerly, as they are at present, similar to those of the Hindoo music. Mr. Joinville, in his observations on the religion and manners of the people of Ceylon, states that "music appears to have been formerly cultivated in Ceylon, and reduced into principles. There are pieces of music to be seen in regular notes in some of the old books in the Pali tongue."[2] The names of the notes are identical with those used in Hindoostan; but I am unable to say whether any traces of the pentatonic scale have been preserved in the Singhalese popular tunes of the present day.

Of the musical systems employed by the Persians and Arabs we have no earlier satisfactory accounts than those dating from the period soon after the conquest of Persia and the introduction of the Mohammedan religion by the Arabs, an event which occurred about the middle of the seventh century of the Christian era. As far as we know, the first writers in Persia who treated music as a science were Arabs. The system expounded by them resembles that of the Hindoos, inasmuch as smaller divisions than our semitones are made use of. They divided the compass of the octave into seventeen intervals; there

---

[2] Asiatic Researches, vol. vii. p. 399.

were consequently two intervals between each *whole tone*. The same system was adhered to by the Persians. However, towards the end of the thirteenth century some theorists adopted a system in which the octave was divided into twelve intervals, like the semitones of our chromatic scale. Kiesewetter believes this innovation to be of European origin, and to have been adopted from the missionaries, who during the thirteenth century were sent by the Popes to various Asiatic courts.[3] This is, however, mere hypothesis, unsupported by any satisfactory proofs, and its correctness will appear the more doubtful if we recollect that the Chinese made use of a similar division of intervals at a very early period. Besides, in most instances where we meet with the same usage or invention, both in an Asiatic and in an European nation, we may be sure that it existed previously with the former, and that consequently, if one nation has borrowed it from the other it must have been the European that was the borrower.

Much interesting information might be obtained on such questions if Oriental scholars would publish translations of some of the most renowned works on music extant in different countries and languages. The translator must, however, possess some musical knowledge, otherwise he is more likely to mislead than to enlighten the musical inquirer. It would be an easy but thankless task to notice instances where, from want of efficient musical knowledge, erroneous notions have been promulgated by men of science.

Amiot gives a list of the titles of about seventy Chinese works on music. In Kiesewetter's disserta-

---

[3] Die Musik der Araber, von Kiesewetter, Leipzig, 1842, p. 14.

tion before noticed almost as many works of Arabian
and Persian authors relating to the music of their
countries are mentioned; and Sir William Jones, as
well as other Orientalists, informs us of the existence
of a number of old treatises in Sanskrit on the music of
the Hindoos. I do not mean to insinuate that the
study of such works alone would be sufficient to
afford us a clear insight into the character and effect
of the music appertaining to those nations. How
little do we know of the real character of the music
of the ancient Greeks, notwithstanding all the expla-
nations which have been transmitted to us! Besides,
the systems put forth in treatises are not unfrequently
mere individual theories of the authors, which
have never been popular, nor ever adhered to in
practice. Sir William Jones states that Soma, the
old author from whom principally he drew his information on Hindoo music "exhibits a system of
his own." And Captain Willard remarks, "During
the earlier ages of Hindoostan, music was cultivated
by philosophers and men eminent for polite literature,
for whom general directions and rules for composition sufficed, after a course of musical education
acquired from living tutors; indeed, the abhorrence
of innovation, and veneration for the established
national music, which was firmly believed to be of
divine origin, precluded the necessity of any other.
But, when from the theory of music a defection took
place as to practice, and men of learning confined
themselves exclusively to the former, while the latter
branch was abandoned entirely to the illiterate, all
attempts to elucidate music from rules laid down in
books, a science incapable of explanation by mere
words, became idle. This is the reason why even so

able and eminent an Orientalist as Sir William Jones
has failed. Books alone are insufficient for this purpose,—we must endeavour to procure solutions from
living professors, of whom there are several, although
grossly illiterate."[4] Kiesewetter, the zealous inves-
tigator of ancient musical theories, also arrives at the
same conclusion, as is evident from the following
remark translated from a dissertation of his on the
music of the modern Greeks :—

"Altogether, I have for a long time been unable
to repel the impression that the executed music of
various ancient and modern Asiatic nations must
have been, and still is, something very different from
the metaphysical or mathematical music of their philosophers, whose theories, the result of mere specula-
tion, must always have borne but little relation to
the practice. I believe we have generally been in-
volved in error, when, from the discovered tracts of
the systematists of those nations, we conceive that we
have acquired a knowledge of the nature of the music
as practised by the people, and when, consequently
we imagine that we understand the latter. I think,
therefore, we ought not to say—the music of the
Chinese, Hindoos, Arabs, Persians, &c.; but rather—
the musical systems (or mysteries) of the Chinese,
Hindoo, Arabian, or Persian philosophers. Perhaps
this applies also to the music of the ancient Greeks."[5]
Almost the same may be said of our own music :
many of the rules advanced by theorists are seldom,
if ever, applied to practice. Supposing, two thousand years hence, some musical antiquary should be

---

[4] A Treatise on the Music of
Hindoostan, by Capt. Augustus
Willard, Calcutta, 1834, p. vi.

[5] Ueber die Musik der neueren Griechen, von Kiesewetter,
Leipzig, 1838, p. 32.

the happy discoverer of any of our present treatises on counterpoint and fugue. How far would his impressions on the nature of our ordinary popular music, as derived from his discovery, be in accordance with the actual truth? If, then, we cannot implicitly rely upon the written records, it is the more important that we should glean information also from the remains of ancient music which are still extant in Asia, and ascertain by comparison whether, and to what extent, the rules of the theorists appear to have been in practical use.

Although we do not possess the same authentic information on the musical systems of the ancient nations inhabitating the south-western districts of Asia as we have of the Chinese and Hindoo systems, nevertheless, indications are not wanting there of the pentatonic scale having been in use at an early period. This might with some reason be expected, considering that it was the oldest scale known throughout the greater part of Asia; that the musical instruments and musical performances of the various nations possessed a certain family type, and that the usual number of strings is the most satisfactorily accounted for. Thus the majority of the numbers of strings which have been ascertainable on the Assyrian instruments are exactly suited for the pentatonic scale, but not for our diatonic scale. Instruments like the harp, asor, and lyre we may reasonably suppose to have been usually tuned in the fixed order of intervals which constituted the common scale, because thus they could be much more effectively employed in all kinds of musical performances than would otherwise have been possible. The fact that instruments whose strings produce only one note each, and the pitch of

which cannot be altered during the performance—
as it can on the tamboura—are, if tuned otherwise
than in the usual scale, of less practical utility, is so
obvious that the Assyrians, with the progress they
had made in music, could not but have been aware of
it, and have acted upon it. Now, the usual numbers
of strings on those instruments appear to have been
5, 10, 20, and such others as represent the number
of the pentonic intervals either once or repeatedly.
Sometimes we meet with an additional string to any
such number, which probably was the extension of
the scale into the octave, which we have already
found in other ancient Asiatic music, which is also
usual in our diatonic series of intervals, and which
suggests itself so naturally, that its adoption must
at an early time have occurred in the progressive
cultivation of music by the Assyrians.

According to this opinion the compass of the
Assyrian harps with twenty-six strings, which I have
previously noticed, would have embraced precisely
five octaves. Assuming c to have been the tonic, the
intervals would have stood as follows :—

c, d, e, g, a | c. d, e, g, a | c, d, e, g, a | c, d, e, g, a | c, d, e, g, a | c.

The lyre with five strings would have had c, d, e, g,
a; and the lyre with six strings, c, d, e, g, a, c.

If these arguments are well founded, the pentatonic
scale must also have been in use with the Hebrews,
the Phœnicians, the ancient Egyptians, and most
likely too with the ancient Greeks.

Of the Hebrews we know on this point only with
certainty, that some of the favourite instruments in
the time of David and Solomon had ten strings; this
number, from the description given by Josephus,
appears to have been augmented at a later period.

If we could place reliance on the correctness of the frets as they are shown on some tambouras represented in Egyptian frescoes, we might gather some further hints respecting the usual order of intervals in use among the Egyptians; it is not, however, probable that the painters should have thought it worth while to observe carefully the proper distances of the frets. Still, some unmistakable indications of the pentatonic scale having been used by the Egyptians as well as by the Greeks are to be found in our best histories on music; among others in Burney's, from which I submit the following extracts, which appear to me all the more convincing, as they are given by Burney not in support of any particular hypothesis of his own, but solely as recording historical facts.

"The Greeks, who lost no merit by neglecting to claim it, unanimously confess that most of their ancient musical instruments were of Egyptian invention, as the triangular lyre, the *monaulos* or single flute, the *cymbal*, kettle-drum, and the *sistrum*, an instrument of sacrifice, which was so multiplied by the priests in religious ceremonies, and in such great favour with the Egyptians in general, that Egypt was often called, in derision, the country of sistrums, as Greece has been said to be governed by the lyre. Herodotus, in tracing the genealogy of the Dorians, one of the most ancient people of Greece, makes them natives of Egypt:[6] and as the three musical modes of highest antiquity among the Greeks are the Dorian, Phrygian, and Lydian, it is likely that the Egyptian colony, which peopled the Dorian province, brought with them the music and instruments of their native

---

6 Herodotus, *Erato.*

country. The profession of music was hereditary among the Egyptians, as was every other profession. This custom was imitated by the Hebrews; and Herodotus tells us that the Lacedæmonians, who were Dorians, agreed with their progenitors, the Egyptians, in this, that their musicians were all of one family. Their priests, too, like those of Egypt, were at once taught medicine, to play on stringed instruments, and initiated into religious mysteries." Burney cites a long and somewhat obscure passage from Plutarch's 'Dialogue on Music,' from which, however, it is obvious that Olympus, who, we are told, composed his music in the Dorian mode, usually skipped over " the *lichanos*, or third sound from the bottom of a tetrachord;" and the old Grecian musicians " abstained from the use of *trite*, or third sound from the top of a tetrachord." Burney concludes this account by observing, " The general fact that these old musicians, composers of the ancient genuine Greek music, which Plato, Aristotle, and all the writers speak of as so excellent and superior to the more modern, did delight to break the diatonic progression, or stride over certain notes in the melody, seems pretty clear: and this surely renders it highly probable that the cast of the old national Greek airs was much like that of the old Scots music. If they had melodies where the *lichanos* was omitted, they must have been *very* like; but even the *trite* omitted gives still a strong Scottish tincture to an air.

For if we suppose the key-note to be *G* instead of *E*,

—a major key instead of a minor,—this omission gives precisely the Scots scale."[7]

Moreover, this scale probably remained popular, in some districts at least, long after music had been scientifically cultivated in Greece, and developed in manifold ways; since it appears still in use and favour in the first century of the Christian era.

THE INTERVALS OF THE NUBIAN KISSAR.

I shall now notice a fact which should perhaps be regarded as less corroborative than it appears to be at the first glance, because striking coincidences are sometimes accidental; nevertheless, in connection with our former evidences, I believe it to be not without weight.

I have already noticed the close resemblance between the Assyrian and ancient Egyptian lyres and the Nubian *kissar*. The modern Egyptians call this instrument *qytârah barbaryeh*, which indicates that it is considered the national instrument of the Barabras or Berbers, who are believed to be descendants of the original inhabitants of Egypt. It occurred to me that therefore the pentatonic scale might still be found on the *kissar;* and this appeared the more probable, as the *kissar* is usually mounted with five strings, while a similar instrument in Abyssinia, the *bagana*, is ten-stringed. I have found this expectation fully confirmed in a description of these instruments by M. Villoteau, from which I shall translate one or two passages.

Villoteau, who was unacquainted with the ancient

---

7 Burney's "History of Music," vol. i. pp. 30, 194.

pentatonic scale, appears to have been greatly puzzled
with the order of intervals on the *kissar*, which he
thought so singular that he says "One may well be
tempted to take this order for disorder, as I actually
did. The first time I had an opportunity of examining this instrument and hearing its notes I found
it tuned as follows :—

I believed that this could not be really its proper
tuning, and that our Ethiopian, not considering this
matter of much importance, must have thought it
sufficient to tighten the strings in order to give them
the elasticity requisite to respond to the touch, and
to vibrate and sound distinctly, without concerning
himself about regulating the sounds in relation to
each other. However, in order to assure myself of
this, I resorted to the same experiment that I had
employed on a similar occasion with the servant of
the Venetian Consul at Alexandria. I slackened all
the strings, to the great annoyance of the Nubian,
and asked him to tune them again. I had not told
him my motive for doing so, and, as he could not
possibly guess it, he was, naturally enough, vexed with
my behaviour. . . . At last, however, he proceeded to restore the strings to their previous condition, tuning each exactly in the same interval as
before ; and this convinced me that it was not accident nor caprice which led him to tune the strings as
above, but that, on the contrary, the order of the
notes was one transmitted and adhered to."

The songs with the kissar accompaniment, of
which I shall give a few specimens, are called by the

Nubians *ghouna*. The performers twangs the strings
with his left hand, while he uses the plectrum with
his right. Villoteau remarks, "The words of the
first song have, like those of the songs of the Barabras, nothing in common with the Arabic language;
but in the following songs are found not only Arabic
but also corrupted Italian words."[8]

NUBIAN GHOUNA.

8 Description de l'Egypte, tome xiii. p. 365, and tome xiv. p. 260.

ton,   do - blé   chan - dé   gan - de -

ton.

ANOTHER GHÒUNA.

Na - - ve   na - ve   be

nahaf . . ya seg - niour el a guid

ya sig-niour el ha - did.

ANOTHER.

Ya se-rou-an a - gui del kour fa-res fa-res el fer -

san.

ANOTHER.

Respecting the *bagana*, or ten-stringed lyre of Abyssinia, I shall merely add that it has, according to Villoteau, only five different notes, like the *kissar*, but each note has its octave.

The peculiar rhythmical kissar accompaniments to the above songs are also interesting, inasmuch as they may give us some idea of the probable Assyrian accompaniments. I have already stated the reasons for concluding that they must have been generally of this kind.

SUBDIVISIONS OF THE WHOLE TONE.

Although, as we have seen, it is highly probable that the musical compositions of the Assyrians were

generally founded upon the pentatonic scale, it does
not follow that smaller intervals than those which
occur in this scale were unknown to them, or were
never used by them. On the contrary, there is reason
to suppose they sometimes employed intervals even
smaller than our semitones. Not only had the Hindoos such intervals at a very early period, as we
know with certainty from some of their old theoretical works which have come down to us, and from
which Sir William Jones, Sir W. Ouseley, and other
writers on Hindoo music have principally drawn
their information, but also the Persians appear to
have made use of similar subdivisions of the *whole
tone*. When the Arabs conquered Persia (A.D. 641)
the Persians had already attained a higher degree of
civilization than their conquerors. The latter found
in Persia the cultivation of music considerably in
advance of, and the musical instruments superior to
their own. They soon adopted the Persian instruments, and there can be no doubt that the musical
system exhibited by the earliest Arab writers whose
works on the theory of music have been preserved,
was based upon an older system of the Persians. In
these works the octave is divided into seventeen *one-
third tones*,—intervals which are still made use of in
the East. Some of the Arabic instruments are constructed so as to enable the performer to produce
these intervals with exactness. The frets on the
tamboura, for instance, are regulated with a view to
this object.

Again, in the vocal performances of several Eastern
nations we meet with a certain disposition to connect
two intervals, at some distance from each other, by
slightly touching the small intermediate intervals.

The singing of the Jews in the synagogue is generally of a similar character. Where this taste is developed, it naturally leads to the adoption of *quarter-tones* or *one-third tones.*

Likewise the ancient Greeks possessed a succession of intervals, known as the *enharmonic scale*, in which a *quarter-tone*, another *quarter-tone*, and a *major third* succeeded each other thus :—

THE ENHARMONIC SCALE OF THE ANCIENT
GREEKS.

The pentatonic character of this scale is unmistakable. It is, in fact, the scale of Olympus (noticed at page 156), into which quarter-tones are introduced. Plutarch, who wrote in the first century of the Christian era, mentions that those musicians who performed in the genuine ancient style did not make use of the quarter-tones, which shows that the more simple pentatonic order of intervals existed prior to the enharmonic, as might be expected.

Thus, there can be no doubt of the employment of smaller intervals than semitones by the ancient Hindoos, Persians, and Greeks.

The Persians were indebted for their early civilization especially to the Assyrians. Mr. Layard observes that the remains which are still existing among the ruins of Persepolis and Susa "prove beyond a doubt that the Persians, who after the fall of the

Assyrian and Babylonian empires succeeded to the dominion of the East, received from the Assyrians their religion, their arts, and their civilization, closely copying them in all particulars. The human-headed bull of the Nineveh palaces is found faithfully reproduced at Persepolis. Slabs sculptured with bas-reliefs of processions, and with single-winged figures, line the chambers and the façades; myths and religious symbols, similar to those found on the monuments of Nimroud, are portrayed upon the walls; and the cuneiform character was used to record the glory and the titles of the kings. Besides, many details of architectural moulding almost identical have been found in the Assyrian and Persian ruins.''

I must leave it now to the reader to decide whether the circumstantial evidence adduced is sufficient to warrant the opinion that the Assyrians, in their music, made use of smaller intervals than semitones.

In anticipation of the objection which may perhaps be raised, that to distinguish such minute intervals would require a more refined ear than the Assyrians can be supposed to have possessed, I would remark that those intervals were most likely discriminated with exactness by theorists and accomplished performers only, which is, according to Lane and others, also the case with the *one-third tones* used by the Arabs and modern Egyptians. The simple and popular music probably contained the pentatonic intervals only. Something analogous may be observed in our own music : the German and English popular tunes being usually founded upon our diatonic scale, without the admixture of chromatic intervals.

DIFFUSION OF THE PENTATONIC SCALE.

The existence of the pentatonic scale at a very early period throughout so large a portion of the world as Asia, and also in Egypt, is a curious fact, not without importance in the history of music, and, moreover, leading the inquirer to various speculations. To conjecture that all the different nations have derived it from one source must appear bold indeed. One might rather surmise it to be an order of intervals so deeply founded upon natural laws as to suggest itself instinctively wherever a certain stage of musical progress has been attained. However, if this were the case, we might expect to meet with it in most nations, or at least in many other nations besides those before specified which we do not. Let us, for instance, turn to Africa: none of the instruments of the Negroes and Kaffres exhibit any traces of it; neither have I detected any in the national airs of these peoples with which I have become acquainted.[9]

To investigate this phenomenon minutely is not requisite for the aim of the present work; I content myself, therefore, with stating in a few words how, in my opinion, it may probably be accounted for.

Evidences of a former connection between several Oriental nations at a very early period are not

---

[9] It is true that, among half-a-dozen balafoes which I have seen, one had the eight intervals, to which it was limited, in the following order :—

But this may have arisen accidentally, as the instrument was in a dilapidated condition. All the others had the diatonic series.

wanting. Philologists inform us of the close relationship existing between several Eastern languages. History records great military exploits at the remotest time,—as, for instance, the invasion of Hindoostan by the Assyrian queen Semiramis, about B.C. 2000, and the conquest of a great part of Asia by the Egyptian Pharaoh Sesostris, about B.C. 1500. Certain religious opinions and ceremonies appear to have been at an early period disseminated throughout various Eastern countries. The Buddhist religion is professed at present by many nations, extending from the western to the extreme eastern part of Asia. Captain Turner says that in Thibet "there is no religious edifice but what is adorned with the head of the lion at every angle, having bells pendant from his lower jaw, and the same figure is equally common at every projection of the palace walls."[10] As there are no lions to be found in Thibet, the representations of these animals point to a former connection with southern countries. Chinese antiquities have been discovered in the Assyrian ruins, and also in ancient Egyptian tombs. Mr. Halloran observes, " It is remarkable, as showing the high antiquity of Chinese customs, that the vases in front of their ancient temples are very much like, both in shape and position, to some figures which appear in the representations of the ancient temples of Khorsabad, as given by Bonomi in his work entitled 'Nineveh and its Palaces.' Bonomi supposes these vases to have been employed for holding water for purification."[1]

In the Nineveh Gallery of the British Museum

---

[10] An Account of the Embassy to the Court of Teshoo Lama, in Tibet, by Captain S. Turner, London, 1800, p. 288.

[1] Eight Months' Journal, by A. L. Halloran, London, 1856, p. 53.

there are, Mr. Sharpe informs us, "several pieces of sculptured ivory, which, if not made by Egyptian workmen, are, at least, copied from Egyptian sculptures, and show how much Assyria was indebted to Egypt for its knowledge of art. One is the figure of the goddess Athor, or of a queen holding a lotus-flower in her left hand, and with the winged sun over her head. Another is an ivory box, on one side of which is an oval ring, crowned with two ostrich-feathers, and within it is written the name of Aobeno-Ra, which would seem to be the Asiatic way of spelling Amun-Ra. On each side of this name is seated the figure of a queen with one hand raised as if in prayer to the god, and the other hand holding the sacred staff of the Egyptian priests, which has on the top of it a dog's head, and a fork at the lower end. Several flat cups or dishes of copper, also brought from Assyria, are ornamented with Egyptian figures, partly chased and partly engraved. One bears the winged sphinx wearing the double crown of Egypt, and the winged sun, together with the scarabæus with outstretched wings, and the ball between its front feet. These were probably divining-cups, used for the purpose of looking into the future, and they remind us of Joseph's divining-cup, which was found in Benjamin's sack."[2]   (See Genesis xliv.)

Again, in some ceremonies or amusements, with which music is generally associated, we meet with the same characteristics throughout the East. For instance, the manner of dancing, described by Sir S. Raffles as consisting in "graceful attitudes of the body, and in the slow movement of the arms and

---

[2] Egyptian Antiquities in the British Museum, described by Samuel Sharpe, London, 1862, p. 190.

legs, particularly of the former, even to the distinct
motion of the hands and fingers,"[3] is very much the
same all over Asia, and may be witnessed even in
Japan, as we are informed by Meijlan, Sherard
Osborne, and others.

Whatever may be thought of the value of such
facts, if considered as evidences of a former affinity
or intercourse between the nations to which they
refer, we may learn from them at least that the
hypothesis of the pentatonic scale having been originally derived from one common source is by no
means so unsupported as it at first appears to be.
Indeed, the more we inquire into the subject, the
more we are forced to accept this hypothesis as probably the most correct.

We have already seen that the pentatonic scale
was in use among the ancient American Indians. It
is true, in the specimens of old Peruvian songs, called
haravi, given in Rivero and Tschudi's 'Peruvian
Antiquities,' no indications of it are traceable. However, any musician at all acquainted with Spanish
national music will perceive at once that these
arrangements too closely resemble the Spanish Sequi-
dilla and Bolero for any reliance to be placed on
their genuineness. The themes are, perhaps, what
they profess to be—ancient Indian melodies, collected
by the first Spanish visitors to the western hemi-
sphere; they have, however, been written down so
carelessly and incorrectly,—as is evident from the
many mistakes in the added accompaniment,—and
so greatly modified to make them more pleasing to
the Spanish taste, that we cannot be surprised if we

---

[3] The History of Java, by T. Stamford Raffles, London, 1817,
vol. i. p. 340.

do not find retained in them what must have appeared
most foreign and distasteful to the arranger. The
musical instruments preserved in museums afford
sufficient evidence of the former existence of the pentatonic scale in America, because we find in them
the intervals of the *fourth* and *seventh* intentionally
omitted.

Now, it may be objected—if this scale was used
by the ancient American Indians, and in Europe by
the Scotch, and if these nations invented it independently, why should not every Oriental nation also
have done the same? In reply to this plausible
objection I would direct the reader's attention to the
following facts :—

Most historians and ethnologists believe the American
Indians to have originally migrated to America from
Asia. Humboldt says, " A long struggle between two
religious sects—the Brahmans and Buddhists—terminated by the emigration of the Chamans to Thibet, Mongolia, China, and Japan. If tribes of the Tartar race
have passed over to the north-west coast of America,
and thence to the south and the east, towards the banks
of the Gila and those of the Missouri, as etymological
researches seem to indicate, we should be less surprised at finding among the semi-barbarous nations of
the new continent idols and monuments of architecture,
a hieroglyphical writing, an exact knowledge of the
duration of the year, and traditions respecting the first
state of the world, recalling to our minds the sciences,
the arts, and the religious opinions of the Asiatic
nations."[4]

---

[4] Researches concerning the Institutions and Monuments of the
Ancient Inhabitants of America, by
Alexander von Humboldt; translated by H. M. Williams; London,
1814, vol. i. p. 146.

Scottish music is too well known in England to require a detailed description here. I shall therefore confine myself to inserting one specimen only, for the sake of comparison with the Asiatic tunes :—

SCOTTISH AIR.

Larghetto.

I've heard them lilt - ing   at   the   ewe   milk - ing,

Las - ses a   lilt - ing be - - fore   dawn of   day.

Now there's a   moan - ing on   il - ka   green   loan - ing, The

flow'rs of   the   fo - rest   are   a'   wede   a - - way.

This song, known as 'The Flowers of the Forest,' is transcribed from the 'Ancient Scottish Melodies from a Manuscript of the Reign of King James VI., published by William Dauney, Esq.' The words are more modern than the melody, which is strictly pentatonic, with the exception of the fifth bar, where the *minor seventh, f,* occurs, through which the melody modulates from G major into C major. Similar occasional introductions of semitones into the pentatonic scale occur also in Asiatic music, as we have already seen.

Traces of the pentatonic scale are perceptible also in Irish national tunes, although to a less extent than in Scottish. The following Irish melody was, according to Mr. Walker, the author of 'Historical Memoirs of the Irish Bards,' written down by a friend of his in the county of Roscommon, from oral communication. The *major seventh, f-sharp,* occurs therein twice, but it does not constitute an essential note of the melody; in fact, it rather gives the impression of having accidentally crept in from carelessly drawing the voice over from the sixth to the octave :—

IRISH AIR, called 'Speic Seoach.'

Mr. Walker remarks, "In no part of Ireland do our old melodies so much abound as in Connaught; that province may be said to be vocal with them."[5] We have therefore an additional reason for consi-

---

[5] Historical Memoirs of the Irish Bards, by J. C. Walker, London, 1786; Appendix.

dering the above melody as a faithful example of
Irish music.

These characteristics of the Scottish and Irish music
have been the cause of various conjectures. They
have been especially attributed to the influence of
ecclesiastical music. Mr. Conran, for instance, observes: " If we compare some of our national original
melodies with those scales [viz. the ancient ecclesiastical modes], we shall perceive, I am inclined to
think, that much of the originality and peculiar construction of those airs may be ascribed to their being
composed in scales or modes corresponding with some
of these modes here given; and I should therefore
conclude that the practice of this species of ecclesiastical music being well calculated to make strong
impressions on the feelings, much of its pathetic character would naturally be imparted to national music
during the progress of its development in Ireland."[6]
Mr. Dauney, on the other hand, more judiciously
observes: "Although it has been truly said that
nothing has a greater influence on the music of a
nation than the music of its church, the use of the
Catholic Ritual in Scotland cannot altogether account
for the predilection which the Scots have never ceased
to entertain for their peculiar style of melody; for if
such an argument were to be admitted, it might
naturally be asked why the same results have not
taken place in Italy, Spain, France, and other countries which were subject to the same regulations, and
under the influence of the Roman Church to a greater
extent than either Scotland or Ireland. Indeed,
the same marked similitude is not to be traced even

---

6 The National Music of Ireland, by Michael Conran, Dublin, 1846, p. 59.

in the ancient music of England. Another view
militates strongly against the adoption of any theory
which would ascribe the invention of the Scottish
music to the See of Rome, and trace its pedigree
to no other source than the Ambrosian Chant, introduced about the year 600. A national music is not
one of those things which a people is much disposed
to receive at second-hand, or to put off or on at the
bidding either of their spiritual or their temporal
masters. It is among the oldest and the most lasting
of their relics. Carried down from father to son,
like an heirloom in a family, it is not likely either
to be lost or bartered even for articles of higher
quality or value."[7]

Again, musicians have endeavoured to explain
those characteristics in music from the imperfect or
peculiar construction of the old Scottish and Irish
musical instruments. Now, the principal popular
instruments were the harp and the bagpipe, both of
which are also in use in Asia. It will be remembered,
we have found the Oriental harp in Ireland; and the
construction of the Persian bagpipe must be nearly
identical with that of the Scottish, since Sir William
Ouseley relates that a Scotch gentleman "played on
it several tunes of his own country, in a very pleasing
manner, without any previous practice."[8]

Mr. Gunn gives us at the end of his book entitled
'An Historical Enquiry respecting the Performance
on the Harp in the Highlands of Scotland,' London,
1807, a prospectus of 'An Enquiry into the antiquity
of the harp, and into the Oriental extraction and

[7] The Journal of the Royal
Asiatic Society of Great Britain
and Ireland,vol.vi. London,1841.

[8] Travels in various Countries
of the East, by Sir W. Ouseley,
London, 1819, vol. i. p. 241.

ancient history of the Caledonian Scots, demonstra-
ing, from the language, ancient religion, supersti-
tious rites, their kalendar and festivals, their remarkable traditions, manners, and customs, and from other
documents and monuments still existing in Asia,
France, Great Britain, and Ireland, that they brought
the harp, together with other arts of civilized life,
from Armenia and the western coast of Asia, into
the southern parts of England, prior to the era at
which our writers commence the history of Great
Britain,' &c. The book has never been published
that I am aware of, and this is the less to be regretted, since, to conclude from the circumstantial
prospectus of which I have quoted the commencement, the author proves himself too superficially
acquainted with Oriental music for the successful
execution of his projected task.

Moreover, a somewhat similar book has been published by Finck, in which the aim of the author is to
show that the pentatonic scale was originally brought
over by the Celts from Asia, and that it was preserved
longer in Scotland than elsewhere on account of the
isolated position of that country, and of similar circumstances.[9]

PREVALENCE OF THE MAJOR KEY.

Another question remains for consideration, viz.,
whether in Assyrian music the major or the minor
key was the prevailing one. In my opinion it was
the former, for the following reasons :—

Most national music is in major; of this I have
had ample opportunity of convincing myself by care-

---

9 Erste Wanderung der ältesten Tonkunst, von G. W. Fink, Essen, 1831.

fully examining all accessible collections of tunes from every part of the world. The generally maintained opinion that the popular songs of a nation are usually in minor is altogether erroneous. There are but few nations possessing more songs and other melodies in minor than in major, while in the music of most nations the major key decidedly predominates. Nor is this surprising, since the major key appears to be the most natural of the two, to conclude from the principal *harmonics* which are softly emitted with any single tone, and which produce together the major chord.

In the Oriental pentatonic scale the interval of the third consists generally of *two whole tones*, as in our major scale, and not of *a whole tone* and *a large semitone*, as in our minor scale. A reference to the examples of Chinese, Hindoo, Burmese, Japanese, and other tunes previously given, all of which have been selected without any reference to the present question, will convince the reader that only a few of them are in minor. In the East, however, we meet not unfrequently with melodies which neither begin nor end with the *tonic*, and in which, in fact, the keynote is not easily ascertainable. Such melodies have generally been considered by Europeans, from the preconceived notion before mentioned, as being in minor, and have been harmonized accordingly.

It is altogether a hazardous proceeding to harmonize any music of this kind according to our own usual rules ; the result must necessarily be unsatisfactory on account of the two semitones of our diatonic scale being wanting. The peculiar characteristics of the music are thereby obliterated without anything beautiful being gained. Many of the well-known expressive Scottish airs have in this way been sadly tampered with.

Moreover, although we may suppose Assyrian, like other Asiatic music, to have been principally in major, it must have possessed a certain plaintiveness, such as pre-eminently appertains to our music in minor; since the two steps of a *minor third*, which occur in the pentatonic scale, would impart to it that character. It will be remembered, that we now use in our minor scale two different orders of intervals, viz., we raise the *sixth* as well as the *seventh* in ascending, or we raise the *seventh* alone. In the latter case the step from the *minor sixth* to the *major seventh*—a step of a *superfluous second*—is, in effect at least, identical with the pentatonic steps of a *minor third* just pointed out. And most likely it may be also partly on this account that the music of Asiatic nations has been described by superficial observers as being generally in minor.

From the nature of the Assyrian instruments we have been led to surmise that the music of the Assyrians must have been especially sentimental and soothing; this is also indicated by the pentatonic scale, which consists of a succession of intervals remarkably melodious and impressive. In proof, we need only refer to the universally admired old Scottish melodies composed in this scale. The Oriental melodies strike us as too strange in construction to convey directly an agreeable impression. After, however, becoming thoroughly acquainted with them, we are sure to discover that they possess peculiar beauties. Of this every one may convince himself by learning one of these melodies by heart, and familiarising himself as much with it as with any of his favourite Scotch tunes, for which purpose I would recommend the Chinese 'Sian Chok,' page 131, or the Javanese

N

'Surung Dayung," page 133, on account of their melodiousness.

They are certainly in many respects different from the Scotch melodies ; which shows that, although the character of the pentatonic scale is remarkably distinctive, this scale is nevertheless not unfitted for the expression of a variety of emotions. Besides, the character of a musical composition is not exclusively determined by the key and scale, but quite as much by the time, tempo, modulation, rhythmical construction, employment of different degrees of loudness, and other conditions. The effect of the Assyrian music may therefore have been widely different from that of the Scotch, notwithstanding the identity of the scale.

NOTATION.

With respect to the question whether the Assyrians possessed a musical notation, we can judge only from analogy, since no evidences of it have hitherto been discovered. Most nations advanced in music, as the Assyrians were, employ some rude means to assist in recalling their musical compositions to memory. The Chinese, for instance, have distinctive characters, which they slightly alter in different octaves. Of the Japanese we are told by Saris, whose account dates as far back as the year 1611, that "their tunes were pricked;"[1] and Captain Turner was informed by the Buddhist priests in Thibet that "their music was written down in characters which they learnt."[2]

---

[1] A General Collection of Voyages and Travels, printed for Thomas Astley, London, 1745, vol. i. p. 481.

[2] An Account of an Embassy to the Court of the Teshoo Lama in Thibet, by Captain Samuel Turner, London, 1800, p. 343.

Even the North American Indians, much less advanced in music, sometimes employ signs written upon birch-bark to assist in remembering their songs, of which examples are given in Kohl's ' Kitchi-Gami,' and in Catlin's 'Illustrations of the Manners and Customs of the North American Indians.' And as we know that the Greeks and other ancient nations possessed some kind of notation, we may conjecture that the Assyrians also, as well as the Egyptians and Hebrews, were not without such a contrivance. Perhaps further discoveries may throw some light on this and other obscure questions relating to Assyrian music, which it would be at present premature to discuss. Some hope of this is held out in the following observation of Max Müller:—

"In a letter, dated April 1853, Sir Henry Rawlinson wrote: ' On the clay tablets which we have found at Nineveh, and which now are to be counted by thousands, there are explanatory treatises on almost every subject under the sun; the art of writing, grammars and dictionaries, notation, weights and measures, divisions of time, chronology, astronomy, geography, history, mythology, geology, botany, &c. In fact, we have now at our disposal a perfect cyclopædia of Assyrian science.' Considering what has been achieved in deciphering one class of cuneiform inscriptions, the Persian, there is no reason to doubt that the whole of that cyclopædia will some day be read with the same ease with which we read the mountain records of Darius."[3]

---

[3] Lectures on the Science of Language, by Max Müller, London, 1862, p. 280.

CHAPTER V.

MUSIC OF THE ANCIENT EGYPTIANS.

Egyptian instruments—Various harps—Bruce's harps—Egyptian name of the harp—The trigonon—The lyre—The tamboura— Peculiar stringed instruments—Pipes, flutes, double-pipes— Trumpets—Drums and tambourines—Curious instruments of percussion—The sistrum—Crotala, cymbals, bells—Vocal and instrumental performances—The Egyptian musical instruments compared with the Assyrian—Opinions of some musical historians.

In the preceding inquiry we have repeatedly had occasion to observe the affinity of the ancient Egyptians music with the Assyrian. I purpose now submitting a short account of the music of the former nation which will more fully confirm what we have already found indicated. Here, also, I shall adhere to the plan hitherto pursued of avoiding as much as possible a repetition of any information on the same subject already given in Forkel's and Burney's Histories of Music, and in similar works, noticing especially those facts which have not hitherto received that consideration which, in my opinion, they deserve.

We have become gradually more exactly acquainted with the Egyptian instruments through the discoveries of a variety of representations of them in sculptures and paintings, as well as of fragments, and even of nearly perfectly preserved specimens of harps, lyres, and other stringed instruments, pipes, flutes, sistra, cymbals, bells, &c.

The following pages contain representations of all

the different Egyptian instruments which have been found.

THE HARP.

The Egyptian harps greatly varied in shape, size, and ornamentation. Fig. 27 represents one of the more simple kind. It is mounted with ten strings, and played on by a female.

The harp represented in fig. 28, which has twenty strings, is more highly ornamented with carving, and more brilliantly coloured, than the preceding. It rests on a low stand, while the performer is seated on the ground.

A similar harp, but much more plain, and raised on a higher stand or leg is shown in fig. 29. It has seven strings and eight tuning-pegs; while another in the same engraving has only four strings and six pegs.

Such inequalities

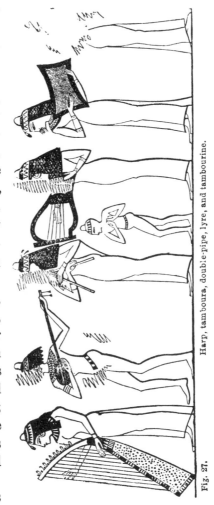

Harp, tamboura, double-pipe, lyre, and tambourine.

Fig. 27.

Fig. 28.   A harp on a stand, a man beating time, and a player on the tamboura.

in the number of the pegs and strings not unfrequently occur, and must probably be attributed to the
.negligence of the painters or sculptors.   We ought

Fig 29.   Two harps.

therefore, not to place much reliance on the correctness of the number of the strings, unless we frequently meet with the same number on several instruments, and unless they are at the same time in conformity with the number of pegs.

Stands of various forms were used for the smaller harps, which enabled the performer to play on the instrument while standing before it, as is shown in the engraving fig. 31, which represents a small kind of harp with nine strings.

Fig. 30.   A harp on a stand.

The Egyptian harps most remarkable for elegance of form and elaborate decoration are the two which were first noticed by the well-known traveller Bruce, who found them painted

Fig. 31.   Tambourine and harp.

in fresco on the wall of an ancient sepulchre at Thebes, which is supposed to be the tomb of

Rameses III., who reigned about 1250 B.C. Bruce's
discovery first became known to the musical world

Fig. 32.   Harp with thirteen strings.

through a letter addressed by him to Dr. Burney,
which, accompanied by a drawing of one of these
harps, without the figure of the performer, was published in the first volume of Burney's 'History of
Music.' Soon afterwards engravings of both instru-

ments appeared in Bruce's 'Travels,' vol. i. This
discovery created a great sensation among musicians.
The fact that at so remote an age the Egyptians
should have possessed harps which vie with our own
in elegance and beauty of form, appeared to some so
incredible that the correctness of Bruce's representations was greatly doubted ; in fact, they were received
with a distrust somewhat similar to that with which
several other communications by this traveller were
at first viewed, which have afterwards been proved to
be authentic. Sketches of the same harps, taken subsequently and at different times from the frescoes,
have been published in 'Description de l'Égypte,' in
Rosellini's 'I Monumenti dell' Egitto,' in Champollion's 'Monuments de l'Égypte et de la Nubie,' and
in Sir G. Wilkinson's 'Manners and Customs of the
Ancient Egyptians,' all of which differ more or less
from each other in appearance and in the number of
strings. The engravings fig. 32 and 33 represent
"Bruce's harps," as they appear in the last-mentioned
work—the first with thirteen and the second with ten
strings.

I notice these discrepancies in the hope that some
Eastern traveller may set the matter at rest by having
a strictly accurate copy, even to the most minute details, made from the frescoes which are still in existence. This would be the only way to render these
interesting representations really valuable in musical
investigations.

Bruce's letter to Burney has been often quoted,
and is well know. The publicity which it has obtained may perhaps be the very cause why the account
of the discovery of those harps given by Bruce in
his 'Travels,' which contains some interesting addi-

tional information, has not received that attention from musical historians to which, in my opinion, it is entitled. I shall, therefore, not apologize for inserting here that portion of it which more immediately refers to our present subject.

Speaking of the tomb of Rameses, Bruce says: " Farther forward, on the right hand of the entry, the panels or compartments were still formed in stucco, but, in place of figures in relief, they were painted in fresco. I dare say this was the case on the left hand of the passage as well as the right. But the first discovery was so unexpected, and I had flattered myself that I should be so far master of my own time as to see the whole at my leisure, that I was riveted, as it were, to the spot by the first sight of these paintings, and I could proceed no further. In one panel were several musical instruments strewed upon the ground, chiefly of the hautboy kind, with a mouth-piece of reed. There were also some simple pipes or flutes. With them were several jars, apparently of potter-ware, which, having their mouths covered with parchment or skin, and being braced on their sides like a drum, were probably the instruments called *tabor* or *tabret* (Gen. xxxi. 27; Isaiah xxx. 32), beat upon by the hands, coupled in earliest ages with the harp, and preserved still in Abyssinia, though its companion is no longer known there. In three following panels were painted in fresco three harps, which merited the utmost attention, whether we consider the elegance of these instruments in their form, and the detail of their parts as they are here clearly expressed, or confine ourselves to the reflection that necessarily follows, to how great perfection music must have arrived before an artist could have produced so complete an instru-

ment as either of these. As the first harp seemed to
be the most perfect and least spoiled, I immediately
attached myself to this, and desired my clerk to take
upon him the charge of the second. In this way, by
sketching exactly and loosely, I hoped to have made
myself master of all the paintings in that cave, perhaps
to have extended my researches to others—though, in
the sequel, I found myself miserably deceived. My
first drawing was that of a man playing upon a harp ;
he was standing, and the instrument, being broad and
flat at the base, probably for that purpose, supported
itself easily with a very little inclination upon his
arm. His head is close shaved, his eyebrows black,
without beard or moustachios. He has on him a loose
shirt, like what they wear at this day in Nubia (only
it is not blue), with loose sleeves, and arms and neck
bare. It seemed to be thick muslin, or cotton cloth,
and longways through it is a crimson stripe about
one-eighth of an inch broad—a proof, if this is
Egyptian manufacture, that they understood at that
time how to dye cotton crimson, an art found out in
Britain only a very few years ago. If this is the
fabric of India, still it proves the antiquity of the
commerce between the two countries, and the introduction of Indian manufactures into Egypt. It reached
down to his ankle ; his feet are without sandals. He
seems to be a corpulent man of about sixty years of
age, and of a complexion rather dark for an Egyptian.
To guess by the detail of the figure, the painter seems
to have had the same degree of merit with a good
sign-painter in Europe at this day. If we allow this
harper's stature to be five feet ten inches, then we may
compute the harp in its extreme length to be something
less than six feet and a half. This instrument is of a

much more advantageous form than the triangular
Grecian harp. It has thirteen strings, but wants the
fore-piece of the frame opposite to the longest string.
The back part is the sounding-board, composed of four
thin pieces of wood, joined together in form of a cone
—that is, growing wider towards the bottom ; so that,
as the length of the string increases, the square of the
corresponding space in the sounding-board in which
the sound was to undulate always increases in pro-
portion. The whole principles on which this harp is
constructed are rational and ingenious, and the ornamental parts are executed in the very best manner.
The bottom and sides of the frame seem to be veneered and inlaid, probably with ivory, tortoise-shell,
and mother-of-pearl, the ordinary produce of the
neighbouring seas and deserts. It would be even
now impossible either to construct or to finish a harp
of any form with more taste and elegance. Besides
the proportions of its outward form, we must observe
likewise how near it approached to a perfect instrument, for it wanted only two strings of having two
complete octaves. That these were purposely omitted,
not from defect of taste or science, must appear beyond contradiction when we consider the harp that
follows. I had no sooner finished the harp which I
had taken in hand, than I went to my assistant to see
what progress he had made in the drawing in which
he was engaged. I found, to my great surprise, that
this harp differed essentially in form and distribution
of its parts from the one I had drawn, without having
lost any of its elegance ; on the contrary, that it was
finished with still more attention than the other. It
seemed to be veneered with the same materials, ivory
and tortoise-shell, but they were differently disposed ;

the ends of the three longest strings, where they joined to the sounding-board below, were defaced by a hole dug in the wall. Several of the strings in different parts had been scraped as with a knife; for the rest, it was very perfect. It had eighteen strings. A man, who seemed to be still older than the former, but in habit perfectly the same, barefooted, close shaved, and of the same complexion, stood playing with both his hands near the middle of the harp, in a manner seemingly less agitated than in the other. I went back to my first harp, verified and examined my drawing in all its parts. . . . . There still remained a third harp of ten strings. Its precise form I do not well remember, for I had seen it but once when I first entered the cave, and was now preparing to copy that likewise. I do not recollect that there was any man playing upon this one; I think it was rather resting upon a wall, with some kind of drapery upon one end of it, and was the smallest of the three. But I am not at all so certain of particulars concerning this as to venture any description of it. What I have said of the other two may be absolutely depended upon. I look upon these harps, then, as the Theban harps in use in the time of Sesostris, who did not re-build, but decorate ancient Thebes. I consider them as affording an incontestable proof, were they the only monuments remaining, that every art necessary to the construction, ornament, and use of this instrument was in the highest perfection; and if so, all the others must have probably attained to the same degree. . . . These harps, in my opinion, overturn all the accounts hitherto given of the earliest state of music and musical instruments in the East, and are altogether, in their form, ornaments, and compass, an incontestable proof, stronger than a thousand Greek quotations, that geometry, drawing, mechanics, and music were at the greatest perfection when this instrument was made, and that the period from which we date the invention of these arts was only the beginning of

Fig. 33.   Harp with ten strings.

the era of their restoration. This was the sentiment of Solomon, a writer who lived at the time when this

harp was painted. ' Is there,' says Solomon, ' anything whereof it may be said, See, this is new? It
has been already of old time, which was before us '
(Eccles. chap. i, v. 10)."[1]
From Bruce's remark that the harp with thirteen
strings " wanted only two strings of having two complete octaves," it is evident he took it for granted that
the Egyptians tuned their harps in our diatonic order
of intervals. Sir Gardner Wilkinson entertains the
same opinion. He says that the harps " are seldom
represented in the sculptures with more than two
octaves "[2]—a statement which implies that he must
be acquainted with the intervals in which they were
tuned. There is, however, no further indication in
Sir G. Wilkinson's work of his having really made so
interesting a discovery.
Dr. Burney, in speaking of the harp with thirteen
strings, expresses himself cautiously, as might be expected from an experienced musician. He says,
" With respect to the number of strings upon this
harp, if conjectures may be allowed concerning the
manner of tuning them, two might be offered to the
reader's choice : the first idea that presented itself at
the sight of thirteen strings was, that they would
furnish all the semitones to be found in modern instruments, within the compass of an octave, as from C to
c, D to d, or E to e. The second idea is more Grecian,
and conformable to antiquity, which is, that if the
longest string represented *Proslambanomenos*, or D,
the remaining twelve strings would more than supply all the tones, semitones, and quarter-tones of the

<hr />

[1] Travels to Discover the Source of the Nile, by James Bruce, of
Kinnaird, London, 1790, vol. i. p. 127.
[2] The Manners and Customs of the Ancient Egyptians, vol. ii. p. 282.

Diatonic, Chromatic, and enharmonic genera of the
ancients, within the compass of an octave; but, for
my part, I should rather incline to the first arrangement, as it is more natural, and more conformable to
the structure of our organs, than the second; for, with
respect to the genera of the Greeks, though no certain
historic testimony can be produced concerning the
invention of the Diatonic and Chromatic, yet ancient
writers are unanimous in ascribing to Olympus, the
Mysian, the first use of the Enharmonic; and though
in the beginning the melody of this genus was so
simple and natural as to resemble the wild notes and
rude essays of a people not quite emerged from bar-
barism, yet in aftertimes it became overcharged with
finical fopperies and fanciful beauties, arising from
such minute divisions of the scale as had no other
merit than the difficulty of forming them. Another
conjecture concerning the tuning of the thirteen
strings of the Theban harp, is that they furnished the
four tetrachords, *Hypaton, Meson, Synemmenon,* and
Diezeugmenon, with *Proslambanomenos* at the bottom.
Thus:

1, 2, 3, 4, 5, 6, 7, 8, 9, 10, 11, 12, 13."[3]

Burney's determination of the thirteen intervals in
accordance with the Greek system might be correct
if the harp dated from time of the Ptolemies; but
it is a thousand years older. At that early period
the pentatonic series was, as we have seen, most likely
the usual one in Egypt. Even the scale of Olympus

---

[3] Burney's 'History of Music,' vol. i. p. 216.

of Mysias, to which Burney alludes, was of a similar stamp. To determine with accuracy how the intervals on the harp with thirteen strings were ordered, is impossible. Perhaps the lowest two may have consisted of the *tonic* and *dominant*; thus, supposing the deepest note to have been *c*—

c, g | c, d, e, g, a | c, d, e, g, a | c.

Or two of the strings may have been tuned in intervals foreign to the pentatonic scale—*i.e.* in semitones or even smaller divisions. The occasional introduction of intervals foreign to the usual scale appears probable from the fact of one or two strings on some of the harps being coloured, or placed more distant from the rest. The Theban harp with ten strings had most likely the pentatonic series repeated in the octave.

A kind of harp with twenty-one strings, represented in the en-

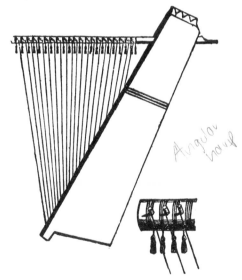

Fig. 34. Egyptian harp in the Paris Museum.

graving fig. 34, was discovered in a well-preserved condition, and is now deposited in the Paris Museum. In the engraving is also shown the manner in which the strings are fastened on this instrument.

All these harps, however different they are from

o

each other in form, have one peculiarity in common
—the absence of the fore-pillar.

The name of the harp was *buni*, or *beni*. In 'Description de l'Egypte' it is called *tebouni;* but the first
syllable is only the article prefixed to the substantive,
te-buni. The name may possibly have been used to
designate stringed instruments in general. It has no
resemblance to our word, *harp*, which may be traced
in the languages of almost all European nations. The
Celtic races, however, have a different word for it.
In Welsh the harp is called *teylin*, and in Irish *clar-
seth.* Conran asserts, however, that the Welsh name
teylin is derived from the Irish language.[4]

In the Egyptian paintings the words *sek an ben*,
"scraper on the harp," have been found written in
hieroglyphs over the figure of a harper.[5]

THE TRIGONON.

The instrument, fig. 35, is most likely the trigonon,
or triangular harp, mentioned by several classical
authors. Burney, in his 'History of Music,' gives a
drawing of a trigonon with ten strings. He observes
that it is called by Sophocles a *Phrygian* instrument,
and that a certain musician of the name of Alexander
Alexandrinus was so admirable a performer upon it,
that when exhibiting his skill in Rome he created the
greatest *furore.* Burney further remarks: "The performer being a native of Alexandria, as his name
implies, makes it probable it was an Egyptian instrument upon which he gained his reputation at Rome,"[6]

---

[4] The National Music of Ireland, by Michael Conran, Dublin, 1848, p. 97.
[5] Introduction to the Study of the

Egyptian Hieroglyphs, by Samuel
Birch, London, 1857, p. 269.
[6] Burney's History of Music,
vol. i. plate v. fig. 5.

—an opinion which is corroborated by the discovery of the instrument shown in our engraving. The trigonon ought, however, more properly to be classed

Fig. 85. Trigonon.

Fig. 36. Kind of trigonon.

with the lyre than with the harp, because it partakes more of the character of the former instrument. A similar stringed instrument is the harp represented on the old Persian sculptures described by Sir Robert Ker Porter, which I have already noticed.

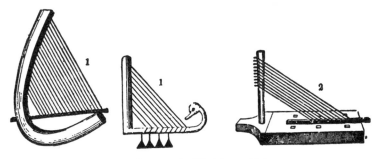

Fig. 37.   Instruments of the trigonon kind.

A curious stringed instrument of a semicircular shape (see fig. 37,) was discovered in the year 1823 at Thebes. It was mounted with twenty strings of catgut, which still emitted sound when made to vibrate. Its wooden frame was covered with red leather. It had no tuning-pegs; the strings were affixed to the upper part of the frame, and were tuned by being wound round a rod which was inserted into the lower part of the frame.

Some of the representations of the Grecian *trigonon* which we find in our Histories of Music exhibit the instrument in the shape of a Greek *Delta* with three bars. In the ancient Egyptian instruments of this class, however, the front bar, which would complete the triangle, is wanting.

THE LYRE.

The lyre of the ancient Egyptians also varies much in shape and in the number of strings. Some greatly

Fig. 38.   Lyres held horizontally.

resemble the Assyrian lyre; others are of a different shape, and are held perpendicularly instead of horizontally. The frame was not unfrequently ornamented with the carved head of the horse, gazelle, or other favourite animal. Some lyres, like that represented in the engraving fig. 39, have been found in a remarkably perfect state of preservation, and are now in the Museums of Berlin and Leyden. That in the Berlin Museum (fig. 40) is 2 feet high; its body is about 10 inches high and about 15 inches broad. It appears to have had thirteen strings instead of ten, like that shown in fig. 39. The lyre in the Leyden Museum is similar, but smaller.

Fig. 39.   Lyre held perpendicularly.

These lyres are entirely of wood, and the frame, as in the Assyrian lyres, is made longer on one side than on the other, for the purpose of tuning the in-

Fig. 40.   Lyre in the Berlin Museum.

strument by sliding the strings upwards or downwards to obtain the pitch required. The strings of the six holes which form the lower row on the lyre in the Berlin Museum contained, probably, the principal

intervals, consisting of the pentatonic scale extended
to the octave; while the strings of the upper row
were tuned in the intermediate semitones, or other
small subdivisions.

Fig. 41. Lyre in the Leyden Museum.

In the engraving, fig.
41, is shown also the
under part of the instru-
ment.

The lyres as well as
the harps, appear gener-
ally to have been tuned
in the pentatonic order,
without the addition of
any foreign intervals.
The most usual number
of strings on the harps
represented in the paint-
ings is, according to Sir
G. Wilkinson, *seven*—
this number "being
found in seven out
of twenty-one harps."[7]

There is, however, no reason to suppose the seven
strings to have been tuned in the seven intervals of
our diatonic scale; because in this scale the *octave* is
so imperatively demanded by the *seventh*, that the
impression is very unsatisfactory if the scale is restricted to seven intervals instead of eight—a fact
which is so universally felt wherever the diatonic
scale is in use, that we do not meet with instruments, even among savage nations, in which it is
made to stop short at the seventh. Moreover, we

---

[7] Athenæum, April 14, 1860.

have already seen that in such matters not much
reliance can be placed on the fidelity of the painted
and sculptured records. Of the before-mentioned
actual instruments discovered, the small harp with
twenty strings, found at Thebes, appears to have had
the pentatonic scale running through four octaves;
and the harp with twenty-one strings, in the Paris
Museum, had probably the same order of intervals,
with the addition of the key-note at the top.

Still, it may be suggested, is it not probable, from
the fact of seven strings occurring most frequently,
that the Egyptians tuned their harps in the same
diatonic series of intervals which the Greeks formed
by two *conjunct tetrachords?*

The Greek tetrachord consisted of a *semitone* and
two *whole tones*, like

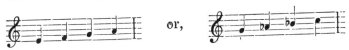

or,

The tetrachords were combined in two different ways
viz., either as *disjunct* tetrachords, constituting a diatonic series of eight notes; or as *conjunct* tetrachords,
containing only seven notes.

DISJUNCT TETRACHORDS.   CONJUNCT TETRACHORDS.

It will be seen from the above example that in the
conjunct tetrachords the highest note of the first tetrachord is also the lowest note of the second.

Now, there is a prevailing opinion among musical
historians, that the Greeks derived their musical
system from the Egyptians. Pythagoras, and other

philosophers and theorists, are said to have studied music in Egypt. I believe, however, that the Egyptian influence upon Greece, as far as regards music, has been greatly overrated. Not only do the more perfect Egyptian instruments, such as the larger harps, the tamboura, and others, appear never to have been much in favour with the Greeks; but almost all the stringed instruments which the Greeks possessed are stated to have been originally derived from Asia. Strabo (book x., c. 3) says: "Those who regard the whole of Asia, as far as India, as consecrated to Bacchus, point to that country as the origin of a great portion of the present music. One author speaks of 'striking forcibly the Asiatic kithara,' another calls the pipes Berecynthian and Phrygian. Some of the instruments also have foreign names, as Nabla, Sambuka, Barbiton, Magadis, and many others."

We know at present little more of these instruments than that they were in use in Greece. Concerning their form and construction there prevails much diversity of opinion. Of the Magadis it is even not satisfactorily ascertained whether it was a stringed or a wind instrument. The other three are known to have been stringed instruments. But they cannot have been such universal favourites as the lyre, since this instrument, and perhaps the trigonon, an inferior kind of harp, are almost the only stringed instruments represented in the Greek paintings on pottery and other monumental records. If, as might perhaps be suggested, their taste for beauty of form induced the Greeks to represent the elegant lyre in preference to other stringed instruments, we might at least expect to meet with the harp—an instrument which equals, if it does not surpass, the lyre in elegance of form.

The representation of Polyhymnia with a harp, depicted on a splendid Greek vase now in the Munich Museum, may be noted as an exceptional instance. This valuable relic dates from the time of Alexander the Great. A drawing of it is given in 'Élite des Monuments Céramographiques, par. Ch. Lenormant et J. de Witte' (Paris: 1846), vol. ii. plate 86. The instrument is, in construction as well as in shape, exactly like the Assyrian harp. It has thirteen strings. Polyhymnia is touching them with both hands, using the right hand for the treble and the left for the bass. She is seated, holding the instrument in her lap. Even the little tuning-pegs, which in number are not in accordance with the strings, are placed on the sounding-board at the upper part of the frame, exactly as on the Assyrian harp. If, then, we have here the Greek harp, it was more likely an importation from Asia than from Egypt. In short, as far as can be ascertained, the most complete of the Greek instruments appear to be of Asiatic origin.

Again, it is remarkable that many of the Greek musicians whose fame is recorded in history were natives of Asia Minor, or of some island adjacent to it. Marsyas, for instance, was a Phrygian; Terpander, Arion, Sappho, were natives of the island of Lesbos. Olympus, recorded as the inventor of the old enharmonic scale, was a native of Mysias, also in Asia. This Olympus, who lived about 1250 years before Christ, was a celebrated composer as well as performer on the flute. The invention of the old enharmonic scale, which is, as we have seen, the same as the pentatonic, was probably in later times attributed to him, because he composed beautiful melodies founded on this scale, which were still known and admired at the time of Plato, Aristotle, and even as late as Plutarch. For a more detailed account of this musician, who must not be mistaken for another distinguished Greek performer on the flute of the same name, who flourished about four centuries later, I must refer the reader to Burney's 'History of Music,' vol. i. p. 280.

Further, it ought to be borne in mind that the theories of Greek musicians and philosophers which have been preserved to us, date from a period about a thousand years later than the time of Olympus of Mysias—the oldest of these treatises being one by Aristoxenus, written not much earlier than three hundred years before the Christian era. The Greeks were a remarkably enterprising and progressive nation; whatever they borrowed from other nations they soon further developed and expanded. The Egyptians, on the other hand, considered it unlawful to introduce any reforms. If, then, the musical systems of the Greeks and Egyptians were identical, this was much more likely the case at the time of Olympus than at the time of those theorists whose speculations have been transmitted to us.

Terpander (B.C. 650) is said to have been the first of the Greek musicians who used seven strings on the lyre, which, before his time, was usually strung with four or five strings. The order of intervals in which he tuned his instrument is recorded to have been the following :—

Some historians mention Orpheus (B.C. 1300) as the musician who first employed seven strings on the lyre.

However this may be, thus much is evident, that the arrangement of the intervals on Terpander's instrument nearly approaches the scale of Olympus, who lived about six centuries before Terpander; and that the further we go back towards the earliest period the more traces we find of the pentatonic scale. Pythagorus (B.C. 550) is recorded to have added an eighth string to the lyre, and to have introduced a diatonic order of intervals, consisting of two disjunct tetrachords. As he is said to have acquired his knowledge in Egypt, some writers have precipitately concluded therefrom that his innovation on the lyre was an introduction from Egpyt. All evidence, however in support of this opinion is wanting, while every ascertainable fact tends, as we have seen, to the opposite conclusion.

After these statements, I leave it to the reader to decide whether those seven-stringed Egyptian harps, dating from a very early period, were not more likely tuned according to the pentatonic order of intervals, than in two conjunct tetrachords like the heptachord of the Greeks.

THE TAMBOURA.

The body of the Egyptian tamboura was either oval, or with the sides slightly incurved, somewhat like our guitar or violin. We find the latter shape also in some of the Hindoo instruments. The tuning-pegs of the Egyptian tambouras are not indicated in the paintings; perhaps because they were situated at the back of the neck, as they are on some Hindoo instruments of a similar class; or the artist may have omitted them through carelessness. In the figure of the tamboura, occurring in the hieroglyphics to which I have alluded, they are distinctly indicated. In the

Fig. 42.   Tamboura.   Fig. 43.   Tamboura.

earlier writings the instrument is made with four

pegs, thus— , and in the later ones it has only two,

thus— If we suppose the

Fig. 44.
Tamboura supported by a strap.

pegs to have been pushed through holes so far as to stick out on the opposite side of the neck—as from the representations appears probable—the former could have had but two pegs and the latter only one.

On a tamboura sculptured on an ancient obelisk now in Rome, dating from about 1500 B.C., of which a description is given in

Burney's History, accompanied by a drawing of the
instrument, from which fig. 45 is a reduced copy,
there are tuning-pegs for four strings, or for two only,
It is probable that the number of strings varied;
three is believed to have been the
usual number. They were perhaps
tuned in the *tonic, fifth,* and *octave,*
like some modern Oriental instruments of a similar kind.

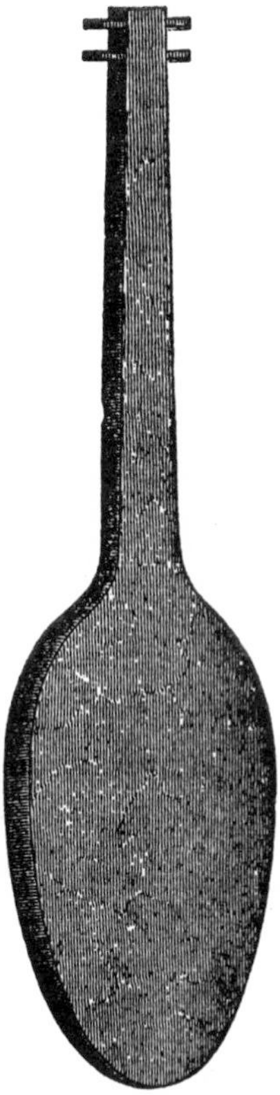

The tamboura was played with a
plectrum, and appears to have been
sometimes, if not always, provided
with frets. In the British Museum is
a fragment of a fresco, obtained from a
tomb in the Western Hills of Thebes,
on which two female performers on
the tamboura are represented. The
painter has distinctly indicated the
frets. On one of the instruments
they are limited to the upper half
of the neck; on the other they extend down the neck as far as to the
body of the instrument. There is
also in the British Museum a small
Egyptian vase in terra-cotta, from
Thebes, 8½ inches high, which represents a female standing and playing a tamboura, whereon the frets

Fig. 45. **Tamboura** from
an Egyptian obelisk.

are distinctly marked over the whole neck, even
where it extends over the body. If this be a
faithful representation of the finger-board—and there
is no reason to doubt its fidelity—a great number of
strictly defined intervals must have been obtainable
upon each string. Dr. Birch, of the British Museum,

describes this finely-modelled and well-preserved vase as made of a peculiar red ware, which "was probably the oldest of all Egyptian pottery." Of the figure he says, "Her eyebrows and the accessories of her dress are touched up in black paint. This elegant specimen cannot be much later than the eighteenth or nineteenth dynasty. The orifice consists of a short cylindrical neck, and the interior contains a viscous fluid."

I may remark here that among the ancient Egyptian figures of pottery are several others with musical instruments. These figures are small, seldom above 6 inches high. Of those which represent deities Dr. Birch mentions "the lion-headed goddesses Pasht-Merienptah, Bast, and Tafne, wearing the sun's disc, a disc and plumes, a serpent, and seated upon a throne, holding a sistrum. . . . . A very common type is a grotesque leonine pigmean deity, the supposed Baal or Typhon, either standing or kneeling, holding a sword, or playing on the tambourine. On his head are feathers or plumes, and a lion's skin is thrown across his back."[8]

It has been mentioned in a previous chapter that the Egyptian name of the tamboura was *nofre*, and that its figure in the hieroglyphics signifies "good." Further proof of this instrument having been held in high estimation may be found in the fact of its figure occurring as an ornament on vases and boxes. On the upper part of the body of the tamboura appear to have been usually four or more sounding-holes. Of the two instruments before mentioned in the British

---

[8] History of Ancient Pottery, by Samuel Birch, London, 1858, vol. i. pp. 58, 86.

Museum, the painter has made one with four, and the
other with six holes, placed in a different order on
each. Sounding-holes would
have been of comparatively
little use had the upper part
of the body been of parchment; we may therefore suppose it to have been of wood,
as on our guitar or violin.
Still, in some instances parchment may have been employed.
The Egyptians evidently had a
variety of tambouras, as may
be gathered from the different
shapes of the body, the distribution or the absence of sounding-holes, and other peculiarities
observable in the representations of this instrument.

Fig. 46. An Egyptian box.
(Berlin Museum.)

All the Egyptian instruments
which have hitherto been found
with the strings preserved had
them of catgut. If wire strings
were known to the Egyptians
they were probably used on
the tamboura, which at the pre-
sent day is mounted with wire strings by the Arabs
and other Eastern nations.

The Egyptians possessed also a tamboura with a
comparatively short neck, resembling our guitar, or
rather the Arabian *oud*. It appears to have been
less common than the tamboura before described.
The instrument shown in fig. 47 is, I believe, the
only one of the kind hitherto discovered. It was

found at Thebes in a dilapidated condition, without tuning-pegs, or indications of its ever having had any. The upper part of the body was of parchment.

The Arabian *oud* has no frets. Its fourteen strings are of lamb's-gut. Two are always tuned together in unison; consequently there are seven different intervals produced by the open strings.

I must not leave unnoticed a painting of an instrument from an ancient Egyptian tomb, now in the Berlin Mu-

Fig. 47.   Kind of guitar.

seum, described by Drieberg as a guitar. From the evident care with which it has been executed, it is believed to be a faithful representation in all its details. According to the drawing in Drieberg's ' Wörterbuch der griechischen Musik,' it has seven frets. The performer was therefore enabled to produce eight different intervals on each string. The frets are placed at equal distances from each other, and the spaces between them are painted in various colours. The discovery is, however, in my opinion, not so important as some musicians are inclined to consider it. The instrument is, in fact, no other than the common tamboura, except that the neck is rather shorter than usual. Neither is its accuracy beyond question. The eight intervals could certainly not have been what has been supposed—a diatonic series, either like the two disjunct tetrachords of Pythagoras, or like our diatonic scale. In order to produce such a series of intervals, the stances for the semitones ought to be smaller than those for the whole tones. Besides, the frets would require to be nearer together at the lower part of the neck than at the upper part. Supposing the distance of a whole tone, from the top of the neck to the first fret, to have been 4 inches, the distances of the other frets, in order to be in conformity with the diatonic scale, would have been nearly as follows:—

1—2.	Whole tone	.	.	.	.	4 inches.
2—3.	Whole tone	.	.	.	.	$3\frac{1}{4}$,,
3—4.	Semitone	.	.	.	.	$1\frac{1}{2}$,,
4—5.	Whole tone	.	.	.	.	$2\frac{3}{4}$,,
5—6.	Whole tone	.	.	.	.	$2\frac{1}{2}$,,
6—7.	Whole tone	.	.	.	.	$2\frac{1}{4}$,,
7—8.	Semitone	.	.	.	.	1 ,,

If, on the other hand, the frets were equidistant, as they are represented, only the step from the open string to the first fret would have constituted a whole tone; the step from the first fret to the second would have exceeded a whole tone; and each following step would have produced a larger interval than the preceding one, so that the lowest would have embraced several whole tones. It seems surprising that these simple facts could have been overlooked by those inquirers who place implicit reliance on the correctness of the representation in question.

PECULIAR STRINGED INSTRUMENTS.

Some of the stringed instruments of the ancient Egyptians differ too much from our own of the present day to be classed with any of them. One of these, when played upon, was borne upon the shoulder of the performer. In shape this curious instrument is not very unlike some of the small Egyptian harps with which we have already become acquainted. Some portions of such instruments may be seen in the

P

British Museum. The best preserved of these, shown in the accompanying engraving (fig. 49), is about 3 feet in length and 16 inches in height. It

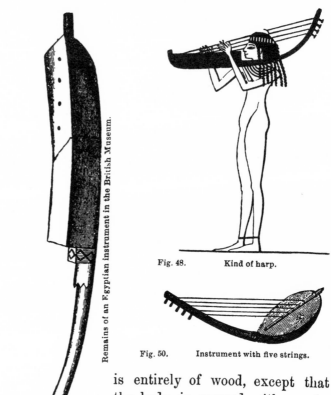

Fig. 48.   Kind of harp.

Fig. 50.   Instrument with five strings.

Remains of an Egyptian instrument in the British Museum.

Fig. 49.

is entirely of wood, except that the body is covered with parchment. The tuning-pegs show that, like the preceding one, it must have been mounted with four strings. In the great French work, 'Description de l'Égypte,' there is a drawing of one of these instruments, in which five strings are given to it.

Another curious instrument of the ancient Egyptians (fig. 50) resembles in construction the *sancho*, a small stringed instrument of the negroes of Guinea.[9] It likewise bears a resemblance to the *valga*, found in Senegambia, Guinea, and other districts of Western Africa—an instrument which is also known by other names, as *wambee*, *kissumba*, &c.   The only difference in construction between the above Egyptian instrument and the *valga* is that the neck of the latter consists or several canes, generally five.   These are stuck into holes in the under part of the body of the instrument, and can be pushed in or drawn out independently o each other.   As each string is affixed to the extreme end of one of the canes, it can be tightened or slackened by drawing
the cane further
out, or pushing it
deeper in ; in this
way it is tuned.
The strings are
apparently made
of the fibre of
a creeping plant.
Some travellers
describe them as
derived from the
fibrous root of a
tree.

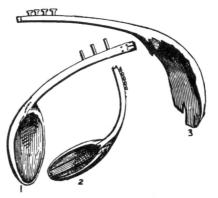

Fig. 51.   Remains of Egyptian   ringed instruments.

Remains of the Egyptian instrument under our notice have been discovered in tombs, in the condi-

---

9 Herr v. Heuglin has recently met with the same instrument among the negro tribes inhabiting districts west of the Bahr-el-Abiad. See Dr. Petermann's ‘Mittheilungen über wichtige neue Erforschungen auf dem Gesammtgebiete der Geographie,’ Gotha, 1863 ; where a drawing of the instrument is given.

tion shown in fig. 51. Two of these are in the British Museum ; and the smallest one, with five pegs, is in the Berlin Museum.

The next instrument to be noticed is a kind of lyre, about 6 ft. high, which stood on the ground, and, like the harp, was played upon with both hands, one on each side of the instrument. From its close resemblance to some Greek lyres (see Forkel's 'Geschichte der Musik,' vol. i. tab. ii. 21; Hawkins's 'History of Music,' vol. i. plate ii. 8; Burney's

Fig. 52.   Kind of lyre.   Fig. 53.   Peculiar instrument.

'History of Music,' vol. i. plate v. 8), and from the number of the strings—eight being an unusual number on the instruments of the ancient Egyptians —as well as from its rare occurrence among the Egyptian instruments, it appears to date from a later period than the others, and to have been, perhaps introduced from Greece.

The instrument fig. 53 is too indistinct to reveal its real nature. The performer might just as well be

taken for a man poking a burning faggot, as for a
musician producing sweet sounds. Possibly the
instrument—for a musical instrument undoubtedly it
is, because it has been found represented as a companion to the lyre—may be a kind of dulcimer. Or,
even more likely, it may be a harmonicon, constructed
of a series of metallic bars, or of wooden slabs,
arranged according to a certain order of intervals.
Instruments of this description are at the present day
common in several countries of Asia and Africa.
Various kinds of them are found, especially in Java,
Siam and Burmah. Also the *balafo*, a favourite
instrument of the negroes in Africa, belongs to the
same class. Indeed, the construction of the harmonicon suggests itself so naturally wherever fondness
for music and some ingenuity are combined, that it is
scarcely likely the Egyptians should have been unacquainted with it, especially as they evidently were
more advanced in music than some of the nations
which possess this instrument.

Although they are all constructed on the same
principle, there is a wonderful variety in the appearance, character of tone, and degree of completeness of
the harmonicons found in different parts of the world.
Those of the Egyptians may therefore have been in
many respects different from any in use at present.

THE PIPE.

Small pipes of the ancient Egyptians have repeat-
edly been discovered, made of reed, usually with four
finger-holes, but sometimes with three, five or more.
Above a dozen of them may be seen in the Leyden
Museum. There are also examples in the British
Museum, one of which has seven holes burnt in at the

side. Two straws were found with it, of nearly the same length as the pipe, which is about one foot long. In some other pipes pieces of a kind of thick straw, or similar material, have also been found inserted into the tube, obviously serving for a similar purpose as the so-called *reed* in our oboe or clarionet. The pipes

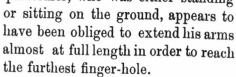

Fig. 54.   Reed pipes in the British Museum.

in the British Museum are in too imperfect a condition to enable us to ascertain from actual sounds whether the Egyptian pipes with four finger-holes possessed the same pentatonic order of intervals that we find in the pipes of the ancient Mexicans and Peruvians.

THE FLUTE.

The common Egyptian flute was of considerable length ; and the performer, who was either standing or sitting on the ground, appears to have been obliged to extend his arms almost at full length in order to reach the furthest finger-hole.

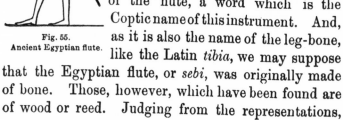

We are informed that the word *sèbi* has been found repeatedly in the hieroglyphics with the representation of the flute, a word which is the Coptic name of this instrument. And, as it is also the name of the leg-bone, like the Latin *tibia*, we may suppose

Fig. 55.
Ancient Egyptian flute.

that the Egyptian flute, or *sebi*, was originally made of bone. Those, however, which have been found are of wood or reed. Judging from the representations, the flute and the single-pipe were played almost exclusively by men. The double-pipe, however, we find in the hands of females also, as was the case among the Assyrians.

The Egyptians evidently had various kinds of flutes, differing in dimension and in the number of finger-holes. Similar varieties exist also among the flutes at present in use in Egypt, called *nay*. It must be remembered that most of the instruments of the modern Egyptians have been derived from the Arabs. Still, some kinds of *nay* appear to be nearly identical with the long flute anciently in use in Egypt. The most common *nay* of the modern Egptians, known as the " Dervish flute " — because it is played by the Dervishes to accompany the songs at their religious dances, called *zikrs* —consists, according to Lane, of " a simple reed, about eighteen inches in length, seven-eights of an inch in diameter at the upper extremity, and three-quarters of an inch at the lower. It is pierced

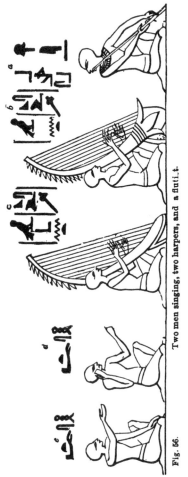

Fig. 56.   Two men singing, two harpers, and a fluti.t.

with six holes in front, and generally with another hole at the back. . . . . The sounds are produced by blowing through a very small aperture of the lips against the edge of the orifice of the tube, and directing the wind chiefly within the tube   By blowing with more or less force, sounds are produced an octave higher or lower.   In the hands of a good performer the *nay* yields fine mellow tones, but it requires much practice to sound it well.''[10]

THE DOUBLE PIPE.

The double-pipe must have been a favourite instrument with the ancient Egyptians, because it occurs frequently in the representations of musical performances.   Its name was *mam*.

On a fragment of an Egyptian fresco-painting in the British Museum, representing an entertainment,

Fig. 57.   Performance on the double-pipe, with a rhythmical accompaniment

one female is playing on the double-pipe, others are clapping their hands in rhythmical accompaniment and are probably singing, while two are dancing to

10 An Account of the Manners and | by Edward William Lane, 5th edi-
Customs of the Modern Egyptians, | tion, London, 1860, p. 362.

the music. The foregoing representation (fig. 57) is of a similar nature.

The Greeks and Romans, who were as familiar with the double-pipe as were the Egyptians, occasionally inserted little pegs or tubes into some of the finger-holes, apparently for the purpose of regulating the order of intervals, or the *mode* in which they intended to perform. A drawing of the instrument, with the pegs, is given in Burney's 'History of Music,' vol. i. plate 6. On the representations of the Egyptian double-pipe such a contrivance is not indicated.

THE TRUMPET.

The Egyptian trumpet appears to have been usually of brass, and of about the same length as the Assyrian. The instrument of an unusual shape (fig. 59), apparently a kind of trumpet, occurs, as far as I am aware, only once in the representations. If this instrument was made of brass, we may suppose the person kneeling before the performer, and holding his hand to his head, to be shielding his ear from the blast. In another group of figures, shown in the same plate of Rosellini's work in which this trumpet occurs,

Fig. 58. Common trumpet of the ancient Egyptians.

is a listener before a performer on the harp, represented in exactly the same posture and with the same expression as the former. The sounds of the harp must have been soft, and the listener is evidently intended to express delight at the music.

This trumpet was therefore probably made of wood,

or even of some softer substance, producing sounds less loud and harsh than brass.

Fig. 59.   Peculiar trumpet of the ancient Egyptians.

THE DRUM.

Of the ancient Egyptian drum we are acquainted with three different kinds. The first much resembles a small hand-drum at present in use in several Asiatic countries.

Fig. 60.   The drum.   Fig. 61. Drum carried on the back.

It was from two to three feet in length, covered with parchment at both ends, and braced by cords. The performer carried it before him, generally by means of a band over his shoulder, while he was beating with his hands on both ends.

The other kind of drum (fig. 62) does not appear in any of the paintings and sculptures with which we are acquainted, but there has been found an actual specimen in the excavations made in the year 1823 at Thebes.

It was 1½ ft. high, and 2 ft. broad. Like the small drum before mentioned, it had cords for bracing it. A piece of cat-gut encircled each end of the

Fig. 62.
Egyptian drum found at Thebes.

drum, being wound round each cord, by means of which the cords could be tightened or slackened at pleasure, by pushing the two bands of catgut towards or from each other. It was beaten with two drumsticks slightly bent. The Egyptians had also straight drumsticks with a handle, and a knob at the end. The Berlin Museum possesses some of these.

Fig. 63.   Drumstick in the Berlin Museum.

The third kind of drum is almost identical with the *darabukkeh* of the modern Egyptians.

The modern Egyptians have two kinds of this drum. One of these is the earthen *darabukkeh*, principally employed by the boatmen of the Nile, as an accompaniment to the *zummárah*, a double reed-pipe, as well as by some inferior story-tellers and such like persons. It

Fig. 64.   Three tambourines and a darabukkeh drum of the ancient Egyptians.

is from 1½ ft. to 2 ft. in length.   The other is described
by Lane as being made of wood, inlaid with mother-of-
pearl and tortoise-shell, " covered with a piece of fish's

Fig. 65.   The darabukkeh of the modern Egyptians.

skin at the larger extremity, and open at the smaller,"
and about 15 in. in length.   This drum is especially
used in the hareems, and appears to be the most like
that which we see in the hands of the female, the first
in the above procession (fig. 64), who probably accompanies her song with its rhythmical sound.

THE TAMBOURINE.

The Egyptian tambourine was either round, like that which is at the present time in use in Europe as well as in the East, and which, as we have seen, was also known to the Assyrians; or it was of an oblong square shape, slightly in-curved on the four sides, and entirely different from our own tambourine. Two instruments of this description, and one of the common kind, are represented in the engraving fig. 64. Sometimes the square tambou-rine had a bar across the mid-dle, which divided the parchment into two equal parts, so that it was in, fact, a double tambourine. Women appear to have played the tambourine more usually than men.

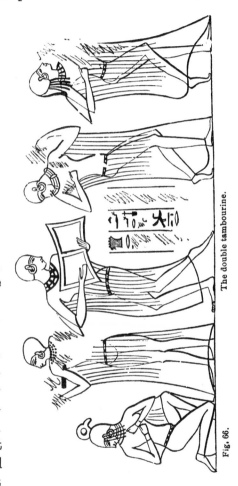

The double tambourine.

Fig. 66.

Doff, or *deff*, is the name given by the Arabs to a
square tambourine still in use, especially in the Barbary States. A parchment of sheepskin is stretched
on a square frame, and four catgut cords are strung
over the inside to increase the vibration, This *deff*
may have been the *toph* of the Hebrews, as well as the
square tambourine of the ancient Egyptians.

TWO PECULIAR INSTRUMENTS OF PERCUSSION.

The instrument held with the left hand by a man,
accompanying the performance of two harpers, is

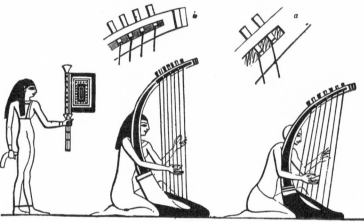

Fig. 67.   An instrument of percussion and two harps.

Fig 68.   Instrument of metal.

most likely a kind of gong,
which was beaten with a
piece of ivory or wood. In
the above engraving is also
shown the manner in which
the strings of the harps were
wound round the tuning-
pegs.

The instrument fig. 68 was most likely constructed of metal, to emit, when beaten or shaken, a sound like a gong or bell; and perhaps, some loose pieces of metal were attached to it, to produce a jingling noise noise like that of the sistrum.

THE SISTRUM.

The sistrum consisted of a frame of bronze or brass, into which three or four metal bars were loosely inserted, so as to produce a jingling noise when the instrument was shaken. The bars were often made in the form of snakes, or they terminated in the head of a goose, as is the case with some sistra in the British Museum. Not unfrequently a few metal rings were strung on the bars to increase the noise; and the top of the frame was sometimes ornamented with the figure of a cat. The smallest sistra which have been found are about 9 inches in length, and the largest about 18 inches.

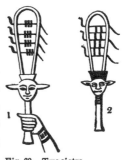

Fig. 69.   Two sistra.

The sistrum was principally used by females in religious performances; and it is remarkable that even at the present time we find it made use of in a similar way by the priests of a Christian sect in Abyssinia, where it is called *sanasel*. Its sound is supposed by the priests to drive away the evil spirits, and it was specially employed by the ancient Egyptians for the same purpose. Its Egyptian name was *seshesh*. The designation for instruments of percussion in general appears to have been *kemkem*, which

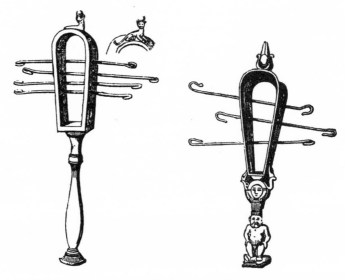

Fig. 70. Sistra in the Berlin Museum.

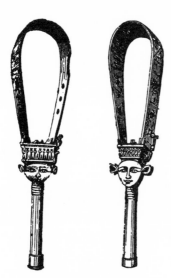

Fig. 71. Sistra without the bars.
In the British Museum.

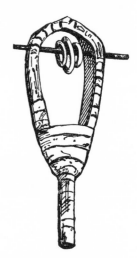

Fig. 72. Model of a sistrum.
Berlin Museum.

is the Coptic name of the tambourine. Villoteau, on
the authority of Jablonski, believes *cencen* to have
been the common name
of the sistrum; and he
suggests that its present
Ethiopian name, *sanasel*
(*tzenacel*, or *cenacel*), and
also the Hebrew *tzeltzelim*,
may have been derived
from the same word.

CROTALA.

Another curious Egypt-
ian instrument, serving
merely for the production
of rhythmical effects, like
the *crotala* of the Greeks,
or our castanets, consisted
of two balls or knobs, sometimes made to represent
human heads, probably of
metal, and hollow, to which
were affixed handles, either
straight or slightly curved.
One of these was held by
the performer in each hand,

Fig. 73.
Abyssinian priest with sanasel.

and the heads were struck together, to mark the time
in instrumental performances or in dances.

In the engraving fig. 74 a double handle is surmounted by a double head, which may have contained
some loose pieces of metal to increase the effect.

Crotala, clappers, or castanets, were made use of by
most ancient nations in religious performances, and are

Q

still thus used, even in the Christian Church. The
Roman Catholics in Santo Domingo repair on Easter
Eve to the cathedral, provided with the *pata*, a wooden

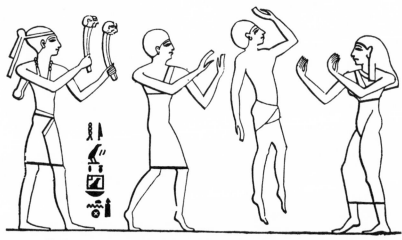

Fig. 74.   Men dancing to rhythmical sound of crotala.

clapper. During the service, at the moment when the
darkness of the place is dispelled by the sudden admis-
sion of many lights, the people hail the commencement of Easter by clattering with their clappers, and
dancing and jumping about in the church. Similar
customs prevail in other Roman Catholic countries.
In Spain these instruments were made usually of
chestnut (castana) ; hence the name *castanet*.

CYMBALS.

The Egyptian cymbals closely resembled our own
in shape. There are two pairs of them in the British
Museum. One pair is, according to the Museum
Catalogue, 5⅓ in. in diameter, and the cymbals are
united by a band of linen.

The other pair was found in a coffin enclosing the mummy of Ankhhapê, a sacred musician, and is deposited in the same case with the mummy and

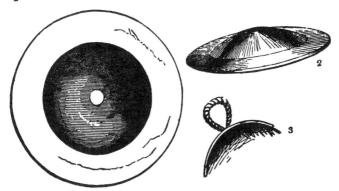

Fig. 75.   Egyptian cymbals in the British Museum.

coffin. In the Catalogue these cymbals are described as being of bronze; but it is probable that brass also, and even an admixture of silver, was sometimes used in the fabrication of such instruments.

BELLS.

Among the Egyptian antiquities in the British Museum are also some small bells of bronze, of which four are represented in the woodcut fig. 76. The largest is $2\frac{1}{4}$ in. in height, and the smallest three-quarters of an inch.

The face with the protruding tongue on the largest represents Typhon, the evil spirit of the ancient Egyptians. All the bells appear to have had clappers, and some of them have a small hole at the side near the top wherein the clapper was fastened, as is actually the case with the lowest of the two small ones shown in the engraving, in which the clapper still exists. This bell is remarkably well preserved, and its tinkling can scarcely have been more clear some thousand years ago than it is at present.

Fig. 76.   Small bells of the ancient Egyptians.

Besides these bells there is another in the same collection, in a more corroded condition, on which also the head of Typhon is exhibited. It therefore appears probable that the bells were employed in religious observances for a somewhat similar purpose as the sistrum.

VOCAL AND INSTRUMENTAL PERFORMANCES.

The information on the music of the Egyptians obtainable from the works of ancient writers is, indeed, but scanty; nevertheless, in connection with the representations depicted on the monuments, it is not without importance. Herodotus, Plato, Diodorus Siculus, and Strabo, each visited Egypt, and most probably ascertained personally what they record. Their accounts are on some points at variance; this may, however, be accounted for by the circumstance of nearly five hundred years intervening between the time when Herodotus visited Egypt and Strabo's travelling there; or from one historian alluding especially to sacred, and another to secular music, or to music in general.

Herodotus (born 484 B.C.) relates that among the several festivals celebrated by the Egyptians during the year, in different towns, in honour of their gods, one of the most important was the festival held in the city of Bubastis for the worship of Diana. On this occasion "men and women embark together in great numbers. During the voyage some of the women beat upon small drums, while some of the men play on the flute. The rest of the people, of both sexes, sing, clapping their hands together at the same time.'

Further, Herodotus relates: "Among other memorable customs the Egyptians sing the song of Linus, like that which is sung in Phœnicia, Cyprus, and other countries, where, however, it bears a different name. But the person they praise in this song is evidently the same whom the Greeks celebrate under the name of Linus. Among the many wonderful things I have met with in Egypt this one astonishes me especially, whence they can have obtained the song of Linus; for they seem to have celebrated him thus from time immemorial. The Egyptians call him Maneros, and they say that he was the only son of the first king of Egypt. Happening to die in the prime of life, he is lamented by the people in this dirge, which is the only song of the kind they possess in Egypt."

In explaining the character of the Egyptian god Osiris, who was put to death by Typhon, but returned to life again, though not upon earth, Mr. Sharpe observes : " The death of Osiris was piously lamented by Isis and her sister Nephthys ; and once a year the Egyptians joined their priests in a melancholy procession through the streets, singing a doleful ditty called the ' Maneros,' or ' Song of Love,' which was to console the goddess for the death of her husband. . . . . This story the Greeks copied, and have given us in the form of the loves and lamentations of Venus, a goddess, for Adonis, who was a mortal. The boar which killed Adonis is no other than the hippopotamus Typhon."[1]

However this may be, there is at least no doubt that the song of Linus was introduced on joyful occasions also. Homer mentions its being sung at a vintage :—

> To this one pathway gently winding leads,
> Where march a train with baskets on their heads
> (Fair maids and blooming youths), that smiling bear
> The purple product of the autumnal year.
> To these a youth awakes the warbling strings,
> Whose tender lay the fate of Linus sings ;
> In measured dance behind him move the train,
> Tune soft the voice, and answer to the strain.
>
> (Pope s ' Iliad,' xviii. 650).

A similar air appears at the present day to be sung on festive occasions in the north of Persia. Mr. Alexander Chodzko states that in Ghilan it is the custom on New Year's Day for boys to sing felicitations before the doors of the people. " It is remarkable that amongst these joyous songs there is a sad one on the death of some foreigner. Its doleful, lengthened tune draws forth a reluctant tear even from the eyes of an indifferent hearer ; and the

---

[1] Egyptian Mythology and Egyptian Christianity, by Samuel Sharpe, London, 1863, p. 10.

impression is the more touching as all around is joyful. On hearing it, one is put in mind of the coffin
which the ancient Egyptians carried around the tables
at their gayest banquets. Their song 'Maneros'
must have been something like the one here alluded
to."[2]

In one or two European countries also we meet
with similar performances. The *vocero* of the country-
people in Corsica, for instance, is a dirge lamenting
the death of a beloved brother or friend. Gregorovius relates that during his stay at Calvi he was
one night awakened by hearing the *vocero* sung in the
streets by some young men, which was intended as
a serenade for a young girl, an inmate of the house
in which he resided. He says: " Singular that a
young girl should be serenaded with dirges; and
the proper serenade itself, with which they commenced, was as mournful as a vocero. It is impossible to tell how overpoweringly touching is the
solemn melancholy of this music in the stillness of
the night—the tones are so wailing, so monotonous,
and long drawn out. The first voice sang solo, then
the second joined, and the third, and at last the
whole band. They sang in *recitativo*, as they sing
in Italy the ritornello. In the ritornello, too, senti-
ments not meant to be melancholy are sung in an
almost plaintive strain; but when this in itself
melancholy kind of music is applied to the vocero,
the whole soul is thrilled with sadness. . . . I shall
never forget the dirges of that night in Calvi."[3]

---

[2] Specimens of the Popular
Poetry of Persia, by Alexander
Chodzko, Esq., London, 1842,
p. 467.

[3] Wanderings in Corsica,
translated from the German of
F. Gregorovius, by A. Muir,
Edinburgh, 1855, vol. ii. p. 31.

Considering that Corsica, as well as Sardinia, was, at an early period, colonized by the Phœnicians, it is not improbable that the vocero may originally have been the Maneros which, according to Herodotus, was popular among the Phœnicians also. Superstitions and usages, apparently of Phœnician origin are said to be still existent in Corsica and Sardinia. A detailed account of those of the Sardes is given by Bresciani in his work entitled 'Dei Costumi dell' Isola di Sardegna, comparate cogli antichissimi Populi Orientali,' published at Naples in 1850. The national musical instrument of the Sardes, the *lionedda*, is a kind of double pipe, which bears a greater resemblance to the instruments of this class which were in use among the ancient Easter nations than to any instrument at present found in other European countries. But, even independently of these facts, the observation of Herodotus respecting the far-spread popularity of the song of Linus is very suggestive, and deserves the especial consideration of musical historians.

On another occasion he mentions that at the festival of Osiris, the Bacchus of the Egyptians, they had processions, the women singing and carrying the images, preceded by a player on the flute.[4] And in describing the customs of the Lacedæmonians, he observes: " In this respect they resemble the Egyptians: their heralds, musicians and cooks succeed to the professions of their fathers; thus a musician is the son of a musician, a cook of a cook, and a herald of a herald. Neither may others on account of the fine quality of their voice apply themselves to the

---

[4] Herodotus, Euterpe.

profession of music, but each adheres to the profession of his father."[5]

The division of the people into castes must have greatly impeded the development of music as an art. There is nothing, except a physical disqualification, to prevent the children of a cook or of a smith becoming as expert in their vocation as their father. But in an art like music, where talent and genius are required, it is very different. These gifts, like mental powers, are rarely transmitted from father to son. It is true we meet with a few instances in the history of our music where a family has produced talented musicians through several generations. This was the case with the Bach family, and also with the Mozarts. Leopold Mozart, the father of the great Mozart, was a distinguished musician; and Wolfgang Amadeus, the youngest son of the great Mozart, has written compositions which might have made him celebrated if his name had not been Mozart. But these instances are quite exceptional: on the other hand, many could be cited where the children of distinguished composers and performers have proved entirely devoid of any talent, and even capacity for music. If, as Herodotus says, the possession of a fine voice did not entitle a person not belonging to the caste of musicians to dedicate himself to the art, good professional singers must indeed have been scarce in Egypt, since they are by no means numerous even in countries where such restriction does not exist.

Plato lived about 400 years B.C. As he is said to have sojourned in Egypt thirteen years, and as he

---

5 Herodotus, Erato.

appears to have studied music scientifically, his information must be considered especially accurate and valuable. In the second book of the 'Laws,' written in the form of a dialogue, he remarks on the subject as follows :—

"*Athenian Guest.*—The plan which we have been laying down for the education of youth was known long ago to the Egyptians, that nothing but beautiful forms and fine music should be permitted to enter into the assemblies of young people. Having settled what those forms and what that music should be, they exhibited them in their temples; nor was it allowable for painters or other imitative artists to innovate or invent any forms different from what were established; nor is it now lawful, either in painting, statuary, or any of the branches of music, to make any alteration. Upon examining, therefore, you will find that the pictures and statues made ten thousand years ago are in no one particular better or worse than what they make at the present day.

"*Clinias.*—You say what is wonderful.

"*Athen.*—Yes, it is in the true spirit of legislation and policy. Other things practised among that people may perhaps be blameable, but what they ordained about music is right; and it deserves consideration that they were able to make laws about things of this kind, firmly establishing such melody as was fitted to rectify the perverseness of Nature. This must have been the work of the Deity, or of some divine man; as, in fact, they say in Egypt that the music which has been so long preserved was composed by Isis, and the poetry likewise."

From these observations it is evident not only that the Egyptians considered some kind of music capable

of corrupting the morals of the people, but also that
in Plato's time the character of the Egyptian music
was different from that of the Greek, and that Plato
admired it greatly.

Diodorus, who visited Egypt about 60 years B.C.,
mentions the invention of the lyre, by Hermes, and
that the god adopted three strings for this instrument
in allusion to the three seasons of the year. The
highest of the three different sounds produced by the
strings represented Summer; the lowest, Winter;
and the intermediate one, Spring. He also tells us
of the universal mournings of the Egyptians on the
death of a king. On such an occasion the temples
were closed, and all feasts and solemnities forbidden,
for the period of seventy-two days. Men and women,
sometimes several hundred together, walked about,
twice a day, throwing dust upon their heads, and
singing mournful songs in praise of the deceased
monarch. Diodorus observes also that it was not
customary for the Egyptians to practise music, because they considered it effeminate and undesirable—
a statement which probably refers only to a certain
class of secular music, since we have in the representations ample evidence of the estimation in which
this art was universally held by them. Strabo, who
wrote his Geography about the time of Christ, states
that vocal and instrumental performances were
usually admitted in the worship of the gods, especially at the commencement of the ceremonies, except
in the temple of Osiris, where neither singers nor
players on the flute or on the lyre were permitted to
perform.[6]

---

6 Strabo, book xvii., Egypt.

I fear, however, I should tire the reader were I to notice all the passages bearing upon the subject found in subsequent writers, as Dion Cassius, Clemens Alexandrinus, who wrote about A.D. 200, and others. I shall therefore substitute a short extract from Dr. Birch's 'Introduction to the Study of the Egyptian Hieroglyphs,' which contains some interesting information relating to music condensed from those writers :—

" The existence of a considerable number of works in the native language was not unknown to the Greeks, with whom they passed under the name of those of *Hermes.* Hence Clement mentions two books of Hermes on music—one containing a series of hymns to the gods, the other the institutes of the life of the king; four others upon astronomy—one containing a list of the fixed stars, a second on the phenomena of the sun and moon; the two others were on the rising of the stars. Another contained a cosmography and geography, the course of the sun, moon, and the five planets, the chorography of Egypt and scheme of the Nile, an account of the supplies of the temples and the lands apportioned to them, touching on measures and the requisites of sacred things. Another of the works referred to the sealing of victims and the instruction of youth; ten others to the honours to be rendered to the gods and other actions of Egyptian piety, as sacrifices, first-fruits, vows, ceremonies, feasts, and similar things. Ten more books embraced the laws of the country and of the gods, and the instruction of the priests. Altogether there were forty-two of these works—thirty-six embracing the philosophical notions of the Egyptians, and the other six medicine. . . . . The

false Hermetic book mentions the secret hymns and
the hymns taught by Isis to Horus. Plato, better
informed, speaks of the hymns of Isis, which were
apparently in the forms of colloquies. Certain books,
which passed under the name of those of Horus and
Isis, are spoken of by Lucian. There were also
ancient lyrical poems, containing the praises of the
gods and ancient heroes, and sung at ceremonies and
entertainments, and deaths, when threnes, or funeral
dirges, composed in rhythm, were chanted for the
deceased. Among the encomiastic odes is mentioned
one in honour of Sesostris, which differed from the
historical accounts. Hymns were also addressed to
the rising and the setting sun, and to Ammon,
to obtain his oracular responses in the Oasis. Of
these the most important were the *Threne, i.e*, the
dirge or lament for Maneros; another addressed to
Saturn; and a chant called the Genethlia, or Birth of
Horus."[7]

Taking all these facts into consideration, there can
scarcely be a doubt that the Egyptians, like the
Greeks, possessed written dissertations on the theory
of music. But it may well be doubted whether from
any such work, had it been preserved, we could have
obtained so accurate an insight into the character of
the Egyptian music as the various representations
of the performances afford. Not only the form and
construction of the instruments have thus become
more familiar to us than they would have been from
mere description, but we are also enabled to ascertain
how the instruments were usually combined so as to

---

[7] Introduction to the Study of the Egyptian Hieroglyphs, by
Samuel Birch, London, 1857, p. 185.

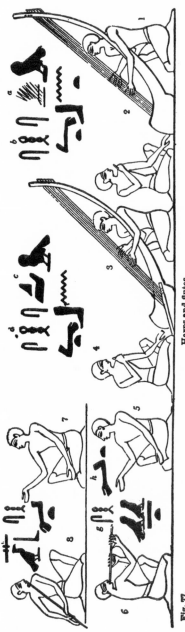

Harps and flutes.

Fig. 77.

form small bands or orchestras. With some of these we have already become acquainted through the previous engravings. One of them, for instance, exhibits a concert of performers on the harp, tamboura, lyre, double pipe, and tambourine. Another shows us a group of females with different kinds of instruments of percussion, evidently accompanying their vocal performances by the rhythmical sounds of tambourines and of the darabukkeh—like Miriam the prophetess, when she and the women of Israel went out in procession, exulting over the destruction of Pharaoh's host.

It may perhaps interest the reader to know that the hieroglyphics in the engraving fig. 77 designate the names of the

Fig. 78.   Harp, tamboura, and double-pipe.

instruments—those over the harpers being the word *buni,* "harp," and those before the players on the flute being *sèbi,* "flute."

The combination of two stringed instruments, the harp and tamboura, with the double pipe (fig. 78), is

Fig. 79.   Harp, two ambouras, and rhythmical accompaniment with the hands.

suitable for compositions of a sentimental character, in which the pipe probably sustained the melody, while the stringed instruments accompanied, with a primitive kind of harmony, such as has been described in the chapter on Assyrian musical performances.

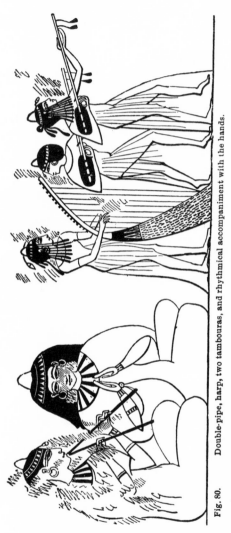

If any further proofs were required to confute the opinion usually expressed by musical historians that the performances of the Egyptians were always in unison, these small bands might afford them. In one of them a harp with ten strings, and a tamboura on which at least three times as many intervals must have been producible, occur in union with a lyre of only five strings. Other representations show combinations similarly suggestive that the performance of a melody in unison, as well as in what is called *unison in octaves*, was almost impossible.

The employment of two tambouras, either alone or in concert with the harp, appears to have been not unusual. In the present group (fig. 80) a double pipe is added, and the effect must have been fine, if it bore any resemblance to that which we are able to produce by blending the sounds of a harp, two guitars, and a flute.

Fig. 81.   Vocal and instrumental music combined.

The instrumental accompaniment to the singing of men and women (fig. 81), consisting of a lyre—in shape similar to those before mentioned which are in the Berlin and Leyden Museums, but mounted with an unusually large number of strings—and of a harp and double pipe, is certainly peculiar. In this respect it is, however, far surpassed by a concert of eight musicians shown in the splendid Prussian work on Egyptian Antiquities, edited by Lepsius. These musicians are all playing on flutes. Three of them, one behind the other, are kneeling and holding their flutes in exactly the same manner. Facing these are three others, in a precisely similar position. A seventh is sitting on the ground to the left of the six, with his

R

back turned towards them, but also in the act of blowing his flute, like the others. An eighth is standing at the right side of the group, with his face turned towards them, holding his flute before him with both

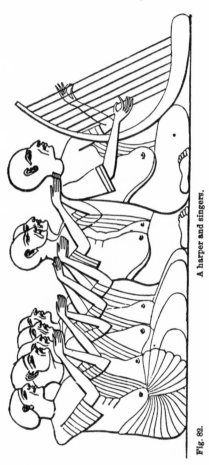

A harper and singers.

Fig. 82.

hands, as if he were going to put it to his mouth, or had just left off playing. He is clothed, while the others have only a narrow girdle round their loins. Perhaps he is the director of this singular band, or the solo performer, who is waiting for the termination of the *tutti* before renewing his part of the performance. And does not the division of the players into two sets, facing each other, suggest the possibility that the instruments were classed somewhat like the first and second violins, or the *flauto primo* and *flauto secondo*, of our orchestras? The occasional employment of a third or fifth, as accompaniment to the melody, is not unusual, even with nations less advanced in music than were the Egyptians.

This representation of a flute-concert is from one of the tombs in the Pyramids of Gizeh, and dates, according to Lepsius, from the Fifth Dynasty. It must, therefore, be earlier than 2000 B.C.

In the same plate of the above work where this concert occurs,[8] we also meet with the figure of the tamboura as one of the hieroglyphic signs of that remote period.

There are in the history of music few facts so remarkable and suggestive as the existence of an instrument of the guitar kind 4000 years ago, evidencing a stage of musical progress in Egypt which some nations of the present time have not yet attained.

In order to enable the reader to form his own opinion concerning the euphony, and the suitableness for vocal music, of the Egyptian language, I shall insert here, in the original as well as in translation, the song of the thrashers to the oxen treading out the corn. This song, one of the oldest metrical poems of the Egyptians which has been found, was written in hieroglyphics over a representation of oxen so employed.

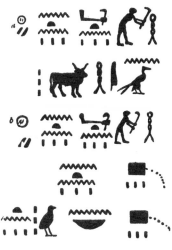

Fig. 88. Song of the thrashers.

8 Denkmaeler aus Ægypten und Æthiopien herausgegeben, von C. R. Lepsius, Zweite Abth., Blatt 74.

Hi těn ēn těn	Thrash ye for yourselves,
Hi těn ēn těn ăūū	Thrash ye for yourselves, O oxen,
Hi těn ēn těn	Thrash ye for yourselves,
Hi ten ēn těn	Thrash ye for yourselves,
Tehā ĕr amū	The straw which is yours,
Khăŭ ĕn nēbŭ těn.	The corn which is your master's.

Dr. Birch, whose translation is here given, remarks: "Verses of four or six syllables are used. There are other parts of this song thus sung by the men engaged in the operations, but the lines are not so distinctly marked."[9]

We have previously had under our notice a group of Assyrians engaged in cutting down palm-trees, stimulated by the music of singers and drummers. Others we have found carrying on their work to the sound of the trumpet. An Egyptian painting from a grotto at El Bersheh exhibits a scene very similar to the removal of the Assyrian sculptured bull. It is, however, considerably older, and is believed to be of the time of King Osirtasen II., who reigned about the year 1600 before the Christian era. A colossal statue, resting on a sledge, is being transported from the quarries by a great number of labourers. Sir G. Wilkinson observes; " On the knee of the figure stands a man who claps his hands to the measured cadence of a song, to mark the time and ensure their simultaneous draught; for it is evident that, in order that the whole power might be applied at the same instant, a sign of this kind was necessary; and the custom of singing at their work was common to every occupation among the Egyptians, as it is now in that country, in India, and many other places. Nor is it found a disadvantage among the modern sailors of

---

[9] Introduction to the Study of the Egyptian Hieroglyphs, by Samuel Birch, p. 266.

Europe when engaged in pulling a rope, or in any labour which requires a simultaneous effort."[1]

Representations such as the above suggest the origin of some of the ancient myths which attribute to music the power of moving stones. Amphion, who is said to have built the walls of Thebes by the sound of his lyre, might be represented similarly to the Assyrian king superintending the removal of the colossus. The traveller Clarke has given a rational explanation of the wonderful power ascribed to Amphion, which I shall here quote, inserting one or two words in brackets for the sake of musical accuracy :—

"In the harmonious adjust of those masses which remain belonging to the ancient walls, we saw enough to convince us that the story of Amphion was not a fable ; for it was a very ancient custom to carry on immense labour by an accompaniment of [instrumental] music and singing. The custom indeed still exists both in Egypt and in Greece. It might therefore be said, that the walls of Thebes were built at the sound of the only [the principal] musical instrument in use, because, according to the custom of the country, the lyre was necessary for the accomplishment of the work."[2]

Moreover, the Greeks had, as is well known, special songs suited to their different trades and rural occupations. Homer describes Calypso weaving and singing :

She sate and sung ; the rocks resound her lays :
The cave was brighten'd with a rising blaze :
Cedar and frankincense, an odorous pile,
Flamed on the hearth, and wide perfumed the isle ;
While she with work and song the time divides,
And through the loom the golden shuttle guides.
(Pope's ' Odyssey,' v. 70.)

1 The Manners and Customs of the Ancient Egyptians, vol. iii. p. 326.

2 Clarke's Travels, part ii. sect. 3, p. 56.

Again, when the companions of Ulysses approached the palace of Circe :—

> Now on the threshold of the dome they stood,
> And heard a voice resounding through the wood :
> Placed at her loom within, the goddess sung ;
> The vaulted roofs and solid pavement rung.
> O'er the fair web the rising figures shine,
> Immortal labour ! worthy hands divine.
>
> (Pope's ' Odyssey, x. 250.)

Moreover, the different kinds of songs used by the ancient Egyptians at their various occupations may be supposed to have been more markedly distinguished from each other than those of most other nations of antiquity; since the division of the Egyptians into castes must have restricted the use of certain kinds of songs almost exclusively to certain classes of the people ; and this must have had the effect of insuring to each kind its own distinctive characteristics.

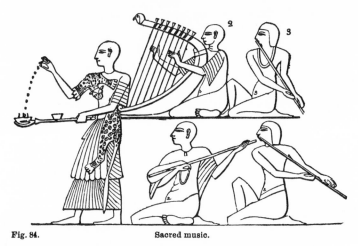

Fig. 84.   Sacred music.

The band of musicians (fig. 84), consisting of a harper, a player on the tamboura, and two flutists, is evidently performing sacred music, while a priest is offering incense. Almost all the various instruments with which we have become acquainted appear to have been employed in sacred as well as in secular music. Among stringed instruments, the harp seems to have been considered pre-eminently suitable for music used in religious ceremonies. The Egyptians had "minstrels of the gods," or sacred musicians, whose functions were connected with the religious observances in the temples.

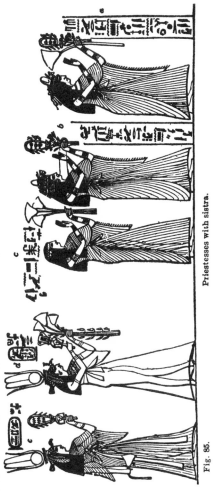

Priestesses with sistra.

Fig. 85.

The sistrum, which was usually employed in religious worship, appears to have been appropriated to priestesses and "holy women," who were sometimes of the highest rank. The two females with the high head-dresses in the engraving fig. 85 are, according to Sir Gardner Wilkinson, the Queens of Ramesis the Great; the others are the mother, daughter, and sister of a priest.

As a specimen of religious poetry, which undoubtedly was sung or chanted by the Egyptians, the first stanza of a hymn to the Nile (taken from a papyrus in the British Museum) may serve:—

SHA EN HAPI.

Nether ek Hapi
Shem em ta an'
Or sankhu kam
Amen sam kek em hru

Hes nu sem
Au shau ammeh
Kam am Ra
Er sankh hu abu neb
S'hur set bu tem
Nau pe haa
Mer en tufa kherp nefra
S'hut teba en Phah!

A HYMN TO THE NILE.

Incline thy face, O Nile,
Coming safe out of the land,
Vivifying Egypt,
Hiding his dark sources from the light,
Ordering his sources;
The streams of his bed
Are made by the sun
To give life to all animals,
To water the lands which are destitute,
Coming all along the heaven,
Loving fragrance, offering grain,
Rendering verdant every sacred place of Phtha![3]

Fig. 86.   Military band.

In martial music principally instruments of percussion, as indeed might be expected, appear to have been employed by the Egyptians. The military band (fig. 86) consists of only five musicians, viz. a trumpeter, a drummer, a performer on an instrument

[3] Birch, Introduction to the Study of the Egyptian Hieroglyphs, p. 268.

which is so much obliterated that its real character
cannot be determined, but which, to judge from
its form and size, must have been of importance in a

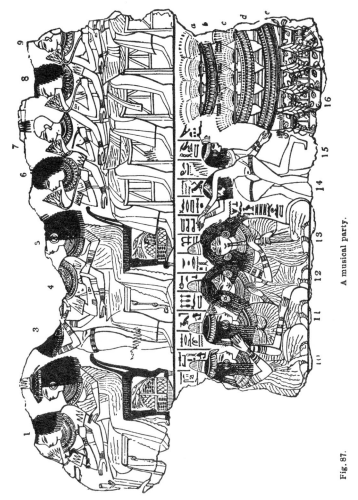

A musical party.

Fig. 87.

military band,—and two persons who are clash-
ing together each a pair of cylindrical maces or
crotala.

The representation of a musical party in a gentleman's house, taken from a fresco now in the British Museum. will be found especially interesting, if compared with our own entertainments of a similar kind. Mr. Sharp has described it thus: "A number of guests, men and women, are seated on chairs, while women servants are handing wine to them, and female musicians. sitting on the ground, play to them, and women dance before them. Many of the guests hold a lotus flower, and one man a handkerchief as a mark of refinement. The servants and dancers are unclothed with the exception of a slight band."[4]

The Egyptians evidently were fond of dancing. Their dances were not always restricted to slow and graceful attitudes, which, as we have seen, generally characterize the dances of Eastern nations; but lively figures, rapid evolutions, and even the *pirouette* (see fig. 88), were sometimes introduced. From the representations it is evident that various dances were in use, differing considerably in character, according to the class of persons by whom they were performed and the occasions on which they were admitted. Sometimes both sexes joined in the dance; sometimes, especially in spirited and vehement dances, only men engaged, bouncing about in wonderful order, without the assistance of music, or perhaps to the rhythmical sounds produced by clapping the hands and snapping the fingers. Again, on some occasions, only women, lightly clad, danced to the sounds of soft instruments before a party of admiring spectators.

The jesters or buffoons (fig. 90) are of interest

---

[4] Egyptian Antiquities in the British Museum, described by Samuel Sharpe, London, 1862, p. 49.

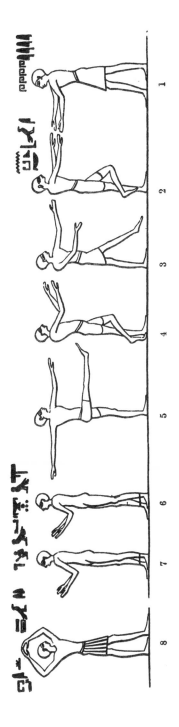

Fig. 88.

Men dancing.

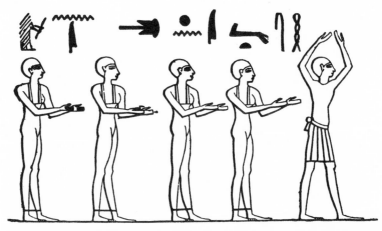

Fig. 89.   A man dancing alone to the rhythmical sounds of clapping the hands.

chiefly in so far as they remind us of the Assyrian mummers described at page 98.   They may be natives of some district in the interior of Africa; but it is quite as likely they are jesters of the lowest caste, who blackened themselves, like the so-called Ethiopian Serenaders of our day, and wandered from place to place to exhibit their antics and low jokes, interspersed with comic songs.

Fig. 90.   Jesters dancing.

In short, through the monumental representations, we are now in possession of irrefragable evidences in proof that the ancient Egyptians, highly susceptible of music, employed it to increase the solemnity of their religious worship, to enhance the pleasures of their social entertainments, to inspire and encourage their warriors, to heighten the rhythmical and pantomimic effects of their dances, and to delight the people in their public festivities, celebrations, and processions.

THE EGYPTIAN MUSICAL INSTRUMENTS COMPARED WITH THE ASSYRIAN.

I now subjoin, for the sake of comparison, a brief enumeration of the Egyptian and Assyrian instruments with which we are more or less acquainted.

ANCIENT EGYPTIAN INSTRUMENTS.

1. The harp, varying in shape and construction.
2. The trigonon.
3. The lyre; various kinds.
4. The tamboura. A kind of lute or guitar.
5. A four-stringed instrument, borne on the shoulder when played upon.
6. A five-stringed instrument, resembling the sancho and valga of the negroes.
7. The single pipe.
8. The double pipe
9. The flute.
10. The trumpet; two kinds.
11. The tambourine; three kinds.
12. The drum; three kinds.
13. Two peculiar instruments of percussion.
14. The sistrum.
15. A kind of crotalum.
16. Cymbals.
17. Bells.

1. The harp, varying more in ornamentation than in construction.
2. The lyre; three different forms.
3. The dulcimer.
4. The asor.
5. The tamboura.
6. The single pipe.
7. The double pipe.
8. The trumpet.
9. The tambourine.
10. The drum; three kinds.
11. Cymbals; two kinds.
12. Bells.

The dulcimer, one of the most important instruments of antiquity, occurs only in the Assyrian list. On the other hand, the Egyptian list contains five more instruments than the Assyrian, and especially a greater variety of stringed instruments. The Egyptian harp was superior in construction; its sounding-board extended in a curve from the upper part to the bottom of the frame, whereby greater power and sonorousness of tone were obtained than on the Assyrian harp. Besides being acoustically superior, it excelled the Assyrian harp in elegance of shape and ornamentation. Instruments so tastefully formed and embellished as the harps discovered by Bruce, and as some of the Egyptian lyres, do not occur on the Assyrian monuments. The Assyrian harp had, however, the greatest number of strings.

Costly materials were sometimes employed by nations of antiquity in the construction of their favourite instruments. Homer mentions a *phorminx* (a kind of lyre called " harp " in Pope's translation), made of silver :—

And now, arrived where on the sandy bay
The Myrmidonian tents and vessels lay;
Amused at ease, the godlike man they found,
Pleased with the solemn harp's harmonious sound.
The well-wrought harp from conquer'd Thebæ came;
Of polish'd silver was its costly frame.

(Pope's 'Iliad,' ix. 240).

As peace and prosperity are especially favourable to the cultivation of music, the ancient Egyptians—a people less warlike than the Assyrians—were the most likely to attain a high degree of proficiency in this art. Hence the superiority of their instruments.

The following observation of Professor Rawlinson, however, does not support this view, but rather tends to point to the Assyrians as most advanced in music. Professor Rawlinson says: "Fully to appreciate the Assyrians, we should compare them with the much-lauded Egyptians, who in all important points are very decidedly their inferiors. The spirit and progressive character of their art offers the strongest contrast to the stiff, lifeless, and unchanging conventionalism of the dwellers on the Nile. Their language and alphabet are confessedly in advance of the Egyptian. Their religion is more earnest and less degraded. In courage and military genius their superiority is very striking; for the Egyptians are essentially an unwarlike people. The one point of advantage to which Egypt may fairly lay claim is the grandeur and durability of her architecture. The Assyrian palaces, magnificent as they undoubtedly were, must yield the palm to the vast structures of Egyptian Thebes. No nation, not even Rome, has equalled Egypt in the size and solemn grandeur of its buildings. But, except in this one respect, the great African kingdom must be regarded as inferior to her

Asiatic rival, which was indeed 'a cedar in Lebanon, exalted above *all* the trees of the field, fair in greatness and in the length of his branches, so that all the trees that were in the garden of God envied him, and not one was like unto him in his beauty' (Ezek. xxxi. 3-9)."[5]

Respecting the music of the *modern* Egyptians, there is reason to surmise it to be more nearly related to the music of the Assyrians and Chaldæans than to that of the ancient Egyptians. It must be remembered that most of the present inhabitants of Egypt are Muslim-Egyptians (also called Arab-Egyptians), a mixed race, principally descended from the Arabs. After the conquest of Egypt by the followers of Mahomed, in the seventh century of the Christian era, the arts and customs of the Arabs were transmitted to Egypt with their religion. We have already traced the affinity of the Arabic music with the Assyrian through the Persian. I shall now submit to the consideration of the reader an interesting observation of Professor Rawlinson, from which it would appear that the music of the Assyrians was closely allied to the Chaldæan :—

"The leaven which was to spread by degrees through the Asiatic peoples was first deposited on the shore of the Persian Gulf at the mouth of the 'Great River' (Gen. xv. 18; Deut. i. 7; Josh. i. 4), and hence civilization, science, letters, art, extended themselves northward, and eastward, and westward. Assyria, Media, Semitic Babylonia, Persia, as they

---

[5] The Five Great Monarchies of the Ancient Eastern World, by George Rawlinson, London, 1862, vol. i. p. 308.

derived from Chaldæa the character of their writing, so were they indebted to the same country for their general notions of government and administration, for their architecture, their decorative art, and still more for their science and literature. Each people no doubt modified in some measure the boon received, adding more or less of its own to the common inheritance. But Chaldæa stands forth as the great parent and original inventress of Asiatic civilization, without any rival that can reasonably dispute her claims."[6]

I must now leave it to the reader to decide whether the music of the modern Egyptians is not likely to be more intimately related with the Chaldæan and Assyrian than with the ancient Egyptian music.

Still, there are a few remains of the original Egyptian musical instruments and performances extant, which have been preserved intact from the influence of the Arabs. I have already mentioned several instruments, such as the kissar, the darabukkeh, the sistrum, &c. The last-named is, however, at the present day only found in Abyssinia. The tamboura and most other instruments have undergone modifications according to the musical system of the Arabs.

In describing the Ghawázee, or common dancing girls of the modern Egyptians, Mr. Lane says : "The Ghawázee being distinguished in general by a cast of countenance differing, though slightly, from the rest of the Egyptians, we can hardly doubt that they are, as they themselves assert, a distinct race. . . . . In many of the tombs of the ancient Egyptians we find

---

6 The Five Great Monarchies of the Ancient Eastern World, by G. Rawlinson, London, 1862. vol. i. p. 216.

representations of females dancing at private entertainments to the sounds of various instruments, in a
manner similar to the modern Ghawázee, but even
more licentious, one or more of these performers being
generally depicted in a state of perfect nudity, though
in the presence of men and women of high stations.[7]
This mode of dancing we find from the monuments
here alluded to, most of which bear the names of
kings which prove their age, to have been common in
Egypt in very remote times, even before the Exodus
of the Israelites. It is possible, therefore, that it has
continued without interruption; and perhaps the
modern Ghawázee are descended from the class of
female dancers who amused the Egyptians in the
times of the early Pharaohs."[8]

Again, if the black buffoons, shown in the woodcut
fig. 90, were Abyssinians, which is not at all unlikely,
they may be the *wattas* of the present day, described
by Mr. Mansfield Parkyns as "musicians and buffoons,
sometimes attached to the courts of the chiefs of
Abyssinia, but also frequently itinerant in their habits,
making professional tours, something after the manner of ballad-singers."[9] True, the Abyssinians are
not black; but it appears to have been the custom
with the ancient Egyptians to paint the human figure
of any African black, except their own, for which
they used the red colour.

Of the modern Egyptian professional singing-girls,
Mr. Lane says: "These are called 'Awálim; in the

---

[7] Sir G. Wilkinson says that this
was not in reality the case, but appears only so from the outline of the
transparent robe being effaced. (A
Popular Account of the Ancient
Egyptians, vol. i. p. 138.)

[8] An Account of the Manners and
Customs of the Modern Egyptians, by
E. W. Lane, London, 1860, p. 379.

[9] Life in Abyssinia, by Mansfield
Parkyns, London, 1853, vol. i. p.
268.

singular, Almeh, or Alimeh; an appellation, as an
Arabic word, literally signifying 'a learned female,'
but, as applied to these female singers, evidently, I
think, derived from the Hebrew or Phœnician word
'almáh, signifying 'a girl' and 'a virgin,' and particularly 'a singing-girl.' 'Al-'alámóth sheer, the title
of Psalm xlvi., and nebálím 'al-'alámóth, in 1 Chron.
xv. 20, should, I doubt not, be rendered 'A song' and
'harps,' or the like, 'adapted to 'almáhs,'—that is,
'singing-girls.' And as Jerome says that alma in the
Punic language signified 'a virgin,' it seems to be
probable that, in old times, the most celebrated of the
singing-girls in Egypt were Phœnicians."[1]

Such conjectures may, on a cursory view, appear
but little to our purpose; but I may say that I have
repeatedly found by experience that, in investigations
like the present, the conjectures of eminent travellers,
ethnologists, and historians are frequently of greater
assistance in arriving at the truth than the confident
assertions of musical theorists. These are often individual views only, based on facts appertaining entirely
to our own modern music.

After what has been said respecting the music of
the modern Egyptians, some specimens of their popular melodies may perhaps interest the reader. A
considerable number of these melodies have been
collected and brought to Europe by travellers. The
singing of the sailors on the Nile, especially, has frequently been noticed and described. This usually
consists of alternate solo and chorus in short phrases,
and varies with the nature of the occupation in which

---

[1] An Account of the Manners and Customs of the Modern
Egyptians, by E. W. Lane, London, 1860, p. 355.

the men happen to be engaged. Thus, one particular air is sung when they shift the sails; another when the boat has struck on a sandy bank, and they are working to set it afloat again; a third when the wind is favourable, and they give themselves up to singing *con amore;* a fourth when approaching a village; and so on.

MODERN EGYPTIAN LOVE-SONG.

Doos yá   lel - lee; Doos yá   lel - - lee;   Doos yá

lel - lee; Doos yá   lel - lee; Doos yá   lel - lee; Doos   yá

lel - lee; 'Eshke   mahboobee   fe - ten - nee.

ANOTHER.

SONG OF THE ALA'TEEYEH, or Male Professional Musicians.

SAILORS ON THE NILE, WHEN ARRIVING AT A VILLAGE.

He Li - sa!

Suef ba-lad al - mah bub   He Li - su!

If any genuine remains of ancient Egyptian vocal
music had been preserved, they would, most likely, be
found among the Copts of Upper Egypt. It will be
remembered that the Copts are descendants of the
ancient inhabitants of the country. They are a
Christian sect, dispersed throughout parts of Egypt,
but in Upper Egypt whole villages are inhabited exclusively by them. The Coptic language is no longer
spoken, but used in religious observances, like the
Latin in the Roman Catholic Church. Through this
language a clue has been obtained to the study of the
language of the ancient Egyptians, as read from their
hieroglyphic inscriptions.

Mr. Lane says, "With respect to the personal
characteristics, we observe some striking points of
resemblance, and yet, upon the whole, a considerable
difference, between the Copts and the ancient Egyptians, judging of the latter from the paintings and
sculptures in their tombs and temples. The difference
is, however, easily accounted for by the fact of the
intermarriages of the ancestors of the modern Copts
with foreigners above mentioned [Greeks, Nubians,
Abyssinians]. The people who bear the greatest
resemblance to the ancient Egyptians at present are
the Noobeh (or more genuine Nubians), and next to
these the Abyssinians and the Copts, who are, notwithstanding, much unlike each other. The Copts

differ but little from the generality of their Muslim countrymen, the latter being chiefly descended from Arabs and from Copts who have embraced the faith of the Arabs, and having thus become assimilated to the Copts in features."[2]

Villoteau, who witnessed some of the Coptic religious ceremonies, expresses himself as by no means edified with the interspersed vocal music, which consisted of a Hallelujah, in which the same word was repeated over and over again, occasionally with as large a group of notes upon one syllable as we find attached to this word in some of our older oratorios. On account of the great length of this composition, written down by Villoteau after hearing it repeatedly performed, I shall here insert only that part with which it commences.

HALLELUJAH OF THE COPTS.

yé   yé yé . . . . . .   yé   lo   go   lo   go   lo .

. . . .   guo   go . . .   ouo . . . .   guo

ouo   ouo . . . .   guo.

Although the Copts no longer possess the kissar and the sistrum, like their neighbours the Nubians and Abyssinians, they make use in their religious ceremonies of the *maraoueh*, which appears to be a modification of the sistrum. This curious instrument I have already described (page 67).

The music employed in acts of worship is perhaps less subjected to change than any other. As, however, the Copts are a Christian sect, it appears improbable that even in their most ancient religious music there should be remains left of the music of their heathen forefathers.

Somewhat similar to the relation of the Copts with the ancient Egyptians, appears to be that of the Yezidis, or devil-worshippers, in Kurdistan, with the Chaldæans and the Assyrians. The language of the Yezidis is a Kurdish dialect, but their religious chants and hymns are in Arabic—a language which is understood only by the priests and chiefs. Their religious vocal performances are usually accompanied by the *Kawals*, an order of priests, with flutes and tambourines. These instruments are looked upon as sacred. Mr. Layard saw the Kawals before and after the performance kissing the tambourine, and inviting the people to do so likewise. The music he describes as on some occasions solemn and impressive, and on others wild and harsh.

It must be remembered that the devil is held by the Yezidis in the greatest awe and reverence. He is only spoken of as *Melik el Taus*, "the Mighty Angel," or *Sheikh Mazem*, "Great Chief;" his proper name, *Shaitan* (Satan) they dread to pronounce.

Mr. Layard observes: " The Yezidis have a tradition that they originally came from Busrah, and from the country watered by the lower part of the Euphrates; that after their emigration they first settled in Syria, and subsequently took possession of the Sinjar Hill and the districts they now inhabit in Kurdistan. This tradition, with the peculiar nature of their tenets and ceremonies, points to a Sabæan or Chaldæan origin. With the scanty materials which we possess regarding their history, and owing to the ignorance prevailing amongst the people themselves, —for I believe that even the priests, including Sheikh Nasr [the high priest], have but a very vague idea of what they profess, and of the meaning of their religious forms,—it is difficult to come to any conclusion as to the source of their peculiar opinions and observances. There is in them a strange mixture of Sabæanism, Christianity, and Mohammedanism, with a tincture of the doctrines of the Gnostics and Manichæans. Sabæanism appears to be the prevailing feature; and it is not improbable that the sect may be a remnant of the ancient Chaldees, who have at various times outwardly adopted the forms and tenets of the ruling people to save themselves from persecution and oppression, and have gradually, through ignorance, confounded them with their own belief and mode of worship."[3]

A German traveller, Herr Wagner, who visited the Yezidis, and who has described their religious observances, relates that during his journey he met with the well-known Bokhara traveller, the missionary Joseph Wolf, who told him he had seen Yezidi pilgrims on the ruins of Babylon, engaged by moonlight in ghastly religious rites, performing strange dances, with peculiar gesticulations, to doleful songs. The missionary added that he recognized in it the literal fulfilment of the words of the prophet Isaiah (ch. xiii. v. 21): "Wild beasts of the desert shall lie there; and their houses shall be full of doleful creatures, and owls shall dwell there, and satyrs shall dance there."

Mr. Layard, in his work entitled 'Discoveries in the Ruins of Nineveh and Babylon,' has published a few specimens of Yezidi music. I shall insert here two of them, which are songs—or perhaps, more properly speaking, chants—of the priests.

CHANT OF THE YEZIDI PRIESTS.

---

3 Nineveh and its Ruins, by A. H. Layard, London, 1849, vol. i. p. 306.

ANOTHER CHANT OF THE YEZIDI PRIESTS.

To seek among the Yezidis for actual remains of Assyrian music would undoubtedly be as futile as to seek for remains of ancient Egyptian music among the Copts, or even more so. Nevertheless, these specimens of songs from Kurdistan and Egypt are interesting, as they in some measure illustrate the present state of music in countries where, at the earliest period, we have found this art cultivated to a considerable degree of development.

OPINIONS OF SOME MUSICAL HISTORIANS.

Most of our principal works on the history of music contain some account of the ancient Egyptian music. Forkel's dissertation, in his 'Geschichte der Musik,' deserves especial notice from the care with which all the facts are stated so far as they had been ascertained in his time. Forkel, it must be remembered, wrote subsequently to Printz, Kircher, Martini, Burney, Hawkins, and other musical historians, and thus had the advantage of consulting their works. The information on this subject contained in Kircher's 'Œdipus Ægyptiacus' (Romæ, 1652) is more curious than instructive. More deserving of attention is the Abbé Roussier's 'Mémoire sur la Musique des Anciens, où l'on expose le Principe des Proportions authentiques, dites de Pythagore, et de .ivers Systêmes de Musique chez les Grecs, les Chinois, et les Égyptiens. Avec un Parallèle entre le Systême des Égyptiens et celui des Modernes' (Paris, 1770). The Abbé believes the Greek musical system to have been founded on the Egyptian, and his conclusions respecting the characteristics of the latter are principally drawn from the former. De Laborde says, in his 'Essai sur la Musique' (tome iii. page 678), that the Abbé Roussier, at twenty-five years of age, did not know even a note of music, but that five years later he was one of the first theorists of his century. The work alluded to certainly contains much interesting information, and has been made use of by most of the later historians.

Some interesting remarks bearing on our subject
are also 'o be found in Rollin's 'Histoire ancienne des
Égyptiens, des Carthaginois, des Assyriens, des Baby-
loniens, des Medes et des Perses, des Macedoniens,
des Grecs' (Paris, 1730), and in Goguet's 'De l'Origine des Loix, des Arts, et des Sciences; et de leur
Progrès chez les anciens Peuples' (Paris, 1758).
During the eighteenth century France was richer in
literature relating to the music of antiquity than any
other country.   De Guignes's arguments, in his 'Mémoire dans lequel on prouve que les Chinois sont une
Colonie Égyptienne,' were soon refuted by Leroux
Deshautesrayes, Pauw, and others.   Had the Chinese,
according to the hypothesis of De Guignes, been
Egyptian colonists, settled in China about 1100 years
B.C., we might perhaps have found a clue to the fact
that the Chinese use the pentatonic scale, which, as we
have seen, the ancient Egyptians also appear to have
used.   We might, with some good reason, expect so
conservative a people as the Chinese to have preserved nearly intact the musical system of the
Egyptians.   Cornelius von Pauw, in his 'Recherches
philosophiques sur les Égyptiens et sur les Chinois'
(Berlin, 1773), the aim of which is to disprove the
theory of De Guignes, treats also of the Chinese and
Egyptian music, expressing an opinion by no means
favourable to either.

Two interesting essays, written by Villoteau—the
first headed, 'Dissertation sur les diverses espèces
d'Instrumens de Musique que l'on remarque parmi
les Sculptures qui décorent les antiques Monumens
de l'Égypte, et sur les noms que leur donnèrent, en
leur langue propre, les premiers peuples de ce pays;'
and the other, 'Mémoire sur la Musique de l'antique

Égypte'—have both been published in 'Description de l'Égypte.'[4]

M. Fétis believes he has made an important discovery, which I shall here briefly notice. "I have not the least doubt," he says, "that this musical notation [used in ecclesiastical music by the modern Greeks] belonged to ancient Egypt. I have in support of my opinion the resemblance borne by the signs in this notation, erroneously attributed to St. John of Damascus, to those of the demotic, or popular characters of the ancient Egyptians. In the system of musical notation in use in the Greek Church there are no *notes*, properly so called—that is to say, signs arranged to represent each a certain sound in the scale—for the Greeks do not accept a fixed diapason, or a normal sound to which all the others are referred. It is true that there is a certain point of departure for all the songs, which may be considered as the principal note in every kind of vocal music, and according to which all the progressions of the voice are regulated; but the singer takes this note as he finds it most convenient, according to the high or low pitch of his voice. The sound which serves as the point of departure in any melody, and· which, as all Greek writers say, is the *beginning*, the *middle*, and the *end* of all music, is represented by a sign which has the name of *ison*. Then, the sign of this sound has an exact resemblance with that sign in the ancient demotic alphabet of Egypt which corresponds to the *delta* of the Greeks. The sign *oligon*, which expresses

---

4 In the octavo edition of Descrip- | than the folio edition, these two essays
tion de l'Égypte, which is less scarce | will be found in vols. vi. and viii.

an ascension of the voice by an interval of one tone, commencing from the *ison*, is one of the characters of the letter N in demotic writing. The *oxeia*, a sign expressing ascension of a sound higher than the *ison*, is nothing more than one of the characters, R, in the same writing. The *kouphisma*, the sign for progression from the third to the fourth tone, is one of the characters representing the letter B. The *petasthe*, the sign of ascension from the fourth to the fifth tone, occurs also in several characters representing the letter T in the demotic alphabet. The *pelasthon*, which expresses the ascending progression from the fifth to the sixth tone, exactly resembles one of the many characters which in the papyri correspond to the *sigma* of the Greeks. The double *kentema*, or *double spirit*, which occurs in many signs in the demotic writing, expresses an ascending progression from the sixth to the seventh tone. The sign for a progression ascending in thirds is the simple *kentema*, which is, in fact, a fragment of the characters in the demotic alphabet, corresponding to the *eta*, the *iota*, and the *sigma* of the Greeks. The progression of the voice in descending from the *ison*, or tonic, to the third below, is expressed by the *aporrhoê*, which in this alphabet corresponds to the letter E. The sign of descending progression from the same tone to the fifth below was one of the characters representing the letter B."

After having pointed out the resemblance existing between several signs employed by the modern Greeks to determine the duration of notes, and certain characters of the demotic alphabet, M. Fétis continues:

"After this detailed analysis of the system of nota-

tion employed in the music of the Greek Church, and
after comparing its signs with those of the demotic
character in use among the Egyptians, can we for a
moment doubt that the invention of ¹this notation is to
be ascribed to that ancient people, and not to St. John
of Damascus? No doubt, I think, will be entertained
on this point. Both the Greeks and the Romans
employed the characters of the alphabet, arranged in
various ways, for musical notation; and this was also
the case during part of the middle ages. The notation of the singing books used in the churches of
Ethiopia, and by the priests of Abyssinia, is to this
day in characters of the *Amara* language, as, in all
probability, it has been since the earliest days of
Christianity; why may we not then conclude that the
ancient Egyptians turned to account the rich varieties
of their demotic alphabet for the notation of their
melodies? and that this notation was preserved in the
music of the first Eastern Christians? Besides, since
it has been proved that St. John of Damascus was not
the inventor of the characters of the musical notation
of the Greek Church, what probability is there that in
the eighth century—when the old demotic alphabet
of Egypt had disappeared, to give place to the Coptic
alphabet, derived from the Greek—what probability,
I say, is there that, with no special inducement, he
sought in an obsolete alphabet for the signs of a notation till then hardly known? I fully believe that
this notation was never lost, but that it was introduced into the music of the Greeks long before his
time. Let us remark the great importance of the
discovery of this ancient notation. Since it cannot possibly be applied except to music overladen

T

with embellishments, and requiring great flexibility
of voice, as we find it at present in the Greek
Church and among some African nations, it gives
us an exact idea of the music of ancient Egypt."[5]

I need perhaps scarcely point out the fallacy of
M. Fétis's conclusion, that if the modern Greeks
employ a musical notation derived from the demotic
alphabet, the characteristics of the Egyptian music
must have been preserved in the Greek. We might
as well conclude that the English language must
resemble the Latin, because it is written in Roman
letters. Nevertheless, his discovery, if well-founded,
would be very interesting, and might possibly lead to
other useful discoveries in the history of music. I
have therefore carefully examined the two principal
sources mentioned by him in testimony of the correctness of his assertions. They are the Greek notation
as shown in tome xiv. of 'Description de l'Égypte,'
and the characters of the demotic alphabet in Champollion's 'Précis du Système Hiéroglyphique des
anciens Égyptiens.'

There are 125 signs in this alphabet, which consist
mostly of lines, curves, hooks, right and acute angles,
and other simple figures, placed in varied positions.
The signs of the Greek musical notation are equally
simple. Might we not then naturally expect to find
a close resemblance between half a dozen of these,
and some of the 125 demotic letters? Besides, even
among those pointed out by M. Fétis, several cannot
be identified without some stretch of the imagination.

---

[5] Biographie Universelle des Musiciens et Bibliographie Générale de la
Musique, par F. J. Fétis, Bruxelles.
1837, tome i. p. lxxi.

I thought it probable that the shape of the Greek signs might have altered somewhat in the course of time, and thus have become less recognizable in the demotic characters. But if this had been the case, we should find the Greek notation as it existed about a thousand years ago—of which, among other musical writers, Burney has given specimens in his 'History of Music,' vol. ii. p. 50—more resembling the demotic characters than it does at present. It is, however, even less like. M. Fétis's assumed discovery must therefore, in my opinion, be considered as a statement unsupported by sufficient proofs.

Indeed, the French writers seem to have surpassed all others in the boldness of their conclusions on such questions. M. Lenormant, after pointing out that the two harpers from the tomb of Ramesis III. (known as "Bruce's Harpers") are performing sacred music before two deities, says : " It is remarkable that the heads which adorn the base of these harps are surmounted, one by the sign of the upper region [of Egypt], the other by that of the lower region ; whence we may infer the existence of two different modes or systems of modulation."[6]

Of the more recent German works containing information on the Music of ancient Egypt, I shall only notice Kiesewetter's dissertation, 'Ueber die Musik der neueren Griechen,' which, though valuable for its many acute observations, contains several assertions which subsequent discoveries have proved to be erroneous.

---

[6] Musée des Antiquités Égyptiennes, par Charles Lenormant, Paris, 1841, planche xiii.

It would be useless to notice here every book in which this subject has been treated. The more important ones I have already mentioned. The best sources for information are the splendid drawings of musical performances in the valuable works of Rosellini, Champollion, Lepsius, and others.

CHAPTER VI.

MUSIC OF THE HEBREWS.

Gradual development of the Hebrew music—Musical instruments—
Diversity of opinion respecting the real nature of some of the
Hebrew instruments—Josephus's account—The chatzozerah—The
shophar—The magrepha—Nebel and nofre—The Hebrew lyre—
Vocal and instrumental performances—Hebrew music of the
present day—Literature of Hebrew music—Eastern origin of our
own music.

SCANTY as our information is on Hebrew music, this
is at least evident, that it was closely related to the
music of the Egyptians and Assyrians. Moses himself, who had been brought up by Pharoah's daughter,
"was learned in all the wisdom of the Egyptians"
(Acts vii. 22); and the singing of the children of
Israel before the golden calf after their departure
from Egypt (Exodus xxxii. 18) was in the Egyptian
manner. The Assyrians were their neighbours, with
whom they frequently came in close contact; in fact,
both nations were of the same descent, had nearly the
same language, and their political condition was also
in many respects similar. During the Babylonian
captivity, although the Hebrews adopted the Chaldæan language, their music does not appear to have
undergone any important modification through foreign influence; so that, after their return to Jerusalem, about seventy years later, a fresh generation
was enabled to re-establish at once in the temple the

musical performances of their forefathers. (Nehem. xii.)

I do not intend to imply by these remarks that the music of the Hebrews has not, in the course of a thousand years, experienced considerable modifications. Indeed, there are, as I shall presently endeavour to show, distinct indications of this having been the case. At the earliest period after the Exodus it was undoubtedly almost identical with the Egyptian music. When Joseph's brethren with their families settled in Egypt, they found the music of that country already developed to a considerable degree. Whatever their own musical acquirements may have been, we can hardly suppose that their descendants did not, in the course of time, adopt the superior music of the Egyptians. Some musical historians, however, express an opposite opinion. Saalschütz, one of the best writers of Hebrew music, conjectures that the Jews, during their sojourn in Egypt, where, from a few families, they gradually became a nation, had preserved to some extent their own music. His reasons for this surmise are embodied in the following interesting remarks :—

"The Hebrews descend from a family in which both vocal and instrumental music were not only known, but also appreciated, and considered as a necessary embellishment in their festivals (Gen. xxxi. 26, 27). Consequently, they possessed a knowledge of this art when they came to Egypt. Again, immediately upon leaving this country, we also find them in the full practice of music. (Exod. xv. 20.) Can there be any doubt, then, that they occupied themselves with music while in Egypt? How otherwise could it

have occurred to them, or how could it have been
possible for them to celebrate with music the happy
termination of the great peril at the beginning of their
wanderings? But, did not the circumstance of their
being in a state of slavery in Egypt prevent their cultivating music? A moment's attention will show
that this question cannot be answered otherwise than
negatively. First, it must be remembered that the
Jews, during the longest period of their sojourn in
Egypt, were a free people. They abode 430 years in
that country. During only the last 80 years of this
time were they living under oppression; in the preceding 350 years they enjoyed full liberty. (See
Jahn's 'Archæology,' Th. ii. B. 1.) During this time
they even carried on wars of their own with Canaan-
itish tribes (1 Chron. iv. 22; vii. 21, 24). They were
also artificers (1 Chron. iv. 21, 23), in which capacity
some of them were even in the service of the king, as
we may infer from the passage in Chronicles just
noticed. Altogether they appear to have stood in
very good relation with the Egyptians, for in 1 Chron.
iv. 18 we even find an instance recorded of a Hebrew
having married the daughter of a Pharoah. Now, as
the Egyptians cultivated music, is it likely that the
Hebrews, with the Egyptian example before them,
should have neglected an art which was domesticated
in their families? Even the eighty years of bondage
cannot have prevented this. The women, it may be
supposed, did not participate in the daily task; neither
did the Hebrews of rank. Thus we are told in Exod.
iv. 27 of Aaron undertaking a journey into a foreign
country; and in verse 29 of the same chapter a con-
vocation is mentioned, to which all the elders of the

Hebrews were summoned. This indicates that the elders, at least, were masters of their own time, that the old patriarchal state of society continued, and that their family life, in which every Hebrew, after his day's toil, had his time at his own disposal, was not infringed. The labour became especially oppressive only after the mission of Moses (Exod. v. 6). Again, the Hebrews, even during the years of their servitude, had considerable herds (Exod. ix. 6, 7; x. 9); there must consequently have been persons in every family who tended the cattle. At all events, the compulsory service cannot have engaged them to such an extent as to prevent every one of them from occupying himself in other ways."[1]

Moreover, there can scarcely be a doubt that, after the departure of the Hebrews from Egypt, their music acquired in the course of time certain characteristics which distinguished it from the Egyptian music, and which originated in the religious views and observances of the Jews, as well as from their intercourse with Asiatic nations, and from other circumstances.

HEBREW INSTRUMENTS.

There are no representations of Hebrew musical instruments, the correctness of which is indisputable. Still, from our acquaintance with the Egyptian and Assyrian instruments, as well as with those used in the East at the present day, we are enabled to approach very near the truth in forming an opinion

---

[1] Geschichte und Würdigung der Musik bei den Hebräern, von Dr. J. L. Saalschütz, Berlin, 1829, p. 67.

respecting the construction and shape of the Hebrew
instruments mentioned in the Bible. Besides those
enumerated in the following list, some others probably were in use with which we are entirely unacquainted.

Some of the instruments mentioned in the Book of
Daniel may have been synonymous with some which
occur in other parts of the Bible, under Hebrew names
—the names given in Daniel being Chaldæan. But
with these also the Jews were probably familiar at a
later period. Max Müller remarks : " The name of
Chaldee has been given to the language adopted by
the Jews during the Babylonian captivity. Though
the Jews always retained a knowledge of their sacred
language, they soon began to adopt the dialect of
their conquerors, not for conversation only, but also
for literary composition. The Book of Ezra contains
fragments of Chaldee contemporaneous with the cuneiform inscriptions of Darius and Xerxes; and several
of the apocryphal books, though preserved to us in
Greek only, were most likely composed originally in
Chaldee, and not in Hebrew."[2]

1. THE HARP.—There cannot be a doubt that the Hebrews possessed the harp, seeing that it was a common
instrument among the Assyrians and Egyptians. But
it is uncertain which of the Hebrew names of the
stringed instruments occurring in the Bible really
designates the harp.

2. THE DULCIMER.—Some writers on Hebrew music
consider the *nebel* to have been a kind of dulcimer ;
others conjecture the same of the *psanterin* mentioned

---

[2] Lectures on the Science of Language, by Max Müller, London,
1862, p. 277.

in the Book of Daniel,—a name which appears to be synonymous with the *psalterion* of the Greeks, and from which also that of the present oriental dulcimer, *santir*, may have been derived.

3. THE ASOR.—This was a ten-stringed instrument, played with the plectrum, and is supposed to have borne some resemblance to the *nebel*. It is therefore probable that it was in appearance similar to the Assyrian instrument to which I have applied the name *asor*.

4. THE LYRE.—This instrument is represented on a Hebrew coin, generally supposed to be of the time of the high-priest Simon Maccabæus. The *kinnor*, the favourite instrument of King David, was most likely a lyre, if not a small harp like the *trigonon* mentioned p. 194.

5. THE TAMBOURA, OR GUITAR.—*Minnim, machalath*, and *nebel* are usually supposed to be the names of instruments of the guitar or lute kind.

6 THE PIPE.—*Chalil* and *nekeb* were the names of the Hebrew pipes or flutes.

7. THE DOUBLE PIPE.—Probably the *mishrokitha* mentioned in Daniel.

8. THE SYRINX OR PANDEAN PIPE.—Probably the *ugab*, which in the English authorized version of the Bible is rendered *organ*.

9. THE BAGPIPE.—The word *sumphonia*, which occurs in the Book of Daniel, is, by Forkel and others, supposed to denote a bagpipe. It is remarkable that at the present day the bagpipe is called by the Italian peasantry *zampogna*. Another Hebrew instrument, the *magrepha*, generally described as a small organ, was more likely only a kind of bagpipe.

10. THE TRUMPET.—Three kinds are mentioned in the Bible, viz., the *keren*, the *shophar*, and the *chatzozerah*. The first two were more or less curved, and might

properly be considered as horns. The *chatzozerah*, was a straight trumpet, about two feet in length, and was sometimes made of silver (Numb. x. 2).

11. THE DRUM.—There can be no doubt that the Hebrews had several kinds of drums, as well as the Assyrians and Egyptians. We know, however, only of the *toph*, which appears to have been a tambourine, or a small hand-drum, like the Egyptian darabukkeh, noticed page 219. In the English version of the Bible it is rendered *timbrel* or *tabret*. This instrument was specially used in processions, on occasions of rejoicing, and frequently by females. We find it in the hands of Miriam, when she was celebrating with the Israelitish women in songs of joy the destruction of Pharaoh's host (Exod. xv. 20); and in the hands of Jephtha's daughter, when she went out to welcome her father (Judges xi. 34). There exists at the present time in the East a small hand-drum, called by the Arabians *doff* or *adufe*,—a name which appears to be synonymous with the Hebrew *toph*. Compare also the description of the square tambourine (page 221).

12. THE SISTRUM.—Winer, Saalschütz, and several other commentators, are of opinion that the *menaaneim*, mentioned in 2 Sam. vi. 5, denotes the sistrum. In the English Bible the word is rendered *cymbals*.

13. CYMBALS.—The *tzeltzelim, metzilloth*, and *metzilthaim*, appear to have been cymbals, or similar metallic instruments of percussion, differing in shape and sound.

14. BELLS.—The little bells on the robe of the high-priest have been already noticed. They were called *phaamon,* and are mentioned in Exod. xxviii. 33 and xxxix 25. The Jews have, at the present day, in their synagogues, small bells attached to the "rolls of the law," containing the Pentateuch,—a kind of ornamentation which is supposed to have been in use from time immemorial. No other Hebrew bells are known. We read, how-

ever, in Zech. xiv. 20 of " bells of the horses," and it
is highly probable that the Hebrews possessed bronze
bells like those of the Assyrians and Egyptians.

The places in the old Testament where these instruments are mentioned are the following :—

KINNOR.—Gen. iv. 21 ; xxxi. 27.—1 Sam. x. 5; xvi. 16,23.
   2 Sam. vi. 5—1 Kings x. 12.—1 Chron. xiii. 8; xv.
   21, 28 ; xvi. 5 ; xxv. 1, 3, 6.—2 Chron. v. 12 ; ix. 11 ;
   xx. 28 ; xxix. 25.—Nehem. xii. 27.—Job xxi. 12 ;
   xxx. 31.—Psalms xxxiii. 2 ; xliii. 4 ; xlix. 4 ; lvii.
   8 ; lxxi. 22 ; lxxxi. 2 ; xcii. 3 ; xcviii. 5 ; cviii. 2 ;
   cxxxvii. 2 ; cxlix. 3 ; cl. 3.—Isaiah v. 12 ; xvi. 11 ;
   xxiii. 16 ; xxiv. 8 ; xxx. 32.—Ezek. xxvi. 13.

NEBEL.—1 Sam. x. 5.—2 Sam. vi. 5.—1 Kings x. 12.—1
   Chron. xiii. 8 ; xv. 16, 20, 28 ; xvi. 5 ; xxv. 1, 6.—2
   Chron. v. 12 ; ix. 11 ; xx. 28 ; xxix. 25.—Nehem. xii.
   27.—Psalms xxxiii. 2 ; lvii. 8 ; lxxi. 22 ; lxxxi. 2 ;
   xcii. 3 ; cviii. 2 ; cxliv. 9 ; cl. 3.—Isaiah v. 12 ; xiv.
   11.—Amos v. 23 ; vi. 5.

ASOR.—Psalms xxxiii. 2 ; xcii. 3 ; cxliv. 9.

UGAB.—Gen. iv. 21.—Psalms cl. 4.—Job. xxi. 12 ; xxx. 31·

SHOPHAR.—Exod. xix. 16, 19 ; xx. 18.—Lev. xxv. 9.—Jos.
   vi. 4, 5, 6, 8, 9, 13, 16, 20.—Judg. iii. 27 ; vi. 34 ;
   vii. 8, 16, 18, 19, 20.—1 Sam. xiii. 3.—2 Sam. ii. 28 ;
   vi. 15 ; xv. 10 ; xviii. 16 ; xx. 1, 22.—1 Kings i, 34,
   39, 41.—2 Kings ix. 13.—1 Chron. xv. 28.—2 Chron.
   xv. 14.—Nehem. iv. 18, 20.—Job xxxix. 24, 25.—
   Psalms xlvii. 5 ; lxxxi. 3 ; xcviii. 6 ; cl. 3.—Isaiah
   xviii. 3 ; xxvii. 13 ; lviii. 1.—Jerem. iv. 5, 19, 21 ;
   vi. 1, 17 ; xlii. 14 ; li. 27.—Ezek. xxxiii. 3, 4, 5, 6.
   —Hos. v. 8 ; viii. 1.—Joel ii. 1, 15.—Amos ii. 2 ; iii.
   6.—Zeph. i, 16.—Zech. ix. 14.

CHATZOZERAH.—Numb. x. 2, 8, 9, 10.—2 Kings xi. 14 ;
   xii. 13.—1 Chron. xv. 24, 28 ; xvi. 6, 42.—2 Chron. v.
   12, 13 ; xiii. 12, 14 ; xv. 14 ; xx. 28 ; xxiii. 13; xxix.

26, 27, 28.—Ezra III. 10.—Nehem. XII. 35, 41.—
Psalms XCVIII. 6.—Hos. V. 8.

CHALIL.—1 Sam. X. 5.—1 Kings I. 40.—Isaiah V. 12 ; XXX.
29.—Jerem. XLVIII. 36.

KEREN.—Josh. VI. 5.—1 Chron. XXV. 5.—DAN. III. 5, 7,
10, 15.

NEKEB.—Ezek. XXVIII. 13.

TOPH.—Gen. XXXI. 27.—Exod. XV. 20.—Judg. XI. 34.—1
Sam. X. 5 ; XVIII. 6.—2 Sam. VI. 5.—1 Chron. XIII. 8.
—Job XXI. 12.—Psalms CXLIX. 3 ; CL. 4.—Isaiah
V. 12 ; XXIV. 8 ; XXX. 32.—Jerem. XXXI. 4.

TZELTZELIM, METZILLOTH.—2 Sam. VI. 5.—1 Chron. XIII.
8 ; XV. 16, 19, 28 ; XVI. 42 ; XXV, 6.—2 Chron. V. 12 ;
XXIX. 25.—Ezra. III. 10.—Nehem. XII. 27.—Psalms
CL. 5.

MENAANEIM.—2 Sam. VI. 5.

SHALISHIM.—1. Sam. XVIII. 6.

MINNIM.—Psalms XLV. 8 ; CL. 4.

SABEKA.—Dan. III. 5, 7, 10, 15.

PSANTERIN.—Dan. III. 5, 7, 10, 15.

SUMPHONIA.—Dan. III. 5, 10, 15.

MISHROKITHA.—Dan. III. 5, 7, 10, 15.

Most commentators are of opinion that the *keren*—
a horn or trumpet, made of ram's horn—was almost
identical with the *shophar*; the only difference being,
that the latter was more curved than the former.
Thus are these instruments usually represented in the
drawings given in our dissertations on Hebrew music.
There appears, however, to be no satisfactory reason
for making this distinction. The *shophar* used at the
present day in the synagogue has not the curved shape
given to it in those drawings. As this instrument

may assist us in forming a correct idea respecting the ancient Hebrew trumpet, I shall presently give a short description of it.

Jobel (Exod. xix. 13 ; Jos. vi. 4, 5, 6, 8, 13) is by some commentators classed with the trumpets ; but is by others believed to designate a loud and cheerful blast on the trumpet, used on particular occasions. If *Jobel* (from which *jubilare* is supposed to be derived) is identical with the name *Jubal*, the inventor of musical instruments, it would appear that the Hebrews appreciated pre-eminently its exhilarating power.

Shalishim is supposed to denote a triangle. *Minnim* appears more likely to imply stringed instruments in general than any particular instrument.

The Chaldæans *abeka* is believed to have been identical with the Greek *sambuka*. Too little, however, is known of the latter instrument to afford us much assistance in forming an opinion respecting the construction of the former. The Greek *sambuka* is described by some writers as of a triangular shape, and mounted with four short strings only ; according to others it was boat-shaped. Drieberg believes it to have been a kind of guitar.

The *mishrokitha* is represented in the drawings of our Histories of Music as a small organ, consisting of seven pipes placed in a box, with a mouthpiece for blowing. It is not improbable that some instrument of the kind was known to the Hebrews and to the Assyrians. The *cheng* of the Chinese, a similar instrument, is asserted to have been in use several centuries before the Christian era. But the shape of the pipes and of the box, as well as the row of keys for the fingers, exhibited in the representation of the *mishrokitha*, have too much of the European type not to suggest that they are probably merely a product of the imagination.

Nechiloth, gittith, and *machalath,* which occur in the headings of Psalms v., viii., liii., lxxxi., lxxxiv., lxxxviii., are also by some commentators supposed to be names of musical instruments. *Nechiloth* is said to have been a flute, and *gittith* and *machalath* to have been stringed instruments. Again, others maintain that the words denote peculiar modes of performance, or certain favourite melodies to which the psalms were directed to be sung, or chanted.

Machol (Exod. xv. 20; xxxii. 19. Judg. xi. 34; xxi. 21. 1 Kings iv. 31. Psalms xxx. 11; cxlix. 3; cl. 4. Song of Sol. vii. 1. Jerem. xxxi. 4, 13. Lament. v. 15) is, in the opinion of some writers, a kind of flute, especially used for accompanying dances; but is more generally believed to signify the dance itself.

Forkel observes that, according to the records of the Rabbins, the Hebrews in the time of David and Solomon possessed thirty-six different musical instruments. In the Bible, however, only about half that number are mentioned. Although it is highly probable that at least some of them were almost identical with those of the Assyrians known to us from the bas-reliefs, it would be hazardous to identify them with any of the latter, on account of the very slight information transmitted to us respecting their form and construction. In fact, from our most reliable source, the Bible, scarcely more can be gathered concerning them than their Hebrew names. The diver-

sity of opinion among Hebrew scholars about the real
nature of most of them is evident even in the first
record on music, where Jubal is mentioned as the
inventor of the *kinnor* and *ugab* (Gen. iv. 21). In
the English authorized version the passage is rendered: "He was the father of all such as handle the
harp and organ. In Luther's German translation
we read: "Von dem sind hergekommen die Geiger
und Pfeifer" (i. e. *the performers on stringed instruments played with a bow and on pipes*). The Vulgate
has "citharâ et organo;" the French translation,
"la harpe et les orgues;" the Italian, "la cetera e
l'organo," &c.

Respecting the illustrations of Hebrew instruments
which usually accompany commentaries on the Bible
and historical treatises on music, it ought to be borne
in mind that most of them are merely the offspring of
conjectures founded on some obscure hints in the
Bible, or vague accounts by the Rabbins.

Equally unreliable are the conclusions drawn solely
from etymological enquiries. For instance, it has been
suggested that the trumpet called shophar must have
been constructed of brass or silver, because *shophar*
means "to be bright." Is it not, however, quite as
probable, if not more so, that the meaning of the word
refers not to the outward appearance of the instrument, but to the brightness of its sound?

The most reliable illustrations of Hebrew musical
instruments are perhaps those which have been copied
from the sculptures on the Arch of Titus at Rome.
But it must be remembered that the arch, in commemoration of the conquest of Jerusalem, was not
erected until some time after the death of Titus, and

that we cannot be sure that the sculptor was actually
acquainted with the Hebrew instruments; or, being
acquainted with them, that he did not consider it
more incumbent on him to please the eye by intro-
ducing modifications of the forms, than to adhere
strictly to the truth. At all events, before admitting
such monumental records as evidences, more caution
ought to be exercised than is usually the case; and it
would be well to bear in mind Burney's remark on a
certain statue of Handel, erected in Vauxhall Gardens
in the reign of George the Second : " The musician is
represented playing upon a lyre. Now, if this statue
should be preserved from the ravages of time and
accident twelve or fourteen hundred years, the antiquaries will naturally conclude that the instrument
upon which Handel acquired his reputation was the
lyre, though we are at present certain that he never
played on, or even saw, a lyre, except in wood or
stone."[3]

Supposing the figures on the Arch of Titus to be
authentic, they may probably be different from the
instruments which were in use about a thousand years
earlier, at the time of David and Solomon, when the
art of music with the Hebrews was in its zenith. If
we compare our own music with that of our ancestors
a thousand years ago, we are surprised at the wonderful change it has undergone. In semi-civilized
nations the arts are undoubtedly for a considerable
time almost stationary; and several oriental nations
are notorious for the tenacity with which they cling
to what has been transmitted to them from time imme-

---

[3] Burney's History of Music, i. 493.

morial. Nevertheless it is not likely that the instruments of the Hebrews—indeed their music altogether
—should have remained entirely unchanged during a
period of many centuries. Some modifications were
likely to occur even from accidental causes ; such, for
instance, as the unpremeditated invention of some
instrument, or the influence of neighbouring nations,
as the Assyrians, when the Hebrews came into closer
contact with them. Thus also may be explained
why the accounts of the Hebrew instruments given
by Josephus, who lived in the first century of the
Christian era, are not in exact accordance with those
in the Bible.

Josephus has been frequently cited as an authority
on matters relating to Hebrew music ; but it would
seem that, whatever confidence he may deserve on
other questions, his statements on the subject of music
ought to be received with much caution. Let us take,
for instance, his account of the preparations for the
musical performances at the dedication of the temple.
Solomon, he tells us, had made on this occasion two
hundred thousand trumpets according to the directions of Moses, and two hundred thousand dresses for
the Levite singers, and forty thousand stringed instruments of bright and precious metal for accompanying
the voice ; all of which he ordered to be kept in the
temple with the treasures.[4]

In comparison with such an enormous combination
of vocal and instrumental music, our most powerful
bands dwindle into insignificance. It throws into
shade even the monster orchestra of which Berlioz

---

[4] See Flavius Josephus, Antiqu., lib. viii. cap. 3.

speaks with prophetic rapture as the *ne plus ultra* in our music of the future, and of which he says, " Its repose would be majestic as the slumber of ocean ; its agitations would recall the tempest of the tropics ; its explosions, the outbursts of volcanos !" &c.[5] It is a pity that Josephus has omitted to inform us how the performers, besides the people, found accommodation within the temple : " The length thereof," we read in 1 Kings vi. 2, " was three score cubits, and the breadth thereof twenty cubits, and the height thereof thirty cubits." The supposition of some writers that the two hundred thousand trumpets were not intended to be used at the inauguration of the temple, but to be deposited in its vaults, is likewise too much in contradiction to the recorded wisdom of Solomon to be seriously entertained.

THE CHATZOZERAH.

Some Jewish literati are of opinion that a certain small figure, occurring on some coins of the time of Simon Maccabæus, is meant to represent the trumpet, *chatzozerah.* There are always on the coin two of these figures together.

Fig. 91.
Hebrew coin.

If they really are intended to represent musical instruments, and not pillars, they may as likely be drums, somewhat similar to the Assyrian sugarloaf drum, but still more resembling a kind of *darabukkeh* found at the present time

, A Treatise upon Modern Instru- | Berlioz, translated from the French, mentation and Orchestration by H. | London, 1856, p. 244.

U 2

among several oriental nations, and also among the
negroes in some parts of Africa, where it was introduced by the Arabs. The above engraving is sketched
from a small silver coin in the British Museum.
There appears, however, to be a doubt whether it
really dates from the time of Simon Maccabæus, or
whether it ought to be attributed to Simon Barcho-
chebas, a.d. 132.

THE SHOPHAR.

The *shophar* is especially remarkable as being the
only Hebrew instrument which has been preserved to
the present day in the religious services of the Jews.
It is still blown, as in time of old, at the Jewish New
Year's festival, according to the command of Moses.
(Numb. xxix. 1.)

In fig. 92 are shown four of these instruments.
Those marked *a* and *b* are from a synagogue in
Germany. They have been copied from drawings
published by Saalschütz, who remarks that the first
represents a shophar made of a ram's horn, and the
second, one made of the horn of a cow.[6] The other
two (marked *c* and *d*) are from the principal synagogues in London, where I have been permitted to
examine them. The first of these (*c*), from the synagogue of the Spanish and Portuguese Jews, Bevis
Marks, is one foot in length. The other (*d*), from the
Great Synagogue, St. James's Place, Aldgate, is
twenty-one inches in length. Both are entirely of

---

[6] Von der Form der hebräischen | die Musik der Hebräer, von J. L.
Poesie, nebst einer Abhandlung über | Saalschütz, Königsberg, 18?5.

horn the latter differs especially from the former, in so far as its tube is not round, but compressed, so

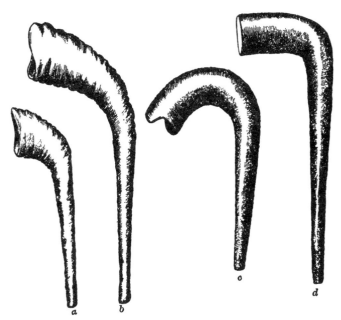

Fig. 92.   The shophar used in Jewish synagogues.

that the cavity is of a long oval shape. There are, besides this, other shophars in the Great Synagogue, which are smaller, and in shape somewhat different from each other; but that which is here represented is the one generally used. On some of them short appropriate sentences in Hebrew are engraved. One, for instance, had the verse from Psalm lxxxi., which in the English translation is rendered " Blow up the trumpet in the new moon, in the time appointed, on our solemn feast day." The psalm in question forms part of the service for the New Year's festival, at which the shophar is blown.

David Levi says: "The reason of the trumpet being made of a ram's horn is in remembrance of Abraham offering his son Isaac, when the angel of the Lord called to him out of heaven, and said, 'Lay not thine hand upon the lad, neither do thou anything unto him; for now I know that thou fearest God, seing that thou hadst not withheld thy son, thine only son, from me. And Abraham lifted up his eyes, and looked and behold behind him a ram caught in a thicket by his horns: and Abraham went and took the ram, and offered him up for a burnt-offering in the stead of his son ' (Gen. xxii. 12, 13) ;—which our received tradition informs us was on this day; and therefore we make use of a trumpet made of a ram's horn, beseeching the Almighty to be propitious to us, in remembrance and through the merits of that great event; and as it is mentioned in Numb. x. 10,—' Also in the day of your gladness, and in your solemn days, and in the beginnings of your months, ye shall blow with the trumpets over your burnt-offerings, and over the sacrifices of your peace-offerings ; that they may be to you for a memorial before your God: I am the Lord your God.' "[7]

The signals blown on the shophar are said to be the same, at least rhythmically, as those which were used more than three thousand years ago. This is the more probable because they are strictly prescribed and adhered to; they are simple, characteristic, and easily preserved traditionally; and they are very much the same in all the synagogues. The liturgy

---

[7] A Succinct Account of the Rites and Ceremonies of the Jews, by David Levi, London, 1783, p. 78.

of the Spanish and Portuguese Jews, known as the Sephardic Liturgy, is different from that of the German and Polish Jews. The fact of their signals being nearly the same furnishes a strong proof of their having been in use anterior to the settlement of the Jews in the Spanish Peninsula, and in northern Africa, which took place at the time of the Mohammedan conquests. And as the signals have been preserved intact, notwithstanding the subsequent persecutions and expulsion of the Jews from the Peninsula, it is not at all improbable that they may have been likewise preserved through many centuries before the dispersion of the Jews throughout the world, when the Jews formed a large community, and when a strict adherence to their ancient religious usages was therefore comparatively easy. In the following examples we have the three principal signals of the shophar:—

SIGNALS IN THE SYNAGOGUE OF THE GERMAN JEWS.

SIGNALS IN THE SEPHARDIC SYNAGOGUE.

The *teruha* consists of rapid repetitions of the *prime*, with a conclusion in the *fifth*. The *tekiha* consists of

a figure of two intervals, the lower being of longer
duration than the higher. This is several times repeated. The *shebarim* is the slowest signal, each note
being sustained as indicated in the above examples
by the pauses. The extension of the *tekiha* and
shebarim into the octave, in the first example, is on
some small shophars not easily executed; this may be
the reason why these signals are also usual as given
in the second example; rhythmically they are exactly
the same in both instances.

THE MAGREPHA.

The *magrepha* is not mentioned in the Bible, but
is described in the Talmud. In tract Erachin it is
recorded to have been a powerful organ which stood
in the temple at Jerusalem, and consisted of a case or
wind-chest, with ten holes, containing ten pipes. Each
pipe was capable of emitting ten different sounds, by
means of finger-holes, or some similar contrivance:
thus one hundred different sounds could be produced
on this instrument. Further, the magrepha is said
to have been provided with two pairs of bellows, and
with ten keys, by means of which it was played with
the fingers. Its tone was, according to the Rabbinic
accounts, so loud that it could be heard at an in-
credibly long distance from the temple. Drawings of
this wonderful instrument, probably originally made
after the description of the Rabbins, are to be found
in several of our older treatises on Hebrew music.
They are all like that given in Hawkins's 'History
of Music,' vol. i. p. 256, which has been copied from

'Sing- und Kling-Kunst, von Wolfgang Caspar Printz,' Dresden, 1690.

Pfeiffer, one of our best authorities on Hebrew music, is of opinion that the magrepha was not an organ at all, but that it was a large kettle-drum which stood between the porch of the temple and the altar, and which was struck to assemble the priests to prayer, and the Levites to the performance of sacred songs, as well as to announce the approach of lepers for purification.[8] Saalschütz, another careful inquirer, declares this to be an error, which he supposes to have arisen from Pfeiffer having been misled by the name *magrepha* being also applied to another instrument, likewise used in the temple.[9] This, however, was not a musical instrument at all, but a large fire-shovel used in removing the cinders and ashes from the altar and temple. In the Talmund, tract Thamid, it is stated that it was the custom for the Levite, at a fixed time, after having used the shovel, to throw it down between the altar and the porch; thereby producing a loud noise, which was heard at a great distance from the temple, and served to inform the people who approached how far the religious observances had proceeded.

In short, it appears uncertain whether the much-lauded *magrepha* was an organ, a kettle-drum, or a fire-shovel. Still, if this question could be decided by a majority of voices, no doubt would remain that there actually was a kind of organ, called *magrepha*, in the temple.

---

[8] Ueber die Musik der alten Hebräer, von A. F. Pfeiffer, Erlangen, 1779, p. 52.

[9] Geschichte und Würdigung der Musik bei den Hebräern, von J. L. Saalschütz, Berlin, 1829, p. 131.

Of the real nature of this instrument, and the Assyrian *sumphonia*, perhaps some idea may be formed from a kind of bagpipe,—a syrinx with bellows (fig. 93),—which has been found represented on one of the ancient terra-cottas excavated in Tarsus, Asia Minor, by Mr. W. Burckhardt Barker. These remains are believed to be about 2000 years old, judging from the figures upon them, and from coins struck about

Fig. 93.
Ancient bagpipe from Tarsus, Cilicia.

200 years B.C. having been found embedded with them. We have therefore before us probably the oldest representation of a bagpipe hitherto discovered. "The instrument," Mr. Barker says, "consists of a vertical row of pipes, the length unknown, as the lower portion is wanting; they are inserted into a small air-chest, which appears inflated in the middle part. The right hand is operating upon it with a kind of cushion or compress, by which the player forces the air into the pipes, and which he seems to apply to different parts at will. There appears to have been a prolongation of the central part of the instrument across the left arm: the loss of this is much to be lamented, as that would have shown us more of its construction, and also how the left hand was employed in playing it. It is firmly fixed to the body; but the upper ends of the reeds are too low for the performer to blow into them with his mouth. The openings in the tops of

the reeds are all perfect; nothing is deficient at that
end. This may be looked upon as the very first application of a pneumatic chest to the Pandean organ,
which still retains its place on the breast of the player,
though he no longer operates upon it with his mouth.
It is most desirable to restore this figure; we should
then see whether the left hand or the foot was employed to blow the air into the machine."[1]

NEBEL AND NOFRE.

A change of the liquid consonants *r* and *l*, one into
the other, is by no means uncommon, and occurs in
the English language, for instance, in the word *colonel.*
Philologists have ascertained that in one of the Coptic
dialects, called Bashmuric, the letter *r* was pronounced
as *l.* The change of *b* into *v* or *f,* and *vice versâ,* is
yet more usual. Even without these known facts,
we may rely on the opinion of Dr. Birch, who has informed me that the word *nebel,* or *neble,* is identical
with the word *nofre* of the ancient Egyptians. Now,
with the *nofre* we are well acquainted. We know
that it was a kind of guitar, closely resembling the
modern tamboura of the East. It would thus appear
that the Hebrews derived the *nebel* originally from
Egypt, and that those commentators on the Hebrew
text of the Bible, who surmise this instrument to have
been a kind of guitar, are most likely right.

One objection, however, may be raised against this
opinion. We find in Psalms xxxiii. 2 and cxliv. 9,

---

[1] Cilicia and its Governors, by W. B. Barker, London, 1853, p. 260.

the asor mentioned as a ten-stringed nebel. Such a number of strings, however, could not have been placed on the nofre, or on any other instrument resembling the tamboura, on account of the narrowness of the neck.

I have already pointed out the impossibility of deciding upon the nature of unknown musical instruments from their names only. Supposing we were unacquainted with the *trumpet marine*, formerly a favourite instruments of the sailors, should we not, from its name, be led to conjecture that it must have been a kind of trumpet? It was, however, a stringed instrument played with a bow, on which sounds could be produced resembling those of the trumpet. Again, the Jew's harp (jaw's harp?) has no resemblance whatever to the harp. In German it is called *Maultrommel*, from which might be conjectured that it must be a kind of drum. Thus also the *nebel asor* may have been an instrument widely different from the *nofre*.

I am anxious to point out these uncertainties and doubts, because they have often been lost sight of in inquiries like the present. It is, however, only by considering them that we can hope to arrive at the truth.

THE HEBREW LYRE.

There appears to be a probability that a Hebrew lyre of the time of Joseph (about 1800 B.C.) is represented on an ancient Egyptian painting, discovered in a tomb at Beni Hassan—which is the name of certain grottoes on the eastern bank of the Nile. Sir

Gardner Wilkinson observes: "If, when we become
better acquainted with the interpretation of hieroglyphics, the 'strangers' at Beni Hassan should
prove to be the arrival of Jacob's family in Egypt,
we may examine the Jewish lyre drawn by an
Egyptian artist. That this event took place about
the period when the inmate of the tomb lived is
highly probable—at least, if I am correct in considering Osirtasen I. to be the Pharaoh the patron of
Joseph ; and it remains for us to decide whether the
disagreement in the number of persons here introduced—thirty-seven being written over them in hieroglyphics—is a sufficient objection to their identity.
It will not be foreign to the present subject to introduce those figures, which are curious, if only considered as illustrative of ancient customs at that early
period, and which will be looked upon with un-
bounded interest should they ever be found to refer
to the Jews. The first figure is an Egyptian scribe,
who presents an account of their arrival to a person
seated, the owner of the tomb, and one of the principal officers of the reigning Pharaoh. The next, also
an Egyptian, ushers them into his presence ; and two
advance, bringing presents, the wild goat or ibex,
and the gazelle, the productions of their country.
Four men, carrying bows and clubs, follow, leading
an ass on which two children are placed in panniers,
accompanied by a boy and four women ; and, last of
all, another ass laden, and two men—one holding a
bow and club, the other a lyre, which he plays with
the plectrum. All the men have beards, contrary to
the custom of the Egyptians, but very general in the
East at that period, and noticed as a peculiarity of
foreign uncivilized nations throughout their sculp-

tures. The men have sandals, the women a sort of boot reaching to the ankle—both which were worn by many Asiatic people. The lyre is rude, and differs a little in form from those generally used in Egypt."[2]

The accompanying figure is a copy of the player on the lyre, as represented in the engraving of the group of strangers, to which the description of Sir G. Wilkinson refers.

Again, the three bearded men with lyres in the Assyrian bas-relief described page 95 are by some

Fig. 94.
The supposed Hebrew lyre.

authorities on such questions supposed to represent Jewish captives. They certainly are in appearance and dress almost exactly like those figures on another Assyrian sculpture which Mr. Layard describes as Jewish Captives.[3] If further researches should confirm this opinion, the lyre in our engraving fig. 7 must be regarded not as an Assyrian, but as a Hebrew instrument. It belongs, however, to a period about a thousand years later than the lyre before mentioned.

How interesting the scene represented in woodcut fig. 95 will become, not only to the musician, but also to the archæologist, and indeed to every reflect-

---

[2] Manners and Customs of the Ancient Egyptians, by Sir Gardner Wilkinson, London, 1847, vol. ii. p. 296.

[3] Discoveries in the Ruins of Nineveh and Babylon, by A. H. Layard, London, 1853, p. 152.

ing reader of Scripture, should further investigation reveal to a certainty the captive minstrels before us to be Hebrews! How forcibly they present to our

Fig. 95. Captive Musicians playing on stringed instruments, supposed to be Jews.
(From a bas-relief in the British Museum).

mind the dejected captives who by the waters of Babylon, having hung their *kinnors* on the willows, sat down and gave vent to their grief!

The cross-bar of these lyres terminates in the head of a goose or duck. The bow of the warrior who

guards the captives is also ornamented in this way.
In fact, the head of an aquatic bird must have been a
common ornament with the Assyrians, since we find
it not unfrequently on implements and on chariots
represented in the bas-reliefs.   Still, it would be pre-
cipitate to conclude therefrom that these lyres must
be Assyrian instruments.   The sculptor may not im-
probably have applied to the Hebrew instrument the
favourite ornament of his country; or the Hebrews
may actually have used the same ornament, as also
the Egyptians did on their stringed instruments.   It
occurs, for instance, in the Egyptian trigonon, as seen
in woodcut fig. 35.

These lyres appear to have had four strings—a
number which, it will be remembered, was also usual
on the most ancient lyres of the Greeks.   Burney has
endeavoured to show that the latter were tuned in
the following order of intervals:—

thus forming a tetrachord.[4]   Other historians believe
the intervals to have been as follows:—

They are led to this conclusion principally by some
remarks of Boethius.   This series is certainly more
likely to have been in use than that mentioned by

---

4 See Burney's History of Music, vol. i. p. 278.

Burney; for the lyre, if thus tuned, could be employed most effectually for accompanying the voice.
Besides, at the present day, the four-stringed instruments met with among different nations are generally
tuned in fifths or in fourths.

True, such an arrangement of intervals on the lyre
appears to be incompatible with the pentatonic scale;
but it should be born in mind that the lowest string
on instruments of this class does not necessarily represent the key-note or *tonic*.   On the four-stringed lyre
the second interval may very probably have been
usually the tonic of the songs for accompanying
which the instrument was chiefly used.   If this
were the case, the lowest note would have stood
to the tonic in a relation equivalent to that of the
fifth.

This view is much strengthened by facts met with
among various nations whose degree of musical cultivation at the present day is nearly on a par with that
attained by most of the ancient nations.   On the
Nubian lyre, for instance, the first string is tuned a
fifth from the second string, which has the principal
interval or tonic of the songs.   (See the musical notation, page 158.)   The Arabs have at present a
system of intervals in which not the first note, *d,* but
the fourth, *g,* is the principal one.

DIATONIC SCALE OF THE ARABS.

X

Further, it is worthy of consideration that such a series of *fourths* or of *fifths* as we know with certainty to have been in use among ancient nations —the Chinese, for instance, according to Amiot, had adopted at a very early period a system of fifths, and the Greeks had, as is well known, combinations of tetrachords—that such a series of *fourths* or of *fifths* exhibits at first the intervals of the pentatonic scale, and after these those of the diatonic scale.

PENTATONIC SCALE.

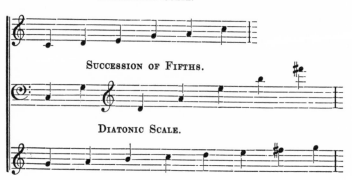

SUCCESSION OF FIFTHS.

DIATONIC SCALE.

PENTATONIC SCALE.

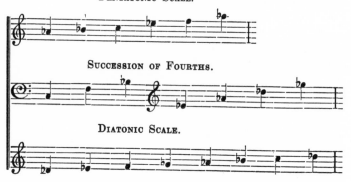

SUCCESSION OF FOURTHS.

DIATONIC SCALE.

Even the two intervals of a fourth on the four-
stringed lyre, which are in the compass of two disjunct tetrachords —

lead, if continued in the same order, first to the
intervals of the pentatonic scale :—

PENTATONIC SCALE.

DISJUNCT FOURTHS.

DIATONIC SCALE.

These facts are pointed out partly with the object
of showing the probability that the Greek system of
tetrachords also was an offspring of the pentatonic
system; but more especially because they afford, in
my opinion, additional indications of the closest
affinity having originally existed between the different musical systems of the Eastern nations.

Further, we have a representation of the lyre on
some Hebrew coins generally ascribed to Simon
Maccabæus, who lived in the second century before
the Christian era. There are five of them in the
x 2

British Museum; two are of silver, and the others of copper. On three of them are lyres with three strings; another has one with five, and another one

Fig. 96.   Hebrew coins with the lyre.

with six strings. The body of the lyre appears in two different shapes, as shown in the engraving fig. 96, which exhibits the three copper coins which are in the British Museum.

The arrangement of intervals on the five-stringed and six-stringed lyre does not require, after what has been already ascertained, any further explanation. The two sides of the frame appear to have been made of the horns of animals, or they may have been of wood formed in imitation of two horns, which originally were used. Lyres thus constructed are still found in Abyssinia. The traveller Bruce states that formerly they were made of the horns of a kind of goat called Agazān, about the size of a small cow, and common in the province of Tigré. He saw in that country several of these lyres "elegantly made of such horns, which nature seems to have shaped on purpose." He says: "After fire-arms became common in the province of Tigré, and the woods were cut down, this animal being more scarce, the lyre has been made of a light red wood. However, it is always cut into a spiral twisted form, in imitation of the ancient materials of which the lyre was composed."[5]

This shape is also usual in the representations of the various Greek lyres; and it may be recognised in a fragment of the actual instrument deposited in the British Museum. This interesting relic was found in a tomb near Athens. The two pieces constituting the frame are of wood. Their length is about 18 inches, and the length of the cross-bar at the top is about 9 inches. The instrument is, however, in a condition too dilapidated and imperfect to be of any essential use to the musical inquirer.

The three-stringed lyre was most probably tuned in the following order of intervals :—

These notes are the lowest of the *harmonics* emitted by a vibrating string, and the first of the *natural tones* produced on a tube like the trumpet or horn. Besides, they are especially suited for accompanying songs or recitations—an object for which the three-stringed lyre must have been principally employed, since it was too limited in the number of its tones to be of material use as a solo-instrument.

Almost all the three-stringed and two-stringed instruments still found in the East are tuned either in *fifths* or in *fourths*. It ought to be remembered that these two intervals are nearly related, in so far as the *fourth* is an inverted *fifth*, and the *fifth* an inverted

5 Burney's History of Music, vol. i. p. 209.

fourth. The two strings of the Arabian *kemangeh* are tuned thus—

The Chinese two-stringed fiddle, *urh-heen,* is tuned in the interval of a *fifth.* The three strings of the Chinese guitar, *san-heen,* are, according to Tradescant Lay, "tuned as fourths to each other." The Japanese *samsien,* a kind of guitar with three strings, is tuned, according to Meijlan, as follows:—

All these instruments have a neck by means of which the intermediate notes can be produced. Instruments with only three unalterable strings, like the above Hebrew lyre, are no longer in use in the East.

The reasons which can be given in support of the opinion that *kinnor* denotes the Hebrew lyre are certainly far from conclusive; still, they appear to be deserving of consideration. The lyre was evidently an universally-known and favoured instrument among ancient Eastern nations. Being much more simple in construction than most other stringed instruments, it undoubtedly preceded them in antiquity. The *kinnor* is mentioned in the Bible as the oldest stringed instrument, and as the invention of Jubal. Even if the name of one particular stringed instrument is here used for stringed instruments in general, which

may possibly be the case, it is only reasonable to
suppose that the oldest and most universally-known
stringed instrument would be mentioned as a repre-
sentative of the whole class rather than any other.
Besides, the *kinnor* was a light and very portable
instrument: King David, according to the Rabbinic
records, used to suspend it during the night over his
pillow. All its uses mentioned in the Bible are especially applicable to the lyre. And the resemblance
of the word *kinnor* to *kithara*, *kissar*, and similar
names known to denote the lyre, also tends to confirm the opinion that it refers to this instrument or to
a kind of trigonon.

VOCAL AND INSTRUMENTAL PERFORMANCES.

With the nature of the Hebrew musical performances we are more accurately acquainted than
with the instruments. Moreover, it is evident from
the Biblical records that the Hebrews had various
kinds of sacred and secular musical compositions,
differing according to the occasions on which they
were employed. To enter into a detailed description
of them would transgress the limits prescribed by the
object of the present essay. The following short
summary will suffice for our purpose.

Sacred Music in Divine Worship was evidently regarded as of the highest importance by the Hebrews.
The number of musicians engaged in the Temple in
the reign of King David is stated to have been four
thousand: "And four thousand praised the Lord
with instruments which I made, said David, to praise

therewith (1 Chron. xxiii. 5). An enumeration of
the whole band is given 1 Chron. xxv., from which
we learn that it consisted of two hundred and eighty-
eight well-practised members, described as "cunning"
in their profession; the rest, making up the number
of four thousand, appear to have been pupils and
occasional assistants of the former.

In the solemn musical performances in the processions conveying the ark, the three principal con-
ductors of the band, Heman, Asaph, and Ethan,
"were appointed to sound with cymbals of brass"
(1 Chron. xv. 19). These "cymbals" (*metzilthaim*)
were most likely a kind of castanets, perhaps resembling the *crotala* of the ancient Egyptians before
mentioned, with the rhythmical sounds of which the
leaders indicated the time and directed the performance.

In 2 Sam. vi. 5 we read: "And David and all
the house of Israel played before the Lord on all
manner of instruments made of fir-wood, even on
harps, and on psalteries, and on timbrels, and on
cornets, and on cymbals." The occasion on which
this combination of instruments was employed was
the conveyance of the ark. The same band is described somewhat differently in 1 Chron. xiii. 8,
where singing is mentioned with the accompaniment
of harps, psalteries, timbrels, cymbals, and trumpets.
This suggests the probability that in some of the
descriptions of Hebrew bands occurring in the Bible,
some instruments—perhaps those which were considered as of minor importance—may have been
left entirely unnoticed, and that therefore the bands,
on some occasions, consisted of a greater number

of different instruments than would appear from the accounts.

Grand, but to our ears painfully loud, must have been the performance which assisted at the solemn dedication of Solomon's Temple: "Also the Levites which were the singers, all of them of Asaph, of Heman, of Jeduthun, with their sons and their brethren, being arrayed in white linen, having cymbals, and psalteries, and harps, stood at the east end of the altar, and with them an hundred and twenty priests sounding with trumpets: It came even to pass, as the trumpeters and singers were as one, to make one sound to be heard in praising and thanking the Lord; and when they lifted up their voice with the trumpets and cymbals and instruments of music, and praised the Lord, saying, For he is good; for his mercy endureth for ever: that then the house was filled with a cloud, even the house of the Lord: so that the priests could not stand to minister by reason of the cloud; for the glory of the Lord had filled the house of God" (2 Chron. v. 12, 13, 14).

Sacred Songs and instrumental compositions, which probably were performed also in family circles, are alluded to in the Bible in a few instances only: "Ye shall have a song, as in the night when a holy solemnity is kept; and gladness of heart, as when one goeth with a pipe to come into the mountain of the Lord, to the mighty One of Israel" (Isaiah xxx. 29). "Though ye offer me burnt offerings and your meat offerings, I will not accept them: neither will I regard the peace offerings of your fat beasts. Take thou away from me the noise of thy songs, for I will not hear the melody of thy viols" (Amos v. 22, 23).

"Is any among you afflicted? let him pray. Is any merry? let him sing psalms " (James v. 13).

Military Music, sacred as well as secular, was evidently considered a necessary requisite in warlike exploits. When Jehoshaphat went to battle against the hosts of Ammon, Moab, and Seir, he placed a choir of singers in the front of his army: "And when he had consulted with the people he appointed singers unto the Lord, that should praise the beauty of holiness, as they went out before the army, and to say, Praise the Lord; for his mercy endureth for ever" (2 Chron. xx. 21).

An instance of the powerful effect of the trumpet upon the Hebrews, in encouraging them on the battle-field, is recorded 2 Chron. xiii. 12, 14; and a peculiar use made of this instrument in war occurs on occasion of the capture of Jericho: "And seven priests shall bear before the ark seven trumpets of rams' horns: and the seventh day ye shall compass the city seven times, and the priests shall blow with the trumpets. And it shall come to pass that when they make a long blast with the ram's horn, and when ye hear the sound of the trumpet, all the people shall shout with a great shout" (Josh. vi. 4, 5). Another peculiar employment of the trumpet in war occurs in the stratagem of Gideon (Judg. vii.), in which three hundred trumpets were used by the warriors.

Triumphal Songs, as well as instrumental performances, usually of a sacred character, celebrating a victory over the enemy, are also frequently alluded to in the Biblical records. Such, for instance, were the song of Moses and Miriam, in which the children

of Israel joined in chorus (Exod. xv.), and the song of
Deborah and Barak (Judg. v.). True, we do not find
it recorded that the last-mentioned song was performed with instrumental accompaniments and dances,
like other songs of the same description; still, there
can scarcely be a doubt that this was the case. David,
after his return from the slaughter of the Philistine,
was greeted with vocal and instrumental music
(1 Sam. xviii. 6); and musical performances of a
similar character are those of Jephthah's daughter
and her companions (Judg. xi. 34); of Jehoshaphat
and his people, on returning from a successful expedition to Jerusalem (2 Chron. xx. 27, 28); and of
Judith and the women, after the death of Holofernes
and the defeat of the Assyrians. The description of
the last-mentioned musical performance, occurring in
one of the apocryphal books, is remarkably illustrative
of Eastern customs, and reminds one forcibly of some
of the ancient Egyptian and Assyrian representations of such performances :—"Then all the women
of Israel ran together to see her [Judith], and blessed
her, and made a dance among them for her : and she
took branches in her hand, and gave also to the
women that were with her. And they put a garland
of olive upon her and her maid that was with her,
and she went before all the people in the dance,
leading all the women : and all the men of Israel
followed in their armour with garlands, and with
songs in their mouths. Then Judith began to sing
this thanksgiving in all Israel, and all the people sang
after her this song of praise. And Judith said,
Begin unto my God with timbrels, sing unto my
Lord with cymbals : tune unto him a new psalm :

exalt him, and call upon his name," &c. (Judith xv.
12, 13; xvi. 1, 2).

Erotic Songs are alluded to in the title of Psalm xlv.,
"To the chief musician upon Shoshannim, for the
sons of Korah, Maschil, a Song of Loves;" and in
Isaiah v. 1, "Now will I sing to my wellbeloved a
song of my beloved touching his vineyard."

Music at bridal processions was probably as usual as
it is at the present day in the East. The prophet
Jeremiah alludes to it in the following passage:—
"Then will I cause to cease from the cities of
Judah, and from the streets of Jerusalem, the voice
of mirth, and the voice of gladness, the voice of the
bridegroom, and the voice of the bride: for the land
shall be desolate" (Jerem. vii. 34).

Funeral Songs and instrumental performances of
doleful music at funerals, combined with lamentations,
processions in the streets, and characteristic wailings,
were also evidently as common as they are at this day
in Asia Minor and in Egypt. Compare, for instance,
the following passages:—

"And Jeremiah lamented for Josiah; and all the
singing men and the singing women spoke of Josiah
in their lamentations to this day, and made them an
ordinance in Israel: and behold they are written in
the Lamentations" (2 Chron. xxxv. 25).

"Man goeth to his long home, and the mourners go
about the streets" (Eccl. xii. 5).

"Yet hear the word of the Lord, O ye women, and
let your ear receive the word of his mouth, and teach
your daughters wailing, and every one her neighbour
lamentation" (Jerem. ix. 20).

"Therefore the Lord, the God of hosts, the Lord,

saith thus: Wailing shall be in all streets, and they
shall say in the highways, Alas! alas! and they shall
call the husbandman to mourning, and such as are
skilful of lamentation to wailing" (Amos v. 16).
Compare also St. Matt. ix. 23.

When king Saul and his son Jonathan, David's
friend, had fallen in battle, David vented his grief in
a touching elegy (2 Sam. i. 19), in which occurs
three times the sentence, "How are the mighty
fallen!" which suggests the probability that these
words were combined with a certain melodious
phrase of the nature of the refrain in some of our
songs.

Popular Secular Songs are found in every nation,
whatever may be its stage of musical development.
There can therefore be no doubt that the Hebrews
must have possessed this kind of music also. Allusion is made in Isaiah xvi. 10 to the songs of the
vintners: "And gladness is taken away, and joy out
of the plentiful field ; and in the vineyards there
shall be no singing, neither shall there be shouting:
the treaders shall tread out no wine in their press; I
have made their vintage shouting to cease." Compare also Jerem. xlviii. 33.

Convivial Songs, as well as instrumental performances and dances, entertained the guests at banquets
and other social festivities. They are alluded to in
Isaiah xxiv. 8, 9:—"The mirth of tabrets ceaseth, the
noise of them that rejoice endeth, the joy of the harp
ceaseth. They shall not drink wine with a song."
The injunction to the master of an entertainment,
"Pour not out words where there is a musician, and
show not forth wisdom out of time" (Ecclus. xxxii.

1, 4), would indicate that music was at least as much esteemed as at the present time, where this rule is not always observed. The custom of celebrating a happy event with music and feasting is alluded to in the parable of the Prodigal Son (St. Luke xv. 25).

In denouncing the debaucheries into which the feasts sometimes degenerated, the prophets also inveigh against the misuse of music on such occasions. "Woe unto them," exclaims Isaiah, "that rise up early in the morning, that they may follow strong drink; that continue until night, till wine inflame them! And the harp, and the viol, the tabret, and pipe, and wine, are in their feasts" (Isaiah v. 11, 12). The prophet Amos censures the ignoble use made of music by voluptuaries "that lie upon beds of ivory, and stretch themselves upon their couches, and eat the lambs of the flock, and the calves out of the midst of the stall; that chant to the sound of the viol, and invent to themselves instruments of music, like David" (Amos vi. 4, 5).

Performances of itinerant musicians were probably common in the streets of the towns. Female musicians are mentioned by Isaiah as performing in the streets, and, perhaps, more frequently in houses for the entertainment of parties, like those seen in some of the ancient Egyptian representations, or like the Hindoo Bayadères, and the Almeh girls of modern Egypt; but their musical accomplishments, whatever they may have been, appear, unfortunately, to have been superior to their moral character. "And it shall come to pass in that day that Tyre shall be forgotten seventy years, according to the days of one king: after the end of seventy years shall Tyre sing as an harlot. Take an harp, go about the city, thou harlot that hast been forgotten; make sweet melody, sing many songs, that thou mayest be remembered" (Isaiah xxiii. 15, 16). Such a class of musicians must Jesus the son of Sirach have had in his thought when he gave the advice, "Use not much the company of a woman that is a singer, lest thou be taken with her attempts" (Ecclus. ix. 4).

Two historical facts are specially remarkable as showing the power of Hebrew music, and how fully it was appreciated. These are, its application as a cure in nervous disorders, and its employment as a means of stimulating the inspirations of the prophets. When King Saul became afflicted with attacks of a nervous malady, his attendants suggested to him, "Let our lord now command thy servants which are before thee, to seek out a man who is a cunning player on a harp : and it shall come to pass, when the evil spirit from God is upon thee, that he shall play with his hand, and thou shalt be well." And we know that the anticipated effect was realised : "And it came to pass, when the evil spirit from God was upon Saul, that David took an harp, and played with his hand : so Saul was refreshed, and was well, and the evil spirit departed from him (1 Sam. xvi. 16, 23). And this was repeated until Saul's affliction became too severe to yield any longer to the beneficial influence of music.

Referring to the power of prophesying evoked by music, several instance might be cited; one, however, will be sufficient. Elisha being required by the kings of Israel, Judah, and Edom, to prophesy before them, his request was for a musician : "But now

bring me a minstrel. And it came to pass when the
minstrel played, that the hand of the Lord came upon
him. And he said, Thus saith the Lord, Make this
valley full of ditches," &c. (2 Kings iii. 15).

Although we possess no such records of the power
of Assyrian and ancient Egyptian music, there can
scarcely be a doubt that it was similarly effective.
Indeed, the fact of musical performances being considered essential requisites in important and solemn
celebrations, as is evident from the monumental representations, in some measure proves this. Neither can
there be a doubt that the effect of music upon the
human heart must have been in ancient times quite as
powerful as it is in our own day.

I have stated already the reasons which tend to the
conclusion that the ancient nations were not so entirely
unacquainted with harmony as is generally supposed.
True, we read in 2 Chron. v. 13, of a musical performance on a certain occasion in the Temple of Jerusalem : "It came even to pass as the trumpeters and
singers were *as one*, to make *one sound* to be heard in
praising and thanking the Lord." This passage is
usually cited in support of the opinion that the musical performances of the Hebrews must have been
in *unison*. Might not, however, rather the opposite
conclusion be drawn from it ? Taking for granted
that a performance in unison is here really meant, is
it at all likely that it would have been specially
recorded if no other mode of combining the voices
and instruments had been known ?

Some hints respecting the character of the musical
performances of other nations adjacent to the Hebrews,
beside the Assyrians, are also transmitted to us in

the Bible. Laban reproaches Jacob: "Wherefore didst thou flee away secretly, and steal away from me; and didst not tell me, that I might have sent thee away with mirth and with songs, with tabret and with harp?" (Gen. xxxi. 27). Laban, who lived about B.C. 1700, was a Syrian. Again, in the book of Job, who is supposed to have dwelt in Arabia B.C. 1500, mention is made of three different instruments in combination, rendered in the English authorized version, "They take the timbrel and harp, and rejoice at the sound of the organ" (Job xxi. 12). The "organ" is the Hebrew *ugab*, which, as we have seen, appears to have been nothing more than a kind of Pandean pipe.

The prophet Ezekiel, while threatening Tyre with destruction, adverts incidentally to the music of the Phœnicians: "And I will cause the noise of thy songs to cease; and the sound of the harps shall be no more heard" (Ezek. xxvi. 13). Perhaps also the passage in Isaiah xxiii. 15, 16, which has already been quoted, may refer especially to certain musical performances common among the Phœnicians. Further, it must be remembered that some of the ancient writers ascribe to the Phœnicians the invention of the *kinnor*, the *trigonon*, and several other of the most remarkable instruments of antiquity.

All that can be gathered from such scanty records tends to strengthen the conclusion previously arrived at, that the principal characteristics of the music in all those nations must have been very much the same. In the ten-stringed instruments mentioned in the Bible we have additional indications of the pentatonic scale at the time of David. Combinations of

Y

various instruments, in performances like those of the
Hebrew and Assyrian, undoubtedly were in use in
Phœnicia and in other countries of Western Asia, also
at an early period.   In reference to the antiquity of
the Egyptian bands, Sir Gardner Wilkinson observes:
"In the earliest sculptures, which are those in the
tomb of an individual behind the Great Pyramid,
between three and four thousand years old, is a
concert of vocal and instrumental music, consisting of
two harps, a pipe, a flute, and several voices; and
during the reigns of the Pharaohs of the eighteenth
dynasty, other combinations frequently occur."[6]   The
Hebrew performances, though similar to these, were
apparently more rude; noisy instruments of percussion and loud wind-instruments, such as the small
trumpet, being usually employed, often in great
numbers, even in Divine worship.   The rudeness of
the Hebrew performances at the time of Moses is
indicated in the conversation between Joshua and
Moses, when the former mistook them for a "noise of
war in the camp;" so that Moses found it necessary
to inform him, "It is not the voice of them that shout
for mastery, neither is it the voice of them that cry
for being overcome: but the noise of them that sing
do I hear" (Exod. xxxii. 18).   The Hebrews evidently
retained their predilection for loud and noisy performances, even after they had made considerable progress
in the cultivation of music.

Considering that it was the vocation of the Levites
to engage in the musical portion of the religious ser-

---

[6] The Manners and Customs of the Ancient Egyptians, by Sir G.
Wilkinson, London, 1847, vol. ii. p. 306.

vices, and that they evidently had ample leisure for
the cultivation of music, it appears highly probable
that they studied this art scientifically as well as
practically. We may therefore suppose that the
Hebrews possessed written treatises on the theory of
music, as well as institutions for the practice of the
different branches of vocal and instrumental music.
They had, as the Bible informs us, schools of the
prophets in various places, in which music appears
to have been taught systematically. One of these
establishments it would appear was at Bethel (1 Sam.
x. 5); another at Naioth, in Ramah (1 Sam. xix. 19,
20, 21); a third at Jericho (2 Kings ii. 5, 7); a
fourth at Gilgal (2 Kings iv. 38); and there was
most likely also one at Jerusalem (*vide* 2 Kings xxii.
14). King Solomon himself was a musical composer,
who undoubtedly had systematically studied the art
(1 Kings iv. 32).

HEBREW MUSIC OF THE PRESENT DAY.

Although the modern Jews cannot be said to possess
a national music of their own, they have retained
several characteristics in their musical performances
which unmistakeably indicate their Eastern origin.
This would scarcely have been possible under the
circumstance of their being so widely and thinly
dispersed among other nations, were it not for the
strictness with which they have always upheld their
prescribed religious rites and ceremonies in which
music is employed. They have, as we have seen,
even preserved one of their old Hebrew musical

instruments, the *shophar*. Moreover, the Jews in Germany possess several hymn-tunes undoubtedly of very high antiquity. Among these is a Penitential Hymn, with respect to which a tradition exists that it was composed by King David. The circumstance of its being somewhat differently sung in the synagogues of Northern Germany, from what it is in those of Southern Germany, speaks more in favour of, than against its antiquity. I shall insert here two readings of this melody; the first is my own notation from hearing it sung in Hamburg, and the second is transcribed from the collection ' Schir Zion,' used in the synagogues of Vienna :—

PENITENTIAL HYMN

AS SUNG IN THE SYNAGOGUES AT HAMBURG.

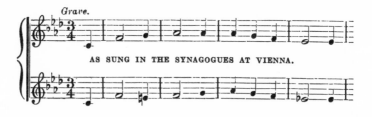

AS SUNG IN THE SYNAGOGUES AT VIENNA.

'Schir Zion' contains, besides compositions of comparatively modern origin, thirty-six ancient melodies; which, however sceptical we may be with respect to their asserted ancient Hebrew origin, are certainly in construction closely allied to the songs of the Arabs and Persians.

The ancient melody to the 'Blessing of the Priests' has been already noticed, page 114. De Sola observes: "A tradition exists with respect to the melody of the 'Blessing of the Priests,' that it is identical with that sung in the Temple, where, as it is known, the priestly choirs were daily wont to bless the people, agreeably to the command to them in Numbers vi. 22-26. That this tradition is supported by great probability, almost amounting to direct proof, will appear from the following considerations: First, that this duty devolved exclusively on the priests—who were a numerous class—who executed it with religious awe and attention, and who, as

a privilege peculiar to themselves, scrupulously transmitted it to their sons. It is therefore highly improbable that, on the restoration of public Divine service,
the priests should have used, or the people would
have permitted them to introduce, any other melody
except the venerated one of the Temple, especially as
the blessing of the people was the only act of ministra-
tion remaining to the priests after the destruction of
the sanctuary. Secondly, we find that, with slight
alteration, this blessing is sung to the same melody
in every Sephardic congregation. And though our
brethren, following the German Liturgy, have more
than one melody for it, they seem to be of comparatively modern introduction; and one of them, said to
be the most ancient, contains unmistakeable traces of
this, which we must consider to be the original
melody. Its simplicity and the repetition of the
same melody for all the words of the *Blessing* (fifteen
in number), are circumstances which will have due
weight, and will be accepted as additional and corroborative evidence for its antiquity by the musical
archæologist and critic.'[7]

Another favourite melody of the Jews, the 'Song
of Moses,' is asserted to be the same which Miriam
and her companions sang after the deliverance from
Pharaoh's host. De Sola gives the following arguments in favour of this opinion:—"According to
a very ancient Spanish work (printed, if I recollect
rightly, in Portugal), 'Some have affirmed that what
we now sing to the Song of Moses is the same

---

7 The Ancient Melodies of the Li-
turgy of the Spanish and Portuguese | Jews, by E. Aguilar and by the Rev
D. A. De Sola, London, 1857, p. 15.

melody which Miriam and her companions sung,' &c.
This legend would not merit any serious consideration
here, except that it undoubtedly proves that the knowledge of the origin of the melody was already long
lost when this ancient Spanish book was written.
And here, again, the acute remark of Dr. Sachs is
applicable, that 'Fable soon occupies itself to speak
where history is silent.' It is therefore highly probable that this melody belongs to a period anterior to
the regular settlement of the Jews in Spain. The
general adoption thereof by every congregation of
the Sephardic Liturgy furnishes also a strong proof
in favour of the high antiquity of its origin :"[8]—

THE SONG OF MOSES.

8 The Ancient Melodies of the | Portuguese Jews, by the Rev.
Liturgy of the Spanish and | D.A.De Sola, London, 1857, p. 16,

mo   mar - ke - bot   Parngho   ve - che - lo   ya -

- ra . . ba - - yam   u - mib - char . . . sha - li -

- shav . tu - beng - u . . . . be - yam   suf.

This melody is, however, so modern in construction, that, if we are inclined to accept Mr. De Sola's views, we must yet remember that it has probably, in the course of time, undergone a transformation sufficient to make it appear almost another tune. The same remark applies, in my opinion, to all the melodies which are asserted to have been in use in the Temple at Jerusalem. Indeed, it may be doubted whether the ancient Hebrews, could they hear them, would now recognise any of them as their own.

Very different is it, however, with the musical performances in the synagogue. These, undoubtedly, have preserved the Oriental type. Thus the characteristic manner of singing, or rather chanting, with the introduction of embellishments—in short, the kind of singing which musicians call *cantillation*, and which may be heard in every synagogue—bears a close resemblance to certain vocal performances of the Arabs and Persians. A Chief Rabbi related to Dr. Burney, that, "being at Petersburgh some years since, the Grand Caliph of Persia was there likewise

on an embassy, and had the service of his religion
regularly performed in a kind of mosque fitted up in
the Czar's palace for his use. That when he first
heard this service performed he found the singing so
like that in the German synagogues that he thought
it had been done in derision of the Jews, and on that
account soon left it. But, upon inquiry, finding it to
be nothing more than the manner of singing common
in Persia, he concluded that the Persians had borrowed this kind of chant from the ancient Oriental
Jews."[9]

Even the peculiar swinging motion of the body,
usually accompanying the singing of the Jews in the
synagogue, which gradually increases with the increasing fervour of the singers, reminds us of the
East. In Egypt, Mr. Lane states, "all the boys, in
learning to read, recite or chant their lessons aloud, at
the same time rocking their heads or bodies incessantly
backwards and forwards; which practice is observed
by almost all persons in reciting the 'Kuran,' being
thought to assist the memory."[1]

If we were exactly acquainted with the musical
performances in the religious observances of the
various Jewish communities in different parts of the
world, we should probably be in a position to determine how much has been preserved since the dispersion
of the Jews after the destruction of the second temple.
Dr. Pickering, the ethnologist attached to the United
States Exploring Expedition, who divides the whole
Jewish family, as it exists at the present day, into
four classes,—viz., the Syrian, Indian, Arabian, and

---

9 Burney's History of Music,
i. 256.
1 An Account of the Manners | and Customs of the Modern
Egyptians, by E. W. Lane,
London, 1860, p. 60.

European,—observes that the Arabian Jews at Aden
have preserved more of the primitive Hebrew customs than any of their brethren elsewhere. Further,
ethnologists describe the Jews in China, Tartary,
and Hindoostan as having spread from early times
through these and other countries of Central and
Eastern Asia. Then, there is in Cochin, Malabar
coast, a colony of so-called White Jews, or Jerusalem Jews, which arrived in that country at a
later date than those of a dark complexion, known
as the Black Jews.[2] What interesting results might
the musical historian deduce from a comparison of
the sacred musical performances of the former with
those of the latter!

Respecting the Black Jews, a recent traveller
says: "Some few of them have a Hebrew cast of
countenance, but by far the greater number are indis-
tinguishable from the natives around. They are
considered by the White Jews as an inferior race,
and not of *pure* caste, and intermarriage between
them consequently never takes place. Their customs,
forms of prayer, songs, &c., are the same as those of
the White Jews, but they do not observe the same
strict Levitical ceremonies, and, having no legitimate
relationship with Hebrews in other lands, they are
looked upon, and pride themselves upon being, a
distinct sect."

Respecting the White Jews, the same writer says:
" Their costume does not at all resemble that of the
natives of India; and as the Jews say that it is the
same as that of their ancestors, there is reason to

---

[2] See The Natural History of Man, by J. C. Prichard, edited by
Edwin Norris, London, 1855, p. 131.

imagine, therefore, that it affords a correct idea of the dress of their sect at the commencement of the Christian era." The Feast of Tabernacles is celebrated by them with great solemnity. The women are in a screened gallery over the entrance of the synagogue. " The service commences with a chant and prayer; a portion of Scripture is read, or rather intoned, by the officiating Rabbi (who wears the Tallith or veil over his turban) ; and the impressive silent prayer follows. The people stand in groups facing the Books of the Law, and, with a constant flexion of the body and an occasional low prostration, hum the petitions very rapidly, and apparently with deep consideration. After some minutes the Rabbi gives the initiative, and they burst forth into a tumultuous, if not irreverent, chant, in performing which they distort their faces with zeal to make themselves heard. After a further pause the men proceed by turns to the end of the building, and with much show of respect kiss the silver cases enclosing the Books, and then the women descend and go through the same ceremony with most touching solemnity."[3]

In Jerusalem there are at the present day several distinct Jewish communities. Among these, the Sephardic, or that of the Spanish and Portuguese Jews, consisting of about 4000 in number, constitutes the largest. The Aschkenasim community consists of Jews from Germany, Holland, Russia, Poland, Bohemia, and other parts of Europe. They all understand the German language, of which they have created a

---

[3] British and Native Cochin, by C. A. L., Cochin, printed at the ' Courier' Press, by B. Fernandes, 1860, p.121.

strange dialect; while the Sephardic Jews, principally
derived from Egypt, Tunis, Tripoli, Morocco, Algiers,
India, and Persia, use the Spanish language. Besides
these, there are in Jerusalem some smaller separate
Hebrew communities, of which the Karaites must be
noticed from their having been resident in Jerusalem,
according to their own account, ever since the destruction of the Temple.   Dr. Frankl, who had ample
opportunity to witness the religious observances of
the Jews in this city, found the singing of the Sephardic Jews closely allied to that of the Arabs, "more
rhythmical than melodious, shrill rather than soft,
and closely bordering on snuffling."   Still, he preferred it to the singing of the Aschkenasim Jews,
consisting of a kind of cantillation, which is usually
called Polish singing.

The same traveller gives an account of the sum-
mons of the Jews in Jerusalem to morning prayer:
"When the oldest rabbi in the institution *Beth-el*, in
which the Talmud is studied the whole night, observes
the first dawn of early morn, he despatches a messen-
ger to the roof of the institution, which commands an
extensive view towards the east.   There he announces
in a loud voice, like the muezzin of the Mohammedans
from the minarets, that it is the hour for prayer.   The
commencement of the Sabbath is announced to the
Sephardim by the cry, 'Ascender' ('Light up'),
and immediately thousands of windows are illumi-
nated, and from the synagogue is heard the fervent
salutation, *Lecho Daudi, likras kalo!*"[4]

---

[4] The Jews in the East, translated from the German of Dr.
Frankl, by the Rev. P. Beaton, London, 1859, vol. ii. p. 62.

Dr. Frankl, having been invited, during his stay in
Jerusalem, to a Jewish wedding, was, on his arrival,
entertained with the musical performance of some
young Jewesses, who were singing an Arab song,
striking at the same time tambourines, to which bells
were attached. In the course of the entertainment,
several young girls performed dances to their own
singing, while the admiring male spectators produced
a rhythmical accompaniment by clapping their hands.
The girls never formed a group; each danced singly.
When a Jewish marriage procession passes through
the streets of Jerusalem, the chanting of the men is
at intervals accompanied by the shrill *Zaghareet* of
the young Jewesses who escort the bride.

O   Zag - - - ha - reet.

During the procession of a Jewish funeral in Jerusalem, Dr. Frankl heard the bearers sing the Psalm,
"He that dwelleth in the sacred place of the Most
High shall abide under the shadow of the Almighty."
On the roof of the house out of which the body had
been removed stood female mourners covered with
long white veils, and singing. As they stretched
out their hands towards heaven, they looked, says
Dr. Frankl, "like the dead risen from their graves in
their white winding-sheets, and chanting a death-song
in wild unearthly chorus." Another peculiar ceremony is the wailing at the wall which formerly
surrounded the Temple at Jerusalem, part of which

is yet standing. Here the Jews assemble every
Friday to express in prayers and songs their affliction
for the destruction of the Sanctuary. Dr. Frankl
relates: "The Jews have a *firman* from the Sultan,
which, in return for a small tax, ensures them the
right of entrance for all time to come. The road conducted us to several streets, till, entering a narrow,
crooked lane, we reached the wall, which has been
often described. There can be no doubt but the
lower part of it is a real memorial of the days of Solomon, which, in the language of Flavius Josephus, is
'immovable for all time.' Its Cyclopic proportions
produce the positive conviction that it will last as long
as the strong places of the earth. Before we reached
the wall we heard a sort of howling melody, a passionate shrieking, a heartrending wailing, like a chorus,
from which the words came sobbing forth, 'How long
yet, O God?' Several hundreds of Jews, Turkish
and Polish costumes, were assembled, and, with their
faces turned towards the wall, were bending and
bowing as they offered up the evening prayer. He
who led their devotions was a young man in a Polish
talar, who seemed to be worn out with passion and
disease. The words were those of the well-known
Mincha prayer, but drawled, torn, shrieked, and mum-
bled in such a way that the piercing sound resembled
rather the raging frenzy of chained madmen, or the
roaring of a cataract, than the worship of rational
beings. At a considerable distance from the men
stood about a hundred women, all in long white robes,
the folds of which covered the head and the whole
figure—white doves, which, weary of flight, had
perched upon the ruins. When it was their turn to

offer up the usual passages of the prayer, they joined the men's tumultuous chorus, and raised their arms aloft, which, with their wide robes, looked like wings with which they were about to soar aloft into the open sky; and then they struck their foreheads on the square stones of the wall of the temple. Meanwhile, if the leader of their prayers grew weary, and leaned his head against the wall in silent tears, for a moment there was a death-like silence. I happened to be near him, and I could mark the sincerity of his agitated soul. He gave a rapid glance at me, and, without stopping short in his prayer, said to me, '*Mokem Kodesch*' (*i.e.* 'holy place'), and pointed to my covered feet. My guide had forgotten to inform me that I must take off my shoes. I now did so, and was drawn into the vortex of raging sorrow and lamentation."[5]

The Hon. Robert Curzon, while in Jerusalem, went on the morning of the day of the Passover into the synagogue under the walls of the Temple. He found a numerous congregation, standing up, with large white shawls over their heads, reading the Psalms. He says: "After I had been there a short time, all the people began to hop about and to shake their heads and limbs in a most extraordinary manner; the whole congregation was in motion, from the priest who was standing in the reading-desk to the porter who capered at the door. All this was in consequence of a verse in the 35th Psalm, which says, 'All my bones shall say, Lord, who is like unto thee?'"[6]

---

5 The Jews in the East, vol. ii. p. 12.
6 Visits to Monasteries in the Levant, by the Hon. Robert Curzon, London, 1850, p. 172.

The traveller Burckhardt, in speaking of the Jews
of Tabaria, or Tiberias, in Palestine, who constitute
about one-fourth of the population of that town, says:
"They observe a singular custom here in praying.
While the Rabbin recites the Psalms of David, or the
prayers extracted from them, the congregation frequently imitate by their voice or gestures the meaning
of some remarkable passages; for example, when the
Rabbin pronounces, 'Praise the Lord with the sound
of the trumpet,' they imitate the sound of the trumpet
through their closed fists. When a 'horrible tempest'
occurs, they puff and blow to represent a storm; or
should he mention 'the cries of the righteous in dis-
tress,' they all set up a loud screaming; and it not
infrequently happens that, while some are still blowing the storm, others have already begun the cries
of the righteous, thus forming a concert which it is
difficult for any but a zealous Hebrew to hear with
gravity."[7]

Alexander Russell mentions that in Aleppo it is
the custom of the Jews on their Sabbath to remain a
considerable time at table singing in chorus, very
much in the same manner as they chant the Psalms
in the synagogue.[8] Also, the Jews in Poland and
Galicia appear to adapt their sacred chants, at banquets, to secular words. The traveller Kohl, when
strolling at midnight through the streets of Stanis-
lawow, a small town in Galicia, was surprised to hear
from a wine-house a chorus of male voices, which

---

[7] Travels in Syria and the
Holy Land, by the late J. L.
Burckhardt, London,1822,p.326.

[8] The Natural History of
Aleppo, by Alex. Russell,
London, 1794, vol. i. p. 63.

appeared to him exactly like the usual chanting of
the Psalms of David in the services of the synagogue.
Having entered the wine-house, he found a picturesque-
looking company of Jews, with fine black beards,
dressed in long black silk *talars*, who were drinking
and singing with all their might.[9]

With the music of the Jews in Syria we are but
superficially acquainted. Dr. Frankl, during his
sojourn in Damascus, was invited to a feast given by
Rafael Stambini, the wealthiest Jew in that place, in
honour of Baron Alphonso von Rothschild, who had
come on a visit from Jerusalem. On this occasion,
as soon as four instrumental performers, playing a
kind of hautbois called *zourna*, the drum, the tambourine, and cymbals, had concluded their extraordinary *quartetto*, the musical entertainment was continued
by a vocal performance in the manner which, Dr.
Frankl observes, "is often scoffed at in the synagogues
of the West as Polish flourishing and snuffling." And
thus, also, was the singing of profane as well as religious songs in Hebrew, Arabic, and Spanish, which
Dr. Frankl heard on a Sabbath in the house of Mr.
Angelo Schemaja, another rich Jew, and the patron
of singers and musicians, in Damascus.[1]

In Egypt there are, according to Villoteau, two
different sects of Jews, strongly opposed to each other
in some of their religious doctrines and rites. The
Rabbanym follow the Rabbinical doctrine, while the
Karaym reject the authority of the Rabbins. Never-

---

[9] Reisen im Innern von Russ-
land und Polen, von J. G. Kohl,
Dresden, 1841, vol. iii. p. 51.

[1] The Jews in the East, vol.
i. p. 275.

theless, their sacred music is the same—a fact which
affords additional proof of the reverence with which
the Jews have preserved the music of their forefathers.
The chants of the Egyptian Jews are principally based
on the minor scale, with the introduction of a *superfluous second,—*

and it is remarkable that some of the ancient melodies
preserved by the German Jews, as given in 'Schir
Zion,' exhibit the same peculiarity, of which I shall
have to speak presently.

Villoteau gives the compass of the notes to which
the songs of the Egyptian Jews, which he heard,
were limited, as follows :—

It will be seen that if the lowest note, *g*, was the
tonic, the melody had a step of a *superfluous second*
from the *third* to the *fourth*—an order of intervals
which, as we shall presently see, is by no means uncommon in Eastern music of the present day. It is,
however, evident, to judge from the above example,
as well as from well-known theoretical laws, that the
interval *d* in the series must be usually taken as
the *tonic* of the melodies.

The Falashas, a kind of Hebrew sect in Abyssinia,

appear to have retained less of the ancient musical religious performances than their brethren in any other country. Even the blowing of the *shophar* at the Feast of Trumpets is not observed by them.[2] There appears, however, to be some doubt whether they can properly be considered as professing the Jewish faith. Dr. Latham observes : " The extent to which the Falashas exhibit a variety of customs common to themselves and the Jews has long been recognised. It by no means, however, follows that they are a result of Jewish influence. The criticism that applies to the Ghás [a negro tribe, Cape Coast, of well-marked Jewish characters in their religious and other ceremonies] applies here. Many of the so-called Jewish peculiarities are African as well, irrespective of intercourse and independent of imitation."[3]

The Jews in the Barbary States have undoubtedly adopted much from the Arabic music. The Rev. J. W. Blakesley mentions a Jewish custom, observed at Tunis on the 1st of May, on which occasion a kind of bower, composed of flowers and wax candles, is carried in procession to the synagogue, the people all the while chanting, and the females uttering the peculiar sound of *ly-ly-ly*, in the manner of the Mahommedan women at wedding and funeral processions. After the arrival of the singers at the synagogue, the whole building is decorated with flowers and the wax-tapers are lighted. The same traveller visited a synagogue in Algiers, and was surprised to find that " the air to

---

[2] Wanderings among the Falashas in Abyssinia, by the Rev. H. A. Stern, London, 1862, p. 190.

[3] The Natural History of the Varieties of Man by R. G. Latham, London, 1850, p. 500.

which the Psalms were chanted coincided almost
exactly with one of the Gregorian tones." The
ritual was in Hebrew, as in other countries, but
the Rabbins preached sometimes in Arabic. In
the town of Constantine he heard the chanting of
the Psalms in the synagogue occasionally accompanied by the ejaculation of *ly-ly-ly* of the women,
which reminded him of similar vocal performances
of the Libyan women mentioned by Heredotus, and
which appears, as we have seen, to have been also
an Assyrian custom.[4]

In Tangier, Mr. J. Cayley, being invited to a Jewish
wedding, found a company, including about thirty-six
young Jewesses, singing, clapping hands, and dancing to the sound of a *kemangeh*, played upon by the
Chief Rabbin, an old man with a long white beard. In
the course of this entertainment a curious ceremony
was introduced: the bridegroom, having been placed
in a chair in the middle of the room, was shaved in
the presence of the assemblage.[5] The Rev. T. Debary
relates that he witnessed at Tangier the festival of the
circumcision of a little Jew boy. During the time of
the ceremony Psalms were chanted. After its conclusion wine was offered to the company, and sprays
of myrtle were thrown among the people for
smelling.[6]

The Jews in Turkey also are divided into different
sects. In Constantinople, Dr. Frankl on a Sabbath

[4] Four Months in Algeria, by
the Rev. J. W. Blakesley, Cam-
bridge, 1859, p. 36.

[5] Lasalforjas, by G. J. Cayley,
London, 1853, vol. i. p. 238.

[6] Notes of a Residence in the
Canary Islands, the South of
Spain, and Algiers, by the Rev.
Thomas Debary, London, 1851,
p 254.

visited the synagogue Bene Hamikra, belonging to
the Karaites. "A handsome boy, about twelve years
of age, in a green caftan, with a red fez and yellow
slippers, walked up to the elevated table covered with
a beautiful carpet, which was brought into the middle
of the synagogue. He fell down on his knees, and,
like a Mussulman at prayers, touched the pavement
with his forehead, and then stood up and sang with a
beautiful clear voice a song of praise to God; the
congregation sang the concluding verse as a chorus.
The boy sang a similar song between the customary
bending of the knees and the head after the *thora*, a
book of parchment (there are no rolls among the
Karaites), had been read."[7]

The traveller Clarke witnessed in the town of
Simferopol (or Acmetchet), in the Crimea, a Jewish
wedding festival, which lasted several days, music and
dancing forming the principal entertainment. On the
day of marriage the bride was blindfolded, and led by
the priest, accompanied by her relations, to a river in
the neighbourhood of the town, and plunged three
times into the water. "After this, being again
dressed, she was led, blindfolded as before, to the
house of her parents, accompanied by all her friends,
who were singing, dancing, and performing music
before her. In the evening her intended husband
was brought to her; but as long as the feast continued
she remained with her eyes bound."[8]

Another curious ceremony, witnessed at the wed-

---

[7] The Jews in the East, vol.
i. p. 153.
[8] Travels in Various Countries, by E. D. Clarke, London,
1810, part i. p. 547.

ding of a rich Jew in the province of Podolia in Russia, is related in the Leipzic 'Musikalische Zeitung.' The band consisted of four Hebrews, playing on two violins, a dulcimer, and a violoncello. They commenced the performance with a soft and sentimental *adagio*, and gradually went on to louder and more passionate music; the object being so to touch the heart of the bridegroom as to make him cry before the whole company; since, according to an old custom, the bridegroom must have exhibited contrition for his former sins before he is permitted to marry. As soon as the musicians, assisted by the relations of the bridegroom, who implored him to endeavour to cry, had succeeded in moving him to tears, the whole company formed a procession to escort the happy pair to the nuptial ceremony.[9]

Blanchini, and after him other writers, have given, among the drawings of various Hebrew musical instruments, a small wooden mallet, which is still used in the synagogue at the Feast of Purim, instituted in commemoration of the deliverance of the Jews from the designs of Haman. On this occasion the book of Esther is chanted. Whenever the name of Haman occurs, the congregation exclaim in a chanting tone, "May his name perish!" at the same time striking the walls and benches with their wooden mallets; which, David Levi says, is done "as a memorial that they should endeavour to destroy the whole seed of Amalek." This ceremony, however, is gradually being discontinued in England, and observed in the

---

[9] Allgemeine Musikalische Zeitung, Jahrgang IV., Leipzig, 1802, p. 346.

22   Feb. 24   p. 363-4

synagogue by children only.[1] The hammer being classed with the musical instruments, suggests the probability that formerly a rhythmical accompaniment to the voice was produced with it, in a like manner as with musical instruments of percussion.

Padre Martini has published in his 'Storia della Musica,' a number of chants from synagogues in different European countries. Some of these must be at least three hundred years old, because the Padre copied them from a MS. collection made in the year 1599 by Ercole Bottrigari, a musical theorist of some renown. The specimens given by Burney, Forkel, and other historians, are most of them transcribed from Martini's work. Again, some interesting speci‑ mens of chants and tunes used in the synagogues of England are given in Nathan's 'Essay on the History and Theory of Music,' and in a collection recently published by Salaman and Verrinder, entitled, 'The Music used in the Services of the West London Synagogue of British Jews.'

A large and interesting collection of chants and songs, as performed in the synagogues of Königsberg in Prussia, entitled 'Schire Beth Adonai,' has recently been published, edited by H. Weintraub. It contains, besides modern compositions, several melodies which are said to be of high antiquity.

Mr. Weintraub observes, that the oldest and most universally used chants are generally in the *Phrygian* and *Mixolydian* Mode; and as the popular melodies of the Arabs, Turks, and some other Eastern nations of

---

[1] A Succinct Account of the Rites and Ceremonies of the Jews, by David Levi, London, 1783, p. 126.

the present day are frequently based upon similar orders of intervals, he concludes that these chants must have originated in the East. He points this out as affording strong evidence in support of the traditional belief of the Jews, that their old chants are the identical ones which were in use at the time when the Israelites sojourned in the Promised Land. I shall insert here one of them,—more for the purpose of showing their peculiarities, than with the expectation of gratifying the musical taste of the reader. This chant is considered by Mr. Weintraub as founded upon the Phrygian Mode. It concludes with a Chorus, which is sung in strict time, while the chant itself, which is intended for a tenor voice, partakes of the character of the Recitative :—

CHANT FROM THE SYNAGOGUE IN KÖNIGSBERG.

Most of these Chants are interspersed with short melodious phrases for the Chorus, in four-part harmony or in unison. It is to be regretted that the compilers of the collections do not indicate with exactness how much they have altered and added. By far the greater number of the Solos and Choruses appear to be their own compositions.

Dr. Burney relates that, when he was in Amsterdam, he betook himself to the synagogue of the German Jews, in order to ascertain how far the musical performances differed from those which he had heard during his travels on the Continent, in the synagogues of other towns. "At my first entrance one of the priests was chanting part of the service in a kind of ancient *canto fermo*, and responses were made by the congregation, in a manner which resembled the hum of bees. After this, three of the sweet singers of Israel, which, it seems, are famous here, and much attended to by Christians as well as Jews, began singing a kind of jolly modern melody, sometimes in unison, and sometimes in parts, to a kind of *tol de rol*, instead of words, which to me seemed very farcical. One of these voices was a falset, more like the upper part of a bad *vox humana* stop in an organ than a natural voice. I remember seeing an advertisement in an English newspaper, of a barber who undertook to dress hair in such a manner as exactly to resemble a peruque; and this singer might equally boast of having the art, not of singing like a human creature, but of making his voice like a very bad imitation of one. Of much the same kind is the merit of such singers who, in execution, degrade the voice into a flute or fiddle, forgetting that they should not receive law from instruments, but give instruments law. The second of these voices was a very vulgar tenor, and the third a *baritono*. This last imitated, in his accompaniment of the falset, a bad bassoon—sometimes continued one note as a drone base; at others, divided it into triplets and semiquavers iterated on the same tone. But though the tone of the falset was very disagreeable, and he forced his voice very frequently in an outrageous manner, yet this man had certainly heard good music and good singing. He had a facility of running divisions, and now and then mixed them with passages of taste, which were far superior to the rest. At the end of each strain the whole congregation set up such a kind of cry as a pack of hounds when a fox breaks cover. It was a confused clamour and a riorous noise, more than song or prayer. However, this is a description, not a censure, of Hebrew music in religious ceremonies. It is impossible for me to divine what ideas the Jews themselves annex to this vociferation; I shall, therefore, neither pronounce it to be good nor bad in itself; I shall only say that it is very unlike what we Christians are used to in Divine service."[2]

The same remark may still be applied to the vocal performances in many synagogues. In not a few instances, however, considerable reforms have been introduced. Indeed, some of the Rabbins have endeavoured to discontinue the *cantillation* altogether, and to adopt simple hymn tunes and part-singing instead. This, for instance, has been the aim of Dr. Abraham

---

[2] The Present State of Music in Germany, the Netherlands, &c., by Charles Burney, London, 1775, vol. ii. p. 299.

Wolff, in Copenhagen, as early as the beginning of this century.[3] Even the venerable tunes of the Protestant Church, the Chorales, have been made use of,[4] and are sung in some synagogues to the accompaniment of an organ—innovations which, on the Continent have contributed to divide the Jews into two parties, the reforming and conservative. The latter has all the more strictly adhered to the ancient mode of singing since the schism.·

It is remarkable that the great susceptibility and fondness for music which the ancient Hebrews evidently possessed have been preserved by their race until the present day. Many of our distinguished musicians, composers as well as *virtuosi*, are Jews, or of Jewish extraction. It would be easy to make out a long list of them; but I shall mention only three celebrated composers—Halévy, Meyerbeer and Mendelssohn.

The Jews, it must be remembered, are limited in their choice of occupation for gaining a subsistence, by their religious laws, as well as, in many countries, by civil laws. This may in some measure account for their so often choosing the art of music as a profession and means of livelihood. Their innate diligence and perseverance in carrying out any fixed plan would, however, not be sufficient for the attainment of those accomplishments in music by which they often distinguish themselves, did they not also possess extraordinary talent for this art. Some of them exhibit

---

[3] See Agende zum Gebrauche beim Israelitischen Gottesdienste von A. A. Wolff, Copenhagen, 1839.

[4] See Melodien zu dem Israelitischen Gesangbuche herausgegeben, von Dr. Kley, Hamburg, 1846. ·

in their compositions peculiarities which remind us of the synagogue. This is, in my opinion, also the case in the music of Mendelssohn, who, though a Christian, was of Hebrew origin. These peculiarities are more easily felt than described. They consist especially in the employment and frequent repetition of short melodious phrases, and passages of a peculiar rhythmical effect, frequently in Minor, and of a certain monotony, which Mendelssohn, however, knew how to render highly interesting by a skilful harmony. I shall insert here two examples of this kind, the first from Mendelssohn's ' Lieder ohne Worte,' book iii., No. 2 ; and the second from his Pianoforte Concerto in D Minor.

FROM MENDELSSOHN'S LIEDER OHNE WORTE.

FROM MENDELSSOHN'S CONCERTO IN D MINOR.

The following characteristic Hebrew song, consisting of *solo* and *chorus*, is taken from De Sola's Collection of the Melodies used in the synagogue of the Spanish and Portuguese Jews, harmonized by Aguilar. This fine composition might easily pass for Mendelssohn's, so much are his style and mannerism in accordance with it:—

ANA BEKORENU.

Mendelssohn has made use also of the pentatonic scale; and this he has done not only where he has adopted or imitated Scotch national melodies, but on other occasions. Thus, for instance, the introduction to ' Œdipus at Colonos ' he commences as follows:—

This example may also serve as a proof how well
the pentatonic series of intervals is suited to the
expression of simple dignity and solemnity. If
Mendelssohn was unaware of its early use among the
nations of antiquity, and if he did not purposely con-
template using it, which is quite possible, the fact of
his commencing with it the introductory chorus to a
classical work by Sophocles is to be considered perhaps all the more as a stroke of genius.

LITERATURE OF HEBREW MUSIC.

An enumeration of all the books which have been
written on Hebrew music would alone fill a large
chapter. Forkel has published in his ' Geschichte der
Musik,' vol. i. pp. 173 to 184, a list of the principal
ones printed before the year 1788. This list he has
extended in his ' Allgemeine Literatur der Musick,'
Leipzig, 1792, where he has adopted a classification
as follows: Works treating on Hebrew music in
all its branches—on the musical instruments of the
Hebrews—on the headings of the Psalms, and on
the terms relating to music which occur in the Psalms
—on the Hebrew accents considered as musical notation—on the music of the Temple—miscellaneous
works treating especially of Hebrew music.

Forkel points out that Le Long, in his ' Bibliotheca
Sacra,' published in the year 1723, has mentioned as
many as 1213 commentators on the Psalms alone;
and he thinks it probable that, during the sixty-five
years which had elapsed since the publication of Le

Long's work, the number of these writers must have increased to at least 1500. As nearly a century has passed since Forkel made this observation, the reader may judge how extensive our literature on this subject must be at the present time.

Another list of the books published on Hebrew music is to be found in 'Dizionario e Bibliografia della Musica, del Dottore Pietro Lichtenthal,' Milano, 1824; and there is another in ' Systematisch chronologische Darstellung der musikalischen Literatur,' von C. F. Becker, Leipzig, 1836. To this work an Appendix was published by Becker in the year 1839. Still it is very incomplete, and the compiler appears to have been unacquainted with many of the books which he notices, and merely to have copied the titles from Forkel, since both writers coincide in several errors, such, for instance, as the misspelling of the names of certain authors.

That among so many treatises, essays, and dissertations on Hebrew music there should be some in which curious theories are advanced, is no more than might be expected. Of these I shall notice two, on account of the discoveries which the authors believe they have made. Speidel, a German divine, published, in 1740, a dissertation entitled 'Unverwerfliche Spuren der alten Davidschen Singkunst,' in which he endeavours to prove that the Hebrews were acquainted with part-singing, and that they called the notes by the names of their vowels. The book is scarce, and I have hitherto not succeeded in obtaining a sight of it. But Forkel ('Geschichte der Musik,' i. 156) has given a detailed account of its contents, with some of the curious compositions in four parts which Speidel

2 A 2

believes he has discovered. Strangely enough, the
ancient Egyptians also are by some historians said to
have used the vowels for designating their notes. If
this was really the case, it would supply an additional
proof of their having possessed the pentatonic scale,
since it would show that they required five names
only for their notes. The statement of Clemens
Alexandrinus (' Strom.' vi.), that the Hebrew songs
were founded on the Dorian scale, is not in contradiction to this opinion, but rather confirmatory of it, since
we find that the old enharmonic scale of Olympus
was likewise considered as a Dorian scale. Neither
is it surprising that Herodotus should have been struck
with the close resemblance of the song of Maneros in
Egypt with the ancient song of Linus in Greece, and
with a similar composition in popular use in Asia
Minor.

In a carefully written essay, entitled ' Versuch die
Melodie und Harmonie der alten hebräischen Gesänge
und Tonstücke zu entziffern ' (published in ' Neues
Repertorium für biblische und morgenländische Literatur, herausgegeben von H. E. G. Paulus,' Jena,
1790), the writer, Gottlob Anton, professes to have
brought to light some genuine specimens of Hebrew
music as it was performed in the Temple of Jerusalem
in the days of David and Solomon. He deciphers
them from the Hebrew accents, which he maintains
constitute a musical notation like our own. And he
ingeniously endeavours to prove that the Hebrews
employed harmony, differing from our own in so far
only as no other chords but *concords* were made use
of. His arguments are accompanied by specimens of
melodies and harmonies obtained from the accents.

The largest and most important collection of dissertations on Hebrew music, published together, is contained in the thirty-second volume of Blasius Ugolino's
valuable work, entitled, 'Thesaurus antiquitatum
sacrarum, etc.,' published in the year 1767. Among
the modern writers who touch more or less upon
this subject, the German scholars Gesenius, Winer,
Joel Löwe, Jahn, and Saalschütz, especially deserve
notice.

EASTERN ORIGIN OF OUR OWN MUSIC.

In the course of the preceding chapters I have
several times had occasion to allude to the affinity
which exists between the music of European and
Asiatic nations. To enter fully into this subject
would require much space, and does not come within
the plan of the present dissertation. It is, however, so intimately connected with the preceding
investigation, that I hope the following remarks, in
conclusion, will not be without some interest to the
reader.

The ancient Egyptians must properly be classed
with the Asiatic nations; their customs were in many
respects similar to those of the latter, and their language was a branch of the Semitic, as was also the
Hebrew and the Assyrian. Besides, the ancients
themselves regarded the Egyptians as an Asiatic
nation.

We have an instance of the transmission, at an
early period, of Asiatic music into Europe, in that of
the ancient Greeks. Most Greek musical instruments

were nearly identical with Asiatic ones; and the names of the oldest and principal Greek modes—the Dorian, Phrygian, Lydian, Æolian, and Ionian—also support the assertion of ancient historians, that the musical knowledge of the Greeks was originally obtained from Asia minor and Egypt. Whether these five modes were originally founded on the five intervals of the pentatonic scale is uncertain; but from what we have seen it appears probable. Again, in other European countries we have found traces of the Oriental harp, and surprising similarities in the peculiar construction and form of old instruments with those of Asiatic countries. And among them we have met with five-stringed instruments of such kinds as, from their nature, we may reasonably surmise to have been tuned in the order of intervals constituting a scale, and which suggest the former existence of the pentatonic scale. Besides the old Russian *gussli* and the Finnish *kantele* already noticed, several others might be pointed out, as, for instance, the Anglo-Saxon harp with five strings, the old Irish *coinar cruit* with ten strings, &c.

We have seen that the pentatonic scale actually exists at present in Europe in the music of some Celtic nations. We have found several names of our musical instruments to be of Asiatic origin. Further, in our Christian Church the intoning, chanting, and antiphonal singing are, in all probability, remains of the ancient Hebrew mode of performing in the Temple. The apostles were Hebrews, accustomed from their childhood to the usages of their nation, and must have been practised in the music which they have been in the habit of using in worship before they became

Christians. And it is not likely that the primitive Christians would have adopted in their worship the musical performances of idolators to which they were naturally averse.

The Romans derived most of their musical instruments from Greece, and afterwards carried them from Italy into other European countries of which they were the conquerors and masters. In Spain the Moors have, at a later period, introduced the Arabic music, of which unmistakable traces are still recognisable in the popular songs and instruments of the country. The Crusaders also are said to have brought from Asia some instruments previously unknown in Europe.

The Gipsies, dispersed like the Jews throughout almost every European country, were formerly supposed to be an Egyptian race; but eminent modern ethnologists tell us that they originally migrated from Hindoostan. The musical talent of these interesting vagrants is well known. As professional musicians we meet with them in most European countries, generally in small bands roving from place to place, and entertaining the people with the national melodies of the country. Thus we find them everywhere, especially in Spain, in Russia, in Hungary, Transylvania, Wallachia, and even in South America. In the northern part of Russia they excel as vocal performers; in the Ukraine, in the Danubian Principalities, and in Hungary they are almost exclusively instrumentalists. It cannot exactly be said that they have preserved anywhere a national music of their own. They have adopted in every country the music of the people among whom they live. Still, there is much in their performances which they appear to have traditionally preserved from their Asiatic forefathers. It is impossible to convey by words an accurate idea of the peculiarities of instrumental music so strange and spirited as that of the Gipsies. Some of its characteristics are a strongly-marked and effective rhythm, the frequent employment of *superfluous seconds*, and the introduction of various kinds of embellishments. When the Gipsies in Hungary perform a favourite national melody, it becomes a *variation*, or rather a *fantasia*, founded upon the simple tune. The introduced passages, *graces, turns, shakes, appoggiaturas* are, however, frequently so original, tasteful, and effective, that these peculiar performances have obtained a well-merited renown. The same mode of treating a melody in extempore performances prevails in Hindoostan, the original home of the Gipsies. This is evident from the accounts of travellers. Captain Willard, for instance, says : " The peculiar nature of the melody of Hindoostan not only permits, but enjoins the singer, if he has the least pretension to excel in it, not to sing a song throughout more than once in its naked form; but on its repetition, which is a natural consequence, occasioned by the brevity of the pieces in general, to break off sometimes at the conclusion, at other times at the commencement, middle, or any certain part of a measure, and fall into a rhapsodical embellishment called *Alap*, and, after going through a variety of *ad libitum* passages, rejoin the melody with as much grace as if it had never been disunited, the musical accompaniment all the while keeping time. These passages are not reckoned essential to the melody, but are con-

sidered only as grace-notes, introduced according to
the fancy of the singer, where the only limitations by
which the performer is bound are the notes peculiar
to that particular melody, and a strict regard to
time."[5]

The employment of two *superfluous seconds* in the
diatonic scale is usual in Turkey, as well as in Wallachia, Moldavia, Hungary, and Transylvania.

There can be, in my opinion, no doubt that this scale
also emanated from Asia, like the races themselves
among whom we find it. The predilection of modern
Eastern nations for the *superfluous second* is clearly
evident from its frequent occurrence in their popular
songs. Instances of its employment we have had in
some of our previous examples, for instance, in the
chorus of the Mewlewi Dervishes, p. 110; in the
Egyptian boatmen's song, p. 261; in the old
melodies of the Jewish Synagogue, noticed at page
338, &c. Though evidences are wanting to prove
that the scale with two *superfluous seconds* is a direct
offspring of the pentatonic scale, this appears not at
all unlikely, considering the close resemblance which
the two scales bear to each other. A *superfluous second*
may, in sound at least, be taken as identical with a

⌄ A Treatise on the Music of Hindoostan, by Captain Augustus
Willard, Calcutta, 1834, p. 34.

minor third. Even in our highly developed music both intervals are generally used, in practical performance, indiscriminately. The two *superfluous seconds* correspond, therefore, with the two *minor thirds* of the pentatonic scale. It is true that this scale occurs also with two *major thirds*, namely, when it resembles our minor scale; in this form, however, it is comparatively but little used.

Here I must draw the reader's attention to a suggestive fact. Most of the ancient scales known to us possess *two steps of a third* in the compass of an octave. In the scales, or *genera*, as they are more usually termed, of the ancient Greeks, this is the case with three out of four. The *diatonic genus* is the only one in which no larger steps than *whole tones* occur. The *chromatic genus* has two steps of a minor third; the *enharmonic*, two of a major third; and the *old enharmonic* of Olympus, two of a major third. In order to facilitate a comparison between the scales exhibiting this peculiarity I shall insert them here together, and shall indicate the largest steps with black notes:—

PENTATONIC SCALE WITH PROGRESSIONS IN MINOR THIRDS.

PENTATONIC SCALE WITH PROGRESSIONS IN MAJOR THIRDS.

CHROMATIC GENUS.

ENHARMONIC GENUS.

SCALE OF OLYMPUS.

SCALE WITH SUPERFLUOUS SECONDS.

Indeed, most of our musical inventions and contrivances appear to have been in use, though less perfect, among ancient Asiatic nations. No doubt the coincidences are in many cases accidental, or rather the natural result of human ingenuity applied to the cultivation of music. Guido d'Arezzo (A.D. 1000) is said to have invented the *solmisation, i.e.* the employment of the six monosyllables, *ut, re, mi, fa, sol, la,* taken from the words of an old Latin hymn. The Hindoos had long before his time the monosyllables *sa, ri, ga, ma, pa, dha, ni,* also obtained from words, "three of which," as Sir William Jones observes, "are, by a singular concurrence, exactly the same, though not all in the same place, with three of those invented by David Mostare as a substitute for the troublesome gamut used in his time, and which he arranged thus: *bo, ce, di, ga, lo, ma, ni.*"[6] The employment of different colours to distinguish the *intervals* is more remarkable. Villoteau describes an ancient Egyptian harp with five blue, six yellow, and ten red strings. The ancient Chinese stringed instrument *kin* had, Amiot informs us, twenty-five bridges, of which five were blue, five red, five yellow, five white, and five black.[7] The contrivances are similar on some of our own instruments. On the key-board of our pianoforte, for instance, the intervals of the diatonic scale of C major are all of one colour, but the chromatic scale requires the introduction of intervals of another colour. And hence, probably, its name, from *chroma,* colour. The ancient Greek chromatic scale appears, however, to have borne less resemblance to our present one than to the pentatanic scale.

Again, the invention of the so-called *harmonic hand,*

---

[6] On the Musical Modes of the Hindus, Asiatic Researches, vol. iii., Calcutta, 1792.

[7] Mémoires concernant l'Histoire, etc., des Chinois, tome sixième, p. 59.

of which a description is given in Burney's ' History of Music ' (vol. ii. p. 90), is also usually ascribed to Guido d'Arezzo. According to Amiot, the ancient Chinese made use of the *harmonic hand*, and in his ' Mémoires ' before mentioned a drawing and description of it will be found. The Chinese also considered the *triple time* the complete, and the *common time* the incomplete one, just as our theorists did formerly. They were also acquainted with the *circle of fifths*, by which we demonstrate the relation of the keys towards each other. Their two-stringed fiddle, *urh-heen*, is tuned in a fifth; the Japanese *samsien*, in the fifth and octave ; and a similar ancient stringed instrument of the Hindoos, the *dwitantri*, described by Sir William Jones in his essay on Hindoo Music, is also tuned in the same intervals as most of our own instruments of a similar kind.

Such coincidences, of which more might be cited, in whatever manner they may be explained, reveal a closer affinity between ancient Asiatic music and our own than is usually supposed to exist. It will be remembered that the Phœnicians—also a branch of the Semitic race—held at an early period trading intercourse with Western nations in distants parts of the world. Should we by fresh archæological discoveries ever become acquainted with their music to the same extent as with that of the Assyrians—of which there appears to be some probability—we may hope to be in possession of further corroborative evidence in support of the opinions advanced in this work.

INDEX.

2 B

2 c